CORA DEVINE

A Sea-Change

A Sea-Change was originally published as an ebook series in three parts:

The Wreck

The Turning Tide

Something Rich and Strange

Cover and interior design by Cora Devine

Published by Morva Press
ISBN 978-1-9160565-0-3

coradevine.co.uk

Also by Cora Devine:

The Fogou

CONTENTS

PART THREE   *Something Rich and Strange*

A SEA-CHANGE

Prologue

It was a matter of maintaining composure at all costs. Kate was determined to leave the dinner party with her dignity, if not her emotions, intact. In her mind's eye she was hauling herself flat on her belly towards the exit like the crawling severed remains of a bewildered zombie, wondering *what the hell just happened...?* But she must not let it show.

She tried to smile without looking brave, and fixed her eyes on Lauren's still-prattling lips, deliberately avoiding the uncomfortable or sympathetic looks from the others. Three hours more. She approximated that it would be at least that long before she could escape her predicament without appearing to have run away. With great effort of will, she resisted glancing at either the clock on the dining room wall, or at the childish blue-strapped watch that she wore, and that Miles had given her, damn him. She did not still wear the watch out of any sense of continuing devotion, but rather because she simply liked it. But it sat heavily conspicuous now on her wrist; a glaring and traitorous declaration of an ongoing attachment.

She felt the anger rise in her blood and she knew, just knew, that there was a triangle of red flush appearing at her throat. Tears were close, and it took the most valiant endeavour of spirit to repress them, as she recalled how the evening had started so well, and how happy she had felt until just minutes ago. After all, she was amongst friends. These friends had stuck by her for years; throughout her pregnancy and the consequent break-up with Miles. Lauren and Marsha,

3

in particular, had listened to her for months on end; had analysed every detail of her heartache. True, they had not looked after the baby as often as they both had promised, but that was understandable since they had been young, and had exciting social lives and careers to maintain. Indeed, it was they who had encouraged her to move on; to find part-time work, and to abandon any notion that Miles might have a change of heart. And now that her daughter was ten years old, it was thanks to these friends that Kate had slowly re-entered the world. It was in their slipstream that she had been sucked back into the heaving eddy of London society.

But all that was before the bombshell. Kate's confused mind mused vapidly on the word. *Bombshell*. It was throwaway; an overused cliché—until it fell on your head. At that moment it felt entirely appropriate, as Kate felt that little bits of her soul were splattered over the white linen tablecloth, smudged across the faces of her friends, and stewing, festering in the coq-au-vin. Only minutes ago, in another world, they had all been laughing with delight at the simplicity of the menu: prawn cocktail, coq-au-vin, pink blancmange followed by cheese and biscuits—and nothing fancy mind you, just plain crackers and cheddar. It had been Kate's idea for Lauren's dinner party to have a 1970's theme; a gesture towards simpler, less competitive times. But now, as they sat stupidly dressed, the men in tank-tops and flared collars, the women in tabards and angel-wing sleeves, it started to feel like the Last Supper for Kate.

Lauren had been talking about the skiing holiday on which they were all going the following week. All, that is, except for Kate, who naturally could not afford to. Not that she minded, since skiing wasn't really her thing anyway. She considered it one of those obligatory holidays that the aspiring middle-classes felt were necessary in order to emphasise their status: skiing in March; second home in France or Italy in the summer; anywhere hot for Christmas. And so it hadn't really bothered Kate at all that she had not been included in their plans, until now.

Miles and Heidi are coming too, Lauren had said.

It was an innocent enough phrase, if technically analysed. Lauren had not sneered or poked her tongue out at Kate as she spoke, but she might just as well have punched her in the nose. *Miles and Heidi are coming too.* Miles and Heidi were going skiing with her friends. With *her* friends. And all of them child-free, Miles included. Kate had thought that there had been a lack of discussion about the holiday over the previous weeks out of a discreet sympathy for her own impoverishment. But now it seemed that their silence had not been out of any concern for her, but rather to hide their own treachery, not only in including Miles, but in secretly being relieved not to be encumbered with the only mother and child in their group.

'I thought you knew,' Lauren said hastily. *She was lying.* 'It was all planned last November at Miles and Heidi's bonfire party. You don't mind, do you Kate? After all, we see enough of *you*, too.' It was impossible not to notice the touch of annoyance, even bitterness in the last sentence.

Kate was still reeling from the second blow. Which bonfire party? Did they often, all of them, still see Miles and his girlfriend regularly...*and all this time?* This was the Miles who had told her when their daughter Isabella was only months old that he "just couldn't do it anymore". The Miles who— independently—had decided that it would be for the best if he broke all contact with Isabella, before she got any older. It seemed that the risk of emotional attachment became greater by the day, and after all—*he just couldn't do it anymore.* The same Miles who had left her broken hearted and reduced to despair.

Why had she not known? Was she really so blind? Of course they should have told her, her so-called friends. The men, granted, were useless when it came to discussing personal matters; but Lauren and Marsha? She thought that the latter, at least, might have warned her of what was afoot. Spontaneously, before she could stop herself, Kate's eyes flickered towards Marsha, who was studying her with a look of earnest pity. *Too late now*, thought Kate, *you should have told me.*

As for Stevie, he could barely disguise his horrified glee, but sat in round-eyed delirium, knife and fork poised in hand, as they all awaited Kate's response.

'Of course I don't mind, why would I?' Kate smiled back across the table at Lauren, but with her heart saying, *you are my adversary now. It's over.* For a second or two Lauren stared frankly at her, as if wondering whether Kate had actually understood what had been said. Or perhaps she was disappointed that Kate's reaction had not been more emotional. No doubt she had prepared herself for shock and disbelief, and Kate was not playing the game.

Kate suddenly thought how ludicrous Lauren looked with her blonde hair flicked and sprayed into flapping boards around her eyes, which were plastered to the brow in spangly blue shadow. Her cheekbones were shiny with creamy tangerine, and her pink lipstick was slimily melting down her chin. *A little piece of my soul*, thought Kate distractedly, although it didn't help to know that she too was also made up like a clown.

'And you know that we did offer you a place first, and Isabella too, if you'd wanted to come,' Lauren continued to justify her betrayal. 'After all, it's very difficult for us,' she said looking around at the others for support, '...always being stuck in the middle when you're *both* our friends. I don't believe in taking sides, Kate.'

'Of course. I understand,' said Kate, although she did not understand. She hadn't known that there *was* a "middle", or that there were "sides". She had thought that it was just her,

Lauren, Marsha, Stevie. Assorted boyfriends. Miles was *her* Ex. He was history, and Kate's history alone for that matter, or so she had thought. Now she realised how foolish she had been to think that Miles would have been so easily abandoned by all. Miles had always been the fun one; the vivacious, charming and sexy one. Suddenly Kate was not the treasured and beloved friend, but the stupid ex-girlfriend of Miles who had got herself pregnant and been forced to drop out of her art degree. Suddenly she was the tragic, foolish character, who had been bolstered throughout her troubles not out of friendship or love, but pity and guilt. *All this time...*

She recalled now how Lauren and Marsha had dutifully reported back on each and every social occasion over the past years where Miles had been present; but how they had done so in such a way as to suggest that although he had *been* there, they had not entered into so much as a conversation with him. Now, in her mind's eye, she imagined them laughing and joking, swapping news, and even...even, talking about *her*. Kate had often suspected that Lauren, in particular, found her tiresome, with her endless reasons for not being able to have as much fun as the rest of them, and that she considered her excuses of financial hardship and lack of suitable childcare as attention-seeking devices. Kate had always suppressed these ungenerous notions, but now embraced her misgivings wholeheartedly.

The meal was long and torturous, given that Kate was required to perform the erstwhile simple act of swallowing food. At one point, and just to add to her humiliation, she accidentally spilt a little wine. Angus, Fred, and even Marsha, who was sitting at the table end, and therefore in no real position to help, all leapt forth with napkins and reassurances, as if she were somehow fragile of mind and had spilt her own blood—having of course slashed her wrists—at the dinner table.

After the meal, they moved to the comfortable chairs by the fireplace, and talked about everything except the skiing holiday. Still with her mind on the clock, Kate joined in and smiled as if nothing was wrong. Angus and Fred were blatantly attentive, but Stevie, shamefully, refused to meet Kate's eye, and instead whispered and giggled with his new boyfriend in the corner.

'This is Luciano,' Stevie had introduced him earlier to Kate, barely able to contain his excitement. 'He's a brilliant design-guru; an artistic ninja. Luciano, Kate used to be an artist too.'

At the time she had laughed it off: ...that she used to be; used to exist. But now she recalled how Luciano's long Mediterranean lashes had lowered behind the frames of his hipster spectacles, and that his beautiful brown eyes had summarily dismissed her.

Finally, Angus and Marsha said that they had to go, making excuses about an early start in the morning. Kate did not hear their reasons why. The distress that she had struggled to contain was slowly weaving around her heart, threatening to reveal itself. She gave it another full ten minutes of excruciatingly good-natured chat with the others, before deciding that she had done enough. As if at last embarrassed into participation, Stevie rushed forward as she put on her coat, and offered to share a cab.

'No, it's okay, I'll walk. It's not that far, and a beautiful night,' said Kate with as much equanimity as she could muster.

'Look, there's no need to be a martyr!' Stevie snapped. 'For God's sake, Kate, we all like Miles. I don't see why we should pretend otherwise just to spare your feelings. It's time you got over yourself and moved on.'

Kate stared at her former friend. He had blown it. They had all very nearly survived the evening intact. All the hard work at self-conscious politeness by the others had been obliterated by Stevie's outburst. Now *his* description, his assumption of

8

her reaction to the news would become the evening's verdict. They would all appropriate his opinion that she had taken it badly—which of course she had, but had meant to appear otherwise. And to think that she had so nearly escaped. A realisation was stirring inside her and she felt the wave of sorrow rise and catch in her throat. This place; all the memories; they meant nothing now. She was walking a high-wire, step by anxious step, and the safety net had been cruelly yanked from under her. Wordlessly, Kate turned to leave.

Lauren fussed after her into the hallway, as if determined not to let her depart in any way upset. 'I'll give you a call in the week, Kate, before...we'll do coffee or something, okay?'

'Before you go on holiday?' Kate could not resist, despite the tremble in her voice.

It was just for a second, but she saw the momentary flash of triumph in Lauren's eyes. And then she knew—what she had always really known—that Lauren, despite Fred, had a secret lust for Miles.

'Okay fine, coffee then.' she said, turning away and opening the door. Another step. With one last reluctant effort she looked back again and smiled. 'That would be really nice.'

But even as she spoke her heart was hardening. The old Kate, that version of herself of mere hours ago would not have been so petty; would have counselled to overlook, to forgive. But as she walked down the stone steps from the Clapham flat to the familiar street below, she knew with prescient clarity that it was for the last time. She would never be back.

PART ONE

The Wreck

"The lowest ebb is the turn of the tide..."

Henry Wadsworth Longfellow

CHAPTER 1

Kate

It had taken Kate O'Neill thirty years to accept that perhaps life was, after all, a bitch. Sure, it had not yet hurled the Big One at her; she had not been required to endure fire, flood or earthquake. She had not been repressed, tortured or otherwise tormented. (In truth, she could not deny that lately fortune had, for once, favoured her, but if anything this only made her more cautious; there might be a price to pay). Instead, life got at her in all the little ways, heaping them on like so many spoonfuls of sugar, innocent-seeming, but ultimately poisonous. Yet she tried to be stoical. Others had it much worse, she reasoned. And she had only suffered *just the one* devastating relationship, so she tried to feel lucky, and appreciative. She counted her blessings. She endeavoured to steer a harmless course through life, in the hope that her karmic reward would be freedom from greater misfortune.

But despite these efforts, she knew she had blown badly off-course. It was fair to say that she had never really controlled the wheel, but rather that her grip had been wrested from the mast, and her once-strong heart flung carelessly adrift. She had weltered haplessly upon life's cruel storm waves, only to be washed up, beaten and in tatters upon its shores. Where she had once been passionate, romantic, and full of hope, now her life was governed by disappointment and the mundane. Yet she coped. She *tried*. But today Kate's resilience was being severely tested by the return of the toothache.

She ransacked the kitchen in search of painkillers, a doomed mission given her aversion to such things. Finally, in desperation, she resorted to the bottle of rum stored at the back of the larder.

The rum had been a house-warming gift from her sister Juliet who had presented it with a flourish and a leer: 'Arrr, me hearty, some tasty grog to wet yer pipe! For we be in piiirate country now...'

Once all the furniture and boxes had been unloaded from the hired van, and were stacked up around them like cargo, the two sisters and Juliet's boyfriend Parker had sat cross-legged in a triangle on the bare kitchen floorboards with large tumblers of the rum, and toasted to "Fair winds and a following sea". Yet, astonishingly, there was still more than half the bottle left.

Kate was sure it was supposed to be whiskey for anaesthetic purposes, but it would have to do. Crying tears of agony, she swigged generously from the bottleneck, spilling more down her neck and onto her sweatshirt than she actually managed to store in the left-hand side of her mouth, where the offending tooth lay. She held the rum there, sloshing and swilling it around her gums, until gradually, the pain was subdued by a stinging, hot, and temporarily numbing sensation. Spitting the rum out into the sink, she repeated the process. The first crack of the heavy brass door knocker thumping against wood further jarred her nerves, fusing the pain to her entire skull. Yet absurdly, Kate could only think of the poor dolphin.

The door knocker was shaped in the form of a dolphin, Maltese in style, with its tail curling aloft and its head plunging downward into the briny deep. It was a thing of beauty, but right now Kate, in her distress, could only empathise as it took an unjust battering. She stumbled into the hallway to be met with the sensation of being shot by poisoned needles in the back.

The cat was not a pet, but appeared to have come with the cottage, and to her mind was completely feral. It would jump on her back at unexpected times, claws remorselessly splayed; or wrap itself like a rabid gremlin around her ankle when she reached the bottom of the stairs in the morning. Her wrists and lower arms were covered with scratches in varying degrees of repair where she had tried to remove the damned thing from her personage. Weren't cats supposed to sit around snoozing prettily in country cottages? This one seemed highly belligerent and intent on laying siege. She vowed yet again to stop feeding it; it was taking her for a great big softy.

'Bloody thing!' she cried, bending double and attempting with one arm to reach the furry assailant. 'Shouldn't even be here!'

'Mum, get the door!' shouted Isabella from the front room. And then again, louder, and dragging out each syllable as though patently addressing an idiot, 'Mu-um, There's-some-one-at-the-do-or!'

'Oh, bog off back to the fields where you belong!'

'*What?*' her daughter's voice was incredulous.

'Not you, the cat!' bellowed Kate.

The unseen visitor banged the unfortunate dolphin against the door again. Finally securing a hairy grip, Kate wrenched the cat from the small of her back and flung it as far as she could along the hallway, away from her pathway to the door. It hit the rug flying, and the momentum took the whole bundle, cat and rug, sliding into the pantry door. Where it might normally have arched its back, hissed, and prepared for a second attack; the cat instead looked stunned at her, before loping off, its body pressed tight to the walls on course for the nearest exit. No doubt it had gone to skulk in the old wood shed to consider its next plan of attack.

15

The torment from Kate's tooth was relentless throughout the skirmish. She stared, wild-eyed, as Isabella and her companion appeared in the doorway of the living room, roused by all the commotion. Isabella's anxious look betrayed her concern that her mother might be about to embarrass her in front of Finn.

'Finn Greenwood-Borlase,' Isabella had earlier announced her new-found friend with pride, as though his name were a grand title and not just a modern splicing of parental surnames. And now the father of Finn Greenwood-Borlase was due to collect his son, who had come to tea after school. She had previously only spoken to him on the telephone to make the arrangements, but that cursory conversation had not prepared her for the man who stood before her now, as she finally and angrily swung the door open.

'Blimey...' Kate muttered under her breath.

'I beg your pardon?' the man said, a concerned expression on his face.

'Ah, never mind...you must be Finn's father?' said Kate, trying to maintain a normal facial expression as the toothache stabbed again.

He was tall, six foot two at the very least, with sun-bleached blond hair that hung unceremoniously down to his shoulders. He stood gently dripping rain in a long charcoal-coloured army greatcoat that would not have been out of place in a First World War battlefield. *Handsome.* The thought drifted briefly into her consciousness, before being ejected by another dagger of agonising pain.

'Yes, Lance Borlase—Look, is everything alright?' He must have seen his son lurking in the hallway behind Kate, for he subtly signalled hello—*are you okay? are you safe?*—with his eyes.

Kate couldn't help a wry smile despite her malaise. Of course he was called Lance. Might as well have been Lancelot. In any case, his name was totally in keeping with his romantic

16

novel cover-boy looks. But the smile was short-lived, and she held a hand to her cheek as her face crumpled again. She felt dizzy and gave a little sway.

'Of course!' she said irritably, and beckoned with one hand, 'I'm Kate. Look, please come in out of the rain while Finn collects his things. Finn, your shoes are in the kitchen by the fireplace, and your schoolbag is on the table.'

'Okay Finn?' Lance Borlase said quietly to his son, as he stepped into the hallway.

Finn nodded in response, but added excitedly, 'Can we just finish our game Dad? We're playing table-tennis on the Wii and I'm winning. Izzy keeps stuffing up,' he chuckled.

'Only 'cos I got the dodgy controller!' protested Isabella.

'No Finn, we have to get going. Help Isabella to clear away any mess, and then fetch your things.' His words were well pronounced and distinct, but underlying this was an illusive accent; a warm rolling Cornish burr.

'Okay,' said Finn sulkily. 'But I've got to go upstairs to choose a game first. Izzy said I could borrow one.'

The two ten-year-olds ran off before further objection could be made, and thundered up the stairs. Kate felt tired and longed to be rid of the visitors. She wanted to give her full attention to thwarting her toothache. But, conscious of her manners, and wanting to make amends for her previous snappiness, she made an attempt at civility.

'Would you like a drink? Tea? Or coffee?' she asked, moving into the kitchen, and assuming that he would follow.

He was oddly slow to do so, and when he did, had to duck his head slightly to get his tall frame through the low kitchen doorway. He did not immediately reply but rather scrutinised the plates still on the table and the remnants of the children's dinner: stodgy flakes of pastry and cold potato and, other than congealing tomato ketchup, no colourful trace of beneficial vegetable matter. Kate squirmed. Pasty and chips had been a *treat*, in honour of Finn's visit. She felt like protesting that she was usually a paragon of healthy living, but instead, guiltily whisked the plates away. Thankfully the children had devoured the cheesecake whole, leaving no trace.

'I've got some herb tea if you prefer,' said Kate. And as an afterthought, 'or perhaps a beer?'

She knew that neither the time nor the occasion was appropriate for alcohol, but her judgement was being severely impaired by the pain, and she didn't have the patience for social etiquette. Besides, most men, in her experience, seemed to want to stand around drinking beer at any given time. And although she never touched it herself, preferring wine, some cans remained in the fridge that Parker had somehow neglected to polish off.

Lance Borlase's scanning gaze fell upon the open bottle of rum on the counter top. 'No thank you,' he said at last. Despite this refusal of hospitality, he sat himself down at the kitchen table, obviously resigned to a wait for his son.

Well, stuff him if he doesn't want any tea, I bloody well do, thought Kate, as she quickly resealed the rum and bundled it to the very depths of the nearest cupboard, as if to persuade that it had been there all along, and its counter-top appearance an illusion. As she put the kettle on, she noticed him glance around the kitchen, assessing. She may have been new to this little cottage, but she still felt a sense of possession, of pride in the dwelling of her choice. Okay, so it needed decorating badly, and the awful curtains with some bizarre print of lambs in the field were a temporary measure; but it had, she thought, an understated charm that was neither predictable nor clichéd.

There were boxes still of unpacked items belonging to the entire house, and not just to the kitchen, stacked on the counter tops and under the table. Despite having been there for two weeks now, Kate was still trying to find a home for everything, and was reluctant to put anything in the 'wrong' place, where it might end up staying for years. There was an old gas cooker where there really should have been an Aga, and a prevalent smell that belonged to past occupants, and not to Kate and Isabella. The light glared from the single light bulb hanging overhead. Again, Kate would not hang a shade until she had found one that was exactly right for the kitchen. It was only just past six o'clock but the low rain clouds outside darkened the September sky, and there was a chill in the air that felt uncommon after the long hot summer. Nevertheless, the persistant beat of the rain, together with the quiet murmurings from the old transistor radio on the window sill, was comforting.

'The children seem to get on well together,' Kate said, as she took a camomile teabag from a box on the pine shelving, and wrestled a mug from the stack of dirty dishes in the sink. 'It's quite unusual for a boy and girl, especially at their age. But I guess Izzy is an unusual girl. She likes computer games for a start. And my parents indulge in buying her all the latest consoles, or whatever they are.'

She stole a look over her shoulder at Lance. It was quite clear from his expression that he was going to make no attempt at small talk. If anything, this only made Kate more determined to cajole him into conversation. For heaven's sake, she had collected his son from school, fed and entertained him, the very least he could do was be polite.

'I'm glad she's made a friend already, it's a difficult age for her to have to change schools,' Kate hammered on. 'She misses her friends in London. It was my biggest concern really about moving—upsetting her life, I mean. I'm kind of hoping that the pros will outweigh the cons in the long run.'

Lance watched her as she poured boiling water into her cup, but still made no response. Sneaking another look at him, she noticed long white crease marks around the outer corners of his eyes, exaggerated by a weather-browned face. *He must smile* sometimes *then*, she mused as she carried her mug to the table, stopping to turn up the dial on the radio. She didn't know much about classical music but recognised Khachaturian's Adagio from Spartacus, a favourite. She thought it was meant to be about roman slaves, but it always reminded her of tall ships on the high seas. She removed a cardboard box full of books from the raffia-seated chair, and sat opposite Lance.

He really was a very good-looking man. Probably in his mid-thirties. Under his coat he wore a T-shirt with a surfing logo, crumpled jeans, thick socks and heavy black boots, loosely laced. His damp locks of hair had begun to form artistic curlicues. With his wide shoulders, narrow waist and long legs, he looked so hilariously like a cartoon hero from one of Izzy's comic books that she might have drawn him.

His eyes were either pale green or blue, and to her mortification, Kate found her own eyes meeting his for longer than might be considered polite, in an effort to decide. She played absent-mindedly with some papers in front of her on the table, a mixture of bills, leaflets and school letters that she had been meaning to sort through. One of the letters from Isabella's new school caught her eye.

'I see the school is having a quiz night in a couple of weeks. Are they any good, do you know? Isabella thinks that I should go and acquaint myself with the other parents. But I feel a bit shy, not knowing anyone. Besides, the quiz nights at her old school were dreadful. I can't believe how competitive some parents are. Are you going?'

'I doubt it,' Lance Borlase answered bluntly.

Kate waited, expecting him to elaborate, but he was unforthcoming, and they fell once more into silence. In these situations Kate somehow felt that it was her responsibility to make conversation. How she would love to have been one of those people who could just sit in mental ease, oblivious to the discomfort of others.

'So, what do you do, if you don't mind me asking?' She was not sure how to address him. "Lance" felt too familiar given his frostiness, and that they had only just met, and "Mr Borlase" far too formal.

Again, his reply was terse. 'I'm employed by the University in Plymouth.'

'Ah,' Kate nodded, frowning once more in discomfort. It seemed that he was determined not to give much away, but she had his measure, or so she thought. He was probably a lab technician—no, an IT technician—a computer geek who spent his spare time surfing and hanging around at the beach. That would explain the image; the long sun-bleached hair and the tan. No doubt he drove a swanky camper van, specially adapted for carrying surfboards and equipped for weekend forays to 'where the waves are'. She was not averse to this lifestyle, and even envied it, but felt that it was a clique to which she could never belong. 'I understand that you're also a single parent...'

As soon as Kate uttered the words she regretted it. Isabella had said that Finn lived with his father and hardly ever saw his mother. But even supposing that this were correct, she would never have dreamed of being so intrusive if it had been a *woman* of such short acquaintance sitting before her. Why did she assume that a man would be less sensitive about his personal situation? She had goofed and she knew it, but the question hung in the air, irretrievable.

'Yes,' was his simple reply.

'Not that it's any of my business, only I was wondering...' she floundered, 'I'm new here and single myself; perhaps we might be able to help each other out? ...With picking the children up from school and such.'

And so, she dug the hole deeper.

What on earth was she saying? Ten minutes ago, Kate had had no such intentions of shared childcare, and if anything would have recoiled from such a proposition had it been put to her. It would normally take her a long time to decide that she liked and trusted someone enough to enter into such an ongoing arrangement.

A dark—or was it contemptuous?—expression flittered across the handsome features of Lance Borlase.

'Look,' he said, 'I don't wish to be rude, but I think that I should make things perfectly clear at the outset. I may be single, but I'm definitely not looking for a *relationship* of any kind. You shouldn't assume that just because I'm a lone parent, and a man, that I need a—*a good woman*—to come along and help me out.'

Kate could not believe her ears. She gaped openly, one hand on her cheek where the tooth throbbed on. They stared at each other for a second or two, both reddening. He clearly felt uncomfortable with what he had just said.

But felt driven to say it anyway.

She had had enough. She stood up, psychologically needing some movement to ease her pain. She paced up and down the stretch of kitchen between the table and the woodburner.

On the radio, the horns sounded menacing, warning of the impending wave ahead.

'For your information, Mr Borlase, I'm not looking for a...a *relationship,* as you put it, either. In fact it's the last thing I want in my life right now!'

The string section increased in intensity as the tall ship attempted to rise up the formidable towering wave. '...Besides, even if I were on the hunt for some poor unfortunate man, now that you've shown how completely *arrogant* you are, rest assured that there is absolutely no chance of my ever being interested in you!'

The crescendo of violins escalated to its zenith then teetered on the peak of the wave before... 'Ever!' she added, to be sure that she had made her point, and just as the cymbals crashed dramatically.

At the same instant, Lance was on his feet, and stood glowering at her. The music played on as the tall ship sailed triumphantly into calmer waters...but in this rural kitchen all was a maelstrom of smashed decorum; thoughts in swirling disarray, and ready to cling to any passing barrel.

Kate was surprised at herself. Not only at how riled she was, although the toothache probably helped to explain that, but also at the fact that she had managed to answer him so eloquently and concisely, and had not stammered with embarrassment, as she would have expected. She felt a little vindicated. Lance Borlase, on the other hand, looked horrified. Visibly at a loss, he was saved from further discomfort by the return of his son.

'Come on then Dad, let's go,' Finn instructed breezily, stuffing on his shoes, and apparently now more than ready to move on.

Isabella followed him into the kitchen and abruptly turned the radio station over. Spartacus segued into an undignified yelping screech before succumbing to some modern dance track.

Lance looked nonplussed for a second and then picking up Finn's schoolbag from the mess on the table, attempted to resume a sense of normality. 'Thank Mrs O'Neill for having you, Finn.'

'Thank you for having me, Mrs O'Neill,' Finn said, parrot-fashion, observing them both suspiciously; two shuffling and awkward parents desperately trying to remember that they were grown-ups.

'You're welcome, Finn,' Kate said, smiling with as much charm as she could summon. 'And it's *Ms* O'Neill, okay?'

What the hell was she doing? Re-emphasising her single—and clearly desperate—status before some snotty clay-brained oaf, that was what!

'But you can call me Kate,' she added hastily.

They all shambled out of the kitchen to where Isabella, despite having commandeered the radio, now waited at the open front door watching the rain. As Lance passed first into the hallway Kate heard a deep voice cry out, followed by a muted curse.

'What the bloody hell...?' Lance's voice trailed off as he realised that the monster that he had pulled from the back of his head was in fact a small tabby cat. He had dropped Finn's bag, and stood there with the cat held at arm's length by the scruff of its neck, whilst nursing the back of his own with the other hand. Any sense of superiority that Kate had felt was rapidly disappearing as the situation developed into farce.

'Oh, It's the cat,' she said, stupidly. 'I'm so sorry.' She stepped forward to take the wretched creature. But then remembering its nature, she hesitated, and drew back again. Lance Borlase stared at her, and without words managed to convey that either she take the struggling cat immediately, or he might throttle it.

* * *

'*That*,' muttered Lance, as he threw Finn's schoolbag into the back seat of his ancient Land Rover, 'is what is commonly described as a madhouse.' He looked back to the cottage entrance briefly, and, reassured that having parked in the lane, they were out of both sight and earshot, continued. 'Are you sure that you get on with this Isabella? Do you *have* to?'

'Yes, Dad, I do and I have to,' said Finn, as he climbed into the front passenger seat.

Lance muttered something inaudible and got into the driver's seat beside him.

'Besides,' said Finn, 'you're exaggerating, as usual. It wasn't a madhouse. And anyway, you should be glad about Isabella. You know I haven't got any friends.'

'Now who's exaggerating? What about Callum and Tom?'

'Yeah well, apart from Callum and Tom.' Finn's mood became sullen. 'I don't get it. You're always on about how I should treat everyone equally. Well, Isabella is new at school and I thought that she might feel left out.'

Lance felt a pang of conscience. His son knew first-hand what it was to feel left out of things. He tried to lighten the mood. 'This has nothing whatsoever to do with her collection of computer games I suppose?' he said as he started the car engine.

'No! Well, maybe a bit. But I like her anyway. She's cool...*for a girl.*'

'Hmm. What about the mother though? She was definitely mad. And quite obviously drunk.'

'Was she? I didn't notice.'

'How could you not notice? She reeked of it. I'll say it again, Finn, I won't mind if you choose not to pursue this friendship.' The rain was easing a little. Steering the car into the empty country lane, Lance floored it with gusto.

'Don't be a snob, Dad. Besides, it's up to me who I choose as my friends.'

'I suppose you think that it's cool to have a friend with an alcoholic mother—and don't go saying any of this to Isabella, by the way.'

'I will. I'll say my Dad says that we can't be friends because her mum's an alcoholic.'

'Finn!'

Finn was laughing now, teasing him. Not for the first time Lance cursed inwardly that he had always spoken openly with his son. True, they had an honest relationship as a result, but it also meant that he had to put up with a lot of cheek.

'You could do with a healthy dose of deep-rooted parental fear,' he said with mock concern, before breaking into a broad smile.

Still grinning in return, Finn turned and reached for his schoolbag in the seat behind, retrieved a dog-eared paperback and started to read. His long blond fringe fell over his freckled nose. Snatching looks at him as he drove through the rain, Lance felt overwhelmed with love for his young son. It came in waves like that, unexpectedly. He loved him, of course, in a general day to day kind of way, but he was always surprised at how a rogue emotion could still hit him out of the blue like that.

'Well? Did you manage to borrow one?' Lance said as they neared home.

'Yup!'

Finn removed the computer game from his pocket and waved it under his father's nose, before returning to his book with barely a break in concentration.

* * *

Kate flung herself onto the bed in abject misery. She held a damp flannel against her cheek and sobbed into the pillow. The bedroom door creaked and she saw Isabella hover reluctantly at the doorway.

'It's alright darling,' Kate said with a tremulous little sniff, 'You can come in.'

'What's wrong?' Isabella said nervously.

Kate sat up. 'It's nothing, just a toothache. But it's giving me a headache too, and well, I've just not had a very good day. There's nothing to worry about, honestly.'

'Why are you holding a flannel on your face? Does it help your tooth?'

'No not really. I don't know why! I think it helps a bit, but I'm not sure.'

26

'Do you want a cup of tea?'

Her daughter's kindness made Kate cry all the more. She gave Isabella a hug and sobbed. 'No thank you. I wouldn't want you to scald yourself.'

'I won't Mum, I'm ten.'

'All the same...but thanks anyway. You're such a good girl. The things that you've had to put up with...'

'Okay, okay, I just wanted to make sure you were alright. If you don't want tea then I'm off to watch the telly,' Isabella said suddenly getting up and moving towards the bedroom door. 'Going to make myself one anyway,' she added defiantly as she left.

Kate burst into fresh floods of tears. She caught sight of herself in the dressing table mirror. Her long nutbrown hair, that had started the morning tied up in a loose knot, was now cascading in less than sexy tendrils in all directions from her head. Her sweatshirt was stained and damp, her eyes swollen, and her complexion grey. Great time to run into *him*, she thought, and threw herself dramatically back onto the bed.

'And *nobody* is called Lance anymore,' she muttered maniacally. 'Ridiculous name!'

She wanted to forget the whole horrible experience of their meeting, but parts of the conversation kept returning to torture her. She burned with embarrassment as she recalled the speech that she had been so initially proud of.

For your information...

...now that you've shown how completely arrogant you are, rest assured...

Kate groaned into the pillow with each recollection. How melodramatic she had sounded. How very Elizabeth Bennet! And what on earth had she said or done to make him think that she was propositioning him? *And then the cat!* It was too much. She was aware of being hungry but didn't dare eat

27

anything. She was in pain. She was deeply unhappy, and she was in Cornwall.

CHAPTER 2

The Breaking Point

By the following morning, the endless drizzling rain had stopped and the rising sun's rays travelled unimpeded across the blue sea. As she walked with Isabella along the cliff-top path to the village school, Kate thought that there was a freshness and expectancy in the air that was more reminiscent of spring, rather than the imminent autumn.

'Isn't it beautiful Izzy?' she smiled at the top of the orange beanie hat bobbing along beside her, its occupant's dark curls escaping around the edges. 'It's one of those just-good-to-be-alive days!'

'You're in a good mood today,' said Isabella, with a note of cynicism in her voice that made Kate wonder at how fast her daughter was growing up. But Isabella was right. Kate's toothache had disappeared miraculously overnight. She walked with the spring-footed step of the newly converted, mentally vowing that she would become a better person, and live a more appreciative life, if only she would never have to bear such agony again.

'Yes I am in rather a good mood, actually. And just look at all this!' she waved her arm expansively above her head, indicating the sky, the turquoise sea to the right of them, and the dry-walled fields to the left. She skipped a full circle in the lane, arms flailing. She was walking backwards now, looking at Isabella, who was busy rolling her eyes skywards. Kate hadn't seen her do this the first time, so Isabella had repeated

29

the action to ensure that her mother was aware of her disapproval.

'Seriously Izzy, in London, you're lucky to ever see the horizon in any direction. Tell me the last time you ever saw this far? In London, it's only the clouds in the sky that remind you that you're living on a planet. You scuttle around in your little cars, in crowded built-up streets...and just look at the colours!'

She turned to walk alongside Isabella again. 'Everything in the city is grey. Grey roads, grey concrete buildings, grey people...'

'Bright lights, bright shops, bright...things to buy!' interrupted Isabella.

'Well, alright,' Kate conceded. 'It's not all dull. But I'm talking about a natural beauty here, not the manufactured, superficial kind.'

'You mean the normal kind. I don't see what's so good about it anyway. It's boring.'

'Oh, Isabella! What about the sea? I thought you liked the sea?'

'I do. But not every day.'

Kate punched her playfully on the arm. 'Oh we'll turn you into a country bumpkin yet!'

'Stop it! You're being really irritating. I think I prefer you in a bad mood—like yesterday.'

Kate knew when to let it lie. They walked silently with their own thoughts for the rest of the way. Kate fully understood Isabella's doubts about their new life. The days were not always so beautiful, and despite falling in love with the cottage, they had spent much of the last couple of weeks feeling isolated and house-bound by cold and miserable weather. As Juliet had said on the day that they had moved (whilst determinedly dragging on a cigarette in defiance of Kate's declarations on the benefits of fresh air): 'Only *you* would move to the seaside just *after* the summer.'

30

Another cause for consternation, and for which she had been foolishly unprepared, was the extreme darkness of the country nights, unadulterated as they were by streetlights, neon and traffic. As a child Kate had always been reduced to tears by total blackness, and had begged her mother every night to leave the hall landing light on.

To her great shame, she had never really grown out of this irrational fear. She had allowed herself, throughout adult life, the indulgence of always leaving a light on, to the point where it had become plain habit. But the silent blackness surrounding the cottage at night felt so invasive, it was almost tangible. The meagre, low energy bulb in the hallway did little to quell her anxiety; and night after night, she had found herself reading through the early morning hours in bed; a veiled excuse to leave the bedside lamp on. On some nights, she only turned it off and finally went to sleep with the first glimmerings of dawn's light at her window. Other times, she would wake in the morning with the book collapsed at her side, and the lamp still glaring wastefully in the morning sun.

The consequent lack of sleep, coupled with the stress of moving house, ensured that she had felt nothing but tired, irritable, and run down since the day that they had moved in. And so it was perverse that she had just had her best night's sleep in two weeks following the trauma of the day before. Now, with the sun warming her face, and breathing in the soft intoxicating air, she felt newly inspired. She made a mental note to pull herself together; for Isabella's sake as well as her own. After all, this was the new life that she had promised herself. It had taken almost every ounce of resolve that she had had to make the move, and it would now require renewed determination if she were to make it work.

All the same, as they approached the outskirts of the village, Kate was aware of the now familiar voice deep in her consciousness saying repeatedly: *this is crazy...this is crazy...what on earth are you doing here?*

She had known virtually nothing real about Cornwall before moving. She had never even holidayed there before. Her perception of the county had a lot to do with romantic visions of Arthurian castle ruins perched on sheer cliff faces, waves crashing dramatically below. It had to do with an image of tanned limbs fishing for crabs in rock pools on idyllic summer days. And worryingly, it had to do with a vague recollection of the entire collection of Winston Graham's Poldark novels that she had ploughed through as a teenager. She risked finding herself genuinely disappointed not to encounter rebellious but principled Georgian types on horseback.

The notion had grown one sodden afternoon in London when she had been so dejected, so jaded and desperate, that she had found herself sitting alone in her car; an old blue Morris Traveller, and a rare source of comfort. Having promised to assist Isabella with some geography homework that evening, and having nothing more suitable, she had popped out to fetch the Road Atlas from the car. But first, given that the lift was broken again, she had had to run the gauntlet of the stairs. First past the cloud of flies surrounding the rotten bins outside a spooky flat on the fourth floor; then past the junkies' abandoned paraphernalia in the glass stairwell and finally she'd had to slip by the two unrestrained and unattended Rottweiler dogs on the ground floor.

The dogs' owner, even when present, was a thin, mean-faced slip of a girl with a fuck-the-world attitude. It was questionable whether she would have either the physical ability, let alone the inclination, to control the dogs should the need arise, and Kate had endured many nervous moments in passing them, especially when Isabella was still small. The potentially starving Rottweilers would focus with a ravenous eye on this little lump of flesh strapped to the pushchair, being noisily but efficiently bumped up the stairs.

And so with practiced, enforced bravery, she had skirted past the dogs, with what she hoped was a convincing air of authority. Trotting down the last few steps outside, Kate had been relieved to see that the car was vacant of the usual gang of teenagers who thought it their absolute right to sit on and slouch against her car; and furthermore to bend or break off the windscreen wipers in a fit of boredom should they so desire. She had slid into the car and gratefully shut the door on the world outside.

The Atlas wasn't squashed into the glove compartment as she had expected, and she had begun to search through the assortment of belongings in the back seat. She referred to the little car as her "handbag". As she reasoned with Isabella, it was better than a normal handbag because you could chuck so much more inside. Apart from the usual driving-related paraphernalia of maintenance manuals and so forth, she kept magazines and children's books, an old cosy jumper and soft ballet-style pumps, and an emergency stash of chocolate bars. Some cushions, and a blanket woven in hot oranges and reds, were slung in the back seat. The glove compartment contained spare make-up and a hairbrush, and in the roomy space at the back accessed by double doors she kept sketchbooks and pencils; and even occasionally a canvas would be transported back to the small flat, symbolic of good intentions.

As she rummaged around, one or two drops of rain fell on the back window of the car, before suddenly and dramatically, the weather turned into a blinding downpour. Finding the Road Atlas beneath one of the seats Kate had put her hand on the cool steel door handle, ready to rush back indoors, when she hesitated.

Why bother? Why go back into that flat, the scene of so much misery and unhappiness? She pulled the blanket from the back seat and wrapped it around herself. She just sat there staring at the rain, and the familiar street. She stared at the tatty high-rises and at the little box-like 'maisonettes', stacked up on top of each other like a wall of children's building bricks, only without the joy of colour. They were designed to a formula for the most basic and necessary standards of existence; the tiny doors and room sizes that would only allow entrance to depressing, small-scale furniture. Mean little windows that only provided the bleakest amounts of light through obligatory net curtains or blinds. How had she got here?

She wondered at the sheer clutter of crammed housing in this one small area, and tried to estimate the sum of occupants. How many families? How many other lives shared this grotty inner-city street? She was shocked to realise that it must have been hundreds. And how many of them did she really know? How many touched her life, or would even say hello to her in passing? She mused for a while on how odd it was that you always seemed to see the same people. She could only think of a handful—ten at most—of her immediate neighbours that she recognised by sight. So who the hell lived behind the other closed doors? How could so many lives pass her by, unnoticed?

One of the known neighbours; a widow who lived alone—*somewhere* further down—shuffled by at that moment, and hesitated as if she thought to say something. But instead, frowning at the downpour, hurried away. Kate was vaguely aware of the oddness of her situation; sitting in the rain in the passenger seat of her own car. But she quickly convinced herself that her self-consciousness was apparent to herself alone. After all, no one else could know of the turmoil in her mind, or that she was in fact paralysed with indecision.

How had she got here? She had, admittedly been rather aimless in life, but surely this had not been part of the plan?

She had let life happen to her instead of taking control. But now Kate felt panicked.

Her natural talent for art had, once upon a time, dragged her in a certain direction; but she had managed to mess that up in peerless fashion. Dropping out of her Fine Art degree course pregnant; *hurrah!* Settling for a tiny one-bedroom sixth- floor flat; *nice move!* Managing to repel her child's father and end up alone; *spectacular!*

Oh, she had not panicked at first. Back then she had calmly assured herself that she would resume her degree once Isabella was...how old? Six months? A year? In the event she could not bear to be parted from her darling baby; the new love of her life. And even once Isabella had started nursery, Kate had found the need for financial security more pressing and so she had found a job. Not just any job mind; she managed to ensure that she found something local, but in the soul-destroying arena of corporate business.

And now her friends had deserted her. Well, disappointed her at least.

'Devastated at the most,' she said out loud to herself. Kate had avoided contact with her treacherous friends over the last couple of weeks, and now they had all gone away on the wretched skiing holiday. They would be there now with Miles and his latest skinny-arsed girlfriend, Heidi. She imagined them all clinking drinks at the bar après-ski, easing their consciences by condemning Kate's resentful behaviour.

Sighing, she looked at the Road Atlas in her lap and turned to the page where her street lay, tiny and unimportant in the spread and sprawl of the city. Interested now, she turned the pages of the book, looking at other towns, fascinated by some of the names, and overawed at the remoteness of some settlements. She made herself more comfortable with one or two of the cushions. Kate had always loved maps. She loved the cool, precise linear drawings and muted colours that

35

somehow conveyed a sense of deep importance. But she also loved the sense of otherworldliness that they held within. Herein lay the possibilities of other lives, of new starts. The regret hit her with such clarity that she began to cry.

There had to be a better way than this. There had to be a way of living life without this constant futile struggle. She thought that she had been doing the right thing, but in this rare moment of lucidity Kate realised that she had been getting it all wrong. She was in bondage; ensnared by necessity into trading her hours—her *life*—in empty commerce; and to what end? Every penny earned was swiftly accounted for by ever rising prices for food, fuel and utilities. And she couldn't see things getting any better. She longed for an alternative; a freedom of choice; a self-sufficiency. Give her a garden and she would grow some food.

Kate would not have said, looking back now, that it was at that precise moment that she had made the decision to move. Perhaps the seed had been sown by her friends' betrayal; although curiously, she did not feel so much grief, or hurt—as they all might have imagined—but rather something inside her had hardened. And with this hardening, Kate realised that she could do whatever she wanted. There were no longer any loyalties to consider; she could be as uncompromising as she liked.

The rain had stopped as dramatically as it had begun, and she had collected Isabella as usual from school. She was a little light-headed from crying, but the city streets were steaming with fresh warm air following the storm, and she felt strangely, if temporarily, released. The wheels would soon turn again, routine would reassert its grip; yet somehow on that lonely afternoon in the car, Kate had turned a corner, and she resolved to remember the feeling. She had no idea at the time how she would make her dream come about; there was no precognition of the act of fate that would soon befall her. But it *was* a dream, and a raft that she could cling to. Either way, the one thing that remained clearly apparent, if she was to save her soul from further decay, was that everything somehow would have to change.

CHAPTER 3

The Hydra

Kate kissed Isabella goodbye at the gates of the small school on the outskirts of the village, and was just turning to go when she felt a tap on her shoulder.

'Excuse me; I'm so glad I caught you. You are the new occupant of Dolphin Cottage, are you not? I'm Alicia Browning.' A woman extended her hand in a formal manner, leaving Kate little option but to respond with a flimsy shake. The woman's hands were soft and her nails impeccably French-manicured.

'Kate O'Neill. How can I help?'

'I would like to welcome you on behalf of the school PTA. I realise that you're new to the town, and no doubt you are still busy settling in—I'm relatively new here myself, so I know what it's like—but I'm sure that in time you will want to become fully involved in school activities.' The woman's accent was not Cornish, but a jolting reminder of the London home counties. 'Between you and me,' she continued, lowering her voice, 'you just can't trust these rural schools to have the children's best interests at heart. They don't have terribly high expectations. I'm sure you'll agree that we all have a part to play in ensuring that standards are up to scratch.'

Kate was not sure that she did agree. She took in Alicia Browning's just-buffed appearance of the well-to-do middle class wife. She appeared to be older than Kate, but that may just have been her authoritarian manner. She wore a long green wax coat fastened, rather unnecessarily, all the way from her welly-booted feet up to her neck. Her skin glowed with what Kate suspected was expensive foundation cream. Her hair too, was well maintained in a set shoulder length bob; a practical cut, but dyed honey-blonde as a gesture towards sexuality. Kate made a mental note to remember to find a decent local hairdresser. And a dentist.

She felt that she was familiar with Alicia's type. In London she had called them "Department Store Wives", because of their constant and snobbish referencing to whichever grand store it was with which they equated quality. These women had forsaken the cheaper, more fashionable shops of their youth, and now purchased everything for the family, the home, and even the dinner, on their store card. Even reports of a downward trend in their favoured shop's profits or reputation could not deter these stalwarts, but rather they would rally to support the cause as if the very fabric of their lives depended upon it. There was something oddly defensive about it; a determination to cling to the principle of a comfortable lifestyle no matter what. All the same, Kate was surprised to be confronted by Alicia's well-groomed manifestation here in Cornwall, where windblown was the norm. Even now, as they stood in the bracing sea breeze, not one hair on Alicia's head lifted.

'I'm sure the standards here are fine,' said Kate. 'It's a lovely little school.'

Alicia Browning frowned slightly. 'Yes of course, but it's no mean feat. It is our duty, as parents, to make sure that our children get a fair crack of the whip, especially when you cannot assume teacher competence these days.'

'Hmm,' said Kate, instinctively rebelling against being informed of her parental duties. 'Of course, teachers have so much more to do now. I mean, it's not like the olden days when they just had to teach. It's all paperwork and testing now.'

'Well yes, perhaps,' said Alicia, although she looked unconvinced. 'But this is why it is even more imperative that we, as mothers, do our bit. I myself listen to my Olivia's classmates read aloud every day. Perhaps *you* could spare a few hours?'

'Hell, no!' laughed Kate. 'I get enough of that at home, not to mention the amount of homework we have to cope with. I reckon it's just a matter of time before the schools send letters home saying: "look, we're too busy, can you just bloody well *teach* the kids, okay?"'

A cluster of other mothers standing nearby now noticeably silenced. It was clear that they had been hanging on every word of Kate's conversation. She despaired of herself. As the newcomer in town they were naturally curious about her, and she had planned to be guarded and reserved; inconspicuous and aloof. So far the plan had worked, yet here she was blathering on, and no doubt sparking off all manner of ill-translated controversy.

'Yeah right! Like they would really expect us to teach our own children,' said one of the women. She stared unblinkingly at Kate, through half-closed heavy-lashed eyelids, while chewing slowly on some gum. *Like a sheep*, thought Kate. And how could the woman possibly not realise that she had been joking?

'Oh, don't be daft Jenifer Trewin, she didn't meant it, did she?' said a third party; a plump woman with hair bleached to the texture of cotton wool. 'She was having a laugh, weren't you my luvver?'

'Yes of course,' said Kate, embarrassed, and to her shame, alarmed that her ally was this large woman dressed in pre-lycra leggings and a black leather jacket adorned with the single word 'Sabbath' on the back.

The woman called Jenifer Trewin stared Kate up and down for a minute, still chewing her cud, before turning away with a flick of her long smooth hair.

'Well, I'm sure we'll find a niche for you somewhere, Kate,' said Alicia, rather sadly, and unable to hide the disappointment in her eyes.

Kate felt immediately guilty. Perhaps she should have welcomed Alicia's gesture. It was possible that no one in the village would ever speak to her again and she would forever be referred to as "the incomer" or god forbid, "the townie".

'Of course,' she said, 'I'll try to come along to the next meeting. I hear there's going to be a quiz night soon. That's being organised by the PTA isn't it? If you're short on any of the teams then I could make up the numbers I suppose? It's a bit difficult not knowing anyone...'

Kate's voice trailed off as the slow realisation dawned that no one was listening to her anymore, but that all heads had surreptitiously turned in the direction of an old green Land Rover that had pulled up at the school gates. The car door opened and Finn Borlase jumped out, trailing his rucksack, coat, and a sports bag behind him.

Gas guzzler, she thought, although Kate was faintly surprised that Finn had not emerged from the trendy van that she had imagined. Grudgingly, she acknowledged that the tyres and nether regions of the car were thoroughly splattered with mud, suggesting a genuine off-road requirement. And although she knew very little about cars, she reluctantly conceded that it was an very old model, resembling something you could imagine scooting across the post-war African plains. And so regrettably, the driver's green credentials were not quite as appalling as she would have them. But she had been right about him in another respect: the back and boot-seats of the large car had been folded to accommodate a haphazard selection of surfboards.

41

She was aware of blond locks and broad shoulders in the driver's seat, before turning away quickly with her nose in the air. After her altercation with Lance Borlase the previous day, she was anxious not to display an iota of interest. But she was astonished at the effect his presence had on the handful of other women still gathered, lingering, outside the school. They had stopped all conversation, yet perversely, assumed an unnatural facade of going about their business. Some stared, narrow-eyed at an imaginary point in the near distance, as though searching for a lost child. One or two of them gave the game away, as Kate spied them nod in Lance's direction, with eyes locked in mutual understanding. Even Alicia raised the spectacles from the chain around her neck to have a peer. They were all, as one, unified in their interest in the driver of the green four-wheel-drive. In fact, Kate was notable amongst them for being the only one determined not to look.

This subterfuge did not prevent Finn Borlase from yelling: 'Hiya Kate!' and waving frantically, before dashing, late for school, into the playground.

Instinctively polite, she waved back grinning like a ninny, and mimicked 'Hiya!'

With all eyes momentarily upon her, Kate read surprise, jealousy and suspicion in turn. Jenifer in particular returned her attention to Kate, with her frosty, fixed gaze.

The Land Rover pulled away quickly with little more than a backward glance from the driver. The women became reanimated, and Kate felt amused at having witnessed such shameless, collective ogling of a handsome man.

'Do you know him then?' Jenifer, flanked by a couple of cohorts, rounded on Kate. Thinking that perhaps they were standing on the wrong side of the playground fence, Kate felt transported back to her own childhood, and her heart beat faster as she observed the unfriendly faces.

'Who? Oh you mean Finn?' she asked coolly, regaining her composure and instinctively reacting to Jenifer's aggressive tone. 'Yes, he's a friend of my daughter's.'

'No, I meant his dad,' said Jenifer irritably. 'Do you know Lance Borlase?'

Kate disliked being interrogated in this way. It brought out the perversity in her. 'Yes, yes I do.' She met Jenifer's languid stare straight on. 'He was over at our place last night actually. Why? Is he a friend of yours too?'

Jenifer's eyes narrowed with barely concealed venom. 'You want to be careful with that one,' she said with vitriol. 'He is not a very nice person. Take it from me; I should know.'

Kate couldn't stop herself now. Jenifer's threatening manner was annoying the hell out of her. 'Hmm. He is gorgeous though, don't you think?'

The two cronies gasped and gaped on either side of Jenifer. Like curling, twisting snakes on the Hydra's head, they looked to their leader for a response. Jenifer flicked her head so that her long hair flew backwards and then fell sultrily over one eye. She put one hand on a hip, arched her visible eyebrow theatrically and gave a wry smile.

'Oh, you'll learn, sweetheart,' she said. And then assuming an air of profound seriousness pronounced: 'You know, beauty is not skin deep.'

The other Hydra heads looked satisfied, but Kate almost laughed out loud at the solemnly delivered platitude. She managed to compose her mirth into an amiable grin. 'You mean it is.'

'Sorry? What?' Jenifer's smile turned into an ugly curl.

'Skin deep,' said Kate. 'Beauty is skin deep. Or so they say, anyway.' And, observing their confusion, she promptly turned and walked away towards the village centre.

CHAPTER 4

A Sea Witch

Kate was still adjusting to the unfamiliarity of her new home. As she reached Pencarra's quaint main street, or Fore Street, she could smell fresh Cornish pasties baking in the morning air. St Piran's flag invaded her consciousness from stickers in shop windows, tourist mugs and key-fobs, from boat-hire signs and from where it flapped proudly atop of masts. Outside shops, surfboards were propped up alongside baskets of seashells and dried starfish. Wetsuits hung drying from upper windows, a contrast to the more traditional sight of fishing nets and lobster pots in the harbour....and everywhere; everywhere was the prevalent call of gulls and the fresh briny essence of the sea. It was all wonderful, but today Kate felt in discord given the recent confrontation, and was still shaking slightly from the rush of adrenalin. Instead of picking up some supplies as she had intended, she turned off down a narrow cobbled lane that she had previously discovered led to a small cove. A signpost and arrow attached to the side of a whitewashed cottage announced it's name: Porthvean Beach.

She sat down on an old weather-beaten wooden bench. Had she continued to the end of Fore Street she would have arrived at the pretty harbour, with its fishing boats, ancient pubs, and charming shops selling pottery and other trinkets for the tourists. But here at Porthvean there was a secluded inlet, and beyond that, on the other side of the headland, a much larger stretch of beach. This, she had learnt, was Porthledden; wider and less sheltered and reputed to be a decent surf break. It could be reached, presumably, by scrambling over the rocky promontory when the tide was going out, as it was now. Otherwise, she knew, it was accessed by a variety of steep tracks winding down from the cliff-top coastal path. Some of these tracks were precarious, having been worn in by centuries of tramping feet—Smugglers! Georgian militia!—or were little more than breaks in the grasses of the huge undulating sand dunes, or *towans*, as they called them. But others had more recently been made wider and more accessible by the installation of reclaimed railway sleepers, in a series of broad steps.

Kate gazed upon the scenery and breathed in the sea air. She felt the sun warm her face, and tried to regain a degree of serenity. But she was cross with herself. How many people had she managed to offend in the short space of two days? She was not doing herself any favours by antagonising the locals. Alicia Browning, at least, had meant well, even if her views might differ a little from her own. And as for Jenifer Trewin...well, she hadn't liked her, but perhaps her warning about Lance Borlase had been justified. After all, she herself had surmised that he was an unpleasant individual.

All too soon, the glory of the early morning sunshine began to be eclipsed by wind-blown clouds, and deprived of the sun's welcoming rays, Kate now felt the chill in the breeze. She was grateful to have worn a jumper on top of her optimistic summer dress. Within minutes the sky and the sea threatened to take on the greyness that, less than an hour ago, she had been scorning the city streets for.

An elderly couple smiled inquisitively at her as they passed along the beach with their dog. They walked sluggishly and talked very little. They stared, speechless, at the sea, and then incomprehensibly, they stared at the rocks. They turned their

45

quizzical gaze back towards Kate for a bit—as if she too were a rock formation, or some strange thing washed up by the tide—before turning slowly away again. They appeared to her to be utterly without direction or purpose. Even the dog seemed half-hearted in its exercise; limping along, obligingly sniffing a rock here or there, as if to show willing.

Oh no. Tilting her head back against the back of the bench and raising closed eyes to the sky, Kate felt her optimism fade and the madness creep back. Isabella had been right. She had taken her daughter away from the vibrancy of London and moved her to a place where nothing was going to happen, ever. They were going to die here of boredom. They would be lonely in their cottage with nothing but the howling wind outside for company—Kate having alienated the entire village—and Isabella would up-sticks at the earliest legal age and take herself back to London. Kate would then worry herself to death about her daughter and become a lonely old woman surrounded by cats—crazy cats that lurked in the shadows waiting to attack.

She was driftwood, stranded; an alien sea-monster; an unnatural thing that didn't belong.

Get a grip, Kate, she told herself sternly, and sitting up straight again. She couldn't afford to let recent incidents bring her down. Think. *Think!* What did she need? Some bread and milk, and locally caught fish for tea. *See how lucky we are, freshly caught fish for tea. Better than over-packaged department store food anytime.*

On sudden impulse she kicked off her canvas shoes, stuffed them in her small rucksack and then strode with purpose across the beach towards the shore's edge. When she reached the flat wet sand where the tide breached, she broke into a run. The action triggered a spontaneous grin, such as she could barely remember. The seawater was still seasonably warm after the hot summer and she relished the feel as it splashed and licked against her bare legs.

46

She noticed, in astonishment, hordes of little blue jellyfish floating on the current, but rather than alarm, she felt a thrill at the *strangeness*. The world was all new and fresh before her eyes. The hem of her dress became wet as she waded deeper into the breaking waves, but she didn't care. She walked the length of the beach in the surf, breathing in the fresh salty air and relishing the sense of freedom.

When she reached the headland, the rocks called to her, with their tantalising natural steps and hand-holds, and she wanted to climb them. The heavy boulders and slabs were still wet and slippery with seaweed down here where the tide had recently been, but it wasn't too far before they made for an easier, drier, climb. She forced her damp, sandy feet back into her shoes, which made her feel like a child again; a memory of some long-forgotten beach holiday. But she wasn't a child, and the realisation made her hesitate. Was this a stupidly rash and reckless thing to do? What if she fell, or twisted an ankle?

But if you don't do it now, then when will you ever? If you can't do it now, then you never will.

Eventually, panting, she found her way to the grassy top, and fell in love. She gasped for breath in the suddenly exposed wind that beat the skirt of her dress and made her long hair fly in a tangle of tentacles, like she was some wild, siren Medusa; a sea witch invoking the elements. But she was transfixed in wonderment at the sight of Porthledden Beach. From this height and angle she could see the approaching lines of surf. The colour changed in bands as each wave came nearer to the shore, and changed again as the sunlight escaped between racing clouds: Paynes Grey became Celadon, Ultramarine and Veridian turned to Cerulean Blue and the palest Mineral Green, and Cobalt Violet stained the Naples Yellow sand. A string of surfers drifted like flotsam just beyond the Zinc White breaking surf; accents of colour. The desire to paint the scene came upon her like a panic.

47

She dropped unsteadily to sit upon a welcoming rock, and to drink in the view. She retrieved a beanie hat from her rucksack to tame her hair, and pulling the long sleeves of her jumper down further, hugged herself for warmth. She felt a strange delight at the exotic tremble in her muscles from the climb, and serene and energised now that her breathing had calmed.

It would be alright.

She would be like the jellyfish, and go where the current took her. In a while, she would climb down to explore this beautiful beach. Later, she would visit the little art supplies shop in the harbour and buy a canvas and some turpentine. And then she would go back to her lovely little cottage and she would start to paint again.

* * *

Lance sat up on his board and steered it to survey the landscape from the water, checking his position against familiar markers. Intermittent clouds cast fleeting shadows across the otherwise iridescent watercolour of sand dune, mudstone and sky. He manoeuvred it back again to face the horizon of the Atlantic Ocean. In places where the sunlight still hit the sea it created tiny pools of sparkling, swirling luminescence that flashed in and out of existence. *Little universes.*

He threw his head back, shaking his long wet hair as he did, and took a deep breath. His hands played idly in the salt sea as the surfboard bobbed on the water between sets. He imagined each particle of water passing between his open fingers, its path disturbed by his intervention, but still held in the larger pattern; still moving inevitably toward its destiny.

Some of the other surfers liked to paddle together for a chat while they waited, but not Lance. A few of his comrades now exchanged amused remarks, rubbed their chins and grinned, knowing that he was deep in thought. Some taunted him, amicably. He ignored them; he was used to it, as were they he.

Instead, he pondered on the double-slit experiment, in which photons or electrons, when measured, revealed their particle quality, but when left un-espied betrayed their wave-like existence. The act of observation made the decision; brought them into being. All the potential outcomes were decided; resolved. But it still defied him how single particles, when fired through the slits one by one, still conspired to make the interference pattern, indicating their wave element. Each electron, or photon, could only arrive at a single spot. How did each subsequent particle fired through the slits 'know' where to land to form the pattern? Was each somehow going through both slits and interfering with itself? Or did it contain a greater knowledge? Did it know of all the electrons that had gone before, and all that were yet to come? Like a breaking ocean wave slowed down to a standstill, only moving by one invisible grain at a time, there was no undoing of the greater force, the *momentum*, behind each particle. The one was still part of the whole, and the wave would still crash, inexorably.

The signs of another set rolling in broke his concentration. He smiled in satisfaction as he noted the height, wavelength and frequency, and then turning, paddled into position. And then he saw her, and groaned. That woman from the day before—Kate O'Neill—was picking her way along the shoreline, seemingly lost in her world, but still stopping at intervals to gaze out to sea. *Landlubbers*, he thought, wryly; so full of wistful, pale romance about the ocean, but never actually getting in. He looked behind again to check the approach of the next wave. It looked perfect. He was in just the right place to catch it and he had priority. He checked the shore again.

His heart sank.

The wave looked to be going left and would carry him in the direction of that bloody woman on the beach. Of course he could feign blindness; just turn straight around and start paddling back out again, but she might take it as a snub and no doubt there would be more petty gossip at the school gates. And besides, he still didn't want her to see *him*. He knew this was unreasonable but was in no mood. After the way she had behaved, she wasn't to have any part of him. But there was no time; he would have to make a decision.

He let it pass, and watched in frustration as the next surfer caught the perfect peeling wave to its end. Damn it! The beautiful slice of stolen energy that should have been his was now heading for the shore and its journey's end. Hundreds, possibly thousands, of miles traversed now to be dissipated in a sonic blast or reclaimed by the receding current. He sat, cursing under his breath as he let the whole set go by, whilst the woman, blithely unawares, inspected seashells in the sand.

CHAPTER 5

Dolphin Cottage

Dolphin Cottage had been a real find. Kate was aware of this over and above all her reservations about the upheaval that she had instigated. When Great Aunt Josephine had died and unpredictably left the house in Alwyne Villas to both Kate and Juliet, their lives had changed fantastically overnight. Initially the two sisters had made jovial talk of sharing the glorious North London home, but it soon became clear that their individual yearnings were worlds apart.

'I'm sorry, but I'm off to Australia,' Juliet had said. Australia was to be preceded en-route by Thailand and Bali, and followed by New Zealand and the Cook Islands, where she secretly harboured thoughts that Parker, who would naturally be accompanying her, might feel sufficiently romantically compelled to marry her. Not that Juliet desired marriage per se, but if she ever were to marry, the ceremony would have to take place somewhere exotic, and preferably display a degree of impulse and abandon, in accordance with her character. *Or her public image*, Kate had thought when Juliet confided these desires in her flighty, throwaway manner.

But since she harboured dubious inclinations of her own, Kate did not criticise Juliet's impulsiveness in frittering away her legacy. Besides, hopefully even Juliet would manage to reserve enough funds to set herself up when she eventually returned from her travels. Their inheritance was relatively substantial. It was not as smart as other houses in the vicinity, but the fact that the house was large, chain-free, unmodernised yet bursting with original features, meant that the offers came rolling in. It was fair to say that the two girls had never imagined such wealth ever coming their way. They had never been "moneyed" people. Their parents were educated but until recently, relatively poor: Grammar school products, who in their youth had thought that enthusiasm and their respective talents, would be enough to project them into a world of middle class respectability, holidays abroad, two cars and adorable children. In truth, it had, eventually. But they resented the long years of poverty raising the girls; their mother, in particular. A politics graduate, she had seen her career slide at a time when she was supposedly burning her bra and changing the world for women.

Susan had never really resumed her intended career as a journalist. By the time the girls were independent, Seamus was doing well enough as a buildings contractor to support them comfortably. They embarked upon a series of ocean cruises and "well-deserved" holidays abroad, culminating in their purchase and restoration of a farmhouse in France, complete with converted outbuildings that they let to holidaymakers as a source of income.

And then, just when they were settling back to reap the rewards of patience and propriety, Aunt Josephine, or Aunt Joe, as she was more commonly known, had skipped a generation.

The old cow! Susan had thought, if briefly, at the time.

Josephine had lived in the house in Alwyne Villas for what had seemed like forever, apparently unaware of the small fortune that she was literally sitting in. Indeed, as time drew on, it may have suited certain family members not to inform or remind her of this detail. Yet she had sailed through all their expectations and left the house to Kate and Juliet.

Of course, reasoned Susan, the resultant money would help Kate out of a dire situation, not to mention Isabella, whom she adored. And she enjoyed conversations with Juliet in respect of her intended travels; glad that at least one of her offspring had not taken the stereotypical hard route of embarking on motherhood too young. In truth, however, she felt robbed. She particularly begrudged Kate's good fortune. Much as she wanted Isabella out of "that dreadful flat", an unattractive part of her had always been secretly jealous of her elder daughter's daring in taking up with a gorgeous Lothario like Miles; and Kate, until now at least, had deservedly paid the price for such audacity. Susan felt that her own current pleasant lifestyle had been hard-earned, if only by its very long time in coming; and that such good fortune should not simply be dropped into anyone's lap. And so it was that despite their recent solvency and comfortable life, Susan had been put out that Seamus' Aunt Josephine had left her property to the girls.

'The thing is,' Juliet had said to Kate, 'I need to travel. I need to see the world. It's important to me. I'm not like you. I couldn't settle in one place and have kids.'

Kate had fought a strong desire to say that she too (and perhaps every parent in the land) harboured dreams of Thai beaches and the clear mountain air of New Zealand. But she had no wish to spoil her sister's excitement. Indeed, she delighted in the fact that Juliet, at least, could now live the dream. Unfortunately, Juliet did not have an equal enthusiasm for Kate's own particular aspiration.

'You're completely crazy,' she had said. 'With the money we'll have, you could buy a house in London! Not as big as Aunt Joe's, but in *London*, for Christ's sake. I know there's a surfing scene in Cornwall, but it's not exactly California, is it? I mean, you could *go* to California for that matter. And as for all those pasties they eat...think of the carbs Kate!'

53

Susan's reaction was even more violently dismissive. Kate found herself firmly told that she should buy a property in London and forget this entire *country* lark. If she moved away now she would never be able to secure a return to London, what with the way house prices rose. It was utterly irresponsible and thoughtless, particularly in respect of Isabella, who for some reason, not apparent to Kate, would suffer needlessly by being removed from the city. Kate suspected that Susan's motives were more likely influenced by her own desire for a chichi, and cost-free, London pied-à-terre. It was with some quiet amusement that Kate realised that owing to the nature of her sudden change of fortune, Aunt Joe's bequest was not quite being recognised as hers alone. And so she listened patiently while Susan instructed her as to her options, wondering when her mother would finally twig that Kate—deservedly or not—could, and would, do exactly as she liked. She wondered, in wild-eyed amusement, what her mother would say if she knew of the full extent of her plans.

And yes, she could have stayed in London, or gone to California, as Juliet suggested. Or Timbuktu if she so desired. But Kate's dream was for a more thorough, life-changing escape. If it worked, then rather than undermine, it might positively enhance Isabella's future welfare.

Samuel Johnson said that "When a man is tired of London, he is tired of life". But perhaps, Kate thought, he could have had no concept of London as experienced by the lesser-privileged at the beginning of the 21st Century. Of course she loved the history, the museums and art galleries. Yes there was an energy, but this was sapped by crowds, traffic and pollution. And more than that there was of late, she felt, an anxiety. She saw it in people's faces; haggard from the expense and perpetual insecurity; wearied from the sheer effort required to traverse its vastness. London exhausted her, physically, mentally and spiritually, but she didn't think that she was tired of *life*.

And besides, she no longer had any ties to bind her. The desire to escape had been strong.

She had honed in on her atlas and singled out Devon, Cornwall and Somerset, possibly Dorset. Being infamously averse to the technological benefits of the Internet—*a complete Luddite*, said Juliet— she had sent letters to various estate agents in these counties expressing an interest in smallish properties with character and charm, including those that might need further work or investment. They were not to know that Kate's plan was not to reap the rewards of property development, but rather to deconstruct; to revert to a simpler, saner way of life. A week later she had been inundated with information on literally hundreds of properties.

So she had decided to restrict her search to Cornwall; to the North coast, where the sea raged tempestuously, or so she imagined. Reluctantly, she resigned herself to the fact that a beach house was sadly beyond her means. It transpired from the sack-loads of Estate Agents' bumph that she'd had to wade through, that this particular dream was going to cost. House prices rose as dramatically towards the coastal areas of Cornwall as they did in the more sought-after areas of London.

'It's a nightmare,' she had said to Juliet on the phone. 'And why do some Estate Agents have this strange antiquated language all of their own? It's all 'twixt this and 'tween that, or '*some* 100 foot garden'.

'Yeah,' said Juliet, 'or "sizeable". "The property benefits from a sizeable garden." What does *that* mean?'

'And why do they always say "older-*style*" house, or "Victorian-*style*" house?' continued Kate. 'Does that mean it's just pretending to be old? Is it Victorian or not?'

In the summer half-term holiday, having already, joyfully, given up her despised office job, she had taken Isabella to view her short-list of around half a dozen properties scattered along the North coast between Tintagel and St Ives. It had taken forever to get there in the Morris, and Isabella, having left her patience behind in London, chastised her mother for the entire journey for not possessing a *proper* car. To compound their consequent ill-humour, the majority of houses that they viewed were a disappointment; nowhere near living up to the expectations aroused by the estate agents' glowing depictions. And certainly, none of them delivered the traditional country dream of thatch or beam, let alone Kate's more nebulous vision of some sort of ramshackle eccentricity.

And yet the countryside that unfolded around them revealed scenes of such increasing beauty and charm, that it left Kate with a peculiar, almost nauseated feeling; a brew of both excitement and serenity.

At their first sight of the sea from a high cliff lane, Kate had stopped the car and wound down the windows to let in the twisting, gusting breeze, and to hear the cry of gulls wheeling high overhead. It was a warm summer's day; sunlit, but fresh by the coast where dreamlike clouds sailed overhead. In the distance small fishing boats made their way back to harbour on the shimmering deep-blue ocean.

And in a sheltered cove a strange tribe of dark-skinned creatures sat waiting, expectant, on the water. They might have been seals, but for their unique, lined-up formation; no, they were neoprene-clad surfers. The waves rolled in in clean, peeling lines of startlingly clear, jewel-coloured water. She longed for Isabella to say something; to voice her approval of such an incredible environment. When she did not, Kate did not prompt. She wanted her daughter to find her own way.

The last of three different estate agents, a Mr Baragwaneth—and Isabella marvelled at the strange name; was she in another *country*?—was a man who clearly took no delight in his job. And so after suffering Kate and Isabella's negative reactions to two other properties, and once having assured himself that they were not planning to squat, had entrusted Kate with the keys to the last one. Feigning other business back at the office, he gave sparse directions, and then left them alone.

They eventually found the obscure, narrow road named Carrick Lane and Kate swerved the Morris into the short earthen driveway to Dolphin Cottage. By this time both mother and daughter were disgruntled with disappointment, and Kate had lost the will to try and keep Isabella enthused. They sat for a while in the car observing; gathering first impressions. Again, the squat stone cottage was not thatched, and neither did it have roses around the door. But Kate thought that she recognised Clematis and honeysuckle reaching up as far as the bedroom windows, where the overgrown, untamed stems drooped and beat against the glass in the summer breeze.

There was a small wooden porch at the doorway; its sides filled not with glass, but with trellis; supporting the well-established climbers. Kate reflected on how most of the exterior woodwork appeared in need of repair. In fact, it had to be admitted that the overall impression was one of distinct shabbiness. And it was certainly no beach house. One could probably only see the sea above the hedges, and in the distance, from one of the upstairs bedrooms. But it was, Kate decided, as near as damn it.

It sat alone, detached, on the outskirts of a fishing village called Pencarra. Kate unfolded the crumpled wad of estate agents' notes that she had carried around all day. The badly copied photograph gave little away; but the text reminded her that the cottage had reputedly been there since the 18th century, but had undergone some rebuilding in Victorian times. It also revealed that it was "in need of extensive improvements". In effect, it had absolutely no modern heating whatsoever.

Perfect, thought Kate, although even she could see the irony. It was a far from normal reaction.

Mr Baragwaneth had supplied the information that the cottage was vacant, and that it had been so for "*some* six weeks now". He also hinted that it would most likely be snatched up by a property developer. 'A cash buyer,' he had stated, with an insinuating look. The previous owner, a ninety-six year old by the name of Amelia Church, had lived there for many years alone following the death of her husband, before being persuaded by her concerned offspring to enter a home for the elderly. She had survived just four months in the home, and the family were now keen for a quick sale to settle the estate.

The cottage had a large overgrown garden that ran all around the house, and, apart from a gap to allow the rudimentary driveway, was almost hidden from the road by a high Cornish hedge, its stone structure overcome with abundant wild flowers and foliage. A huge Ash tree dominated the grounds, serving as a landmark. An old round wooden garden table and two matching chairs sat abandoned, disintegrating and lop-sided outside one of the front windows—*a window that was low-enough to climb in and out of as if it were a doorway*. Kate immediately imagined herself doing just that. Feeling a flicker of inspiration, and praying that they weren't completely rotten, Kate contemplated rejuvenating the window frames and door in a deep sky-blue paint. Then, if she were to white-wash the exterior walls, and perhaps plant some window boxes with trailing geraniums or bougainvillaea....

'...I'd have the perfect little Greek Island villa,' she muttered sardonically. Well, maybe not white paint. There was something of a timeless dependability about the thick granite stone; a cool and solid retreat from the summer heat, that would as equally be a warm shelter in the winter.

'Come on, let's look inside,' said Isabella.

A sign over the door confirmed the name "Dolphin Cottage"; it was painted in a style that reminded Kate of old wooden boat-names; hand-scripted, quirky and charming. Her hand reached instinctively to touch the beautiful dolphin knocker, and she had a strange feeling of recognition. Kate turned the key in the lock, and the weathered tongue-in-groove boards that made up the front door shuddered, but obediently fell from the grasp of the door-frame to which they no longer fitted comfortably. The hallway was long and narrow, but the walls were delightfully wood-panelled and painted in an ancient white, long since turned to a yellowy-cream. The air was warm and musty.

On her right there were two doors, the first of which led to a large kitchen with a wood-burning stove, and the other to a bathroom. The *only* bathroom, she realised, referring briefly to her scanty notes. That was okay; it was just the two of them, and they knew how to use stairs. To the left was the living room; not so spacious, and dominated by a large stone inglenook fireplace; but it had the potential to be cosy in a shabby-chic sort of way. Further along the hallway on the left there was a staircase that twisted up and around to the three bedrooms.

'Could do with an airing,' said Kate. Isabella said nothing, but pushed past her and headed up the stairs to inspect the bedrooms, as she had done in each previous house that they had viewed; her prime objective being to secure the best bedroom in any given house for herself.

Kate stood still in the hallway, her mind full of ruminations. There was an old-fashioned slightly grimy wall-phone, complete with dial. It made Kate smile. She disliked mobile telephones; both for their flashy throw-away, ever-upgrading designs and for their bossy intrusiveness. She had given in to having one at all only because Juliet, in frustration, had bought her one. But she still stubbornly refused to renew it even though the battery life was diminished, and the ringtone barely audible. It was *vintage*, she gloated in response to Isabella's chiding remarks.

She moved towards the old telephone and picked up the receiver—its moulded shape instantly, aesthetically comfortable to her hand—and put it to her ear. A high pitched shriek indicated that the line was out-of-order, but not completely defunct...she could have it reconnected.

Isabella thumped back down the wooden stairs, clearly excited. 'Mum, it's really weird, come and see!'

Kate followed Isabella upstairs and found herself in another narrow panelled hallway leading off into the three bedrooms. It was immediately obvious which bedroom Isabella preferred, as she dived into a huge room that was divided, nonsensically, into two levels, forming a 'step' in the middle of the room.

'Well this is odd...' said Kate, puzzled.

'It's like a stage!' said Isabella, 'I'll have a drum kit and guitars up here!'

'We'll see about that!'

'Anyway, Do you get it?'

When Kate looked blank Isabella said, 'Close your eyes and come over to the window.'

Too weary to contradict her daughter's logic, Kate complied. Impatient, Isabella grabbed her stumbling mother's arm and guided her to the window.

'Now, keep your eyes shut! What do you think you will see out of the window? When you open your eyes I mean.' Kate could sense Isabella's own eyes sparkling.

'Er, the car I suppose,' she said, 'the car in the driveway, and the front garden.'

'Wrong!' said Isabella triumphantly. Kate opened her eyes and was taken aback to see a view that she had not anticipated, but which must have been overlooking the gardens at one side of the house.

60

'It works in all the bedrooms,' said Isabella, 'Come and see.' The bedrooms were indeed a conundrum, as none of them overlooked the view that one would have expected of them.

'It must be something to do with the stairs,' said Kate. 'They must curve around further than you would imagine. Or less...?'

'It's freaky!' cried Isabella. 'It's all wonky! It's...it's like a magic cottage!' And with that, she raced back downstairs, where Kate could hear her clattering about, opening and shutting cupboards and doors. Kate smiled. The advantage of having off-loaded the Estate Agent was that they could explore without inhibition. She walked slowly into the other decent-sized bedroom, which presumably was to be her own if they were to go ahead and buy the place (the third being impractically small). Faded paint was the only decoration to bare plastered walls. Her footsteps resounded in the empty room as she crossed the dark wooden floor to the window. It was a pretty little bay window, with a deep sill that you could sit in, something that she suddenly remembered hankering after as a child. And the view, this time, was of the front garden, the hedges and fields beyond; and finally, in the distance, as she had suspected, the sea. It was lovely.

She thought of Amelia Church, newly married and happy with her husband. *Was* it a happy, loving home? She thought of her bringing up her children, perhaps even giving birth to them here in this room. Perhaps they had struggled; for it had certainly been no rich man's home, despite what the current market value might suggest. And yet it was a small slice of paradise to the likes of Kate. What a shame for Amelia, she thought, to have had to leave her home at the last. She thought also of Aunt Joe, defiantly rejecting the family's well-meaning offers to accommodate her, or perhaps, move in with her, "for her own good".

Back downstairs again, Kate ventured towards the back of the cottage, where at the other end of the hallway, a half-glazed door led through to a tile-floored utilitarian room fitted with an old porcelain sink and ancient wooden work top. There were two doors leading off into good-sized store cupboards. She imagined that these were larders, and that the room had once been some sort of pantry area; or even an outbuilding. But she was drawn now, her heart beating wildly, through a further half-glazed door to the very back of the building, where unbelievably, magically, someone had had the imagination to install a large conservatory. On entering, she found the stale fustiness even more intense. There was another wood-burner in here; but it was covered in ages of dust, suggesting abandonment years before Amelia Church's demise. Kate suspected that the conservatory was, in its entirety, the Victorian addition that had been referred to; and as such was relatively modern, and not in keeping with the period of the rest of the building. However, it was large enough to qualify as another room. And it seemed to call to her: lovelorn and shabby and in need of attention; a little like herself. If Kate had not been convinced of the cottage's charms thus far, then it was the conservatory that had finally seduced her. The garden beyond was wild and unkempt, but it was south-facing. The conservatory, despite the gathering layers of dirt on the glass panes, was bright, warm, and filled with light.

Light and space. This was where she would paint. She would clean her brushes and jam-jars at the pantry sink. It was too perfect. The composed adult in her fought an overwhelming desire to ring Mr Baragwaneth there and then and put in an offer. She was panicked at the thought of another buyer usurping her, but the pessimist in her felt compelled to check the entire place thoroughly.

'I'm just not this lucky,' she said aloud.

Later, having inspected the cottage several times over, Kate and Isabella had sat down amidst the long grasses and summer meadow flowers of the wild back garden, and considered.

'Well, Izzy,' said Kate, picking some grass from Isabella's dark curls, 'what do you think of this one?'

'I love it!' cried Isabella, 'I've just got to have that bedroom—it's brilliant! Please Mum, let's get this one; *please!*'

Kate sighed. Isabella was only thinking of the here and now, as her age decreed. She had immediately forgotten the distance, the long journey that they had travelled. Perversely, given her well-voiced objections on the way, she was no longer thinking of what she would be leaving behind. Kate often sought Isabella's opinion on matters that really ought to be her decision alone. It was a habit from the years that they had spent alone together, when Kate, lacking in confidence, and more importantly, adult companionship and support, would sound out her young daughter for ideas and advice. But it would be unfair to put this one on Isabella; it was too big a decision.

They drowsed in the afternoon sun, Kate with eyes closed and face upturned to the gentle summer breeze. Isabella lay on her back using one arm as a pillow, chewing a long grass and kicking one crossed leg up and down rhythmically in the air. The excitement pulsed through her veins as she dreamed of that bedroom, and of how she would make it her own. The drone of the bees and the rustling of the grass were a heady mead wine to Kate's starved senses. She felt her limbs relax.

This is where I go to in my head, she thought. This was a special place of calm and peace. To complete the fantasy there should be a hidden rustic gateway leading down some stone steps to a deserted beach, where she could wander slowly through the surf...

Isabella's scream brought her back to reality and onto her feet in seconds, as the creature tore its way through the long grass, and was gone.

'What is it?' shrieked Isabella. 'Has it gone? It jumped right on my stomach!'

'I think it was a cat,' said Kate. 'Don't worry, it's gone now.'

'I bet it was a rat,' said Isabella, her eyes wide. 'I could have been bitten by a rat!'

'I'm sure it wasn't; don't be so melodramatic! It was a cat, that's all.'

But Kate trod furtively back through the jungle of a garden to the cottage, her moment of tranquillity soured and suddenly conscious of the threat of grass snakes, amongst other things. Back at the car she stood and took one last look. The fantasy and the reality were two different things; in her heart she knew this. She could always go back to London and try to carry on with the life that she had, and knew. She could always fester and die.

She drove thoughtfully back into the village and caught Mr Baragwaneth about to lock up shop. Too late, Kate realised her "vintage" phone had died and that he had probably been trying to call her. Clearly aggravated, Mr Baragwaneth hustled them back inside, complaining that they were late and pointedly bolting the door behind them as if to prevent an onslaught of undesirable latecomers—although the streets outside were deserted.

'I'd like to buy Dolphin Cottage,' said Kate, once they were all seated, and in her most grown-up voice; the one she used when addressing Isabella's school teachers, or applying for a job on the telephone. 'And I'd like you to take it off the market straight away.'

Mr Baragwaneth peered disdainfully at the single parent sitting before him. 'Of course you're welcome to put in an offer, but be prepared to be disappointed. As I said, there's been a lot of interest, and a mortgage could take many weeks to arrange...'

'I'm offering the full asking price,' said Kate. Then noting the estate agent's supercilious eye, she coolly added: 'Cash buyer.'

And then she smiled conspiratorially at Isabella, who beamed right back at her.

CHAPTER 6

Jem

Jem Farrow took advantage of the gap between patients to gaze through the open french windows onto the garden and the sea beyond. *Christ*, how he would love a cigarette. He didn't even smoke, not since his teenage years anyway. But metaphorically he wished he could stand at the french windows, leaning in a sensual, gallic way, and dragging on a Gauloise. Maybe he'd sport a rebellious few day's stubble. He didn't often get a break. If anything, his patients usually overran their scheduled times, and he would end up working through lunch, then leaving exhausted at the end of the day. His thoughts by then would be a confused amalgam—he allowed himself a smirk at the analogy—of rotting teeth, bad breath, what to grab for his dinner, and the football match on television that evening.

His choice of meal was always heavily prejudiced by the type of wine that he was going to intoxicate himself to sleep with that night. He kidded himself that the wine was a mere trimming, to complement the meal; but in reality the opposite was true: the food was really a mask to disguise his ever-increasing alcohol consumption. He rarely, if ever, these days ate beans on toast—although he quite liked beans on toast—because beans on toast went with a cup of tea. Whereas, if he were to chuck some fresh egg pasta in a pan, and rustle up a not bad (if he said so himself) Marinara sauce, then he could justifiably indulge in a bottle of Chilean Merlot. Likewise, if he were to think, *sod it, I've been working all day, and what's the point in cooking for one?*—then he couldn't possibly drink anything but an ice-cold Australian Chardonnay with his takeaway prawn dhansak. And it didn't even matter that Chardonnay was losing its popularity amongst the masses, because he knew what he liked. He was a man of opinion and taste. Yes, a man of character.

'Fuck, I'm a sad case,' he muttered, bending over double in his chair to bring elbow to knee, and fist to brow.

He was interrupted in these thoughts by Nicky, his trainee assistant, bringing in the next patient. He startled momentarily, before replacing his surgical mask over his nose and mouth in a perfunctory manner, and studying the next set of notes in the pile. But apart from the personal information at the top of the large pink card, they were blank.

'Ah, you're a new patient, are you?'

'Excuse me?' snapped the woman who was gingerly easing herself into the dentist's chair.

Uh-oh. She was clearly a phobic. Jem sighed. Why had he ever thought that it was a good idea to become a dentist? Ninety percent of the people that he encountered in his daily work hated having treatment in varying degrees of rationality. And he worried still more about the ten per cent that cheerfully and gratefully sat through root canal work.

'It's just that your notes...I've not seen you before have I?'

'What?' said the woman less politely. Beads of sweat were beginning to form on her forehead. She had that nervous, hostile look in her eyes that he had become so familiar with. A shame, for they were quite pretty eyes. Lovely really, if only they did not look quite so wary and fearful.

'What are you in for?' He ventured.

The woman looked despairingly at him. 'I'm sorry, what did you say?'

67

Of course, of course, it was the mask. He sighed. Once more that day, Jem Farrow sighed. He knew that nobody understood a bloody word that he said through his surgical mask. But he wasn't going to remove it. Apart from the risk of being splattered with globules of bacteria-infested spittle, he had a cold, and hygiene required that he wear it. Oh he knew he could remove it to chat before any procedures commenced, but sod it. If the rest of the world was going to be bloody-minded, then so be it. He could be bloody-minded too.

'What exactly is the problem?' he mumbled, but with an air of scholarly superiority.

'Toothache,' blurted the woman in the chair, visibly trembling.

He couldn't resist. 'Sorry...didn't catch that?'

'*Toothache!*' the woman shouted. 'Here!' and she indicated with her forefinger in a jabbing motion that looked so much a personal insult to himself that it made him pause.

Jem entered into professional mode. 'Open wide...yes, I see... hmm.'

The woman's eyes queried anxiously.

'Yes there's lots of work to be done here,' said Jem gleefully through the mask, for which he made no allowance, no effort to raise his voice or pronounce his words more clearly. 'How long have you had the toothache?'

Jem knew it was wicked to ask questions when the patient had their mouth wrenched open and occupied by a mouth mirror. He tried to hide his amusement as the patient struggled to reply.

To his surprise she snatched at his hand, pulling both it and the surgical instrument away from her mouth.

'Please speak up,' she said. 'I can't understand you.'

Jem eyed her curiously. *Well, alrighty then...* 'The toothache. How long?' he bellowed.

"Thank you. For a while now – it comes and goes. Been okay for a couple of days now, but back again this morning."

68

'Hmm, I see. Now, if you wouldn't mind...?' He indicated the mouth mirror which he held aloft, poised and ready for action. The woman acquiesced and he resumed his inspection.

'We'll have to fill that dreadful hole,' he boomed cheerfully. 'Temporarily at least. Other than that you may have an abscess. Get an X-ray on your way out and we'll send it off to the lab, and take it from there. In the meantime I can give you painkillers and some antibiotics to see if that will help, otherwise...it all depends. Do you want to save the tooth?'

Jem absolutely *loved* this question: "Do you want to save the tooth?" Hundreds of pounds' worth of salvage work or fifty quid to take it out. He would watch in devilish pleasure as each patient wrestled with their vanity at the expense of their purse.

'But I'll take an impression first,' he continued, '...for the inlay. And...you're going to need remodelling on that chipped tooth.'

The woman beseeched him with her eyes, presumably not daring to interrupt again, and he grinned secretly to himself.

'Seriously,' Jem yelled, his brow furrowed in deep professional concern. 'You weren't thinking of just leaving it were you?'

He began. He was methodical now, performing a symphony of dentistry in perfect harmony with Nicky, and unperturbed by the tense clenching and unclenching of his patient's fists. This elegant flow of unspoken understanding between Jem and his young assistant was based on a competitiveness, rather than a strong bond of communication: neither of them wanted to be the one to mess up first. Jem was aware that Nicky was unimpressed by his status, or his relative good looks. The fact that he did good business in such a small village was not so much because dentists were scarce, but because many of the village women found that his lazy bedroom eyes and thick dark hair helped to distract somewhat from the indignity that they suffered at his hands. But at thirty-three, he knew that he was already an old man to Nicky, and that she considered him a tragic loser, and an example of how *she* would never turn out.

Jem's thoughts now raced ahead, determined not to appear slack under Nicky's nineteen-year-old judgmental gaze. He would have to give the woman at least four injections of local anaesthetic, and he did this first in anticipation of the forthcoming drilling and filling. Perhaps this was a little excessive—unnecessary even—but she looked jumpy. Better to subdue and reassure with mass loads of painkiller than to risk a mistake brought about by twitchy, nervous anxiety. She would have no excuse now. After that he took the impression of her teeth, urging her to bite down hard on the dental plaster; and then forcing her, after a long minute of saliva-dripping humiliation, to wrench her teeth free; daring her not to lose half of them in the process.

'Bite down hard now' he said again, after adroitly filling her tooth with the temporary dressing, and inserting a cotton wad.

Her teary eyes blinked at him in confusion. 'Whah? On your thinger?'

It took a couple of seconds for him to realise that, suffering from the numbing effects of the anaesthetic, the woman thought that the cotton wad in her mouth was in fact, his finger. It was too good. 'Yes, that's right,' he nodded with grave authority, struggling to keep a straight face behind the mask.

'But...but...' the woman protested as best she could.

'Do as you're told, please,' he drawled in a bored but authoritative, and very loud tone.

Eyes wide now in bewilderment, the woman nevertheless did as she was told. She bit down.

Jem could contain himself no longer. He threw off the mask. 'It's not my finger, you daft head, it's a cotton dressing!' he chuckled. Nicky looked disapproving.

In befuddlement, the woman slowly began to register her mistake, and as realisation dawned, she started to smirk lopsidedly, as much as the numbness in her cheek would allow.

'Okay, I thee... Ah'm thorry! Ah gueth it wath okay to bide down then...' She could hardly get the words out, for giggling.

For Jem it was infectious. He started to shake with suppressed laughter. 'I can't believe you actually did it! You could have taken my finger off!'

'Yeth!'

'Come back next week and we should have the inlay and x-rays back from the lab,' said Jem, struggling with each word, and removing the wad from her mouth, before collapsing, helplessly, with mirth.

'Okay!' said the woman, staggering out of the chair. 'Do I make an appointment at the dethk?' Every word was punctuated with a hiccupping chuckle.

Jem tried desperately to think of something else, as he attempted to write the prescription; to break out of the nonsensical fit of giggles. He didn't even really know why it was so funny, but the mere thought of the whole silliness reduced him once more to childish hysterics.

'Yes, at the desk,' was all he could manage, in delirium.

Nicky frowned on at the pair of them, conscious of being left out of the joke. She had no idea what they were laughing at, but one thing she was sure of was that Mr Farrow was behaving in a most unprofessional manner, and what little respect she already held him in diminished several degrees further. She really would have to get her CV updated and go for that other job.

After the woman had left, guided by Nicky, for her X-ray, Jem filled in her notes. He tried very hard to clear his mind in readiness for the aged hag who had replaced her in the chair. It would not do to chortle his way through trying to bolster and reincarnate what remaining teeth *this* one had left. He studied the name at the top of the record card for the woman with the potential abscess but lovely eyes.

Kate O'Neill.

And not that it meant anything other than professional interest, but he checked that his receptionist had properly filled in the address and telephone number for this new patient. Then he turned to face the toothless witch and promptly burst out laughing again.

CHAPTER 7

Wreckers

Kate was still grinning unevenly as she left the dentist's surgery and strolled along the quayside. With the numb half of her face unresponsive, several people gave her strange looks as they passed her by. *Maybe that's it*, she thought. *Maybe I needed to laugh so much that I'll laugh at anything.* She had a bit of time to kill before collecting Isabella from school and thought that she might investigate the little row of quaint, but compelling harbour-front shops. She hovered like a shy child outside Blue Wave, an artist's co-operative and gallery right on the harbour front. On more than one occasion previously, she had ventured in to view the paintings and prints on display, but the woman on the counter had always looked too formidable to approach. On this day, the gallery was occupied by a scruffier, more laid-back looking middle-aged man. Kate had discovered during her previous aborted forays into the shop that there appeared to be only one man involved in the co-operative and that he went by the very proper artist's name of Wendron Laity. Assuming this to be him, Kate finally summoned the courage to question him on their set-up. The crumpled artist was obliging and explained that there were six of them involved and that they took it in turns to man the shop while the rest of them worked in their private studios.

'Are you in the profession?' he asked kindly, looking at Kate curiously above half-rimmed glasses.

But despite her mind screaming *I could do this! I want in!* Kate merely mumbled,'Er, well, sort of...I dabble. Thank-you for your time,' and then browsed her way timidly towards the door.

I dabble! Kate mentally kicked herself once outside. *I dabble!* The most idiotic, inane thing to have said! She might just as well give up now if that's how seriously she took herself.

Procrastination had set in as far as her artistic intentions were concerned. She had purchased brushes, canvasses and paints, and had erected her easel in the conservatory. She had spent an unfeasible amount of time setting up her supplies for ease of access, and arranging her sketchbooks and paper into the drawers of an old pine chest. She had sharpened every one of her pencils, but yet inspiration, or rather *beginning*, eluded her. Eventually she had distracted herself with decorating and furnishing Dolphin Cottage.

Already she had sanded and repainted the panelled hallways in a fresh, brilliant white, enhancing the limited available light. The kitchen had been transformed by a coat of grass-green paint on the plastered walls, and a distressed yellow on the pine cupboards and shelves. The sheep-curtains remained, and were starting to look worryingly permanent, not to mention deliberate. The cardboard boxes had been shifted from the kitchen to the small living room, but remained unpacked. Realising that she was desperately short of furniture, she had made a mental note to visit an antique shop that she had spotted on the harbour front.

It stood tightly sandwiched between a take-away Cornish pasty shop and one of several public houses; a tiny ancient inn called The Ship. As Kate stood surveying the exterior, some local fishermen, still in their waterproofs, who sat on the wooden benches outside the inn, eyed her brazenly. The shop, like most of its neighbours—old fisherman's cottages, sail lofts and customs houses—bore the look of some past connection with the sea. It was a battered galleon of a building; tall and narrow and wonky, and with a protruding upper floor for the prow. A simple driftwood board, stained sea-blue, and then more decoratively inscribed with the single painted word "Wreckers" served to display the shop's name. Peering through the window to the dark, eclectic clutter beyond, Kate could not be sure that her assumption of an antiques shop was correct. The name gave a somewhat ambiguous clue as to the content or form of trade; but surely it could not contain the plunder of the reputed and possibly murderous act of wrecking? That was all centuries ago, wasn't it? The gang of fishermen, who had possibly, given unsocial working hours, been drinking for some time now, called to her in an addled and over-friendly manner. *The wreckers*? Cursing her overactive imagination, Kate smiled shyly and then hurried on into the shop.

The interior took the form of a succession of poky rooms spread over several floors. Up and up they went, each joined to the other by a narrow oak staircase that creaked as though it were indeed moving through the oceans wide. The upper floors were filled with pine chests and dressers, huge heavy wardrobes and gilt mirrors; or magic mirrors, as Kate would have called them when she was Isabella's age.

Back downstairs again she found smaller treasures of gemstones and antique jewellery, perfume bottles and soft silk gloves. Old musical instruments were displayed amongst driftwood, draped ship's rope, props and pulleys. There were telescopes and sextants, portholes, compasses, ship's lamps and bells. Where there was space the walls were hung with old paintings of seascapes and ships, and faded photographs of lifeboatmen, miners and bal-maidens. A large carved ship's figurehead—a golden haired mermaid with a green tail—was suspended from a beam on high. Kate loved the place and explored with unqualified thoroughness. The shopkeeper, a

75

young woman, was reading a book, but Kate felt sure she could feel her eyes hot on the back of her head.

Briefly, Kate felt herself touched by melancholy. There was a poignancy transmitted by these relics of past lives. But did these gloves really play a part in some grand drama of emotion, or were they merely cast-offs, barely worn or cared for by their owner? It did not pay to be foolishly romantic; she had learned that much, at least. But the alternative too, was hard to bear. Namely that all these beautiful treasures were just dead things; and their owners too, dead forever...and that there was no meaning.

There were some clothes hanging from a rail to one side of the oak table that served as the shopkeeper's cash desk, and Kate gasped as amongst them she spied several unusual dresses, medieval in style, but far more expensively produced than the usual fancy-dress shop options. Her fingers instinctively reached out to touch the blood-red yet cool silk of one gown that had a V-shaped bodice, and long tapering 'Anne Boleyn' sleeves. It was a princess dress; straight from the pages of her childhood books.

'I don't believe it,' she said out loud. 'This is a princess dress!'

The shopkeeper raised her head from her book and smiled. 'Yes it is, isn't it?

Kate eyed the young woman questioningly. Did she really know what she had meant? Could she really understand that this gorgeous dress exemplified all the fantasies of a six-year-old Kate, and all that she had once fully expected to wear as an adult?

'But where did it come from? It's so beautiful. Is it real?' Kate shied away now, withdrawing her hand from the lush and possibly expensive fabric.

'Antique? No, I'm afraid not,' said the woman, standing up. Kate could see now that underneath the blanketing white-blond tresses of her long hair, she wore a sapphire-blue dress, in the same style as those hanging on the rail. 'Actually, I made it. I made them all. She waved an elegant hand lightly in the direction of the row of dresses. On her fingers she wore rings of coloured gemstones.

'Really?' Kate was genuinely impressed, if a little wary of this strange young woman in medieval garb.

She had bright cornflower-blue eyes that complimented the colour of her dress. The very front parts of her hair were woven into two small neat plaits that met at the back of her head, where they became entwined; and braided into a blue ribbon. The crisp material of her dress rustled as she moved around the desk to where Kate was standing, and took the red dress from the rail.

'This one would look fantastic on you with your dark hair', she said thoughtfully, holding the dress up at arm's length in front of Kate.

'Well, maybe,' said Kate, aware that the woman was naturally after a sale. 'People always say that I suit red, but I don't know...I find it hard to carry off. It's too...bold. Besides, I doubt it would fit. And I'm not sure when I would ever wear something like this. It would have to be a fancy-dress party!'

'Yes, I know,' sighed the woman with resignation. 'I get a lot of that...I do a recycled range, if you're interested; more modern and funky in design. Most of my antique style dresses go to theatre companies and the like, but I do think it's such a shame that ordinary women don't feel that they can dress like this every day.'

'Like you do?' asked Kate tentatively, and smiling at the long blue dress.

'Yes!' her laugh was spontaneous and unexpectedly hearty. 'I'm on a one-girl crusade to reintroduce glamour and romance to the lives of modern women!'

Kate had, until this point, been totally unconscious of her own attire, but now felt desperately drab in the thrown-on mother's uniform of faded jeans, sweatshirt, canvas trainers and, of all things, *of all things*, a cagoule! There was a time when she would not have been seen dead in one. Had the practicalities of life overtaken her to such an extent that all sense of personal style was lost forever? Yes, it was true that the clothes she wore were comfortable and non-inhibiting; and yes, it was raining lightly outside; but why, oh why, a bloody cagoule?

Kate had entered into motherhood vowing not to become like The Drudge. The Drudge was a woman that she didn't know, but had observed passing each day along the street in London, with a straggle of children in tow. Although the children looked healthy and well-cared for, the woman walked hunched over her buggy, struggling with each step in timeworn court shoes that had very likely been the height of fashion in her working, child-free days. Every muscle from the chin down had atrophied and become overrun by hanging layers of flab. Her hair lay in greasy straps with no discernible parting, or deliberation of direction. Her clothes, it seemed, were chosen simply because they went on, and were not in any shape or form an expression of personality.

Was she, Kate, becoming The Drudge? She quickly shook off this painful thought. Kate would dearly love to wear a long red silk gown. She knew in her heart that it would make her feel feminine. Not necessarily sexy, but intrinsically, fundamentally feminine. She imagined the feel of the material moving and flowing against her legs as she walked, and of her hair softly brushing her skin where the deep curve of the neckline exposed her shoulders and the top of her back. Simply put, it was a beautiful dress, and she too might be a thing of beauty if she were to wear it. She was sorely tempted to buy it.

'It really is a gorgeous dress' she said. 'You're very talented. But I shouldn't be tempting myself.'

78

She thought of her lack of furniture and the cardboard boxes gathering dust at the cottage. She had enough money left from her inheritance to live on for an indefinite period, but with no other income as yet she would have to show restraint. The girl smiled understandingly, and Kate watched in disappointment as she replaced the dress on the rail. *Even now*, thought Kate, *I am last on the list*. Despite her relative wealth now, she still had to make mundane little sacrifices.The legacy of poverty was not only the fear of its reoccurrence, but also the miserly grip in which it held her natural exuberance; her *joie de vivre*. It rattled her. She didn't want to be like this.

Reminding herself of her objective, she shook off the thought. 'I'm really here for some furniture. There's a bookcase upstairs that I'm interested in...'

'Show me,' said the woman, giving Kate an odd sideways look.

Comprehending, Kate said, 'Sorry if I sound a bit odd, I've just been to the dentist. I'm still numb on one side of my face.'

'Ah,' said the blonde woman, lifting the long skirt of her dress to ascend the narrow staircase. 'So you met Jem, then.' It was a statement and not a question.

'Jem?' queried Kate, following.

'Jem Farrow, our dentist,' said the woman brightly. 'He's a good friend. Well, friend of my brother's more precisely, but we all hang out together in the same gang.'

'Oh, I see,' said Kate, not sure how else she should respond to this flow of information. She couldn't recall ever having come across a dentist so attractive. It was humiliating really, to have him pick over the evidence of one's decadent attitude to oral hygiene. But he had laughed with her. She had been really quite taken aback by this. It was almost surreal the way that he had dropped his guard; that barrier of professionalism that necessarily existed in such circumstances. And despite the queasy feeling caused by the anaesthetic and the nasty metal-like taste in her mouth, the rare laughter-induced endorphins still raced around her system, and she smiled at the memory of their joke.

'This is the one I meant.' Kate indicated a large, deep, oak bookcase that had glazed doors to the top half, and panelled ones on the bottom. She wondered why the woman should assume that she had only just met the dentist. Was it so obvious that she was a newcomer to the village? Of course it was, she surmised. The indigenous population of such a small place could probably spot a tourist or stranger in an instant. And of course, they all knew each other too.

'Ah, a good choice,' the young woman continued in her friendly manner. 'It's a bit battered but very practical, I reckon. In actual fact, this came from the school. They refitted and refurbished the whole building in the summer holidays, just before your Isabella started there. Luckily I managed to salvage some of the furniture before it got thrown in a skip.'

Kate looked surprised. 'Isabella? You know my daughter?'

Momentarily confused, the woman suddenly laughed again, although nervously this time, and touched Kate's arm lightly.

'I'm so sorry, you must think me very rude. You're Isabella's mother aren't you? I've seen you around but forget that we haven't been introduced.' As Kate's expression remained nonplussed, she offered, 'I'm Vivien Borlase. Lance's sister? Finn is my nephew. We had Isabella over to play at Tremeneghy last Friday after school. We made carrot cake.'

'Of course,' chimed in Kate, recollecting Isabella's diatribe on how *they* never made cakes together. Lance had returned the favour of inviting Izzy to tea, but had rudely just dropped her back at home with no more than a toot of the car horn, and then driven away as soon as Kate had answered the door. 'So you're the aunt who made the cake...Isabella said that you looked like a fairy!'

And she wasn't wrong, thought Kate, but Vivien, not in the least offended, once more displayed her gutsy laugh at this description. Kate tried to recall Isabella's excited report on her day spent at the Borlase household. Distracted as she was at the time by the arrival of an errant fuel bill relating to her old flat, she had barely been listening when Isabella had tried to explain how Finn lived with his father, his aunt, and his grandmother in an old stone house with a weird name that looked like a castle.

'How can they do this?' was all she had said at the time. 'I had the meter read when I left, I paid the bloody bill. Why are they still sending me more? And who the hell is Miss Buttkiss? That has to be a made up name to start with!' On telephoning the gas company Kate learned that Miss Buttkiss was indeed the new tenant of her old flat, who had rather easily persuaded them that Kate was still responsible for her bill. By the time she had finished giving vent to her anger and frustration on the unfortunate call-centre operator, Isabella had withdrawn, pointedly, to her room, leaving Kate guilt-ridden.

Another mistake. Another foundation laid for the wall of resentment that she feared would build between them during Isabella's teenage years. She wished that she had listened to her daughter; that she had sat her down with a cup of tea and a biscuit and shared her delight in every aspect of her visit. In truth, she found it irksome that Isabella seemed so enamoured of the Borlases, who apparently all lived together in a big creepy house. It was odd. But she was patient in the belief that Izzy would soon make other friends, with whom she, Kate, would feel more comfortable.

Looking at Vivien now, she could see the family resemblance. The flaxen locks and good looks should have been a giveaway. But despite herself, she liked this woman.

81

Her engaging openness and easy laughter were in direct contrast with her brother's cold-faced conceitedness.

They agreed a price on the old school bookcase, together with a convenient delivery date. Vivien chatted about Isabella's computer game skills, which were evidently the main reason for Finn's admiration and interest in her. Kate returned compliments about Finn's good behaviour and charming manners.

'Stay for a pot of tea next time Isabella visits Tremeneghy,' offered Vivien.

Kate smiled and nodded politely, but then deftly, too quickly, escaped into the bright sunshine of the cobbled wharf. She felt guilty at the hasty exit. It was hard to dislike the bright, good-natured Vivien, at least on first meeting; and despite herself, Kate felt a fleeting lament for bygone days; for the memory of sharing long intimate chats with friends over endless cups of coffee or bottles of wine. But she steeled herself. Had she withdrawn so far from her faithless London friends only to replace them anew? No—she admonished herself—she was not lonely, it was just her nature to be melancholy. The sun bounced around the bobbing harbour boats and a gull cried mournfully overhead. It was the *world*'s nature to be melancholy. And so Kate dismissed the dull pain in her heart.

CHAPTER 8

Tremeneghy

Kate sat on the rickety wooden chair outside the kitchen window and watched as her own little patch of the planet turned gently away from the October sun. Golden light and long shadows cast a magical tint over the garden. A disdainfully discarded letter from Marsha lay on the table at her side.

Marsha, being aware of Kate's notorious lack of response to e-mail and text had slyly tracked her down in pen and ink. Although Kate was cross at being found—and secretly suspected Juliet—she was oddly unmoved by Marsha's lengthy protestations of the group's innocence, and accusations of petty unreasonableness on her own part. She sipped from her glass of red wine and relaxed.

'Fuck 'em,' she muttered under her breath, and grinning rebelliously at her uncharacteristic use of profanity.

The sun's receding rays cast every leaf on the Ash tree into intense profile, and the green leaves shouted their last hurrah against the cobalt sky. Such beautiful colours, she thought, in half-stupefied wonder. She wondered how much firewood the tree might provide. There had been a fair amount of spent, fallen branches around its base, and Kate had dutifully collected as many of these as she could before they became damp, and stacked them up in the wood shed. The shed already contained a small supply of neatly chopped and seasoned logs; a sad reminder of Amelia Church's sudden departure before the last onset of winter.

But what would she do when they ran out? What did Kate know about sourcing wood or chopping logs? Well she would have to find out. Staring dreamily at the sky, Kate mused on how to balance her desire for independence from fuel companies with her "carbon footprint". At what point would her open fires become a scourge on the planet? And more pertinently, when in the coming winter months would her daughter retaliate and demand that she install central heating? She had already found herself told off for the apparently torturous labour involved in sorting rubbish for recycling, and vegetable peelings for the 'pig bin'.

'Can I just point out that we don't have any pigs?' Isabella had said loftily.

And so Kate had explained, yet again, that she intended to make compost; and once again had endured the arch cynicism at the suggestion that she might actually produce something resembling a home-grown vegetable.

Isabella was sitting now some yards ahead of her on a blanket on the grass, reading a magazine, and filling her belly on popcorn. Kate knew that she was way beyond the battle of trying to get her daughter to bed at what her own parents would have called a decent hour. True, it was a school night; but they were both relaxed, and it seemed pointless to disrupt their mutual content. And deep down, in her black little heart, Kate knew that she didn't really care. Here, within the cottage environs, in their own private universe, they would do as they pleased.

The surrounding countryside was beautiful. The sea indeed crashed passionately against the coastline, resulting in stunning crags and rock formations, and the grassy sand dunes were alive with wildlife. It was commonplace to spot seals in jagged coves or even in the harbour, to where they followed the fishing boats, looking for pickings from the fresh catch. And if you were lucky, you might spot dolphins or basking sharks from a clifftop perch. In Carrick Lane a balmy verdancy prevailed. In the garden there were still flowering herbaceous perennials that she liked to imagine Amelia Church had so thoughtfully planted, carefully lifting and separating every few years. Other flowers appeared to have spread their seed from the garden into the lane outside, and integrated with the wild flowers and fungi in the Cornish hedge. Late rambling roses scaled the trees and defied the boundaries of the garden to arch across the lane.

Kate's knowledge of plants had been limited, but she had read countless books on the subject since her arrival in Pencarra, so thrilled was she to have her own garden. She absorbed the information readily and unconsciously, and her knowledge swiftly grew. Looking around her now, she felt supremely relaxed in her new environment after the hardship of previous years. Whatever doubts and insecurities she faced beyond in this newly adopted land of hers, she instinctively felt that within the confines of Dolphin Cottage she was at home. She tried to think of how to progress. Despite her relaxed mood and enjoyment of the sun's last rays, a nagging conscience, ever present, yet elusive, destroyed her near-complete fulfilment.

What is it? What do I want? she thought, the wine inducing a philosophical pretence to her thought. *What more can I possibly want than this?* She had Isabella. She had a garden. She had peace. She was free.

Of course, there was work to be done. The garden needed clearing and planting. But she would go carefully, and wait to see what plants, as yet unseen, the spring and summer brought. She would start with just a few raised beds for vegetables; see how she went. The tiny greenhouse with shattered panes would do for a few tomato plants; and she would have a section for fruit bushes; raspberries and blackberries; and Isabella could have a strawberry patch. But this was all to come; the hard work of making ready lay before her. It wasn't this daunting task that unsettled her. It would take time of course, but hopefully they would not starve. Kate's plan was an aspiration, not a religion.

She had no mortgage; another subject for vehement reproach from her mother. Kate, it transpired, knew nothing of the ways of the world and was naïve in the extreme for not keeping the bulk of her capital in a high interest account, and then working to pay off a mortgage. After all, that was what everybody did. Susan stopped just short of telling Kate that she was lazy and work-shy. Kate protested that she far more valued her freedom and her time, and to Susan's great frustration, pronounced no desire to profit further from her capital, even if there existed such a thing as a high interest account in the current financial climate. Instead, and if she had her way, she would spend as little as humanly possible on food and fuel. She would live cheaply and learn crafts; she would make furnishings and weave baskets. She would burn candles instead of electricity. Well, *except for her night light*...

Kate could stretch to the boundaries of her courage for the sake of her beliefs, but preposterously, she could not yet overcome this deep-rooted and absurd fear and abandon the comfort of her lamp. Perhaps she could search Wreckers for an old-fashioned gas lamp? Or install a windmill to generate her electricity? There *were* possibilities.

Susan had made some of her most scathing remarks about the "good life", and announced that Kate had always been stubborn. But Kate, stubbornly, was immovable. And sitting here now, in the cottage garden with so much potential, she was still undaunted. So what was the source of this uneasy feeling?

A man? No. She dispersed the fluttering thought before it could settle, as instinctively as if she were shooing a pigeon trying to land on her head. She recalled the unbidden attempts, over the years, of her London friends to match-make her. It had always resulted in excruciating failure.

'They're just trying to help,' Juliet had said at the time.

'I don't really understand dating,' had been Kate's response. 'Why go out with someone you have no instinctive desire or passion for? Relationships are complicated enough as it is, so surely they ought to at least *start* with passion? It ought to be worthwhile getting into the whole thing in the first place...'

Juliet had sighed and shaken her head in despair.

No. Men were trouble, and if anything, a distraction from this deeper nagging dissatisfaction.

Perhaps it was guilt induced by her newly leisurely lifestyle, but the last thing she wanted was a job. It was not labour that Kate was averse to, just meaningless labour. She would far rather spend an hour in penniless creativity than to sell that hour to futile toil. No; to give in to guilt would be cowardly and conformist, and besides, she had her work cut out. She reminded herself it was important to refurbish the cottage, making it a homely and delightful environment for Isabella to finish her growing up in. There was a lot of catching up to do in this respect. She wanted brightly coloured rooms and quirky, charming furnishings. She wanted a herb garden and fresh flowers in every room. She wanted homemade chutney. She and Isabella would return from long hot days on the beach to salads fresh from the garden, and in winter she would welcome her daughter home from school with walnut cake or scones and clotted cream...

And yet it was hard to throw off the shackles of convention. She vaguely imagined that it would be wrong to fritter away the remains of her inheritance in daily living. She had, she was told, the future to think of and a child to rear. People were always bemoaning the cost of putting children through school and the like. Kate tended to take one day at a time, but was becoming progressively aware of this *future* that she should be worried about, and in not worrying about, was risking untold of horrors to come. But she thought of her previous soulless job in the personnel department of a large retail company and winced.

Deadlines, working parties, endless meetings; where previously ordinary-seeming people would transmogrify into company androids, spewing personnel-speak in sentences so convoluted that surely no one truly understood their meaning? Kate would feel like one of the crowd gathered to admire the Emperor's new clothes, but unlike the boy in the story, had not the courage to speak the truth. In the management training department where Kate had worked, momentous importance was attached to the most trivial of matters—when considered on a life, the universe and everything kind of scale.

She recalled the gloomy, opaque brown glazing of the office windows and the unnatural, antiseptic air-conditioning. It could have been the most gloriously hot summer's day outside, or a beautifully bitter winter's one. The non-climate of the office remained constant as the hours and days of her life melted away.

Even the work had been meaningless. Sending poor sods on "bonding" courses they didn't want to do, to enable them to keep jobs that they hated anyway. Surely a return to this was not to be her fate. Frankly, she'd rather be a cleaner, or a waitress; good honest work, at least. Or maybe she could be a...a fisherman; or a small-holder; a baker or a maker; an artisan; an *artist*. Good fortune had bought her a little time, and opportunity was staring her in the face.

It was as if life wanted something back from her. This uneasy feeling wouldn't leave her alone until she had discovered, and achieved the unknown; the hidden agenda. She really should start to paint in a serious manner. This was her talent and she had neglected it shamefully. There really were no more excuses. No pleas of poverty, depression, or lack of time; and she drunkenly resolved to awake phoenix-like in the morning to a new era of creative activity.

Her enthusiasm sadly dissolved the next day, aided by the onset of a crashing headache and energy-sapping dehydration. She shot a resentful look at the empty wine bottle on the kitchen table. It stood there, proudly indignant, protesting its innocence. But Kate had another, more immediate dilemma to confront. Tonight was to be the evening of the school quiz.

Isabella, having spent the last couple of weeks persuading her that she should behave *like a normal parent* and go, now seemed intent on undermining what little confidence Kate had.

'You're not wearing that are you?' she cautioned, later that afternoon as Kate tried to get ready.

Kate had felt uncomfortable enough in the plain black skirt and blue shirt that she had considered part of her work "uniform" back in London. It was not an outfit that she had ever enjoyed wearing, but felt that it would make her appear respectable and mature—for Isabella's sake.

'You look really boring,' Isabella continued. 'Why don't you ever try to be fashionable? You're not that old, for God's sake.'

'I was trying to not embarrass you actually,' sniffed Kate. 'And don't blaspheme.'

'Why not?' retorted Isabella, 'We don't go to church. And you say 'God' all the time.'

Kate sighed. 'God, you can be a handful at times...' she said under her breath.

'See?' Isabella was triumphant. 'You say it all the time!'

'Oh, for God's sake...'

'See, you did it again!'

'Shut up and listen!'

'Shut up? Shut up?!' Isabella pounced immediately. 'You see how you speak to me? You think I'm bad and you wonder where I get it from!'

'Isabella,' said Kate, 'Isabella! Listen to me, please!'

Reluctantly, Isabella stopped mid-tirade, and adopted a sulky *you can make me listen but you can't make me hear* face.

Kate resisted the urge to scream "I'm only doing this for you, you know", as the memory of her own parents' martyred recriminations bobbed up from the depths of her subconscious.

'For one thing, I don't think you're bad,' pleaded Kate, 'I don't know where you get these ideas from. I love you; *to bits*. And secondly, I'm going to be late. I need to know what to wear, right now, and I don't want an argument about every little thing...'

'You see! You always blame me for everything!'

It was hopeless. Kate threw off the admittedly hateful garments and slid thankfully into her comfortable jeans. But instead of putting back on the sweatshirt she had worn all day, she grabbed a little-worn baby-pink mohair jumper from her wardrobe. She loved this jumper, but never felt quite right in it. *That's because you look sexy in it,* she silently rebuked herself. But she had no more time to analyse and fret. If she did not go right now, she would tell herself that it was a stupid affair anyway and not go at all.

Thankfully by the time they were en route, the tiff had vanished and been forgotten, for in a minute she would have to face the bloody Borlases. They had offered, via Finn, to watch Isabella while Kate was at the school. It would be satisfying if just once she could present these paragons with a positive and happy image of mother and child.

'Well, here we are; Tremeneghy!' said Kate, with forced cheeriness as they arrived at the Borlase household, and was rewarded with a big smile. Although it had not been an accurate description, she could understand why Isabella had decided that the house was a castle. It had originally been the gatehouse to an old Priory, she had heard. Her eyes were drawn to the roof, where there was a circular room topped by a strange white dome structure. But apart from that, the stone walls and mullioned windows indeed inspired images of cavernous rooms filled by huge fireplaces, and of winding staircases lit by flaming torches. But there were no turrets, drawbridges, or moats. In fact, the house sat, incongruously close to the road, on one corner of a leafy crossroads. Peaceful banks of ferns lined the narrow lane outside, and Kate had been unsure where to park, before deciding that an onslaught of fast-moving traffic was remote, and had settled the little blue car directly opposite the house entrance.

'I still think it's a bit weird,' she whispered to Izzy as they crossed the road. 'That they all live together, I mean.'

'Maybe they think we're weird,' replied Izzy, with a giggle.

Kate swallowed hard as they approached the sombre, heavy oak door. There did not appear to be anything resembling a modern door bell, and so taking a deep breath, Kate lifted the heavy iron knocker and let it thump twice against the solid wood. She reassured herself that it was only going to be a quick drop-off, and that she would not have to enter the house. But she was to be foiled. The door was answered by Finn, who after a mumbled greeting ran off chattering with Isabella into the dark recesses of the house, leaving the door open. Kate stood foolishly on the doorstep. Hell, what did she do now? She could hardly just disappear without a word. And yet, to wander uninvited along the stone corridors...

Tentatively, she took a few steps inside, gently closing, but not quite shutting the door behind her. She was annoyed at Isabella for running off and leaving her unannounced. The long corridor facing her was adorned halfway along its length with a display of fresh Agapanthus flowers in a simple glass vase on a wooden table. The walls were hung with painted portraits, possibly of past Borlase family members.

Their sad dead eyes gazed imploringly at her. *Look at you, you wimp,* they accused, *afraid to walk along a corridor, never mind* "seize the day!" *And we're dead, while you're being pitiful. Life was* so *wasted on the living.*

'They're in the kitchen, I think,' said an assertive, yet tremulous voice behind her left ear, making Kate jump. An elderly lady stood in the doorway of a parlour—such houses did not have "sitting rooms"—a china teacup and saucer balanced defiantly on frail bony fingers. She wore a gardening apron over her dress, and house slippers on her feet.

'Go on,' she said waving her free index finger towards the far end of the corridor. 'Down the steps to the right.'

'Thank you,' said Kate, and made to introduce herself, but the woman had already turned on her heels and disappeared into the vastness of the room from whence she had come. Kate felt dismissed in every sense of the word. But armed with permission to venture further into the house, she put a bold, faintly indignant, step into her stride.

She descended the spiralling stone steps as instructed. At the bottom was an open door, arched and medieval-looking with ornate black iron hinges and large ring-pull handle. She entered into a den of warmth and light. The house must have been built on different levels of land, for despite being the basement, the far end of the kitchen was a bank of glass doors leading to a small section of garden where a grapevine-covered pergola sheltered a private patio for al fresco dining. Vivien, gulping from an oversized coffee cup, waved hello and beckoned her on in. Isabella and Finn sat in the corner with their backs to her, already engrossed in a computer game and seemingly oblivious to her presence.

'There you are!' Vivien beamed at her. 'Nice to see you again; I thought you'd gone! I'd offer you a coffee, but I think we're going to be late.'

'We?' said Kate, confused.

'Yes, I thought I'd go with you. It's not really my scene, you know, but I'm happy to help out. I'm representing Lance, if you like. Especially since he...well, Lance doesn't exactly get along with some of the other mothers.'

Of course. Jenifer Trewin and her cronies.

'I'll be glad of the company,' Kate said, meaning it, and thinking of the ordeal ahead. 'But...what about the children?'

'Oh, that's alright, Lance is upstairs, and my mother Lillian is around somewhere too. Besides,' said Vivien indicating the children, 'I doubt that they'll move from where they are right now for a couple of hours at least.'

'I think I met your mother,' said Kate. 'Briefly.'

'Sounds like Lillian. She doesn't waste time with small talk. She's usually too busy. But she knows we're going out and she won't neglect the children, so don't worry. I'd like to say the same for Lance, but he gets so engrossed in his work.'

Vivien raised her eyes to the ceiling as she spoke, as if to indicate Lance's unseen presence upstairs. Right on cue, Kate heard the heavy scraping sound of a chair against wooden floorboards, and the sound of footsteps pacing the floor directly above the kitchen.

'Lance's study,' explained Vivien.

Study? Rather grand for a computer-geek surfer, thought Kate.

Vivien grabbed her bag, an embroidered and jewel encrusted affair; and a delicate blue cardigan from the back of a kitchen chair. *At least she's not in fancy dress today*, thought Kate as she observed Vivien's pretty vintage tea-dress and ballerina pumps. Still, it had to be admitted that Vivien effortlessly oozed style and confidence, and could probably have carried off the wearing of her granny's Crimplene two-piece with aplomb.

Kate was anxious to get going. She had braced herself for the possibility of meeting Lance Borlase again for the first time since their heated exchange of words. She had expected that he might answer the door, or at least come to greet her hello. She had intended to be the epitome of politeness and courtesy, and thus shame him for his previous outspoken behaviour. But now her nerves were failing. She felt her anger rise at his rudeness in not even acknowledging her presence, and did not trust herself to behave so impeccably should she encounter him now.

* * *

From his study window on the ground floor, Lance Borlase could safely observe his sister and Kate leave the house from his position at the computer. The window was open, and the breeze considerately parted the fine muslin curtains that were the only obstruction to his view. His hands were poised on the home keys, his head positioned directly before the screen, with his forehead tipped slightly downwards. If the two women were to turn at that exact moment and look directly through his study window, he would appear to be deeply engrossed in his work. Only his eyes followed them across the road to where Kate was busy introducing Vivien to her car. When they had gone, he decomposed his position and stretched. Then he relaxed into his more usual working position of staring into space, hands clasped on head, and one long leg bent up over the other, the ankle resting on the opposite thigh. He chewed on his pencil and gently swung the rotating chair from side to side.

Vivien would berate him later for not coming down to say hello to Kate, he knew. She had previously scoffed at his declaration that Kate was crazy, and a drunk to boot. He was

94

paranoid, she had said—Isabella's mother was a perfectly nice woman, and he had obviously caught her on a bad day. Well, maybe a very bad day. He wasn't to be so judgmental, and should learn not to be so candid—so very *blunt*.

Lance smiled as he remembered his sister's lecture. He adored Vivien and was ever grateful that there was at least one woman in the world who came some way to understanding him, and to whom he never had to offer explanation. Even his mother, he suspected, considered him to be a little peculiar. But he valued Vivien's opinion, and it puzzled him that she appeared to like this awful woman. Mind you, the awful woman certainly at least looked a lot better than she had when they had first met... Scrubbed up well, as they said.

Lance had not spent too much time reflecting on his run-in with Kate, considering her to be unworthy of even the energy required to do so. But now, as he hazily recalled and analysed the detail of their conversation, the first uneasy stirrings of self-doubt began to invade his framework of conviction. On paper, Kate's words to him would have appeared innocent enough. But there had been a nuance; a hint at something else...hadn't there? He felt the distant tide of embarrassment swell as he ventured to think, for the first time since the incident, that he might actually have been mistaken. And if he had been mistaken, then his own response must have appeared...*arrogant?* Was that the word she had used?

Vivien was right, he was too candid. And although he preferred to think of himself as forthright, and honest, he had to admit that there were times when he should keep his counsel, and his thoughts, to himself. And yet... No. He fought the tide. There had definitely been a nuance. Isabella's mother's approach had been presumptuous and brazen. Lance did not like to play games, especially when it came to affairs of a personal nature. And women, he had learned, played games with skill and ruthless mastery. Leah played games. Jenifer Trewin had played games. He shuddered at the thought of *that* disastrous episode. No. He would trust his instinct on this one. His equilibrium restored, he returned to the business of preparing the notes for his lecture in the morning.

After only five minutes he crept downstairs to the kitchen and prepared a plate of crusty bread, cheese and grapes. He threw a couple of bags of crisps and some cheerful, throwaway remarks at the children. Then, on consideration, he grabbed a glass and a half-finished bottle of wine from the fridge. Having thereby ensured that he had sufficient supplies, he skulked back to his study, grabbed his notes and took them to his observatory at the top of the house, where he'd be safe from the possibility of any encounter on Kate's return.

CHAPTER 9

The Quiz

Pencarra Junior School was buzzing with activity when Kate and Vivien arrived. Alicia Browning was shouting loudly above the throng, and gesticulating wildly to direct the masses to their appropriate team tables. They found themselves herded towards a group of "leftovers"; being those who had not previously formed a team with friends. Once all the 'official' teams had been seated, Alicia approached them and, somewhat impatiently, divided them roughly into groups of six. With a barely-disguised tone of regret, she announced that Kate and Vivien would have to be in "her" team. The sensation, for the latter two, was akin to being forced to pair up with the class teacher, because none of the other children would hold your hand. Their other teammates were Angie, the bleached-haired woman who had defended Kate at the school gates, and who still wore her 'Sabbath' leather jacket; Angie's partner Don, and Alicia's husband Nigel. It occurred to Kate that despite Alicia's obvious involvement in organising the event, she still found herself consigned to a team composed of remnants. Neither had she been selected to sit with the other officiating PTA members at the long table on the stage, where the questions were to be put via a microphone and squealing PA system.

A pale, poker-faced young woman in a long hippy dress and bead necklaces announced the procedure in an uncomfortable tone. The quiz would take place in sections, each covering a different subject matter. Each team was to have a captain, responsible for filling in the answer sheets and returning them, as each instalment was completed, to the table on the stage for marking.

Without discussion, Alicia assumed the role of Captain, and announced that their team would be called "The Academy". Kate squirmed. The absurd pomposity of the name was highlighted, as one by one, the other teams revealed their names to be The Beach Bums, The Pirates, The Rum Smugglers, and The Kooks. The table next to theirs was occupied by The Surf Chicks, a team captained by Jenifer Trewin, and comprised of her clone-like friends. *The cronies*, thought Kate wryly.

As they settled around their table, Angie and Don produced from several carrier bags a small party-load of chilled cans. Lager and cider were generously proffered around the table. Kate and Vivien, grateful for any anaesthetising antidote, eagerly accepted a can of cider each. Horrified, Alicia refused; and Nigel, although accepting the offer—and in stark contrast to the eagerness with which the others pulled rings and gulped—left his can unopened on the table.

Alicia quietly seethed. Although it was customary for alcohol to be indulged in at school quiz nights, she thought that it could only jeopardise their chances of winning. And besides, tins were dreadfully uncouth. Wistfully, she remembered the polite bottles of low-alcohol wine that she and her friends at Olivia's old school in Surrey had preferred on these occasions. Surveying the faces around the table now, she realised, bitterly, that she ran the risk of being associated with any drunken shenanigans that might occur. And she had so hoped to gain favour with the more long-term members of the PTA, now presiding from the stage. She wondered if it was too late to reorganise the teams, but requests for silence were made over the P.A. system, and the quiz began.

'What is the name of the main surfing beach of Pencarra?' The hippy woman self-consciously pronounced each syllable into the whining microphone. The resultant groans all round signified how easy to answer was this first question on local history and environment, and the Captains' pencils scribbled in unison the answer of Porthledden Beach. However, the questions became progressively harder, and Kate, the newcomer, sat in ignorance for the majority of this section, a wasted member of Alicia's team.

'In what year was the present Pencarra village hall built?' the woman posing the questions struggled to be heard over the ever-increasing din arising from the tables below her, as the by now lubricated contestants warmed to the event and arguments over previous questions persisted.

'I know that!' cried Kate, suddenly springing to life. She leant across the table, and said in a loud whisper, 'it was built in 1935.' Kate had happened upon a local history book in the small village library, and in a effort to familiarise herself with Pencarra, had briefly studied its contents. It had been a slimline paperback affair, not much more than a brochure really, filled mostly with Victorian photographs, and by chance, a picture of the opening of the new village hall.

'Oh no, I don't think so,' said Alicia. 'It would be much older than that. Nigel, what do you think?' and she turned to face her husband. 'Nigel is an architect,' she added by way of explanation.

Nigel, who had taken little part in the proceedings so far, shrugged in a detached manner. 'I suppose...with the kind of bricks used and the general design and layout, I would tend to say...yes, definitely sometime in the fifties.' His eyes were distorted and alien behind the large thick lenses of his glasses.

'Could you give us a year, Nigel?' said Alicia, pen poised ready for his answer.

Again Nigel shrugged as though he couldn't care less, and obviously hedging his bets announced, '1955. I would say 1955.'

Alicia smiled approvingly at him, then head down, put her pen to the answer sheet.

'Hang on a minute!' said Kate. 'It was 1935. I saw it in a book. In the *library!*' she emphasised. She looked to her other teammates, being locals, for support. Vivien smiled apologetically and held her palms up in ignorance, while Don, who seemed to be able to drink without actually swallowing, opened his throat to pour down another can of lager. Angie just looked amused.

'Perhaps you made a mistake,' said Alicia, with an exasperated smile.

'No, I don't think so,' said Kate, 'Besides, you said yourself that it would have been older, and in a way you're right because there used to be some sort of market or meeting place on the site, I can't remember the details...'

'Shush!' Alicia scolded, 'I've already written down the answer and they're about to ask the next question!'

Kate gasped in indignation. But none of her teammates seemed to notice as she sat with hands on hips, appalled at being so patronised. They were already listening intently to the next question, and so Kate mustered up the maturity to let it go. It was only a stupid school quiz, after all. Feeling miffed, but determined not to be seen as sulking, she forced herself to join in again. By now the quiz had moved on to the category of "entertainment and sport", whereby Don and Angie visibly perked up and took more of an interest.

'*Name five British Gold Medal winners from the London Olympics, 2012.*'

'Oh well, there was Ben Ainslie, and Andy Murray of course...' said Alicia simultaneously writing the answers down.

'Jessica Ennis,' said Don.

'Yes, good!' said Alicia, 'I was just about to say that...'

'Who were the girls who did the rowing?' said Vivien, 'There were a few of them I think; I felt quite inspired at the time. Oh, what were their names?!'

Kate frowned sadly. 'I know the ones you mean, but I can't remember their names either.'

'Quickly!' snapped Alicia.

'Well never mind then,' said Kate, 'Just put down another track athlete—Mo Farah, or Greg somebody...'

'Who? You don't sound too sure,' said Alicia.

'Rutherford, that was it,' said Kate. 'Put down Mo Farah and Greg Rutherford. Oh come on Alicia, everyone knows that!'

Alicia looked at her dubiously. But as time was moving on, she reluctantly put Kate's answers down, muttering the disclaimer, 'Well, I'm not sure, but we'll have to put *something* down I suppose.'

'Quiet!' said Vivien, somewhat slyly, as the 'quiz-mistress' prepared to set the next question.

'*Who directed the films Mr Deeds goes to Town and Mr Smith goes to Washington?*'

'Oh! Oh! I know!' cried Vivien, bouncing up and down in her chair and putting her hand up like a child in class. Then remembering to whisper, she said, 'It was Capra; Frank Capra!'

'Now wait a minute, let's think,' said Alicia with her eyes closed, and clasping her pen between the two palms of her hands, as if deep in prayer. 'It was Pressburger and...Pressburger and...damn it...Nigel?'

'Powell,' said Nigel, once more roused from his indifference by the command of his wife's voice.

'Powell! That's it, Pressburger and Powell!' cried Alicia, happily scribbling on the answer sheet. Kate fought the urge to grab the pen and paper from her manicured fingers.

And so it went on. The questions on music found Don and Angie in their element. Kate was impressed at the encyclopaedic and broad spectrum of knowledge that Don, in particular possessed. He gave his answers briefly and confidently, his faculties apparently in no way impaired by his considerable alcohol consumption.

Drummer in Blondie?

'Clem Burke.'

Second Pogues album?

'Rum, Sodomy and the Lash.'

Water Music?

'Handel.'

Kate observed that on each answer he was met with doubt and outright incredulity from their team captain. It appeared that if Alicia did not know the answer to a question herself, she found it unacceptable that one of her teammates might. Don took it largely on the chin, only shaking his head slowly in ironic disbelief as Alicia continually pooh-poohed his answers. Kate and Vivien had at this point withdrawn their contribution to such an extent that they almost empathised with the emphatically resigned Nigel. Angie, completely unfazed by any sense of decorum, laughed loudly and boisterously throughout. That she was laughing at Alicia alone was not entirely clear, Kate felt uneasily. Yet Alicia sat regally holding court, unperturbed by, or unaware of, the fury that she incited with almost every utterance. Things came to a head with a question on rock music.

'Right, that's it!' announced Don, his hands held up in protest, 'I'm sorry, but I'm not having it! You can question me and my intelligence all you like, Madam, but when it comes to The *Sabbath*...if you're saying, nay, *telling* me that I know nothing about Black Sabbath then I'm not having it. I'm just not having it!'

And with that he turned his chair completely around, so that he sat with his back to the rest of the table, his legs crossed and arms folded. He drank more ferociously than ever from the endless supplies of lager and refused to be coerced into answering any more questions. Alicia appeared genuinely shocked at his behaviour. Her voice quivered a little as she nevertheless continued to preside over the team's answers.

Jenifer Trewin and the rest of The Surf Chicks on the next table tittered and whispered to each other, nodding at Don, who sat resolute in his mutiny against his teammates. Kate noticed that Jenifer was looking directly at her, with a smirk on her lips. It was disconcerting. In a reflex action, Kate turned and looked over her shoulder at the table behind them, on the off-chance that Jenifer was looking beyond her at some other amusement. She turned around again with lowered lashes, knowing even before she raised them again, that Jenifer was still staring at her with barefaced challenge.

Angie laughed on.

Kate looked around the packed school hall at the faces, ruddy and excited. The noise, like that rising from a swimming pool full of schoolchildren, was exhausting. Angie's mocking laugh rose up with the cacophony of other voices and rang around the high ceiling. Kate felt suddenly very alone. How did she come to be here in this place with these strange, disagreeable people? The quiz-mistress announced that there would soon follow a short break before they began the second half.

Second half? How much longer could it possibly go on? Like some mad, sweat-soaked nightmare, it felt as though she had endured days of delirium already. Only Vivien noticed the look of desperation on her face, and smiled back at her kindly.

When the break finally came, Vivien grabbed Kate's arm outside the queue for the Ladies' toilets and simply said, 'Come on, let's get out of here.'

'But...what about the team?'

'Ah, who cares?' scowled Vivien. 'Exasperating old bag doesn't deserve us anyhow.'

Kate was downhearted. The whole point of the evening had been to try to kindle relationships with other parents, for Isabella's sake. As such it had been an unmistakable disaster. But the cold night air outside was refreshing after escaping the cauldron of heat and frayed tempers inside the school hall. They had a short walk to where Kate had parked the car, but they walked unhurriedly, enjoying the crisp clarity of the air. Slowly, the silence of the night soothed their ears, which had been buzzing with noise from the school.

'So...why is your shop called Wreckers?' Kate asked uncomfortably, by way of conversation. 'I hope you don't mind me saying so, but it does imply that your goods are somewhat—well, ill-gotten!'

Vivien laughed. 'Well, it really doesn't hurt the trade, you know. You'd be surprised how many tourists rather like the idea that they're purchasing illegal treasure. But really, the use of the word has changed; nowadays it means beachcombing or marine salvage. You know, picking up the flotsam and jetsam that arrive upon the shore. Or in my case, good old-fashioned antique dealing. But there's no shenanigans. No decoy lights used to run ships aground, I assure you! Some latter-day wreckers even catalogue all their finds; or display them. It's like receiving messages from across the ocean.'

Almost an art form, thought Kate, but did not say. Instead she stopped abruptly in her tracks. 'Wow,' she said quietly, her head upturned to the night sky. 'Look at those stars. Isn't it amazing?'

Vivien smiled. 'Now you sound just like Lance.'

'What do you mean?'

'Oh you know; Lance and the stars. The galaxies; the Cosmos; the meaning of everything. Schrödinger's bleeding cat.'

'What are you talking about?'

'Physics, of course,' said Vivien. 'That's what he does. I think his official title is Theoretical Physicist, which actually always sounds like a sort of made-up job to me. Or is it Cosmologist? He's a professor of one and doctor of the other, I'm not sure which, I forget. He has to go to the Uni to give lectures and stuff, but he gets to work from home a lot, which as far as I can tell involves a lot of sitting around thinking! But it allows him to be there for Finn...'

'And go surfing!' Kate quipped, although she was ruminating over this new information.

Vivien looked at Kate's puzzled face, '—didn't you know?'

'No,' said Kate honestly. 'I had no idea, I thought...'

'What?'

Kate checked herself. She could hardly say, *I had your brother down as some weirdo surfer who potentially posed for women's erotic magazines!* 'I...didn't think at all really,' she admitted.

'What do you do?' asked Vivien, taking Kate by surprise.

'Me? Oh well, um...I'm an artist,' said Kate, and immediately felt overcome with guilt and shame. But she had said it now. She had to follow through. There was a part of Kate that believed that if she took herself seriously then she could in fact be whatever she chose to be. But the truth was that as far as being an artist was concerned, she was unpractised, unsold, and as such, an imposter.

'Well, not a very successful artist,' she added, hoping to dilute the previous statement. 'I mean, I paint; but it's hard to earn a living from fine art these days.'

'You should try selling your paintings down at the harbour front in the summer,' said Vivien, as if the possibility of Kate's being a professional was not remotely unbelievable. 'Quite a few local artists make some sort of income that way. And I could hang some at Wreckers, if you like? What sort of stuff do you do?'

Kate gulped. 'Er, expressionist, I suppose; only not in the familiar sense. I'm no Kandinsky. My work's quite detailed, but expressionist in an, um, emotional sense. I'm really looking forward to doing some seascapes, I er, love the energy here...'

'I see,' said Vivien with a nod of understanding, and again displaying the sort of nonchalance that implied that her life was simply swarming with emotional expressionistic artists. It occurred to Kate that it probably was. Apart from Blue Wave, there were several small art galleries in the town. Being a newcomer, it might not be so hard to pass herself off as a professional. She could be really evil and invent a successful career.

They reached the car with Vivien still extolling the virtues of having a "talent" like Kate's, and woefully regretting that she herself was hopeless when it came to pencil and paper, or brush to canvas. Kate was desperate to change the subject. Vivien was a woman who knew about antiquities; who could conjure up a dress from any given period with little resource; and here she was lathering praise upon Kate: Kate the unworthy; Kate the charlatan. Desperate to restore her peace of mind, Kate decided that she would now have to work night and day to produce a few half-decent canvasses to justify her boast. It was the only way out, and as such, might just be the prompt that she needed to "find" inspiration.

They arrived back at Tremeneghy and Vivien insisted on Kate coming in for a coffee. Once more Kate found herself descending the stone steps into the warm, welcoming kitchen, with each step dreading what, or more specifically whom, she might find there. But she needn't have worried. The room was occupied solely by the children, who had barely moved from where they had sat when the two women had left, sprawled on beanbags before a television in one corner of the kitchen. The only indication that any time had passed was a collection of discarded crisp bags, chocolate bar wrappers and juice cartons that formed satellites of effluence around their own private planet. In low voices they discussed technicalities of their game that were way beyond Kate's comprehension. Her only attempts to enter and understand this world of computer games had been hysterically ridiculed, as Kate had either killed Lara Croft in seconds flat, or repeatedly crashed her virtual car into a wall, like some maniac banging her own bloodied head with a hammer. At this point she would usually have the controls scornfully whipped from her hands, and replanted in Isabella's more skilled, dextrous ones.

'Isabella, *please* pick up all this rubbish,' said Kate sternly. 'You should be ashamed!'

'Sorry!' said the two children in a practised tone, and dutifully began to clear up the mess surrounding them. There was a dreamy, trancelike state about their motions; their minds still locked into the game that they had been playing. Isabella would not ask Kate about the quiz night until they were alone at home, Finn being far more deserving of her immediate attention. Kate felt the familiar guilt at leaving Isabella for hours in such inactive, mind-frazzling leisure. But then, there was nothing much wrong with Isabella's mind, she reminded herself, thinking of her daughter's quick observational skills and sharp tongue.

Vivien put the coffee machine on and urged Kate to make herself comfortable at the kitchen table. Kate could not help but be impressed by the ambience of the kitchen. Although it was large, it had a low ceiling and so remained cosy. It was painted in a soft chalky yellow that managed to look warm without being too bright. It comprised of wooden shelves, cupboards, a range cooker and a large pine table at one end; and a disarray of easy chairs, cushions and bean bags surrounding the television at the other. But what Kate admired most about the room was that it was not in the least ostentatious; but rather every mug, chair, or random mosaic tile secured above the worktop looked as though it had been inherited, or had otherwise been acquired over time, and as such had some history, or meaning. What was it that William Morris had said? "Have nothing in your home unless you either know it to be useful, or think it to be beautiful"...something like that anyway. She thought of her own kitchen with its clutter of belongings and effects; the heaps of discarded clothing and newspapers; the wads of letters and junk mail stuffed into every available drawer or shelf space.

'Well, that was an experience!' said Vivien, placing a mug of coffee before Kate. 'Can you get over that woman? Who on Earth does she think she is?' But Vivien smiled as she spoke, giving the impression that she had hugely enjoyed the entire evening. In retrospect, Kate too, had to raise a smile.

'I wonder if she's noticed that we've gone?' she said cynically.

'Well, I doubt it. And even if she has, she's probably glad of it. We were only dragging her down.'

'But she'll get all the glory if the team wins!' said Kate with feigned concern.

'Ah yes,' said Vivien, her nose emphatically in the air, 'Alicia's Academy!', and they both giggled.

'So tell me,' said Vivien, as they warmed both physically and to each other. 'What brings you to Pencarra?' She looked Kate directly in the eye as she spoke. For one wild moment, Kate was tempted to pose dramatically and cry, *why, to paint, of course!* But she restrained herself. She had said too much in that respect already. But how could she answer Vivien's question? How to explain the slow, gradual decline that encompassed her time with Miles; dropping out of her Fine Art course; her life in the grotty flat, alone but for a young child? It was not so easy to sum up such disenchantment. And would Vivien understand her sense of betrayal at the hands of her friends? It would sound trivial to anyone else, and not convey the depth of the wound.

'I was really, truly, desperate,' she said, 'to get away from London. Not just London, but from cities, and from people. I mean, I hope every day that's it's not just a phase. I genuinely worry that I may not have made the right decision, especially where Isabella's concerned. But it was such a strong impulse at the time. And then when we found the cottage, well that was that. If we hadn't found it, then who knows?'

'Hmm. Amelia Church's old cottage,' said Vivien pensively. 'Yes, it's a nice place, if a bit... in need of work. It still seems a bit rash, if you don't mind me saying so.'

'Oh?' said Kate, and then a little defensively, 'So you don't recommend life in Pencarra?'

'Oh no, I absolutely love it!' exclaimed Vivien. 'And don't get me wrong. I think you're very brave, I'm just curious as to your motives. We get a lot of people who come down here from up-country—our friend Alicia and her husband for instance. But they don't all end up staying, for various reasons. They don't like being cut off from the shopping facilities, and the weather can be a shocker. But on the whole I think they just don't fit in. They miss their old friends and social life. You really have to be prepared to start from scratch I think, if you're going to make it work.'

Once more that evening Kate felt depressed. Alicia was trying to "make it work". The woman had actively thrown herself into the community, not only joining in with school activities, but who knows what other committees and institutions she busied her days with? It was not a scenario that Kate could see herself imitating, and even less so after tonight's disastrous effort...

'Well, I like it,' she said defiantly. 'I do worry, but I like it. I love the wild weather as much as the good. I love the space around my home, and the fact that there's no one living on the other side of my wall. Although perversely, I hate the darkness at night. There are no street lights! How do you walk along the lane at night with no street lights? I mean aren't you constantly afraid of attack?'

'You are strange!' laughed Vivien. 'You've just been raving about the stars and yet you're scared of the dark?' She shook her head in mock pity, as she cradled her coffee. 'It's because it is so dark that you get to see all those beautiful stars!'

'I know!' said Kate. 'I know it's illogical. And I know that my fears are city fears. I've been indoctrinated with the philosophy of expecting the worst; of being wary, and nervous, and suspicious! I hope to get over it.'

'So coming here is a kind of therapy, you mean?' said Vivien. Then after a pause she said. 'Don't worry about fitting in around here, Kate. You possess the requisite degree of eccentricity.'

'You mean I'm nuts,' said Kate.

'Quite.' Vivien replied, in all seriousness.

CHAPTER 10

Schrödinger's Cat

Autumn leaves were falling; yet despite the low sun's blinding rays and long shadows, to Kate it still felt like springtime. All was fresh and new, and she was finally getting her life in order. She had cleared the overgrowth in the garden, hopefully not damaging any plants not yet seen. She had filed all her papers pertaining to the house sale and to Aunt Joe's will, paid all her outstanding bills and diarised school dates. She had even knocked out a few paintings. Before the days became too cold, and lacking any other inspiration, she decided to paint some pictures of her new home and gardens.

She had been reflecting on the day when she and Isabella had moved in, when she had been stopped in her tracks by the sight of a humble snail, making its way slowly across the porch step. With no realisation of the bane that he and his several-thousand brothers and sisters were to become to her, she could only stare like a small child, in first-time wonderment.

Kate could seriously not remember the last time she had seen a snail. Indeed she had begun to doubt that she ever had, but suspected that her memories had been supplanted by children's books and nature programmes. Or perhaps she had simply never noticed such things until they had become removed from her life. She had also gulped back tears at the sight of a spider and its fragile dewy web that straddled the porch. With great import, she had deliberately and carefully avoided breaking the web. Isabella however, was not amused to encounter several larger, blacker varieties in what was intended to be her dream bedroom.

'Oh, don't worry about spiders;' Kate had said at the time. 'Spiders are our friends. They eat flies. And before you ask,' she went on, anticipating Isabella's question, 'no, we do not like flies. They are our enemies, okay?'

It was Kate's intention to try to capture some of that feeling of freshness and wonderment in her paintings; although quite how to do this, she wasn't sure. She had always worked with the notion that if she *felt the feeling* whilst painting, then that experience would transfer, through her brushstrokes, via some sort of empathetic osmosis, onto the canvas. But it wasn't the sort of thing she felt inclined to say out loud.

Dishearteningly, the first results, rather than "fresh and wonderful", veered more towards twee and cloying. *You're just unpracticed*, she reminded herself. *Don't give up*. Sure enough, the more she painted (albeit urged on by her sinful boast) the more her confidence and skill returned. She began to notice detail; small flecks of undercoat on the sills where the paint had been drilled off by years of weather; an almost imperceptible lean to the porch where the Clematis grew heavier on one side; the perfect, inexplicably pleasing balance of the design and structure of the building. Nature burst through at every given opportunity, despite her clearing operations. Hacked back bushes assumed new, graceful shapes within days. Strange and beautiful alpine-like plants emerged from cracks in the walls. She started to become engrossed, losing herself in deep thought as she worked. The very concentration required to paint was almost a form of meditation, and left her feeling more satisfied than any shopping spree, or night out clubbing would have. They still weren't great paintings, but being her own worst critic, she could tell that she was at least improving.

One sunny, but very cold morning, a van pulled up in the driveway. Working at her easel in the garden—in muddy boots, a woolly hat and *three* jumpers over her jeans—Kate found herself confronted by the robust frames of Lance Borlase and, of all people, *her dentist* marching towards her.

'We meet again!' her dentist spoke first, extending his hand for her to shake. Without his infernal mask, he confirmed the curly, sexy grin that she'd noticed on previous visits to the surgery. 'How's the tooth?'

'Oh fine,' said Kate coyly, and gingerly taking his hand. 'Thanks to you!' And it was indeed fine; the infection had cleared and the tooth been restored and saved. But even as she spoke she winced. Why did people talk in clichés? Were they so influenced by the culture of television and the media? She wished that she had an original vocabulary with which to stun people with her wit and insight. Especially when one such person was Lance Borlase, looking coldly at her as he did now.

'My name's Jem, by the way,' said her dentist, still smiling warmly at her.

'I'm Kate,' she said foolishly, 'But...you know that don't you?' She smiled back, grateful for his friendliness and, it had to be said, his good looks.

'Ahem,' coughed Lance, with no attempt at subtlety, 'We've brought your furniture. If you show us where you want it, we'll get moving.'

Of course; the old school bookcase. Vivien had said that she would arrange the delivery, and Kate had asked that it wait until she had finished sanding down the floorboards in her living room. This had proved to be a monumental job that she had started by hiring a floor sander, and finished by hand, scrubbing away stubborn patches of ancient and blackened floor polish with endless little scraps of sandpaper. The floorboards were not exactly pristine, but luckily none had needed replacing, and they now gleamed with two coats of durable varnish, ready to receive their furniture.

Kate certainly had not foreseen that the bearers of her goods would comprise the two most good-looking men she had seen since arriving in Cornwall. If only Juliet could see her now, she chuckled inwardly. She would never believe her unless she saw them with her own eyes. Kate directed the two men to the appropriate position in the living room, and then ducked into the kitchen, leaving them to it. As she placed an overfilled kettle on the hob, she realised, to her horror that she was trembling with nervousness. And was it any wonder? Apart from having to endure the dreaded, unpredictable Lance Borlase in her home once more, she also had to contend with—and she tried hard to stop the blush—an attractive man. Or to be more precise, a man that *she* was attracted to. She couldn't remember the last time that she had felt this way. Just like with the snail.

Pull yourself together, O'Neill. Had she learned nothing? Surely she had progressed beyond falling for good looks and a sexy smile? She made some mental notes: no flirting, no aspirations, no getting carried away with false imaginings.

It took the two men no more than five minutes to transport the piece of furniture, but since Jem, at least, had gratefully agreed to tea, Kate found herself having to make conversation whilst they removed scarves and hats in the warm kitchen, before sitting down at the table. Kate remained standing, as she waited for the overloaded kettle to boil. The situation began to feel uncomfortably familiar, and she wondered distractedly where the cat might be lurking. She had decided by now that Lance, in his arrogance, was probably never going to apologise to her for his previous behaviour. Indeed he barely saw fit to even mention the incident, such was his self-assurance. It frustrated her still, to think of it. She had been unfairly tried and sentenced; cheated of the chance to defend herself.

'How's Finn?' She enquired tentatively.

'He's well,' replied Lance.

Kate smiled sardonically. Had she really, just a moment ago, considered him unpredictable? As before, he was terse and short with his reply, and she wondered, again, how he could possibly be related to Vivien.

'So what the hell is Schrödinger's cat all about anyway?' she asked, provocatively hell-bent on getting him to open up and realising that small talk was not the way.

Lance looked at her in surprise. 'Well...'

'I mean, I know *of* it, of course,' she added hastily, 'I just don't get it.'

But before Lance could answer, Jem butted in laughing. 'Oh don't tell me he hasn't already bored you with that? What was it?—Correct me if I'm wrong, Professor—an experiment where, get this; the scientist locks his cat in a box, and depending on...something scientificky...the cat is both dead and alive at the same time! Is that it?'

'Not quite,' said Lance, testily. Then, appearing reluctantly drawn, he went on. 'It's a thought experiment. In other words, Erwin Schrödinger didn't actually perform the exercise, but thought through the process of what would happen if the cat, unseen, was subjected to a radiation-induced release of poison in one instance, or not, in another.' Observing their blank looks, he offered: 'It's a sealed environment; just the cat, a potential radioactive particle and some hydrogen cyanide. The cat, for the purpose of argument, cannot affect the outcome, nor can the outside world. It all rests on the detection by a Geiger counter of a single decayed atom.'

'Right,' said Jem. 'That's it. So; if the atom is detected, the poison is released, and the cat dies; if not it stays alive?'

'Oka-ay,' said Kate, 'so, then what? He opens the box and gets a dead cat? Or not. What's the point?'

Lance sighed. 'The point is that while the box is sealed, the cat, in theory, is in a state of coherent superposition. It is only the action of observation that decides the final outcome; until then the cat has a condition of both existence and nonexistence. You don't know until you open the box.'

Kate stared, nonplussed, at Lance. He stared right back as if confronted with the height of idiocy.

'Because the wave function collapses,' he deadpanned. It was obvious from his expression that he knew he was wasting his time.

'Oh come on!' said Kate, laughing. 'You're not serious! If the cat's dead, it's dead, whether you open the box or not!'

Lance's handsome features took on a pained look of heavy resignation, and he sighed. 'As I said, it's not a real experiment. It's designed to try to explain a thought process, more properly applied to subatomic particles and waves. It attempts to illustrate the very bizarre nature of quantum mechanics. And yes, the absurdity. I believe Schrödinger himself was attempting to emphasise exactly that by translating the Copenhagen Interpretation to a classical level.'

'He's like this all the time, you know,' said Jem. 'Really needs to get out more.' And with that he shot Kate a devastating smile, his eyes fixed firmly onto hers. She smiled back amicably, but felt her blush rising nonetheless as Jem still did not avert his eyes. It was the kind of blush that even if barely noticeable on the outside, on the skin of her neck and cheeks, instead rose up inside her like a power surge, intensifying every action and electrifying her eyes. Horrified, she realised that Lance had noticed the exchange, and his cool gaze caught her eye for a fraction of a second, before he discreetly turned his head, and peered idly out of the window. Gratefully, she sensed that the water in the kettle was finally coming to the boil, being attuned, as she was, to the little worried-sounding change in pitch that it made as it

116

summoned the energy to blow its whistle. She turned away to clatter about with the teapot and cups.

'Nice place you've got here,' said Jem to her back.

Hardly original, thought Kate, but remembering her own cliché-ridden efforts, made an allowance.

'You've made some improvements,' said Lance, and then hesitated before adding, 'since I was last here.'

What? Could this be true? Had Lance Borlase actually spoken to her unnecessarily and of his own volition? Kate did not reply, but eyed him suspiciously for a second before continuing with her task.

'I'm impressed,' he added quietly.

But with little conviction, thought Kate. 'Thank you,' she said, eyeing him suspiciously. Yet she allowed herself a little pride. It was true that the cottage was undergoing a slow, but beneficial, transformation at her hands.

Nervously, Kate placed on the table the pot of tea, three cups with saucers, a small jug of milk, spoons—so many things! Why had she not just stewed teabags in mugs as she usually did?—and, lacking anything else for sweetening, a storage jar of Muscovado sugar and a jar of honey.

'Help yourselves!' she urged, stepping back from the table with a swing of her arms. In truth, she did not trust herself to pour without missing the cups, or scattering sugar all over them. 'I'll er, see if there's any biscuits...' and she banged the cupboard doors open and shut.

'Shall I pour yours?' Jem enquired politely.

'Er, yes...just milk please,' said Kate gratefully. She gave up trying to find any biscuits, and accepted her cup of tea from Jem, desperately trying not to let her hand touch his as they made the exchange. Similarly, for fear of her knees accidentally brushing against the tangle of long male legs on the nearest sides of the table—and the far side suddenly seeming a long-distance obstacle-course away—she instead stood and leaned back against the kitchen cupboards.

Abandoning the tricky saucer, she kept both hands firmly clenched around the hot cup, and desperately resisted the urge to fiddle with her hair. Apparently this was a dead giveaway that you fancied someone, according to something she'd read somewhere. She felt very warm. Kate had put the gas cooker on full blast that morning, as well as lighting a fire in the stove, imagining that she would be cold after coming in from the garden. But now, with the brilliant sunshine streaming through the window, the kitchen suddenly felt ridiculously hot. Kate wished that she had discarded a couple of layers of clothing while the men had been in the other room, but no way was she going to start stripping off now. Worse than the fear of any suggestiveness involved—and that was certainly a risk not worth taking when Lance Borlase was in the room—was the anxiety that she would grab two layers by mistake, and then perhaps get stuck with the jumpers over her arms and head; and then the bottom layer would ride up revealing...oh heck, which bra had she put on that morning? Probably best to sweat it out then.

'Your artistic nature shows in your interior decorating skills,' said Jem, his eyes skipping around the green and yellow kitchen.

'Oh, not really,' said Kate, 'I just kind of splashed this up. I didn't give it a lot of thought or anything.'

'It's lovely,' said Jem. 'Very unusual, but it works. What are you painting, by the way?' He gestured with his thumb over his shoulder at Kate's easel, visible in the garden through the window.

'Oh, just a painting of the cottage,' said Kate feebly, and then joked, 'I'm doing some chocolate-box-covers for the tourists.' Even as she spoke she cringed. She was barely more than a tourist herself. It was a bit soon to start patronising. But Jem merely laughed courteously whilst Lance drank from

118

his cup of tea and maintained a studied display of interest in the view from the window. Kate suppressed her paranoia.

'Actually, I'm not all that brilliant or successful an artist', she ventured, by some way of amendment for her Big Lie, 'but I do love painting.'

She resisted adding, melodramatically, *it's my life!*

'You know, I'd love something like this in my kitchen; it's a mess,' said Jem forlornly. Then, as if suddenly inspired, he suggested, 'I don't suppose I could persuade you to decorate for me?'

Lance looked at Jem for a second in surprise, explicitly raising one eyebrow, before resuming his air of indifference.

'I mean, I'd pay you of course,' continued Jem, unfazed. 'It would be a proper business deal.'

Kate was caught off-guard. 'Oh, I don't know,' she said, 'I really don't feel qualified.'

'Nonsense! But I don't want to pressure you. Promise me you'll at least think about it. I'm serious.' Once more Jem gazed directly into her eyes.

He's doing it again!, thought Kate in exasperation. In her experience it was quite a difficult thing to do. You had to *consciously* look into someone's eyes when you spoke to them, rather than more generally at their face, or in their roundabout direction. It was certainly not something that Kate herself would ever do *lightly*. There was a power involved that should not be wielded at random.

Could it really be that Jem was flirting with her? Or perhaps he had an eye defect? Kate concluded that in all probability he was like this with everyone. No doubt it was a technique that he employed cynically on all women, and she wasn't falling for it. But she assured him she would consider the proposal and quickly changed the subject. The surfing conditions, she had discovered, were always an easy topic for local discussion, and sure enough, she managed to distract him into a protracted lament at how a good swell was long overdue.

'Are you done?' Lance asked eventually, indicating Jem's teacup.

'Er, yeah, sure,' Jem acquiesced, downing the remnants of lukewarm tea. Then he stood up and stretched emphatically, revealing a tantalising glimpse of midriff where his jumper rose. He was not quite as tall as Lance, but hunky, thought Kate, with a cuddliness about him that looked good in jumpers and cardigans. He would be lovely to snuggle up to on a sofa by a blazing fire...*stop it now!* Kate forced herself not to start fantasising such things. That way madness lay. Not to mention heartbreak, humiliation and despair.

Desperately she fixed her eyes instead on the rangy figure of Lance as he put on his beanie hat and scarf. Grudgingly, she conceded that his good looks had not diminished in the weeks since they had first met. She had half hoped that on further consideration, he would prove to possess a vulgar leer, a psychopathic twitch, or some other ugly habit that would render his features disgusting. But his eyes were a pale seafoam green—*green; they were definitely more green than blue*—and his cheek and jaw bones contrasted masculinity against the softly hanging blond hair.

He looked back at her, impassively. 'Vivien said to call her if there's any problem with the bookcase. She'll be happy to take it back if it's too big.'

'Oh no,' Kate said, 'It'll be fine; I love it! And I need the storage space. But I'll ring her anyway, just to say thanks. And thank you too—both of you.' She allowed herself a peek at Jem.

'No problem,' said Jem. 'And think about what I said, won't you? Otherwise, I'll see you at your next appointment!'

Oh crap. He was still her dentist. It was inconceivable that she could ever sit in that chair again with her mouth agape while he bore down on her, eyes a-smoulder. She would have to think of a way to wriggle out of it somehow.

On the way out, Lance paused for a second or two by the art print that Kate had hung in the newly decorated hallway, a discerning—or was it disdainful?—expression on his face. The temporary blockage that he caused in the narrow passage left Kate unnervingly close to Jem, as she found herself trapped between the two of them.

'*Lorenzo and Isabella*, or *The Pot of Basil*,' muttered Lance. 'After the Keats poem. It's reputed to contain phallic symbolism.' And he looked sideways at Kate, with those judgemental eyes, before turning and striding towards the door. Jem gave a comical shrug and a roll of the eyes, and grinned at Kate once more. She smiled back in complicity.

Once they had gone, Kate returned defiantly to the simply framed Millais print in the hallway. Phallic symbolism? Hah! Trust Lance Borlase to pick up on that bit of...of...*tittle-tattle*, and miss everything—everything—else. Lorenzo gazed forever at his loved one imploringly, whilst she, Isabella—her daughter's namesake—remained demure and with eyes downcast in fear of her brothers' discovery. So what if Lance Borlase despised her taste in art? Okay it might be unfashionable, but she loved the Pre-Raphaelites, *and* the poetry of Keats. What did he know anyway? "Wave function collapses" indeed.

Inexplicably disturbed, she paced the kitchen floor for some time, unable to settle on a chair, replaying every word of conversation with Jem, and drinking in the potent, lingering essence of testosterone in the kitchen. She had to do something to snap out of it. There was something nagging at the back of her mind...something she had been meaning to do. Ah, that was it!

Ring Juliet!

CHAPTER 11

Juliet

Juliet's trip around the world had not yet got under way. The planning alone had involved much discussion and argument, and tears had been shed. Parker had a number of fashion modelling jobs lined up and was reluctant to jeopardise his career by disappearing for a year. Juliet, who could hardly wait to jack in her secretarial job at a solicitor's office in the city, had been telling her work colleagues for weeks now that she was "out of here". Frankly, it was becoming embarrassing.

'When exactly are you going?' demanded Lucinda, popping up from the adjacent work-space to Juliet in the large open-plan office. 'We'll have to arrange the leaving do, and that will take time. Unless of course you're prepared to just go to the other place...' She was referring to a bar called The Udder Place in nearby Milk Street, and which served as their local after-work watering hole. But somehow Lucinda didn't seem to get the joke.

'The *Udder Place* is fine,' Juliet said, pronouncing emphatically. 'I really don't mind where we go. Keep it cheap and cheerful.' Even as she spoke Juliet was torn. Part of her wouldn't have cared much if she never set eyes on any of her work colleagues again, especially when they came in the form of Lucinda's snooty round-faced features. (Why did people with particularly round faces always opt for pudding-bowl haircuts? It was one of life's perplexities; like the way people with ginger hair always insisted on wearing pink—Juliet was not one for politically-correct thoughts and she allowed herself a smirk). But another part of her knew that you were networking until the last minute. If she wanted the same status of employment upon her return, she would have to keep playing the game. Besides, she quite looked forward to being the centre of attention. It would be fun deciding what to wear, and flirting with the Senior Partners, who no doubt would have told their wives that they were working late.

Some of the secretaries—or *assistants* as they preferred to call themselves—who worked at Rutherford and Strang unfailingly accompanied their bosses on numerous after-work "business meetings". It was expected. Not that these meetings weren't genuine; there was always a client or business associate to impress. The solicitor would ask his assistant to attend on the premise of her being made familiar with the case, and so that they would be able to put a face to a name. But everyone knew that they were there as decoration. The suggestion that the solicitor in question hoped to convey was that he was sleeping with his secretary, although this was not necessarily the case. Those, like Juliet, who had so far managed to avoid being singled out for this kind of attention, openly despised those who considered it flattering, or even more misguidedly, a career move.

The trick was, for Juliet, to maintain the interest of her bosses without being conned into prostituting herself. She did this by behaving in a vivacious and flirtatious manner, which she alternated with cold intellect; a dry—to the point of arid— wit; and sheer, conscientious hard work. In short, she scared the life out of them, and all but dared anyone to try to compromise her.

'Anyway,' said Juliet, petulantly, 'we're not going away now until the spring, so I suggest you put your efforts into planning the Christmas party instead.'

'Oh,' said Lucinda, a little put out. She hovered a while, as if reluctant to let it be. 'But you *can't* go to Australia in the spring, or you'll miss their summer! That's ridiculous. You'd need to go *now* to catch their summer.'

As if I don't know, Juliet thought bitterly; but try telling Parker that. And why couldn't Lucinda mind her own bloody business? Bitterly, she realised that it was her colleague's way of pointing out that she *hadn't gone yet*. The old bag was taunting her.

The telephone on Juliet's desk rang and she quickly grabbed the receiver, grateful for the interruption. 'Rutherford and Strang, Solicitors, Litigation Department, Juliet speaking, how can I help you?' Juliet recited the rehearsed spiel down pat, whilst giving an apologetic look to Lucinda, who grudgingly sloped off.

'Hi Jules, it's me!' came the familiar voice on the line.

'Kate, hi!' said Juliet, immediately dropping the professional tone. 'How's life in the sticks?'

'Fine. Great. We're really settling in.'

'Hmm. If you say so.'

Juliet was still cynical about her sister's decision to move to Cornwall. Moving to the countryside was like moving back in time, as far as she was concerned. She held in contempt the middle-class professionals that she had known, who, with burgeoning offspring, had moved to Devon or Dorset in an attempt to recreate some sort of nostalgic idyll of bygone days. But she made some allowance for Kate, in that she *wanted* it to work out well for her.

'So what's the gossip?' her sister asked, sounding oddly stressed; or excited or something. Her voice seemed to have a superficially raised pitch to it.

'Oh, the usual,' Juliet said grumpily. 'Parker has to go to Milan for a shoot, and *I* can't go. Not unless I pay for my own ticket and hotel accommodation of course—he has to share with another model. And even then, he says we'd never see each other because he'd be working.'

'The perils of dating a supermodel,' joked Kate. And it was a joke. Parker was by no means anywhere near supermodel status, but that didn't seem to prevent his agency transporting him hither and thither as though he were an international star. Yet despite the vast amounts of money that they spent on him, very little of it seemed to come his way.

'Work is hell,' continued Juliet, lowering her voice somewhat. 'Lucinda is *working late* with some new sleazoid litigator, though Christ only knows what kudos he gets from traipsing *her* ugly mug around town.'

'Do you know when you're going away yet?' asked Kate.

Juliet raised her eyes to heaven. 'Spring. That's the latest anyway. I really don't want to talk about it, it's too depressing. Anyway, that leaves me free to come and visit you for a cosy, quaint Cornish-cottage Christmas!'

'Oh.'

Almost three-hundred miles away Kate paced the floor of the narrow hallway, as much as the receiver coil of the old wall-phone would allow. 'I, er, hadn't thought...well of course you'd be welcome.'

This wasn't entirely true. Much as she loved her sister, Kate placed great emphasis on this being their first Christmas at Dolphin Cottage. Despite her well-voiced opinions on the commercialism of the season, a softer part of her was anxious to instil a few traditions in Isabella's fast-developing mind. She wanted to wipe clean the memories of miserable past years and replace them with those akin to some imagined Victorian idyll. She envisaged roaring open log fires, sixpences in puddings, carols in the local church and snow in the fields.

If Juliet, or more specifically, Juliet and Parker, were to invade them, then no doubt excess and debauchery would ensue. They hardly seemed able to avoid substance abuse on any given occasion, and Christmas demanded it all the more so. Kate pictured Isabella, her eyes shining, rushing downstairs on Christmas morning in her tartan pyjamas to find herself having to negotiate drunken bodies, beer cans, precariously balanced ashtrays or worse...

'Isn't Mum expecting us to go to France for Christmas?' said Kate, who had been secretly hoping that Juliet would play family representative, leaving her, Kate, free to make her excuses and stay at home.

'Nah!' said Juliet. 'She only invited us out of a sense of duty. She's got all her mates coming over for a big week-long party. She won't want us around cramping her style.'

'Oh,' said Kate, starting to feel backed into a corner. 'Well, if you're sure you won't feel bored...'

'Don't worry!' said Juliet, who did not possess the requisite lack of self-esteem to suspect that she might not be entirely welcome. 'If it's really dull, we can just hole ourselves up and get drunk!'

Kate sighed inwardly. She would have to make the best of it. On the plus side, Juliet was good company, and it was true that she, Kate, needed to let her hair down a bit. Her mind raced. She supposed they could camp down in the spare bedroom. It was minuscule; only barely big enough to house the bashed-up old computer that she reluctantly kept for Izzy's sake, and some bookshelves. But it would only be for a few days. Perhaps she could have a small party? Kate's supposed reclusiveness was temporarily forgotten and all pretension towards solitude flew out the window as she contemplated the need to entertain Juliet and Parker. Pride, it seemed, would be an enemy to her intentions. She could invite Vivien, and perhaps Jem? Of course she'd have to invite Lance too, out of politeness, but naturally he wouldn't come...

'Hey, you still there?' said Juliet on the other end of the line.

'Yes! *Sorry*,' Kate said quickly 'I was just thinking about maybe having a...' she hesitated to use the word "party", '...a few friends over for drinks or something. I never did have a proper housewarming. That's if you're definitely coming?'

'Friends, eh?' Juliet chuckled, 'What kind of friends? Is the local pig farmer making eyes at you? Let me guess, he's approaching sixty years old; he couldn't wed before now because Mother was still alive, and it wouldn't do to have another woman in the house. But now she's croaked and the only available local women are all his cousins. Not that he wasn't tempted, of course, but then the fancy lady from London arrives on the scene with a secret history and a *bairn* in tow...'

'Juliet!' cried Kate. 'Stop being so patronising! Not to mention prejudiced. And they don't say "bairn" down here...'

'Okay, okay!' Juliet laughed. 'So go on then, who are the "friends"?'

'Never mind,' Kate said, disgruntled. She had been hoping for a good gossip relating to the two gorgeous-looking men who had just vacated her kitchen. But her enthusiasm waned as she realised that Juliet would cheerfully ridicule. She suppressed a bud of regret for the loss of Stevie, who would have been all ears. 'But I'll have you know,' she added mysteriously, 'that I'm finding Cornwall to be quite the land of discovery. Oh, yes indeed!'

'What *are* you going on about?' said Juliet, and then hissed, 'Look I have to go now—getting "looks" for prolonged personal phone call. I'll speak to you soon. Love to Izzy, byee.'

Juliet didn't hear Kate's response as she threw the telephone receiver back onto its cradle and looked busy with some papers on her desk.

It didn't occur to Juliet that her sister might have rung for any reason in particular. She mulled over the idea of Cornwall for the Christmas holiday. It would probably be mind-numbingly tedious, but it would impress the sentimental fools that she worked with. She could make it sound incredibly romantic, and thus stave off any suspicion that there might be any problems between her and Parker, and also make her life sound interesting and fun-filled. Yes...a romantic Cornish break for Christmas, and *then* off travelling the world. Satisfied, she decided to take a walk to the ladies washroom to check her appearance.

As Juliet surveyed her immaculately made up features, and her neat, precision-cut bob that accentuated the sleek, shiny blackness of her hair, Lucinda bustled in and stood beside her in front of the mirror. She started vigorously applying a too-dark burgundy-red lipstick. She had a luminous ruby spot on her nose that became hideously highlighted by the deep shade on her lips.

'Tsk. Got to work late tonight,' said Lucinda, rolling her eyes as if it were a great nuisance. When Juliet didn't respond, but merely continued to arrange her hair, first behind and then in front of her pretty, pixie-like ears, she went on: 'Honestly, it's the second time this week. Crispian doesn't seem to think I have a life of my own. But I suppose I should show loyalty. It *is* a very important client, after all. We're going to the Barbican tonight. Hope I get something nice to eat!' She finished with a honking laugh.

Juliet imperceptibly paused, but for only a moment. Was *she*, Juliet, supposed to be jealous? It was contemptible.

'Lucinda,' she said, 'Crispian is an out-and-out *sleazoid*, who looks as though he wears fishnet stockings and a suspender belt under his pinstripe.' And with that, she coolly turned and left, leaving the washroom door swinging in her wake.

CHAPTER 12

A Night On Earth

Isabella O'Neill sat with her feet curled up underneath her on the wonky wooden table outside the kitchen window. Wrapped in a blanket, she was also wearing two pairs of thick socks, a hoody over her pyjamas, and her fleece hat and scarf. A hot water bottle stuffed under her hoody burned against her stomach. She felt perfectly warm except for the cold November night air that she sucked through her nose into her lungs, and she quite liked that. In fact she positively drank it in, her little nose upturned to the stars like some wild nocturnal animal.

It had taken ages to sneak downstairs, avoiding all the creaking boards, and to quietly open the kitchen window and climb out. Her only concern, apart from avoiding being caught, was that there might be rats about. Huge black rats. As a precaution she always left the long glass doors of the window ajar so that she would be able to dive backwards into the cottage in an emergency. Besides, she liked to think that although she hated rats, it would not be beyond her abilities to fight them off. Or to kill them, even. To assist her in this eventuality, she kept a large chef's knife on the table beside her, but wrapped in a towel—another safety precaution; she wasn't *silly*.

Isabella knew that Kate would go spare if she were to catch her outdoors at this hour. She felt like Huckleberry Finn, but without the smoking pipe. (Although she quite liked the idea

129

of smoking a pipe, but everybody these days knew how bad it was for you.) And, unlike Huck, she hadn't had the nerve to make her escape via her bedroom window; but still. On this latest of many instances, she sat entranced by the sight that had enraptured her imagination; filled her young mind with questions and her heart with love. The stars...countless endless stars. The whole of her galaxy lay before her...well, this part of it at least. She hadn't known, in London, where most of the twinkles in the sky were airplanes, just how much there was to see. It puzzled her that adults, who kept going on about the importance of learning stuff, could lie in their beds, their curtains drawn, on such a beautiful clear night as this. She imagined what it would be like, if it were normal for crowds of people to congregate outside on clear nights. They would gather to teach, to learn—but most of all to wonder about the stars.

It would be like some gigantic bonfire party; only without the bonfires, naturally; for everywhere, including all the cities and towns, would have to turn out the lights to see the spectacle. There could be advance notices given on the weather reports, like they did if there was an eclipse, or a meteor shower.

It will be an especially clear night on Thursday, so all you stargazers out there, remember to check the notices on your local town hall or library for the evening's meeting points.

She frowned. How did grown-ups become so disinterested, so boring and so *scared*? Her mother was always scared. She was scared of the dark, for goodness' sake. At *her* age! And she worried constantly about Isabella, in particular. She was always checking on what she was up to, and with whom she walked home from school. She said ridiculous things like "don't drown" whenever Isabella went for a swim. "Be careful not to get blown off the cliffs" was the latest, on the walk to and from school, and if there was only the slightest sign of a breeze in the air. In fact, she had probably heard the words "be careful" more than any other in her short life. It was crazy because in all the best books and films, reward was always gained by following adventure and daring. You had to take chances in life; everyone knew *that!*

But if Kate were to catch Isabella sitting out here in the cold in the middle of the night, her first words would not be, "Hey, why didn't you wake me? It's beautiful! Hold on while I make some cocoa, and I'll join you!"

Fat chance. Instead, Isabella would be treated to a lecture on the perils of catching pneumonia. And then the *knife* would take some explaining... Or perhaps she would be given that other old favourite, namely that she "could have gone missing". What was all that about? She knew, from what she had overheard on news reports, that children sometimes were abducted by strangers; but she couldn't imagine why. Maybe they had no children of their own and were lonely? Or more likely, she thought, like the fairy tales of old, they put you to work in their house, cleaning and cooking, and wearing rags. She was vaguely aware of darker motives, but did not allow her thoughts to go there. And of course she didn't *want* to go missing, but honestly, it was so dark out here at night that no passing abducting stranger would even know she was there. In fact, thought Isabella ruefully, we would be practically invisible if *she* would only turn off her bloody lamp! She glared crossly up at the only slither of light coming from her mother's bedroom, and which was ruining her almost perfect view of the sky. Didn't Kate realise that the light acted as a beacon, guiding and beckoning any potential kidnappers to their door?

Isabella vowed solemnly never to lose her fascination with the universe, or to become afraid. And one day, she would own a big telescope that she would keep on the top floor of her house, like Finn's dad did. Lance—he allowed her to call him Lance—actually had several telescopes that he kept in a special room that had a domed roof that opened to the skies. His telescopes were connected to a computer, and he said that this meant he could track stars, or even whole galaxies, and take pictures. One smaller telescope was on wheels, and this he would shove outside at a moment's notice, through some large doors onto the flat roof. Lance said he had had the house specially changed in this way just so that he could look at the stars. Isabella loved this room—the observatory, they called it—and on the several occasions that she had been allowed up there with Finn, had felt privileged and important. Isabella thought that Lance was probably the best grown-up that she knew. Well, apart from Kate, she conceded; but grudgingly, and only out of love.

* * *

Less than a mile away, Finn Greenwood-Borlase lay awake in bed staring at the vintage poster on the wall that depicted King Kong scaling the Empire State Building, with Fay Wray struggling pointy-toed and aghast in his huge hand. Did Gorillas have hands, or were they paws? His thoughts turned, as they often did, to the day when he would go there himself— to New York. And not only there, he would go to Sydney to see the Opera House; to the Pyramids in Egypt; the Taj Mahal in India and to Ankhor Wat in Cambodia. There were so many other places that he wanted to visit: Mexico; Peru; Easter Island... He had made a list. He would get so excited just thinking about the travels and adventures that he would have, that sleep became impossible. The world seemed so vast and thrilling and full of promise. When he had finished travelling—after many years of course—he might settle down. For a while anyway. Probably in New York. He would make buildings, bigger and better than anyone could yet imagine. Only *he* would use much better materials.

Finn was fascinated by cob houses and the way that they seemingly could be moulded almost straight up out of the ground. He thought an awful lot too, about termite colonies, and the towering mounds that they built. His imaginary buildings of the future owed everything to these ruminations. Of course, once he had set out in the world, Finn didn't think that he would ever come back to Cornwall. Well, except to see his Dad, and Aunt Vivien and Grandma. And to surf, of course; that was a no-brainer.

But he would never get married and have children. What was the point if you couldn't do what you wanted to anymore? And if you *did* do what you wanted, then you wouldn't always be able to see your children, and that was just a bummer. His mother had a fantastic career, or so everyone said. She was on the TV anyway, so that must be good. Anyway, she never seemed particularly happy when she did visit him, and he supposed that it was a nuisance for her to have to interrupt her work to come and see him at all. He tried very hard not to make her feel that she had to stick around. And it seemed to work, because she was always happiest when saying goodbye again. She would smile, and stroke his hair, and make funny cooing noises. But she wasn't sad, and she didn't cry, not ever.

* * *

In the heart of the village Jem Farrow sat sprawled on his sofa amongst the debris of his evening's diversions. A late-night semi-pornographic movie was showing on the television. It was something that he should have been thrilled about, but which for some reason he instead found deeply depressing. Yet he couldn't summon the will to turn it off. The uneaten rinds of a too-dry pizza lay on a plate on the coffee table, next to the barely touched and now soggy Caesar salad. An emptied bottle of Pinot Noir also sat, next to his idly placed foot, on the table, steadily oozing a ring of red stain onto the pine surface. It was the second bottle he'd opened that night. The dribble of wine that still remained in his glass offered no enticement. He would polish it off, naturally, but the anticipative enjoyment had worn off. What was it that he had had drummed into him, in his school economics lessons? *Marginal utility*; yes, that was it. Discovering the decreasing marginal utility of a bar of chocolate had been one of the more exciting lessons in economics.

'What was it?' he said aloud to himself, as though practicing for the real thing; for that time when he would regale a *real* person with his witty anecdotes. 'The marginal utility of a chocolate bar is the...um...period of enjoyment attained within the first two mouthfuls, when desire it at its greatest. I think? After that, it's downhill all the way, mate. You become full, but you keep eating. Until you're positively sick of the muck. But you still finish it off.'

It suddenly occurred to Jem that there was probably a marginal utility period for sex. Not for the act itself which could never be described as marginal in any way, but well, for a sexual *relationship*. He ran a mental list of all the women that he had slept with.

Sarah Legge: a year. But then that had been a relationship comprised of lengthy periods of anticipation, culminating periodically with great satisfaction, usually when her parents were out for the night. The fact that these nights were usually followed by another wilderness of little action, meant that the still inexperienced Jem looked forward eagerly to the next opportunity. So the positive marginal utility of that relationship remained for some considerable time.

Dolores Prince. Oh Dolores Prince! There were still stirrings of something at the thought of her lips and eyes; or more particularly, the way she would look at him. Dolores had stolen his heart and his reason at Uni, but dropped him from a great height back into reality when he realised that he was not the only one to entertain her affection. She had still been willing, but somehow it was never the same. He had entered a period of negative marginal utility.

He had arrived back in Cornwall in a flurry of fresh expectation and hopes of starting anew. This enthusiasm carried him for many years, and he could not deny that he'd had fun, moving from each fading relationship to new, exciting conquests. In short, he had loved the bachelor life. But lately he seemed to have hit a dip, and a new pattern was emerging. Cheryl Scobey; Debbie Pellow; Jenifer Trewin...a month; two weeks; one night, respectively. The list went on. It was thoroughly depressing. The possibility of a full-time, even *married*, relationship seemed to have sailed effortlessly beyond him.

His thoughts turned to Kate O'Neill. Yes, she was lovely; yes, he was attracted. Somehow he couldn't stop himself from flirting with her. Lance had mocked him after they had delivered the bookcase. He recalled the words "obvious" and "desperate" being thrown back at his protestations of innocent friendliness.

Desperate, indeed! Lance didn't know; *he* didn't understand. It was in Jem's nature to...to continually throw himself at love. Caution to the wind and all that. He was...an optimist; yes that was it. And that was a good thing, wasn't it?

'I'm like some exotic insect, that gets eaten by its mate,' Jem spoke aloud again. '...an insect, yes; the name of which escapes me just now. But an exotic one anyway, that is compelled to follow its mating instinct, despite said instinct also being its doom...' and with that he fell off the sofa with a painful thud onto the beige shag pile carpet, and lay there, one foot still on the table, whilst his fellow insect, the house beetle, crawled around him.

* * *

Kate O'Neill wiped tears away from her sodden cheeks with the back of her hand and then reached for a tissue from the box on the bedside table. She blew her nose loudly. She noted from the alarm clock that it was nearly 1.30 in the morning. Her library copy of Tennyson's *Idylls of the King* lay dog-eared and tear-soiled on the bed beside her, where she had flung it down. It had already been made grubby by flecks of sloshed camomile tea, and grease-stained from where she had carelessly left it upturned and open on the kitchen table, right where Izzy had recently been buttering a sandwich. Kate reckoned that she was the most slovenly of all borrowers, and fully expected to one day have her library membership publicly revoked, when she dared to return one tatty copy too many. She had, in the past, even recognised her own stains on books that she had borrowed years previously. Whereas it would have been harder to point a finger at the culprit in London, here in the tiny domain of Pencarra, she risked exposure on a regular basis.

She pulled at another tissue and dabbed at her eyes, desperate to regain control of her emotions. But it was *so, so* unfair. Why should Lancelot have to leave Elaine when it was obvious that she was the one who really loved him? Guinevere wouldn't be caught dead getting her hands dirty nursing him back to health after he had been wounded. Guinevere was just a spoiled brat, toying with Lancelot's affections. It was so obvious that she was bored, not least of all by her elderly husband, Arthur. And it's not as though Lancelot could refuse her attentions—her being the Queen and all that, and him being bound by the conventions of courtly love. And to think that it was Guinevere's selfishness that caused Arthur and Lancelot, *good friends and allies, don't forget,* to fall out and ultimately bring about the fall of Camelot. And all the while poor Elaine had to suffer the unendurable pain of being apart from her Lancelot.

136

Kate took a deep shuddering breath and sobbed again. The pain that she felt was actually physical, and centred somewhere around the region of her heart. Modern thinking would decree that it was stress that caused the pain and would ultimately result in her short life span. But Kate knew better. The characters in her medieval imaginings did not entertain the belief that the soul lived in the heart for no reason. That was where they felt the pain or elation of emotion, and it was their emotion that propelled and motivated them. It was also what made them vulnerable.

Somewhat recovered, Kate considered for half a second that she should be brave, turn out the light and go to sleep. But instead she settled back into her pillows, picked up the book again and muttered: 'That Guinevere was *such* a bitch!'

And then she continued to read.

* * *

Lance Borlase kicked back with his long legs and the chair wheeled him gracefully away from the telescope where he had been studying The Pleiades for the last hour. Sometimes when he had to think, it helped to return to basics; to the love of astronomy that, as a boy, had set him on his life's path. He often lost track of time in the observatory and he only now noticed that his neck ached and that he was cold. Standing up, he slung on an extra jumper. It was one of the many articles of clothing that had collected in these very private quarters, having at some point previously been discarded from his person, but never since reclaimed—least of all for washing purposes.

He moved over to the large glass doors that opened out onto the flat rooftop and viewed the night sky now unaided. His old childhood friend Orion the hunter chased Pleione forever across the universe. He never tired of the view, despite

137

knowing it intimately, as he did. There was nothing, he thought, more grounding, more focusing, than contemplation of the cosmos. It helped him a great deal, when weighing up the relative importance of other aspects of his life. He had problems, yes. For a start he would far rather be concentrating full time on theory and not be obliged to also teach at the University. He had had other opportunities, of course, but all had involved moving away from Pencarra, and whilst he had Finn to consider, he depended on the support of his mother and sister. He could have taken Finn away with him, but baulked at the idea of paid childcare, and always had done. Finn had already lost the companionship and influence of a mother, and Lance was anxious, but determined that his son should feel secure in a strong, loving, family environment. Besides, he was convinced of the advantages that Cornwall had to offer in respect of a carefree, outdoors childhood. After all, It was such a childhood that he himself had enjoyed.

Except that he, Lance, had had the company of brothers and sisters. His elder siblings, Tristan and Bronwen, had long since settled in Oxfordshire and Gloucestershire respectively, where they had set about producing four children apiece, and gave every impression of having successfully achieved fulfilled middle-class lives. They returned now to Cornwall with their families only for summer holidays, and occasionally at Christmas time. They would also usually venture down for the "Summer Ball"—a title employed with heavy irony by the younger generations of the family to describe the party that the Borlases traditionally held at Tremeneghy every midsummer night.

Lance mourned the fact that Finn had no brothers or sisters. The fact of his separation and subsequent divorce from Leah had ensured, increasingly it seemed, that Finn would never enjoy the special companionship of siblings. That his son's childhood was so different from his own made it all the more difficult to deal with. He had had to get down on the floor and play. He had endured the mind-numbing boredom of pushing tiny cars around a road mat for hours and become expert at constructing exciting track layouts for model trains. He had suffered jigsaw puzzle ennui and the trials of making robots from cereal packets. But he had also shown Finn how to find crabs in rock pools. He had taught him to play chess, and to surf. He had, he hoped, inspired with his knowledge of the universe, even if Finn's interests lay in more earthly pursuits. In all, he had trodden the tricky path of being both father and best friend.

Only...being best friends with a young child was a lonely existence for a thirty-three year old man. Initially, after his divorce, Lance had had available women thrown at him in a far from subtle manner by well-meaning friends. This took the form of a succession of dinner parties, and ill-advised blind dates. They had all come to nothing, not least of all because Lance was reluctant to expose Finn to a stream of "friends", who might inevitably end up disappearing from their lives. And then there had been that whole embarrassment with Jenifer Trewin. He still felt angry whenever he thought about the effect that it had had on Finn.

All in all, Lance recognised that he had become decidedly choosy where romance was concerned. The trouble was, while he was busy being selective, time had passed. He had come to realise that life went on for some considerable length beyond thirty, and that there was time yet to realise his ambitions in respect of his work. But it saddened him to think that if he ever were to meet and marry someone new, perhaps even have more children, it was already too late for Finn to benefit from the friendship and shared memories to be had with siblings who were close in age.

He surprised himself with a deep sigh. He would be fine. As long as he had his study, his work, he would be fine. On the whole he had a good life, and an easier one than most. Lance was acutely aware that all the loneliness; the exasperations and career frustrations that he encountered were no different from those that were experienced, more usually, by *mothers* throughout the land.

He returned his thoughts to the beautiful clear night sky. There was so much more that he wanted to know. There were more questions than answers. He would feel cheated if, during his lifetime, he did not find the answers to at least some of the perplexities that constantly occupied his thoughts.

He had become disenchanted with string theory as it seemed unprovable, although new discoveries on quantum entanglement were exciting, and might shed some light. But for now it was in the realm of Dark Energy that he concentrated his energies. As far as a unifying theory was concerned he was convinced that if such a thing could be discovered, it would have to be simple, and beautiful, and clear. It was thrilling to imagine that the answer to everything could be just staring everyone in the face. Yet Lance recognised naïve hopefulness for what it was: longing for the final adventure in the story; the ultimate climax when all would be revealed. His contemporaries were forever chasing this ultimate prize: a unified theory of everything. However, Lance seriously doubted that such a final answer could ever be arrived at, because it seemed to him that it was the nature of the universe to constantly present new, and ever more complex puzzles. You found what you were looking for; what you tested for. And just when you thought you had a sensible and logical system worked out, a new revelation would turn the whole thing on its head; would present new rabbit holes to fall down. Add to that the fact that they were observing it all from such a slight, insignificant viewpoint...well, it was all part of the wonder and excitement of the subject. Yet it made it relatively tricky to teach, for nothing was ever concrete.

And besides; it all depended on what you were looking for...

What was he, Lance, looking for? And if he looked, would he find it?

Reluctantly conceding fatigue, he left the observatory and crept downstairs to his bedroom. On the way, he looked in on Finn, who lay silent in the dark. Lance watched for the gentle rise and fall of his chest , indicating life. It was the long-standing habit of a parent, even though the fragile slip of life that had been his baby had long since grown into the most robust embodiment of health. He stole quietly away, only stopping briefly to smile outside Vivien's bedroom, from whence came the gentle snore of a soul in deep sleep. It was something more to be grateful for; his sister had suffered long enough from guilt and sleepless nights. He resolved to be positive. Everything would be alright in the end...wouldn't it?

CHAPTER 13

Captain Carter's

Vivien had invited her to lunch at Captain Carter's, a huge barn of a bar that had been converted from an old quayside warehouse, and which, Kate was told, threw its large glass doors open to the cobbled street in the summer. Captain Carter's, Vivien had instructed, was the kind of place that became full and rowdy in the evenings, but did a wonderful line of mostly seafood dishes at lunchtime only. It was frequented by all the local artists, artisans and bright young things, who would sit easily alongside families, and with fishermen just arrived back from the morning's catch. Vivien said that it was the only place to be, until the height of summer, when it became overrun with tourists.

Kate had been reluctant, but unable to refuse Vivien's affable overtures. Yet despite herself, she loved Captain Carter's immediately. The menu was simple to the point of contrariness. The decor was rustic and plain, with an eclectic mix of second-hand tables and chairs, and just the right amount of fishing nets and lobster pots strewn about the place.

Vivien swept in wearing a romantic dark-green hooded cloak. As she passed along the rows of tables to where Kate sat she was met with a series of greetings and salutations. From crusty old fishermen to laid-back surfers; from leather-clad bikers to fashionable young girls, it seemed she was popular with all.

'Hi!' she beamed at Kate. 'I'm so glad you agreed to come!'

She removed her cloak to reveal a long grey and rose-coloured dress, once again medieval in style, and complemented by green suede boots. Around her forehead she wore a thin dark-green band also fashioned out of suede. Had anyone else dressed in this manner they might have appeared slightly crazy, but Vivien carried it off with characteristic self-assurance. And Kate, *Kate* had met this vision for lunch dressed in her jeans and faithful old sweatshirt.

It was mortifying. Yet Vivien appeared oblivious to her companion's peasant rags. She was greeted with warm enthusiasm by the young waiter who came to take their order, a warmth that was extended, by association, to Kate. He promptly brought the wine they had selected, and Kate took a swift, grateful glug. She did not understand why she felt so nervous; Vivien could not have been more genial. She chattered away, filling Kate in, conspiratorially, on whom everyone was, and what they all did. She motioned subtly with her eyes as she spoke, or with a discreet flick of her long hands, to where her subject stood propped up at the bar, or sat idly at a table, gazing out to the grey sea.

On the far side of the room, sprawled over a couple of wooden settles surrounding a large corner table, were a group of young men. Well, they were probably in their thirties, but were essentially young in a way that had not existed in previous times. Kate still imagined *real* grown-up men to be of a certain rakish species that dressed in suits with trousers that came up to their armpits, and wore hats at a jaunty angle. There was a certain gruff sophistication to this image, that allowed for stubble and the smell of cigars and whiskey. Sadly, it was an image only personified by the likes of Clark Gable and James Stewart in the old black and white movies that she loved so much. Kate had never met a real-life equivalent.

These present day manifestations of manhood were dressed in what Kate could only suppose to be the winter version of surfing gear. They wore hoodies and slogan-bearing T-shirts over long-sleeved merino jerseys, and baggy military-style trousers in place of board shorts. They had waved hello to Vivien when they came in, before taking up residence on the corner settles, where they drank virtuous smoothies or coffees—'They say it's going to be pumping,' Vivien explained. 'They'll be waiting on the tide.'

Kate felt a little uneasy as she noticed the group of men surreptitiously eye her over their drinks. It was a strange experience to be noticed so regularly after the anonymity of living in a large city.

'The one with the tattoo on his cheek is Gabe,' said Vivien discreetly. Kate's eyes sought out the tattoo—a small blood-red heart—and then the face belonging to it. It was an interesting, sharply defined face, with a few fading scars and surrounded by locks of black hair that swept back off his face and down to his jaw line. Kate could tell, even at this distance, that he spoke carefully and thoughtfully. But there was something else; a glint in his eye, a bold confidence that made her suspect—with extreme prejudice but embattled experience—that he was an emotional minefield; incapable of commitment and dangerous to get involved with.

'Gabe's an American,' continued Vivien. He's been here for a few seasons now—works at the surf school. He lives in a completely run-down cottage on the other side of the village. Well, I say cottage, but it's no more than an old shed really! Right on the coast and plenty of room for surfboards, but it's got no mod cons to speak of at all. Gabe says he likes it like that, that he doesn't need anything more. You know, "all I need is the sea and a daily handful of grain", sort of thing.'

'Very Zen.' They both laughed, but Kate privately registered an interest. Was it possible this Gabe person might be a source of advice?

144

'Don't get me wrong,' continued Vivien. 'He's okay. He knows the surf and is a fantastic teacher. He's just very intense sometimes. He and Lance have become close. I suppose you could say they've bonded!'

Kate groaned inwardly, but didn't show it, instead casting her eyes down at the plate of delicious-looking prawn risotto that was placed before her by the waiter. It amazed her how Lance Borlase managed to be friends with anyone. And not just because of his manner, but because he never seemed to go out anywhere at all.

'Who's the one with the dreadlocks?' Kate asked, picking at her food, before finally selecting a supreme forkful of creamy, lemony rice, prawns and parsley.

'Oh,' said Vivien, taking her turn to study her plate. 'That's Derry.'

'Well?' Kate said expectantly. 'What's his story?' As she spoke she noticed Derry, who had sadly not mastered the art of subtlety, look over his shoulder at the two women for the umpteenth time. He was a big man, with a large face and features. His sandy-coloured dreadlock braids reached down to his waist, and although tied back with a strap of leather, one or two spidery locks escaped at the front to spring madly across his face.

'Derry...' said Vivien, and then stopped abruptly, apparently lost for words. 'Derry,' she said eventually, 'is a good man. He *likes* me, if you know what I mean.'

'Really?' said Kate, intrigued. Then taking in Vivien's glum face, proposed, 'I take it you don't feel the same way?'

'No, I don't,' said Vivien, without the slightest presence of malice, but with the candour that Kate had come to expect of her. 'I mean, I love him dearly, he's an old friend. But just not in *that* way, y'know? It makes things difficult sometimes. I start to think that he's over it, and then we'll go somewhere as a crowd and...I only have to be the least bit friendly towards him and he's off again; pleading and protesting love. It makes me uncomfortable, but I don't want to hurt his feelings. I just wish that he'd...well, fixate on someone else.'

'Is there...anyone special in your life?' asked Kate, suddenly curious, and aware that Vivien never mentioned a partner. 'Tell me to mind my own business...' she added light-heartedly.

'No, that's okay,' said Vivien. 'There was someone once. His name was Max. We were together for a couple of years, but he was away a lot. He was a soldier you see. Anyhow, whenever he was home we fooled around and had a lot of fun together. But all that came to an end when he stumbled across an IED in Helmand Province.'

Kate was stunned. 'Oh no; that's terrible.' Turning ashen, she put down her fork and fumbled for words. 'I'm so sorry; I shouldn't have asked...'

'Don't be sorry,' said Vivien. 'You weren't to know.'

'What happened to him?' Kate said, afraid of the answer.

'Well he's alive,' said Vivien, in a hardened, far-off voice. 'But his injuries were...life changing. That's the euphemism they used; at the hospital. It was extremely tough for him, as you can imagine. Those were terrible, terrible days—*long* days—when I would visit him but barely know what to say, or what to do. And then...' and at this point Vivien moved closer to Kate across the table and almost whispered, '...one day, without warning and in front of his family who were gathered around his hospital bed, he asked me to marry him.' Vivien's eyes locked onto Kate's and searched for understanding.

Kate gave a moment's pause. 'And what was your answer?'

'I said yes,' said Vivien, drawing backwards again in her chair, with a small shrug of helplessness. 'At first, I said yes. What else could I do? The poor man was in an awful state, and I wanted to do the right thing, I really did. Of course, Max's family were in tears, and proclaiming how romantic it all was.

146

They started straight away with the arrangements. I think it gave them a sense of...hope. For the *future*.'

Kate was silently disturbed. Was it really romantic? Perhaps the truly romantic and heroic action would have been for Max to finish with Vivien; to tell her to leave and never come back; to give her her freedom and her life back. Kate shuddered to think of how real life differed so much from fantasy. Her heart ached to think of all the lives—young lives—ended or ruined by war. She thought of Max, coming to terms with the terrifying prospect of a life so dramatically changed. He must have feared loneliness; of losing the companionship that he had so far taken for granted. Were his actions those of love, or of desperation?

'So, what happened?' Kate asked gently.

'Well, I freaked,' said Vivien. 'In all the time that I had known Max I never once doubted my affection for him. But once I had agreed to marry him, I mean the *minute* I agreed, I heard this tiny voice that came from deep inside me that was screaming, NO! I mean, I could actually hear it, like an alarm bell ringing in my ears. I only say 'tiny voice' because it felt like it was coming from somewhere so distant—primeval almost. But it was really *screaming* at me! "No! No! NO!" Like that. This little voice was stamping its feet and tearing its hair out.' She took a swig of her wine and looked thoughtful. 'I tell you it was freaky, like a panic attack or something.'

'Maybe that's exactly what it was,' offered Kate.

'Naturally I felt dreadful,' continued Vivien. 'This poor man kept asking about what kind of ring I'd like, and about the venue and which of my friends I'd ask to be bridesmaids. He stopped talking about his own dire situation and started totally obsessing about our wedding. In the end, I confided in Lance; explained how I was feeling.

'And then I told Max. I told him that I wasn't ready for marriage. I said that I was too young, and it wasn't something that I had even considered up until then, and if he was honest, he hadn't considered it either.'

'So, is that what Lance thought? I mean is that what he advised?'

'No, but it was the easiest way to let him down. The things I said weren't untrue, but neither were they the real issue. I didn't touch on the real issue.'

'And that was?'

'Lance said that the voice I kept hearing was my instinct. He said my whole being was rebelling against the idea. Well, he said it in his own inimitable way, but that was the gist. He said that it had nothing to do with whether or not you had considered marriage before, or how old you were, or how long you had known someone. He said that you would just know in your heart that it was right. No one would be able to talk you out of it, no matter how unsuitable the match might appear. He said that when the right person asked, the tiny voice would say "yes", and would say it immediately, and without doubt.'

It took a considerable effort for Kate to not scoff out loud. She almost threw down her fork in disgust. So, Lance had persuaded his sister that she should trust her instinct. What a load of pretentious claptrap. To Kate's mind, Vivien had been panicked by the reality of Max's injuries, and the lifelong commitment that they would entail—just as Miles had been scared off by the reality of parenthood. To romanticise what was essentially basic fear into something more noble, was self-serving and delusional. There was no ultimate soul mate; Kate had found this out the hard way. You just took your luck where you could find it and faced any problems that you encountered head on. But she didn't say any of this; for it was a grim story of little redemption. Instead she said, 'Are you over it now?'

'Yes, kind of. Only...it's not a nice feeling. It's not something you're ever going to feel better about. I know it was the right decision—for both of us—but the guilt...' Vivien appeared lost in thought for a second, then spoke. 'The one thing I've learned is that you should never get involved with someone unless you're sure of your intentions.'

'You mean like some Victorian patriarch demanding to know a suitor's intentions towards his daughter?'

Vivien managed an ironic laugh. 'Yes! Or towards his *son!*' She gulped down some more wine and, since the waiter was busy, motioned to the barman for another bottle by brazenly waving the empty one in the air.

Kate searched for some common ground on which to empathise. 'I sort of agree with you,' she said. 'In as much as I don't think that you should ever sleep with someone unless you're prepared to have their child.'

'Aha,' said Vivien dramatically. 'This couldn't be related to your own experience, by any chance, could it?'

'Well...yes!' Kate said laughing, and hoping to lighten the mood. 'Entirely related! I'm not saying that you should go all out and have the child to justify the sleeping with, if you follow me...' she continued, the wine beginning to take its toll. '...Just that you should ask yourself whether you would be prepared to do so if you *did* accidentally get pregnant. If the answer's "no", then you shouldn't be doing the sex.'

'Wow,' said Vivien, in wonderment, and not without some incredulity. 'So, it's a kind of benchmark? Others would say that your thinking is not entirely liberated, Kate.'

'I know,' Kate smiled. 'It's just that it is such a big thing, having a child. I never thought that it would be like this. I mean—and I know this sounds naive—I thought that when I found the man I loved...'

'...Your soul mate!' corrected Vivien with a nod.

'Yes, whatever. I just thought, like everyone does, I suppose, that we would get married, have six adorable children and live... I'm not even going to say it.'

'Happily...ever...after!' said Vivien waving her empty glass as if in a toast to the barman who had suddenly appeared with

149

the second bottle of wine, and was peering at the women dubiously.

'But I'll tell you something,' said Kate, when they were alone again. 'Women, or at least girls—*young* girls—are deluded into expecting something that doesn't exist. We're all influenced by cinema and romantic novels into thinking that there's one special person out there who will make all our dreams come true. And our mothers are in on it too! Can you believe that mine taught me how to eat spaghetti correctly in preparation for the day when a prince—a *prince*, no less—would take me out to dinner. As if princes ate spaghetti anyway!'

'If they were Italian...?' suggested Vivien, topping up Kate's glass with long slugs of the wine.

'Hmm, but at the time I kind of had the whole traditional handsome prince thing going on in my head—straight from the pages of Sleeping Beauty, complete with white horse and feathered hat. I couldn't see where spaghetti came into the picture.'

'I'm not sure who had higher hopes, your mother or you!' Vivien winked.

'Oh but it's all pooh!' Kate tutted. 'It's all nonsense. Mothers should be telling their daughters not to be seduced by romantic notions. They should be teaching them to look out for themselves. And if they insist on believing in the love myth they should at least be practical enough to splice their genes with a man who shares basic moral values and...and who doesn't care if they have spaghetti sauce in their hair! You know what? I *still* can't eat spaghetti without getting in a mess, and I wouldn't have it any other way!'

And then they both laughed, and papered over the serious element to their conversation, as they laughed and gossiped to the bottom of the bottle.

CHAPTER 14

A Walk in the Rain

She wore an old cotton print dress that had, over the years taken on a soft consistency. A-line in shape, reached just to her knees. The neckline was rather low-cut, but Kate was pleased to see that the front-fastening buttons no longer strained around her breasts, as they had done some years ago, and at which time she had consigned the dress to the pile at the bottom of the wardrobe. She turned around, slowly viewing her mirrored reflection from all angles. On her feet she wore a pair of wedge-heeled espadrilles. They had long laces that were wound repeatedly around her ankles, like those of roman sandals. Hardly the height of fashion, but it was interesting, she admitted, to see herself in different attire.

There was no need or necessity for her to dress in a particularly feminine way. Kate felt like a child who was dressing-up, practising for the day when she would become a real woman. It was all Vivien's fault. Despite her grand intentions for the hermitical lifestyle, Kate had become drawn into the glamorous company of Vivien, and felt herself inspired, or perhaps shamed, into making more of an effort. Not that Vivien ever made comment; only that she herself was usually so wonderfully presented that Kate felt like the poor cousin, the fat friend and both ugly sisters rolled into one.

Even as she contemplated these thoughts she became aware of the crunch of footsteps on the ground outside,

151

followed by the inevitable clack of the knocker. She rolled her eyes in exasperation. Instinctively she knew what it meant: it was the world come banging at her door, dragging her out to where there was risk and pain. She should never have agreed to go to Captain Carter's.

Vivien stood smiling amicably in the little trellised porch. Behind her, near the entrance to the cottage, a group of others stood chatting. 'Hey there, Kate! We were passing by on our way to The Old Oak and I thought you might like to join us?'

'To see a tree?' said Kate, nonplussed.

'No, silly,' said Vivien. 'It's a pub! What do you think? It's not that far, but we ought to get cracking if you're coming.'

'What about Izzy?' Kate asked, her mind racing. She partly wondered if it were feasible, and partly wanted an excuse.

'She can come too,' said Vivien, 'They're okay about children at the Oak. And Finn's coming too...you see?' Vivien turned and pointed towards the small assembly gathered beyond. Kate looked. She recognised Gabe, the American, and Derry, from Captain Carter's. They were talking to a petite, pretty, elfin-faced girl, with short-cropped dark hair whom Kate had not seen before. Then she saw Finn standing with his father and with a lurch of horror realised that the final party member was Jem Farrow. He stood with hands in his jacket pockets, chatting with Lance. She watched as he extracted one hand to run it through his dark curly hair, and the resultant pang of excitement it caused made her hesitate.

'That sounds great!' she managed, 'Give me a minute, I'll just go and get Izzy. I won't be long...'

Once concealed inside the shady confines of the cottage, she fought off another attack of nerves, and then went upstairs to find Izzy. She hoped her daughter would say that she was busy and didn't want to sit in a lousy pub with her *mother's* friends anyway; Izzy was however all too easily persuaded from her room by the news that Finn was there. Dashing downstairs again, Kate became aware of her attire, and wondered if she should change back into something more practical, namely her faithful jeans and sweatshirt. After all, even Vivien had looked relatively normal and everyday, in leggings and one of her colourful recycled tunics. But *what the hell,* thought Kate, panicked at the thought that they were all waiting for her. She could be spontaneous couldn't she? And if she was going to embark upon a more feminine way of dressing, then she might as well start now. Besides, the day was relatively mild for the time of year, and if she just slipped on a little knitted cardigan, that would be alright wouldn't it? After all, she was only going to be sitting in a pub, and frankly, there was no way on Earth that she was wearing that bloody cagoule again.

Fastening the top two flimsy buttons on an even flimsier cardigan, Kate locked up the cottage and then sauntered, a little wobbly in the wedge heels, behind Isabella towards the others. They had already begun trudging idly away, seemingly indifferent to her presence, let alone her inner turmoil. Isabella soon found Finn, but Kate was happy to keep a low profile, and kept to the back of the group as they made their way along Carrick Lane.

Vivien was up ahead, apparently deep in conversation with Jem. The two were out of earshot, but Kate watched Vivien's face as Jem spoke: she was nodding; the tiniest of frowns crinkling her brow. Then her look became serene, knowing, and understanding. Suddenly she broke into a wide smile and touched Jem's arm briefly and gently. Their conversation appeared to have ended, but they continued to walk apace, their shoulders bouncing off each other. Kate wondered what Derry was thinking. And annoyingly, she herself felt slightly peeved. Vivien had said that Jem was an old friend, so it was possible that there was something more to it. After all, she hardly knew these people, and Vivien, despite her direct nature, and even the revelation about Max, had hardly given

Kate her entire life story. Even as she pondered these things, Kate admonished herself for even entertaining such thoughts.

You will not *talk yourself into believing you're interested*, she reprimanded, as they turned off the lane onto a waymarked footpath that weaved between farmland fields. *You don't even know the man, and he's probably a complete idiot when you do get to know him. A creepoid,'* she thought, slipping into her sister's language. It made her smile.

Juliet would deduce the measure of a man after only minutes of close scrutiny, and then would promptly declare him to be anything ranging from a dysentery-causing *amoeboid* to an 'utter shag'. In Juliet's world, to be a 'shag' was the highest accolade.

Kate's smile faded. Nowhere in Juliet's vocabulary was the word for hero; or faithful, honest, or sincere. No word for serious, or intellectual. Men were either complete creeps or they were worth shagging. It was very depressing.

'Hey, how're you doing?' Kate was disturbed from her thoughts by an American accent. Gabe—*the dangerous one*—had dropped back from the party, possibly curious, to talk to Kate.

'I'm doing just fine,' said Kate brightly.

He eyed her, sideways on, his dark, almost black eyes assessing her. Kate turned her face away to the hedgerows to hide her smile. His appearance, which might have been intimidating, she found amusingly passé. At the school gates of London, almost everyone and their grandmother sported tattoos or piercings of some kind. No, it was not his exterior that she found threatening.

'I'm Gabe,' he said. 'And you are...Katie?'

'It's Kate...pleasure to meet you.'

'Likewise...' said Gabe, still looking intently at her as they walked. 'I hear your girl wants to surf.'

What? Since when? And why did this stranger presume to know anything about what her daughter wanted?

'I wasn't aware,' she said haughtily.

'I'm willing to teach her,' said Gabe, ignoring Kate's manner. 'If it's fine by you, she can join in on some of my classes. No charge.' And here he grinned. 'Well, maybe mate's rates, as you people say...'

'I...don't know *what* to say,' Kate stumbled. 'It's the first I've heard of it. If you don't mind, I'll speak to Izzy first and...well, I'll let you know.'

'Hey, no sweat!' said Gabe, holding his hands up in surrender. 'Do what you gotta do. Let me know.' He smiled politely, but picked up his step a little and subtly edged his way back toward the pack as if looking for shelter. He had done his bit. He had attempted conversation with the uptight newcomer and was now absolved of all duties.

Kate felt her despondence settle again like a fog covering a hill, and as if in sync, the weather became increasingly damp and cloudy. Surveying the fields and lanes ahead, she wondered for the first time just how far this "Old Oak" was. Despite what Vivien had said, they had gone some distance already, and there was no sign of civilisation in sight. The others marched on, joking and gossiping, and Isabella looked happy in Finn's company. Kate alone was lost.

As they entered an overgrown part of the trail, the sky darkened and the air became cold with mist. The track narrowed here and the party assumed single file. The earth under their feet became hazardous with tree roots and sodden with thick mud, churned up by previous travellers on horseback or foot. Kate struggled in the doomed espadrilles, which, having survived so many past seasons, were now going to be hopelessly ruined. Once or twice her ankle gave way as she encountered a stone or misjudged her footing on the uneven track. Her toes started to freeze and she wrapped her arms around herself, shivering in the skimpy cardigan. Where the hell was this stupid pub? Devon?

155

And then—inevitably—it began to rain. Kate had not yet become used to this gradual inclination towards rain since living in Cornwall. Yes, it sometimes showered heavily, without warning. But most of the time there was a gradual, subtle accumulation of damp air and fine mist, until before you knew, it was silently and steadily raining. It was so light that you could scarcely call it rain; but it seemed to come from all directions and consisted of such small particles that it invaded every pore of your clothes and skin and hair. Mizzle, they called it.

One by one, all the others, except Lance, who wore his long "in-the-trenches" coat, stopped walking and reached into rucksacks or pockets and pulled out tiny coloured parcels that, once shaken and pulled about, revealed themselves to be Pac-a-Macs—or *cagoules*—which they all quickly put on.

Kate muttered an obscenity under her breath. She was starting to shiver. Thankfully Isabella, at least, was wearing a sensible anorak.

'Didn't you bring a Mac?' called the elfin-faced girl, in an unnecessarily loud voice. Immediately all eyes were on Kate. Mercifully she resisted the urge to yell in response, *No, I effing well didn't!* But instead shrugged lamely and adopted a pathetic expression that said: *what can I say? I am an idiot.*

Lance Borlase stared at her—that look again—and then took off the military greatcoat. Wordlessly, he held it out to Kate to hold, and she took it without thinking. Then he removed his thick black jumper to reveal a plain white T-shirt and, for the time of year, implausibly tanned arms. Brusquely grabbing the coat back from Kate's arms, he shoved the jumper at her.

'Put this on,' he instructed. 'It's waxed.' Then looking at her uncomprehending features he explained, 'It's waterproof.'

Kate met the green-eyed gaze with a complex of emotion. She wanted to protest but was hesitant—he might deliberately misunderstand her again. But since he was already throwing on his overcoat again and marching away, his blond locks flying, she quietly complied and put the garment on.

She was immediately grateful for having done so. The jumper was much too big for her, and out of proportion to the length of her dress. It was also a bit bulky, what with the cardigan underneath as well. But it was immensely warming from the minute that she put it on. She hadn't realised how cold she'd become. *Ah well*, thought Kate, as she rolled up the sleeves; *so I'm badly dressed again. What's new?*

And so they trudged on. The sound of the children's laughter drifted back on the air and reached Kate at the back of the procession. It was still chilly; but being greatly warmed by Lance's thick wiry jumper, Kate began to enjoy the monotony of the walk, and her mood lifted. It was strange how even in silence it was possible to acquire an affinity with one's companions. Eventually they reached more open fields and the rain started to subside. Vivien deliberately strode to the back of the line and smiled warmly at Kate.

'I'm so sorry,' she said, 'I've left you alone all this way. I couldn't get away.' She didn't elaborate. But for once, Vivien didn't have to indicate her meaning with her eyes, or with a gesture from her long, expressive hands; Kate had noticed Vivien resume her deep conversation with Jem.

'It was kind of you to ask us along,' said Kate, warmly. She was not going to pry. What did she care about their going's on anyway? *Keep a distance, Kate.*

Finally, they came upon a steep decline that led into a valley, wherein stood an ancient inn, planted like a deep sofa-button within the gently sloping curves of the surrounding hills.

'The Old Oak...' said Vivien.

Although it was only early afternoon, the sky was gloomy with the mizzle. The allure of the warm orange lights beckoning from the pub windows summoned them on, and they picked up their step.

All that is, except Kate, who picked her way slowly down the rocky track trying not to slip in her ludicrous shoes.

CHAPTER 15

The Old Oak

Once inside the pub, the warmth, noise and conviviality enlivened them all, and the dreariness outside was swiftly forgotten. The pub was amazingly full. Kate wondered at how so many people had bothered to travel so far to such a secret, hidden place and at this time of year. Stripping off their raincoats and seizing upon a spare table in the corner, the group divided into those who would remain at the table with the children, and those who would venture to the crowded bar. Kate, not sure of the etiquette, floundered amongst the latter.

She rummaged around in her bag, fumbling for her purse. Should she buy herself and Isabella a drink, or would they get a round in? She felt a complete shipwreck. She knew that, thanks to the rain, her hair was now an unruly mop of straggling curls. And now that she had stopped walking, she realised that her legs were freezing, and her footwear rendered ridiculous with mud.

Suddenly, Jem was at her side. 'Kate! It's good to see you again.'

'Jem! Hello!' Kate somehow managed to utter, still mindlessly engaged with her purse, but suddenly utterly forgetful as to her purpose there.

'Hello!' he mimicked, sounding amused. 'I'm glad you could come.'

'Oh, really?' Kate said shyly, desperately suppressing the inevitable blush.

'Of course,' he said, with exaggerated sincerity, and looking mildly wounded. But then he quickly smiled; a warm affable grin.

Instinctively, Kate shot a look towards where Vivien sat chatting with the elfin woman. But she appeared unconcerned, so Kate allowed herself to feel more comfortable.

Lance appeared beside them.

'What would you like to drink?' he said, looking at each of them in turn. As usual his manner was precise and direct. He said no more, nor less, than the requisite number of words necessary to make his meaning clear. He might never make a poet, but Kate began to suppose that he might actually be able to explain the cosmos in layman's terms. Jem gestured towards Kate, his palms upturned expansively, indicating that she should go first.

'I'd like a white wine please,' she said to Lance. Since it was a pub, rather than a wine bar, she decided to play it safe: 'Chardonnay? A New Zealand if possible? Otherwise just Australian or Chilean or something; but cold. It has to be really cold. Actually...have they got a wine list?'

'Good idea,' said Jem. 'In fact I'll join you, if you don't mind. We could share a bottle?'

'You're on!' said Kate enthusiastically, and warming to his friendly demeanour. They both turned to look at Lance, who was surveying them patiently as if they were a couple of fussing children. He gave them a weary look, before turning to the bar to make the order.

'So you like a good wine?' Jem asked, but awkwardly, as if by way of conversation.

'Oh yes, I truly love wine. I rarely drink anything else,' Kate was aware that she sounded flustered. 'Alcoholic that is...I mean I do drink tea, coffee—even water's been known.'

'It's okay,' laughed Jem, 'I know what you mean. Wine is truly on a different level from beer or lager. And I don't really get along with spirits...'

'Phantom or alcoholic?'

'Not a fan of either, but I suppose I meant alcoholic.'

'Ugh! Pah!' said Kate, feigning disgust, 'Evil, evil stuff!'

'You're right, they should call it that; say it like it is; the evil spirits.'

She giggled. 'Wine is altogether different. It is the...the soul of the land, the very essence of nature, distilled...'

'Although *not* distilled,' added Jem, with a tilt of his head, and warming to the pretence.

'No, no of course; *not* distilled. Er, captured then. The very thingy of nature *captured* in, um...'

'A bottle?' offered Jem.

'Quite! And thankfully so,' said Kate, relaxing despite herself, and delighted that they were being silly again. She could not restrain her most natural beaming grin. And when Jem returned it, she felt the stirrings of something long-forgotten.

'Sweet, medium or dry?' They were interrupted by Lance, who suddenly leaned between them, his tall body still half-turned towards the bar.

'Sorry?' asked Kate.

'Your wine,' stated Lance. 'Would you like it sweet, medium or dry?'

'Well, it depends on what grape it is!' declared Kate. 'Is there a wine list?' she asked again, in agitation.

'No,' said Lance, with suppressed impatience.

'It's all here, love,' verified the barman, observing her consternation, and tapping an ugly plywood box on the wall behind him. He then proudly confirmed: 'Sweet, medium, or dry.'

Horror-struck, Kate craned her neck to look beyond the portly, waist-coated barman to the box, where her worst fears were confirmed by the sight of three upside-down bottles attached to optics, sporting dodgy, cheap-looking labels. With creeping dread and disappointment, she realised that the wine would not only be lukewarm but, she suspected, reconstituted from concentrate or powder.

'Which one would you like, love?' The barman persisted. *As if nothing was wrong!*

'Well, none actually,' said Kate. Then, in desperation, suggested: 'Have you got any red?'

Sullenly, the barman turned and took from the counter a single bottle that contained just enough red wine for perhaps a glass. He started to pour.

'No wait!' cried Kate. 'Maybe something that hasn't been open for weeks?'

The barman, speechless, looked at Lance now with a subtly raised eyebrow, as if to say that this was all a bit irregular; and since he was in charge of the order, could he not control this difficult female? When Lance said nothing, he turned away, muttering something about going to have a look "out the back". Kate felt sheepish. Most of the others had acquired drinks and secured seats on the old sawn-off tree trunks and planks that had been fashioned into stools, benches and tables.

'Don't worry,' said Jem, with a placatory look, 'I'm sure he'll find something better.'

'I don't mean to make a fuss,' said Kate, feebly apologetic. 'But you have to think: how long had that bottle been there? And the white wine looks disgusting to start with. I don't want to get ill!'

'Why don't you just have a beer?' said Lance. He didn't snap, or display impatience, but there was enough in his stony tone to imply that a fuss was precisely what she was making, and furthermore, that he disapproved.

She stared at him. The green eyes were unflinching. 'Because I don't drink beer!' she snapped, and displaying much less control than he.

'Actually,' said Jem slowly, his eyes darting quickly from Lance to Kate, 'the beer here is really good. In fact, they're famous for their real ale; got their own microbrewery. That's probably why they're not too fussed about the wine! I'll have a pint, Lance mate. Cheers.'

Kate admitted defeat. 'Okay, okay!' She made a dismissive gesture with her hand. 'I'll have the beer!'

'Go and join the others,' said Lance, 'and I'll bring your drinks over.' He fixed his gaze directly on Kate. 'I'll explain about the wine.'

Rankled, Kate moved obediently with Jem towards the others. There was no room left at the table that they had all squeezed around, but just beside that, were two of the rudimentary stools, which squatted at the bottom of a huge upright beam that she initially supposed supported the ceiling. But on closer inspection, the "beam" turned out to be the remains of a real tree trunk. *The Old Oak*, supposed Kate. A pattern of branches, leaves and acorns had been painted on the ceiling, and suggested that the pub had originally been built around the tree. The sawn lengths of oak that she and Jem now perched themselves on, gave the impression that the surfaces had been softened and polished not by sanding and varnishing, but by many years of customers' backsides.

At the table, Kate could see that Isabella was noisily draining the contents of a bottle of coke through a straw. Their eyes met; Isabella's in knowing rebellion, and daring Kate to complain about her ordering an unhealthy sugared drink. On the table lay several bags of crisps, ready for the children to attack once their thirst had been sated. Being just a little too far away from the others, and unable to join in their conversation, Kate racked her brains to think of something to say to the man sat beside her. The two of them were faintly ridiculous, crouched on the low-slung stools. Kate's knees stuck up towards her chest, and she fiddled nervously with the bottom of her dress, anxious to ensure her decency. Then she fidgeted with her hair—oh no, a giveaway sign!—pushing and tucking it behind her ears. She cleared her throat. But still no words came. Jem smiled at her, and looked as if he were just about to speak, when Lance arrived with the drinks. There was no table, so Kate found herself having to balance a heavily overflowing pint of oxblood-coloured liquid, whilst still trying to avoid flashing her knickers.

Lance sought out an ordinary wooden chair from the other side of the pub, and now stood clasping it hesitantly at the edge of the gathering. Conceding that there was no room left at the table, he reluctantly placed the chair opposite Jem and Kate. The two men immediately struck up a conversation about football. Feeling as though she were eavesdropping, Kate struggled to ascertain which teams they were talking about.

'Sorry, which cup match is this?' she ventured during a likely pause. Kate quite enjoyed watching a game of football now and again, but her interest waned commensurately with her confusion as to which competition she was watching.

The two men looked at her, startled.

'Er, not the World Cup, obviously, I know that much,' she continued. 'But otherwise, is it the F.A. cup, the league cup, or the European cup? Or the UEFA cup, the Champion's League, or the cup-winner's cup?'

Lance and Jem remained frozen and unresponsive. It was as if they were convinced that they had been talking in code and had now been surprised by a spy in their midst who was attempting to infiltrate their circle.

Kate attempted some levity. 'Or maybe the second-to-bloody-last in the second division cup-winning cup-winner's cup? It seems to me to be designed so that almost everyone can win one trophy or another, just so that none of the little boys will have to go home, muddied and heartbroken, without a prize. It's all about bums-on-seats, really!'

Lance and Jem exchanged looks, and Kate knew she had gone too far. No doubt they were liberal men who *didn't mind* women watching the football—but to question it? Such sacrilege!

Jem eyed her curiously, with just the faintest of smirks. 'It's...we were just talking about a local non-league match. No seats for bums I'm afraid. No-one even comes to watch us play!'

'Ah. I see.' Kate decided to keep her mouth shut and instead concentrated her efforts on taking tiny, busy sips of the beer. Hell, no wonder they called it bitter. But she was going to have to quickly shed some of the load, otherwise she was either going to slop some into her lap, or drop the unwieldy glass completely.

At the table they were talking about surfing. The petite girl, who was called Salima, was nodding her neat little head furiously, whilst Gabe spoke quietly and reverentially on the subject. Kate didn't understand a word. Eventually, she turned back to the two men that she sat next to.

'..So you're really going to do it?' Jem was saying. 'Build a quantum computer? That's amazing.'

'Not myself,' said Lance, 'a friend and colleague of mine at Imperial...although I am in close talks with him. As I said, recent experiments in dark matter may indicate exciting new hope for progress.'

'What's a quantum computer?' said Kate.

Lance gave her that look again; the look that suggested that he was about to waste his prodigious intellect on an undeserving monkey brain. 'It's...complicated,' he said.

'Try me,' said Kate brightly.

165

He stared at her, and then shaking his head began: 'A standard computer can only work as efficiently as it can be programmed to. It can only mimic and replicate our thought processes—as human beings—to a greater speed perhaps, but still with limitations. It can only process information to a certain level. A quantum computer will be able to consider...all possibilities...and all at the same time, before providing the answer, instantaneously. It's hugely challenging to create a stable environment. But there is a possibility that once we work things out, the prototype might be able to help us to develop...well, itself.

'Wow,' said Kate.

'Um...' said Jem.

'The implications for all fields of science could be staggering,' continued Lance. 'But more than that, we are delving into an area we still don't fully understand and asking it to explain itself. In short, a quantum computer may be able to explain quantum mechanics.'

'Mind-blowing,' said Jem.

'What if...' said Kate slowly, '...it's the other way around? What if everything in the quantum world is the true universe, and we are part of the computer that they've created to understand what the hell *our* level of existence is? Sort of like a "reality computer"?'

Jem laughed aloud, shaking his head. 'They? Who are *they*?'

Kate chuckled. 'No really,' she said. 'Think about it, there's all this stuff, this *matter* lying around and no-one knows why. So you create a self-replicating organism made of the stuff itself to go and take a look; to find out what it's all about through experience. And then, y'know, report back.'

'And how does that work?' asked Jem.

'I'm still working on that part,' said Kate, grinning, 'but it's not going so well. We've all developed egos and existential angst.'

166

Lance was still scrutinising her in that intense manner. 'So you're saying that space-time is a construct to contain us—in this "reality computer"—that it only exists for the purpose of human experience and has no bearing on the greater truth of a perpetual quantum state?'

'Yeah...yeah that's what I'm saying...that thing you just said,' Kate grinned at Lance, willing him to lighten up.

For a second there was a flicker of recognition in the seagreen eyes, and she almost thought he might smile.

'Have you thought any more about my proposal?' said Jem's voice suddenly at her ear.

Kate turned with a jolt, her careful efforts gone to waste as she inevitably sloshed some beer onto the borrowed jumper. She quickly looked at Lance, who politely turned away. But it was too late; he had *seen*.

'Excuse me?' she said, thrown by the sudden change in subject.

'For you to decorate my kitchen; I was serious, you know.'

'Oh,' said Kate, and then, thinking on her feet, said, 'Well, I suppose I could... so long as you realise that I'm an amateur. I don't want to wreck your house!' She had, after all, given it some thought over the last couple of weeks, and her thinking had progressed from scorn at her own pretentiousness, to thinking that maybe it wasn't such a bad idea. It was all very well to stand around painting pictures, but this venture might provide some hard cash. And naturally, she would insist that Jem was not around to get in the way when the work took place.

'Kate,' said Jem—and she tingled at the intimate way he said her name—'believe me, it couldn't possibly be any worse than it is. Come over and have a look before you decide. Honestly, it's appalling. You'd have to see it for yourself before you made a commitment. Right Lance?' He looked at his friend for confirmation.

167

'It's not so bad,' said Lance. 'It's functional.' Then after a mere second of consideration, his taciturn expression burst forth in the widest of grins and he laughed aloud. 'No, it's not! It's not even functional; you're right, Jem. Do your worst Kate, he needs all the help he can get.' He was still smiling.

Kate was stunned. She noticed for the first time properly his teeth; which were white, but by no means straight (a flaw!). She noticed the creases in his cheeks caused by the broad grin, and how the crinkled white lines around his eyes jumped into action and betrayed their origins. It was the most peculiar experience to see him so animated. He must have noticed her gawking at him, for he appeared to quickly check himself; and after coming up from a swift swig of his pint, resumed his usual, guarded composure.

Salima twisted her tiny body around to lean over the back of her chair, and addressed Kate loudly.

'You're from London? What part are you from? I've been to London a lot? I know it really well?' Salima's speech was fast and matter-of-fact, and she used the worn-out fashion of a raised inflection at the end of each sentence, rendering every utterance a question.

'What clubs have you been to? Leah and I always go clubbing when I stay at hers? She lives in Shoreditch? We get into all the celebrity parties, her being in the business and all? Have you been to Koko?'

Kate wondered if she were actually required to reply, and smiled wanly as Salima continued.

'Leah knows everyone, and she's just so cool? She knows, like, really, really famous people? But I suppose, they're just, like, normal to her?'

And so she went on. Kate responded politely, managing to stay on just the right side of not admitting that in the last ten years or so she had not ventured into any nightclub; that in fact she rarely went out into town; and that she had never, in all her years in London, met anyone remotely famous. Well, except for when she had seen that actor strolling in Covent Garden. Or some footballer strutting his stuff down the Kings Road in studded black leather. Or there was the time that she and Miles had spotted a faded rock star in a pub in Croydon, but since that was technically in Surrey, it probably didn't count. But Salima did not appear to notice Kate's lack of name-dropping, and happily regaled her with tales of her exploits with this "Leah" person. It seemed that alongside the visits to Sushisamba and The Duck and Waffle, shopping expeditions to the latest high fashion outlets were de rigueur.

Once or twice Kate thought she noticed a certain tension; an exchange of looks between the others at the mention of Leah, but nothing was said. Lance, in particular, became noticeably ill at ease. He leaned over and quietly suggested to Finn that he and Isabella might like to explore the small pub garden. It had stopped raining and there were, he assured them, rabbits to be seen, in hutches. The children looked unimpressed, but dutifully trotted outside.

Kate kept on nodding and smiling as Salima talked, but found her mind wandering. How different it all was, from her own experience of inner city life. Her experience was of run-down Irish bars sporting flock wallpaper, noisy bands, and aggressive, alcoholic regulars whom you learnt how to pacify and not provoke. Her experience was of paying over the odds for a bottle of wine in the dubious local shop, where loitering, swivel-eyed gangster-types hung out. Her experience was of struggling around a crowded supermarket, pushing a heaving pushchair up the hill and then bumping it, groceries, child and all, up ten flights of stairs because the stinking, urine soaked lift was broken, again.

'...and so, remember,' Salima was concluding with a bright smile, 'always bring a mac when you go out and about in Cornwall? It always rains!'

Kate snapped back into the here and now, clearly having missed a great deal of the monologue. She smiled wryly at Salima. 'Thanks. I will.'

Later, back in the cocoon of Dolphin Cottage, and weary from the long trek home, she reflected on the rest of the afternoon. Lance had—*rather too eagerly*, Kate thought in resentment—grabbed one of the seats vacated by the children and joined in on the surfing conversation. Derry, poor man, who had been struggling to keep up a casually indifferent approach to Vivien, had in time succumbed to what she supposed was his more natural inclination of round-eyed adoration. As for Kate, her conversation with Salima had done nothing to assuage the impending dejection that was always circling, brewing, around her. She was loathe to be reminded of her ties with London, and of the past.

She thought of Jem. Although his company had been uplifting at the time, she wished now that she had been cooler, more offhand. She hoped he didn't think that—apart from a mutual interest in her teeth— there was anything between them. And yet, it occurred to her that perhaps she might be misreading the signals from *him*. It was possible that he might only be paying her attention out of politeness. Kate felt her self-esteem plummet once more as she pondered this possibility. Like storm clouds rolling in from the horizon, she became consumed by an irrational, brooding compulsion. Naturally this feeling had nothing to do with her decision to finally agree to decorate his kitchen. It would be a business transaction, no more, no less. And of course she would make this absolutely clear at the outset.

CHAPTER 16

The Net Loft

And so it was that Kate found herself standing in a kitchen so grimy, and so overcrowded with stacks of kitchenware in desperate need of a home that it was going to take her at least half a day to stash everything out of the way. It was not as if Jem did not possess the latest mod cons. Kate observed both a juicer and an Expresso coffee machine lurking amongst the blue stone plates and elegant wood turned bowls that lay in heaps on every counter surface. But instead of creating a cool display of graceful minimalism, in Jem's kitchen these ostensibly desirable items more resembled the second-hand paraphernalia of a charity shop. Every grater, peeler, slicer or dicer ever designed lay strewn about haphazardly.

And there were bottles everywhere, both empty and full. They were predominantly wine bottles, but Jem also had plentiful supplies of spirits and mixers. Little bottles of Angostura Bitters and Curaçao lurked amongst the cups and glasses in the dreadful brown wall-cupboards.

So much for the evil spirits, thought Kate.

There were countless packets of special pastas, exotic quinoa, dried black seaweed and the like. These had all been opened, but lay about unsealed and unfinished. Overhead, there hung a mock-antique drying rack on a pulley, impractical for the low ceiling, and Kate had to duck to avoid hitting her head on it. Hilariously, and despite the modern

171

penchant for hanging cooking pots or dried herbs, the only thing attached to the rack by way of a lanyard on a luminous green bungee coil, was a corkscrew. Clearly there was one thing that Jem was always going to be able to find in the wreckage.

'Oh no, what have I done?' she groaned. Sighing deeply, she resigned herself to a morning of hard labour before she could even begin to contemplate what lay beneath the squalor, and more importantly, what she could possibly do to improve and enhance it. Her own kitchen had been a straightforward painting job, and as such its transformation had been a pleasurable task. What she was supposed to do with fake tweed-effect surfaces and beige tiles portraying harvest loaves and mushrooms, she wasn't quite sure. And it was difficult to ignore a section of shredded, red-patterned vinyl that had been stuck to one wall. It looked as though an earlier attempt to strip it off had been understandably abandoned. The lino on the floor was similarly scored and torn, and it curled up at the edges where it had been badly fitted. Her first compulsion was to turn and run, but she had told Jem that she would look the room over, and if possible, make a start that same day.

It was unfortunate that she had insisted, as a condition of her accepting the job, that Jem should make himself scarce. He could have helped her to clear up this mess. But she had avoided the possibility of flirtation by insisting that she couldn't work with people there to distract her. Even so, hadn't he said as he had shown her up the stairs to the flat that he had "cleaned up" in readiness for her? She had almost run back downstairs to confirm that it was in fact the kitchen that he wanted decorated.

Jem lived in a converted net loft in the harbour. Some old and crumbling stone steps led up from the outside, to the first floor living quarters, where a hand painted sign sure enough confirmed "The Net Loft". The ground floor, originally a fish cellar, had been refurbished as Jem's dental surgery and waiting room. Kate had sighed at the shamelessness; the sheer effrontery at turning such a lovely old building into something as prosaic as a dental surgery. The original window frames had been replaced with horrid metal ones, a crime committed during the conversion, she supposed. But thankfully the original granite stone walls, together with some half-hearted window boxes and a tiny but pretty patio garden to one side, saved the building from being an entire mess.

The entrance to The Net Loft led straight into the shambles of a kitchen, but she hadn't been able to resist a peek at the rest of the flat. Made confident of being undiscovered by the distant screeching sound of dental tools from downstairs, she lurked guiltily for a while in the living room. Compared to the kitchen, it was relatively uncluttered. A grotesque black and yellow imitation leather sofa, worthy of any bastard landlord, dominated the room, sadly distracting even from the exposed granite wall. The only real challenge to the pure kitsch of the sofa was a pair of curtains that hung at the incongruously metal windows. The curtains were badly in need of a clean, and portrayed an oversized blue daisy design that, giving Jem the benefit of the doubt—and remembering her own sheep-curtains—Kate concluded were fashionably retro. The only other pieces of furniture to speak of were the black ash television and music system units, and a much-stained coffee table. Piles of CDs and DVDs devoid of their cases were scattered on every available surface. Old vinyl records and their discarded covers lay ill-assorted on the carpet.

Well, what did you expect? Kate asked herself. It was your stereotypical bachelor pad. All the same, she grimaced at the deep-pile, coffee coloured carpet. It really was better suited to a bedroom—provided it was not hers. She decided not to dwell on what food remains and insect life were harboured there.

Venturing on, she didn't dare to put more than her head around the bedroom door, which lay temptingly ajar. No excuses that she might have prepared in her head would have justified her being caught with her nose in his underpants drawer. Unsurprisingly, the bed was unmade, and clothes lay in heaps everywhere. There was a whiff of damp socks and mould. She was taken aback that instead of the funky modern duvet covers that might be expected of a young-ish single man, Jem's bedclothes were covered in a peachy floral design. The walls were covered in Magnolia-coloured woodchip wallpaper, and a couple of pink country-style lamps sat on either side of the bed, perched precariously on cream painted cabinets. The lamps looked like the type that would topple at the slightest provocation. Kate was disappointed. She had expected, or perhaps hoped, for sturdy manliness. The lamps should have had huge round globes cast from stone or metal, for their base. They should have rested on solid cherry-wood cabinets and not flimsy ply. And the bed should have been, well, okay *unmade*; but unmade with cool white linen sheets. Did the man really not have a clue? Perhaps Jem just needed a little help. He was probably terribly overworked. Kate's cynicism immediately kicked in. *Stop making excuses for the lazy slob.*

She had seen enough. The bathroom was a horror that could wait until the need was required. She returned to the kitchen and decided to make herself a coffee—if indeed the means to make a coffee could be found amongst the debris—before getting down to some serious work. Eventually, as she stirred her coffee, she peered nervously around the dire kitchen and conceded that inspiration had not found her. Not one single idea for improving Jem's kitchen had entered her head; other than getting the professionals in. But then there was a budget involved, and that was why she was there. Setting her cup down on the grimy kitchen table, she collapsed into the chair, held her head in her hands and groaned again. *What am I doing here? Why did I ever think that I could do this?*

174

She contemplated admitting defeat: '*I'm sorry Mr Farrow, but your kitchen is revolting beyond salvation.*' Instead, she found herself ruminating on the possibilities open to her, as she methodically began to clear up the kitchen.

The tweedy cupboard doors and worktops could not be painted, and so would have to go. Staring at the dark brown interiors of the cupboards, Kate toyed combining chocolate with turquoise. It was an intriguing combination that she had nonetheless admired in Aunt Joe's house. However, what had worked well in the living room of an Islington town house that sported Chinese vases as though they were bric-a-brac, might not have quite the same effect in this chaotic kitchen.

By lunchtime, Kate was beginning to have the stirrings of an idea, when Jem came bounding noisily into the flat, carrying a large brown paper bag. Dressed in a navy knitted sweater and brown corduroy trousers, and with his dark curls bouncing across his forehead, he looked like an oversized "Julian"; an Enid Blyton character, clutching a parcel of hard boiled eggs and ginger beer. Except that Julian was unlikely to have sported such a darkly suggestive, subliminal message in his gaze.

'Kate,' he said, as if it were a statement, and she hoped that he hadn't actually heard her gulp. Then he appeared to stop in his tracks and exclaimed: 'Wow, it's looking amazing! What have you done?'

'Nothing,' said Kate, puzzled. 'I've just um, tidied up and cleaned a bit. I'm still thinking about...' *torching the place,* she thought, '...what it needs. To lift it, so to speak.'

'Well, I have complete faith in you,' he said, plonking the bag on the little square table that she had just cleared. 'You know that don't you?' And he gave her yet another smouldering look.

'Er, business dried up for the day?' asked Kate, trying to divert him.

175

'Not at all,' said Jem. 'I just thought, as it was lunchtime, that you might fancy a bite to eat, so I got some takeaway. And, erm...' he produced a bottle of wine from the paper bag, together with two crusty bread sandwiches, which Kate recognised as being Captain Carter's famous "door-stoppers". 'After all,' he grinned, 'you can't have goat's cheese and strawberry salad sandwich and beetroot crisps without wine!'

Kate's appetite responded right on cue. It did all look incredibly appetising. And now that she had cleaned up a little, the concept of actually eating in the kitchen no longer filled her with dismay.

'Thank you,' she said, and then understanding his perplexed look, turned to one of the wall cupboards and produced two squat blue-glass wine goblets.

'Aha!' cried Jem, 'Christ, I haven't seen these for a while; thought I'd broken the last of them, actually!'

'I've put all the drinking glasses in the same cupboard,' said Kate, thinking that she was probably going to have to give him a detailed itinerary of where everything was.

The tiny note of sarcasm went over Jem's head. 'It's just Pinot Noir,' he said as he pulled on the bungee-corkscrew, rattling the whole drying rack. 'I hope that's okay?'

'Perfect,' Kate replied with a smile. That pulley-maid thing was definitely going to have to go.

They ate in silence for a minute, smiling awkwardly at each other now and again.

'Is your sandwich okay?' asked Jem. 'I didn't know what you liked...'

'It's gorgeous.' said Kate, when she had finished chewing on a mouthful.

'Would you like more salad? I have a bag in the fridge...' and he half stood up to get it, as he spoke.

'No! No thank you, this is fine!' Kate had seen the contents of the fridge.

To her relief Jem sat down again. 'So... How are you settling in? Not missing the big smoke?'

'Nope!' said Kate, with feeling. 'At least, I haven't had any major regrets. A couple of wobbly moments perhaps, but on the whole...I haven't really had time to think about it. It's so wildly different here to the environment that I've come from. Everything is a new experience, even the little things. It's all still exciting and I guess I've been kind of caught up in that. To tell the truth, I don't like to think too much about London, in case I lose the momentum.'

He regarded her thoughtfully. 'I don't really understand you. Everyone around here wants to *go* to London. Haven't you noticed? There's very few young people here, between the ages of say, eighteen and twenty-five. Apart from Uni, they all take off for London, or New York or somewhere, just as soon as they have the means. It's a crying shame, but there's no work, you see. No work, no money and no housing. And Pencarra might be a fine place to grow up, but it's hardly the hub of excitement.'

'It depends on your perspective, I suppose,' said Kate. '*I* came here. I longed for somewhere like here. What's-her-name, Alicia Browning and her family came here. Gabe came here. How about you? Have you ever left Pencarra?'

'Of course!' said Jem, with mock indignation. 'I was up in that London, I'll have you know; did my training at King's College. I did enjoy it, it was a great experience. But once I qualified, I found it...I don't know; too competitive I suppose. I knew that dentists were scarce in Pencarra and that people often had to travel, so I suppose it was an easy option in my case. It's easy to build up a patient list if everybody knows you— and they're desperate!' He chuckled. 'A captive clientele!'

'And what about the others?' asked Kate, curiously, 'Vivien, Derry...were they never tempted to try out the big wide world?'

'Again, yes!' said Jem, 'Take Derry. He might seem like he's never left the shire— Cornish to the bone that one—but he's been all over the world, you know. A surfer, you see.'

The relevance of this was lost on Kate.

Seeing her expression, Jem added,'Chasing waves. Especially warm ones! Indo, Australia, Costa Rica, Cali... That's how he met Gabe—Santa Cruz I believe—a fellow nomad and surfing nut. Anyway, Derry told Gabe to try out Cornwall's waves, and he's been here ever since.'

'If only he knew,' said Kate.

'Knew what?'

'That it's only Cornwall! I mean, no offence, and all that, but of all the places for a traveller to wind up. I suspect he probably sees it through very romantic eyes.'

'Unlike you?' said Jem, with a grin.

She laughed. It was true. It was superior to think that only *she* could see through the tourist-industry image of family campsites, cream-teas and fudge; that only she could appreciate the wild, unspoilt beauty, and deep historical import of the land, with its myths and legends.

'Okay, you got me,' she said in a pseudo-American accent. 'And the others?' she persisted, before attempting another bite of the gargantuan sandwich.

'Well,' said Jem, considering, 'Vivien studied at Exeter; and she's travelled a bit for work; but Vivien will never leave here,' he stated confidently. 'She belongs here. I've never known anyone so sure, so...less full of doubt.'

Kate thought about Vivien. Jem was not wrong. Vivien was almost witchlike in her confidence. There was a serenity about her that was a refreshing antidote to the more insecure kind of glamour. But Kate knew that beneath the calm exterior she had agonised over Max; so she said nothing.

Jem continued: 'No, Vivien doesn't hanker for the "big wide world", as you put it—rather patronisingly, I might add! Not sure I like your tone young lady...' He gave her another devilish look.

Kate winked at him. 'And Lance?'

'Well, Lance went up to Oxford—or was it Imperial? Both probably, knowing him. But I expect you knew that already?' Jem said in a bored voice. Kate shook her head.

'After that he lived in Plymouth, near the Uni. But of course he always came back to Pencarra for Leah. Think they both moved to London for a short while, and then...let me see, did they come back here when Finn was born? Yes I think so. It was all a bit confusing and messy. But ultimately, Leah took off for London, and well, Lance stayed here. With Finn.'

'Leah?' Kate's curiosity grew.

'Yeah, Leah. Finn's mother. Lance's wife? Well, ex-wife to be more accurate. Christ, it's funny to say that. I can't quite believe how long it's been since they were divorced. I've always thought of Lance and Leah, Leah and Lance; you know, as a couple. But I suppose...' he said, relaxing back in his chair, and swirling the wine around in his glass, '...I suppose it's been quite a while now.'

'Wait a minute,' said Kate, 'Is this the same Leah that Salima was talking about in The Old Oak?'

'Was she? Don't remember,' replied Jem. 'But Salima and Leah are friends, so probably, yeah.'

Kate was wickedly amused. 'So, you're saying that Lance was married to the woman who apparently cavorts herself around all the predictable West End watering holes? The woman who seems to have no discernible vocation, yet lives the high live as if she were born to it?' Salima's vivid descriptions were coming back to her. 'This woman is Finn's mother?'

'Well, yes,' said Jem, a little reluctant to recognise the description. 'Leah Greenwood. Leah Greenwood is Finn's mother. Didn't you know?'

Kate's jaw, rather unimaginatively, fell open. The penny did not only drop, but spun, clanged, and reverberated to a halt. Of course! Leah *Greenwood!*. How stupid of her. How come she had not made the connection before? How had she not seen the link between the Christian name that Salima had so irritatingly overused, and the surname that she had heard little else of since coming to Pencarra: Finn *Greenwood*-Borlase? Isabella had recited it religiously on every single occasion that Kate had had the temerity to refer to him as simply Finn Borlase. It was true that there wasn't much of a likeness—Finn being altogether an incarnation of his father—but could it really be that Finn was actually the son of up-and-coming television presenter, Leah Greenwood?

'No!' she cried in disbelief.

'Seriously, you didn't know?' repeated Jem. 'I can't believe no one's told you before, especially with you being so pally with Vivien. Christ, she's practically all anyone ever talks about around here. Nobody else remotely famous has ever come from Pencarra, at least not that I know of. Mind you, she's a bit hoity-toity now, got her nose right up in the air. It's hard to think that she was ever one of us. Lance won't hear anything bad said against her, of course. I reckon he still loves her despite everything...'

As Jem talked, Kate was assembling a picture in her mind of the woman that he was referring to. She was someone whom Kate had paid little attention to before; mostly, it had to be said, out of contempt. But now she mentally compiled an impression from a montage of images: early morning television appearances doing something daringly wacky; shouting from an outside broadcast, her long smooth chestnut hair blowing sexily across her face; a bit of weather reporting, her hair scraped back now in a bun, and her ample lips plastered in glossy maroon lipstick. Free falling from airplanes. Scantily clad on a beach in winter. There was nothing this woman wouldn't do for attention.

More recently she had become involved in what Kate referred to as "humiliation TV". She was a hostess on a programme called Confession Box. Kate had only ever watched it once or twice, being initially drawn by its sheer awfulness, but now finding it too dismal to bear. The programme took the form of a game show, whereby people were induced to confess their most shamefully embarrassing experiences, not only to a studio audience, but to their husbands, wives, lovers, or parents. The winner—of a cheap holiday—was voted for by the studio audience, and by anyone else watching the programme that cared enough to either call or vote online. Kate found it genuinely disturbing to think that anyone ever bothered. Even more depressing, was that the winner was generally the competitor who managed to provoke the most distress in their loved ones.

Cameras zoomed in for close ups of grey-haired Mother sobbing into a handkerchief, whilst desperately clutching Father's hand. Father meanwhile, who had, after all, been through the war and a lot worse besides, sat stoically bearing all, eyes focused straight ahead, as he mentally fended off his beloved child's admissions of carnal degradation as if he were seeing off enemy blows. And all the while the audience screamed with hysterical laughter.

The game show host was some lightweight wannabe who paraded a succession of flashy designer suits, and who, despite being utterly without humour, displayed his cosmetic dentistry nonetheless in a permanently fixed grin. It was Leah Greenwood's job to prise every last bit of emotional anguish from the poor demented relatives. She did this by employing the subtle art of shoving a microphone up their nose and pleading: "But can you tell us how you *feel*? How you *really, really* feel?"

And *this*; this was the woman that Lance Borlase had married! Kate grinned wryly, but her eyeballs were popping at the revelation as she took a long, hard swig from her wine glass. She found it harder than ever to imagine that Lance was not in fact, perhaps secretly, an erotic male dancer. It was the only way that she could imagine him with the likes of Leah Greenwood. As such, they would make the perfect couple. And yet, there was a serious manner about Lance that she found hard to reconcile with his ever having been married to...*Leah Greenwood!* She made a mental note to call Juliet with the gossip. Yet strangely, despite her amusement, she also found herself a little—what was it?—disappointed?

'So, what do you think?' Jem said, with a worried look on his face, and interrupting her thoughts.

'I'm sorry,' said Kate, 'What did you say?'

'I said,' Jem spoke slowly and carefully, his eyes fixed on hers, 'Would you care to have dinner with me sometime this week?'

CHAPTER 17

Lancelot

A
ll was not well with Isabella. She had become withdrawn and sulky. When she did speak, it was to complain—not unreasonably—about the cold.

'I cannot believe you!' said Kate, quietly fuming as she changed pillowcase covers.

Her daughter lay on her back on the bed, her head and neck supported by her old teddy bear. She was virtually motionless, except for the ever fast-moving fingers that gripped her computer game control panel.

'Look at you!' continued Kate. 'You look dead from the neck down. You should be out and about. Don't you realise how lucky you are to have all this space to roam in?'

Izzy answered with a silent glance toward the window where the December wind buffeted the sides of the cottage, and the ever-present threat of fine rain hung in the air. She slowly turned her head back to the screen in front of her with just the smallest twitch of her eyebrows.

'So, what's a little bit of weather?' Kate persisted. 'You should be climbing trees, or...or wading through rivers.' Kate allowed herself to imagine an Isabella, rosy-cheeked in an oversized cuddly jumper, finding dens and secret places, and dreaming her dreams from the lofty tree tops, hidden and unseen. Or in the summer, by lazy rivers, dressed in green Wellington boots, a pretty patterned pinafore and headscarf, and with a little fishing net clutched expectantly in her delicate hands. Ideally, she should have a brood of ducklings that followed her everywhere, or perhaps a sickly lamb that she had hand-reared and befriended.

'All sounds a bit *dangerous* to me,' said Isabella sarcastically, and interrupting Kate's unspoken reverie. 'I mean, I could *fall* from a tree, or *drown* in a river.'

Kate sighed. Isabella never missed an opportunity. She was alluding to their ongoing argument about Izzy taking up surfing lessons. Isabella had recently, and cannily, added horse-riding to her ongoing campaign to break her mother down. The plot was, no doubt, based on the assumption that by arguing the two together, she just might pressure Kate into giving in to one. And so, once she had exhausted all Kate's objections to her throwing herself to the mercy of the cruel sea, she would appear to concede, and announce—in a very mature manner—that perhaps Kate was right, and that maybe horse-riding would be a better option after all.

On this occasion Kate refused to be drawn. She tried another tack. 'Shall we take that trip to Truro on Saturday?'

Isabella was growing and Kate had promised her that they would go to a town with some "proper" shops, so that she could buy some new clothes. It was also Isabella's birthday soon, and so a good excuse for spoiling her.

'Hmm...I suppose so,' said Izzy dejectedly.

'Come on, it'll be fun.' Kate sat down on the end of the bed. 'We'll shop till we're stupid, and then have a really gluttonous lunch. And you can have whatever you want. As a birthday treat.'

It was a good hand to play; Kate was not known for wanton consumerism. But Isabella just looked sullen and uncompromising.

'Poor Izzy,' said Kate, suddenly overcome with remorse. 'You miss your friends, don't you?'

'Yes,' said Isabella, who finally cracked and turned to face her mother. It was just one word, but her voice croaked as she

184

bravely fought back tears. Now the onslaught came. 'I haven't got any friends here,' she sobbed pathetically. 'Except for Finn, and he can't hang out with me all the time because he's got Tom and Callum.'

'Well, can't you all be friends together?' suggested Kate.

'No!' cried Izzy.

When Kate looked puzzled, Isabella explained. 'They're *boys*, Mum! They're okay sometimes, but I don't want to shame Finn by being around all the time!'

'Well, what about the other girls at school?' Kate spoke gently, knowing she was treading on sensitive ground. 'What about Olivia Browning? After all, you have a lot in common. She's from London you know. Well, Alicia said Kingston-on-Thames which is technically Surrey, I think, but it's a London borough. And she's had to be the newcomer too.'

'Olivia Browning? Ugh!' said Izzy, sitting up in disgust, and punching her poor innocent teddy bear right in the face. 'She's so full of herself. She thinks she's it, just 'cos her mum and dad have got loads of money. And she's actually got a horse, so *she* can go horse-riding. At least she's allowed to go horse-riding. I'm not allowed to do *anything*.'

And so, all roads led to discontent.

'Oh Izzy, I'll think about it, okay? I've already said so, haven't I?' Kate was stern now, determined not to be drawn into further debate. 'Perhaps in the spring...'

'Oh, *Spring!*' cried Izzy, flopping helplessly onto her back again, her upturned eyes beseeching the heavens. The spring was a lifetime away.

'I just think that these activities are better suited to clement weather,' Kate explained, 'especially surfing.'

'I've told you!' Izzy wailed at her. 'You can surf all year! You wear a wetsuit. *Everybody* does!'

'Right that's it,' said Kate, getting up. 'I'm not having this conversation over again.' She scooped up the dirty linen from

185

Isabella's bedroom floor, and fully laden, used her foot to lever open the door. 'Think about what you'd like for your birthday,' she shouted back over her shoulder as she clattered down the wooden stairs.

'A *wetsuit,*' muttered Isabella, under her breath.

Downstairs in the kitchen, Kate tried not to let the conversation upset her, as she stuffed the dirty laundry into the washing machine. After all, Izzy was at an age where nothing was to her liking. But all the same, she felt the guilty pangs of self-doubt. If Kate had followed her mother's advice and bought a house in the London suburbs, Isabella could have entertained herself with the shops, cinemas, and bowling alleys. She could have gone swimming in the safe environment of a sports centre. Perhaps even at her young age, Isabella was already too old for the simpler pleasures that Cornwall had to offer, and Kate reluctantly conceded that her daughter was not going to be asking her for a pet duck. But surfing? In truth, Kate rather liked the idea of a lean, supple Izzy mastering the surf, or experiencing the freedom of galloping a horse along the beach or over the moors. But she wasn't ready for it yet.

Oh, she knew that in time Isabella would have to take charge of her own life, and of course she wanted her to be confident and happy. But she just wasn't ready. From the moment that Isabella had been born, Kate had felt overwhelmed by the sudden, sheer responsibility for another life. Here was this tiny, beautiful thing that could just die, if she, Kate, were to prove inadequate. As the usual trials of parenthood had unfolded, inevitably, over time, Kate's anxiety had grown.

There were the long nights spent panicked by a raging temperature, when she would lie awake at her daughter's side, praying to any god that might be listening to return her child to good health. She had felt the heartbreak of seeing her young daughter in tears, when playmates were unkind. She had foreseen the future become unravelled and distorted because of her own failure to provide, stimulate, or entertain. The world was such a hard, ruthless place, and Kate could not easily abandon the role of protector. Indeed, she had always thought of herself as selfless when it came to Isabella's desires and needs. But now she wondered if she were not committing an act of gross selfishness, from which their relationship might never recover.

It was after all she, not Izzy, who had so strongly desired to move to Cornwall, and now Izzy was feeling stifled with boredom. And yet Kate could not conceive of going back to London. Whereas Izzy's spirit was withering, Kate had felt her own begin to bloom again with every breath of salty air, or clear light-filled morning. Perhaps Izzy would settle down when she started at the village High School in September. The transfer, unlike the undignified scrap that was the applications procedure for school places in London, had been thankfully uncomplicated.

Wearily, Kate forced herself to think on something else. Sitting down at the kitchen table she noticed that the cat was happily nestled on top of the basket of clean white washing that she had carefully folded, unironed, ready to be put away. Heating an iron, she had decided, was a costly and unnecessary ritual, and the biggest waste of her time. Although she had, after only one attempt at hand washing and wringing her clothes dry, rather rapidly decided that the washing machine could not be so easily forsaken. Shivering, despite a fire in the wood-burner and the oven being on, she stared at the cat blindly. Her thoughts, not for the first time, wandered to that of a nice big wood-burning range. The cat stared right back at her; challenging her indignation through yellow half-closed eyes. It purred loudly, boldly shedding long hairs and dragging its claws through the linen, thus rendering the whole laundering process meaningless.

187

Sighing, Kate dragged her sketchbook from across the kitchen table and perused the drawings that she had made for Jem Farrow's kitchen. She stared at them hopelessly, head in hands. She liked her ideas, but in truth, wished that she had never started the project. It was bad enough to have posed as a serious artist, never mind interior decorator. And then there was Jem, himself. She had managed to persuade him that his suggested dinner date would be better undertaken once she was no longer in his employ, so to speak. She had muttered something unconvincing about professionalism; but in truth, she was stalling. She wasn't sure why.

Already Kate was starting to feel less intimidated by his presence. This was in no small way influenced by her intimate knowledge of his repellent living conditions. As she gained control of her confidence, Kate had determined not to offer any encouragement to his attentions. But as her shyness gradually fell away, she found herself, despite her intentions, falling into easy conversation with him on each encounter. They laughed, joked, and enjoyed a teasing banter. She had to admit, she enjoyed his company, in which she felt witty, vivacious, and deeply interesting. He, in return, was open and confiding. He belittled his love life endlessly. He berated himself for his lack of vision in becoming a dentist. He protested that government policy left him no choice but to run a private practice, and that he longed to one day put his skills to more altruistic use. And he reassured Kate that she was well-liked in the town by those who had met her and why on earth would she think otherwise?

'I had a really bad first encounter with Lance,' she had said. 'We just had this whole misunderstanding. Well, at least he misunderstood me.' She'd paused to think and then laughed. 'Either that or he's so vain that he thinks every woman is after him.'

Jem had smiled. 'Well, he *is* used to the attention.'

188

'What's the story with Lance and Jenifer Trewin?' Kate had not restrained her curiosity; but rather suspected that Jem, a lively gossip, might willingly divulge.

'Whoa!' he'd said. 'I know it's a small village, but boy, does word get around.' He'd considered her, whilst toying with the glass of the wine that had become part of their daily lunchtime ritual; his expression grave, as though assessing her trustworthiness. Kate had forked salad into her mouth innocently.

'It was nothing really, at least, not as far as Lance was concerned,' Jem eventually said. 'They had a fling. An affair. I think Lance just wanted to play the field for a while, after Leah. But it got nasty. He finished it rather abruptly, and Jenifer was, shall we say, *upset*. The worst thing was that Jenifer's son is in the same class at school as Finn, and the two children were aware of the whole thing. Apparently there was some name-calling; some bullying. A bloodied nose...'

'How awful!' Kate had been horrified. 'How could they have been so indiscreet?'

'Well, I think Lance just blundered into it. His mind is really always on his work, and I expect Jenifer was just a distraction. I don't suppose he even considered the consequences. But of course, while his head was in the sky, Jenifer was telling all her friends—that is, just about every other mother at the school—about how well it was all going. When he dumped her she was humiliated.'

'No wonder Lance gets all the attention at the school gates!' Kate had sniggered at how parochial she sounded.

'He does? I heard he got cold-shouldered...'

'That too. It's a weird combination of both from what I've seen. He is studiously ignored, if you know what I mean.'

'Well, quite. I imagine he's not Mr. Popular.'

So that explained Jenifer's warning to Kate. She had felt, deep down, that there was probably something inherently

189

dodgy about Lance Borlase. It was inevitable really. What were the chances of his moral integrity being on a par with his good looks and supposed intelligence? As Juliet would have said: *he reckoned himself.* But out of loyalty to his sister, Vivien, whom she liked, Kate had dropped the subject. Instead she, rather coyly, hinted that she had thought there was a *frisson* between Jem and Vivien? She remarked that they had appeared rather close on the walk to The Old Oak.

He had observed her curiously for a moment, a playful look in his eyes as he habitually swirled the wine in his glass. Then he grinned broadly. 'I was asking her all about you, you daft head!'

And so her lunches with Jem did her self-esteem no harm whatsoever; but was it flirting? Was she flattering her ego to the cost, ultimately, of his disappointment? If only she could be more like Juliet.

'You look too far around the corner,' Juliet had more than once said to Kate. 'You're always trying to cover every eventuality. Why can't you just wait and see what happens?'

Because I don't want to fall again, Kate thought, recalling Juliet's words. *I don't want to fall and get hurt.* She might have been a fool in her time, and had made mistakes. But she was damned if she was going to make the *same* mistakes. It was a dispiriting thought, but if Juliet were in Kate's position, she would have shagged Jem stupid by now.

Frustrated, she abandoned the sketchbook and paced around the kitchen, and then out into the hallway. She flung the front door open wide, and strode across the garden in the chill air. Up and down the garden she walked, like some demented wind-up toy. What was wrong with her?

Just then, Lance Borlase's car swung through the gap in the Cornish hedge and pulled into her garden. He looked discomposed as he locked the car and strode towards her.

'I've come to do your logs!' he half-shouted awkwardly.

'My what?' said Kate, bemused.

He was close to her now, and spoke more softly. 'Vivien said that you needed some help with chopping your firewood. I thought she'd told you that I'd be dropping by?'

'No!' said Kate defensively. It was true that she had told Vivien of her ineptitude with the axe, and they had had a good laugh about it, but she hadn't known that Vivien would send Sir Galahad, or rather Sir Lancelot, to help her out.

'I see,' said Lance, looking sheepish. 'There's...been a misunderstanding. I'll go.'

'No, it's okay,' said Kate. 'I didn't know you were coming, but I really would be grateful for some help with the wood. That's if you don't mind?' She kept her voice even and her expression impassive, determined that he should not misinterpret her meaning again. She would make it clear that she had no aspirations in respect of him whatsoever.

'Of course I don't mind,' said Lance with equally laboured courtesy, 'that's why I'm here.' He was looking directly at her, and Kate noticed a register of surprise in his eyes, which he quickly disguised.

'This way?' he asked, gesturing towards the dilapidated shed.

Kate showed him where the axe and the woodpile lay and let him get on with it. She couldn't help but be amused by the turn of events. As she watched Lance surreptitiously from the kitchen window, she wished again, rather wickedly, that Juliet were there to witness the unlikely sight of this astonishingly attractive professor flexing his muscles for her sake.

When he had finished, Lance came to the house and knocked on the window of the kitchen, where Kate still anguished over the sketches for Jem's kitchen. She got up and opened the front door. She ought to offer him a drink or something, by way of thanks, but was loathe to get drawn into the polite cup of tea routine again.

'That's done then,' he said, betraying little sign of having partaken in heavy manual labour. 'I'll be off, now.' And he turned to go. Just then, Isabella poked her head around the door, and under Kate's arm.

'Lance!' she squealed, 'I didn't know you were here! Where's Finn?'

'He's at home. And I'm just leaving,' said Lance; but not without affection.

Isabella ran outside and took his hand in her own. 'Please don't go,' she pleaded. 'I want to talk to you.'

'Leave the man alone, Izzy,' said Kate, taken aback by Isabella's familiarity.

'But it's important,' said Izzy, turning to Kate with a warning look in her eyes. She pulled Lance a step or two back towards the cottage before releasing him. 'It's about my birthday present.' She paused as if expecting another challenge, then announced grandly, 'I've decided what I want. I want a telescope.'

'Oh right. A telescope!' said Kate, trying to hide her confusion. *Where the hell had that come from?* 'And in five minutes time, it'll be something else no doubt?'

'No, I mean it,' said Isabella, slowly. 'Lance can teach me how to use it.'

Kate threw an apologetic look at Lance. 'Izzy,' she said sternly. 'You can't just assume these things. Mr Borlase is a very busy man...'

'Oh he's not that busy,' said Isabella flippantly, 'he's already told me loads about the stars, and he had the time to do that.'

'Oh really?' Kate was bewildered. She raised her eyebrows at Lance Borlase as if to suggest that the ball was in his court.

'Yep,' nodded Isabella. 'For example, do you know why the sky is dark?'

Oh great, she was being tested in front of a bloody physicist. By her child.

'Um, is it because the stars are so far away? It takes too long for some light to reach us.' said Kate.

'Partly,' said Isabella. 'But also because of the red shift. The further away they are, they become infrared and our eyes can't see them anymore. Even if all the light from all the stars in the universe reached us we couldn't see them all. Unless we had really powerful infrared glasses, maybe...' She looked hopefully at Lance. Kate tried hard not to look boggle-eyed.

'May I make a suggestion?' Lance spoke tentatively. 'Try binoculars.'

'Binoculars?' said Izzy and Kate in unison. It must have been for a mere second, but Lance Borlase smiled, ever so slightly, at the dual onslaught of female puzzlement that stood blinking before him.

'Yes. And, sorry Isabella, I don't mean for seeing the most distant stars but rather for more local observation.'

He spoke to Kate directly. 'Buy a good quality pair of binoculars, and perhaps a tripod to stand them on. She'll see a lot more of interest that way; the face of the moon and so forth. It's a good way to start, and I can help you choose a decent pair. There's no point investing in a good telescope until you know what you're doing.' He took in their nonplussed expressions, before adding, 'And of course, I'd be happy to answer any questions that Isabella might have.'

Kate looked at her daughter. Izzy appeared to be summing up the proposition, probably weighing it against the likelihood of acquiring either a surfboard or a pony.

'Okay!' she said at last. 'Binoculars would be cool...to start with. If that's alright with you, Mum?' she said to Kate, finally remembering to be ingratiating.

'Oh...fine!' Kate said, smiling broadly in cynical resignation. Once they were alone, Izzy was going to get a lecture on not railroading her mother.

Lance said that he would lend Kate some brochures and recommended a good shop in Truro. Isabella immediately commented that that would be ideal, since they were planning a trip to Truro soon anyway.

Back in the kitchen when Lance had gone, Kate questioned her daughter about her sudden interest in astronomy. 'You're not getting confused with astrology, are you? You know— horoscopes and all that.'

'Of course not,' said Isabella indignantly.

'It's not that I object,' continued Kate, half to herself, 'but I don't want you to waste your birthday present on a whim. On the other hand, it's good if you're taking a genuine interest. It's great, really. But how come you've never mentioned it before? How come I had no idea?'

'Oh, Mother dear,' said Isabella shaking her dark curls, and smiling pityingly. 'There's so much that you don't know about me!' And with that, she turned and flounced off, trying to look mysterious.

Ah, the arrogance of youth. Kate was sure that there had once been a time when she, herself, had been mysterious. She was sure that she had once had secrets, and dreams, and wild ambition. She leant back against the warmth of the oven and tried not to feel old. As she fumbled with her long sleeves, she realised with creeping horror that the jumper she wore was the one that Lance had lent to her on the day that they had walked to The Old Oak. She had always intended to return it, but since he had not asked for it back, and as the days had grown colder, she had found herself increasingly reaching for it. It was the most enticingly warm and comfortable garment, if not the most glamorous. It was especially useful on days when she stood painting for hours on end in the conservatory. The more often she wore the jumper, the more grew the need to wash it before it could be returned to its owner. But could you actually wash a "waxed" jumper? Kate had no idea. And while she pondered on whether or not it should in fact be dry-cleaned, she continued to wear it. In short, she had started to treat it as her own.

Kate suddenly recalled the expression of surprise that had passed across Lance's face when he had arrived, and her eyes grew wide with alarm as she noticed the many tiny flecks of paint that were now splattered across the once black jumper.

CHAPTER 18

Comfort & Joy

The next couple of weeks were grey and cold. The land was covered in a thick blanket of cloud that let almost no light through. Kate cursed the fact that she had not installed better lighting in the conservatory, where she painted. As it was, there was only a light bulb fitting attached to what had once been the outer wall of the cottage.

Isabella, meanwhile, regularly resorted to her duvet, complaining that she was freezing and possibly afflicted by Seasonal Affective Disorder. She also grumbled that she had, so far, been unable to use her brand new binoculars, because of the perpetual cloud cover. Her eleventh birthday had passed with relatively little fuss. The trip to Truro had been a successful, if wearying day. Isabella found the shops, already lit up with Christmas lights and decorations, to be the perfect antidote to the grey, characterless weather.

Kate had forsworn against making any comment on exploitative foreign sweatshops or on contributing to landfill sites; and so she bit her tongue at the parade of useless junk on offer. Her mind, so recently and happily removed from the worst aspects of consumerism, and her eyes more accustomed now to the beauty of nature, saw afresh the awful, wasteful, plethora of *stuff*.

There was so much stuff. Vast arrays of plastic moulded toys; soon to be redundant mobile phones and games consoles; the latest grotesque doll with attendant accessories.

Added to this were the seasonal Christmas baubles and tinsel. She picked up and turned over in her hand a gaudy, clay-moulded image of Santa Claus's face. It served no purpose other than to grin cheerily from the mantelpiece.

Ugly sofas; overblown, over-designed, and yet inexplicably mass-produced. "Get your sofa in time for Christmas!" the banners inexplicably urged. "Buy now, pay nothing for a year!". How many Christmas mornings, she wondered, were truly ruined by the lack of a new sofa? Was it really such a failing? And where did all the ugly sofas go to die?

Where too, the needless, garish grinning reindeer head on a stick? Closer inspection revealed this particular monstrosity as not only a mechanism for dispensing chemically coloured sweets, but also as an extending-arm device. The reindeer could presumably grasp your next handful of crisps in its mouth whilst simultaneously pooping sugar tablets. Surely there was no serious demand for a crisp-reaching, sweet-shitting reindeer head? The more she stared at it the more Kate thought what a singularly pointless contraption it was. She longed for some bygone time when baskets were weaved from willow, and pots turned from wood; items of beauty and use. The Ancient Greeks adorned their practical pots and vessels with illustrations of myths or of daily life. Perhaps they too were traded, but at least created with care and artistry, and not made to be throwaway.

She thought of that melancholy mausoleum of mankind, The British Museum. She loved the ancient artefacts, but what future exhibition could possibly give import or meaning to the excavated treasure of...a freakish, plastic, reindeer-headed, totem? It would be the End of the World show; a warning to some future civilization of this one's sheer folly and greed. The plaque would say that they did not know when they had enough stuff, but kept spewing it out like some uncontrollable tumour; too afraid to trip up the wheels of commerce. Even as

Kate dreamed of hand-carved furniture, made to order, vast containers of *stuff* made their way around the world, to settle menacingly at Southampton Docks, awaiting distribution.

A warning look from Izzy, and Kate halted in her thoughts, masking them with a smile.

And they had had fun. They didn't stop for so much as a coffee until Isabella had exhausted every glitzy shop in town, and their feet ached from all the tramping around. Isabella lingered in the hip surf shops, having decided that dressing from head to toe in Billabong and Roxy was some recompense for not being bought a wetsuit—did her mother not realise how embarrassing it was to be named O'Neill and yet *not even surf*?

Secretly Kate wished that Isabella had the strength of character to throw off the labels and dress in a more individual style. But she had to admit a sense of pride and camaraderie as she watched her long-legged daughter, the embodiment of youth, model a succession of fun and carefree styles. *If only there was not so much waste.*

They had rounded the day off with a leisurely feast of pizza and ice cream, and bought a huge chocolate birthday cake to take home for supper. Later that night, Isabella kissed and hugged her mother with affection, before going to bed, for once content.

The occasion of Isabella's actual birthday was marked by a visit from Kate's parents, who had planned to stay overnight on the sofa bed. Kate had offered her own room, but it had been deemed unsuitably far from the bathroom. In the event— and despite previous assurances that she was quite capable of "roughing it"—Kate's mother was horrified by the lack of space, and complained bitterly about the cold.

Eventually, both parents retreated to the warmth of a room at one of the village pubs. They stopped in again for a coffee early the next morning, before hurrying to catch the ferry back to France later the same day. The visit, although short, was still long enough for Susan to harangue Kate once more about her foolish move to Cornwall, and to insult her decorating attempts in the kitchen as being "a bit gaudy". If only Kate had bought a nice little house in the London suburbs. As it was, it transpired that Dolphin Cottage was a freezing, falling-down hovel on which Kate had completely wasted her inheritance.

'I just don't understand how you could have paid so much for a house that doesn't even have central heating!' Susan said, as she cradled her coffee cup. 'It's so impractical; so unrealistic! It may seem charming now to light fires in every room, but believe me, you'll soon get tired of that. If you'd had to suffer the hardship that your father and I did growing up, you'd know that. There's nothing romantic about trying to light a fire on a cold winter's morning, I can tell you. And you have the oven on all the time.' She gave a disapproving nod towards the old fifties-style gas cooker. 'I dread to think of the bills you're going to get. Isn't that defeating the object?'

'You wouldn't say that if it was an Aga,' Kate replied sulkily. 'How come it's okay to gather around a posh expensive range for warmth, but not a perfectly reasonable and working gas oven?' Even as she spoke, Kate kept her fingers crossed that the beaten-up cooker wasn't about to blow up in her face.

And she was being perverse. She could have told her mother that her long term plan was to install a range that would burn solid fuel—that she had already asked Vivien to keep a look out in case anything suitable came into Wreckers. Or she could have told Susan that she had only put the damn cooker on this morning anyway to allay her mother's constant declarations of impending hypothermia. But the truth was that Kate found herself doing a lot of baking these days...it wouldn't do to admit it to Susan, but it *was* difficult to keep the fire in the wood-burner constantly on the go; and on the coldest of days she justified the extra cost of the oven by making slow-cooking vegetable and bean stews, apple and blackberry pies and baked potatoes. Isabella would arrive home from school not only to a wealth of warming smells but a veritable winter feast.

'And I'm sorry, but I don't like this green,' Susan continued, looking in revulsion at Kate's grass-green kitchen walls.

'Well, I do,' said Kate, emphatically, 'It's cosy and warming in the winter; and in the summer, it'll bring the lushness of the greenery outside right into the room.' Kate, who could hardly wait for the warmer months, stared wistfully through the large kitchen window, while Susan only looked sceptical. Admittedly, the barren winter landscape outside did not do the vision much justice.

'Well it's not too late to come to us for Christmas,' said Susan, with a shiver.

Seamus, Kate's father, made no criticism of the cottage, but merely smiled indulgently at both women throughout. He did, however, spend some time inspecting the structure of the building, and agreed that it seemed sound enough.

'It'll need general repairs of course,' he said to Kate, when they were alone. 'I'll be happy to give you any help and advice, love. And if you should decide to have heating installed, then please allow me to take care of it for you. It would be my treat.'

Seamus, although technically retired, still kept his hand in where his building expertise was concerned, and he had undertaken much of the renovation of their French farmhouse himself. 'And I should point out,' he continued, 'that if you're serious about conserving energy then you probably should have all the windows replaced with double glazed...these old frames are a bit draughty.'

'Oh come on Dad!' Kate cried, 'I know as well as you do that buildings need to breath...as do people! I'm not going to sit in a sealed box. And don't you dare mention PVC to me!'

Seamus smiled, although Kate was not sure if it was at her passion or her folly.

When they had gone, Kate sat by the kitchen stove on an old Windsor chair that she had recently bought from Wreckers. She hugged her knees to her chest and sighed deeply. She didn't want to be so relieved that they were gone. She loved her parents, but their visits were oddly stressful. Thankfully, her mother had at least shown unreserved affection to Isabella.

She looked at the stack of vintage "cider cups" that they had obligingly brought over from Brittany. They were cream coloured, and decorated with only the simplest design of thin red and black stripes around the rims. Kate already possessed plenty of the little bowl-shaped cups herself, but was planning to use this new batch to accessorise Jem's kitchen.

To her relief the kitchen project was almost complete. Kate despaired of making any further improvement, yet Jem had been increasingly impressed by each stage of development. Kate suspected that the root of his joyous enthusiasm lay in the fact that the kitchen was actually now clean and tidy. She would take the cups round the following morning, and add a few final finishing touches. Then on Saturday afternoon, she was to attend a 'private function' as Jem laughingly put it.

He had invited a small gathering of friends—"Just the usual mob"— to drink champagne and celebrate the "official opening" of his new kitchen. In reality, it was just an excuse for a pre-Christmas drink, but Kate was dreading it all the same. She anticipated the polite remarks and strained efforts to compliment her handiwork. She was also nervous; bearing in mind that as her "professional" relationship with Jem came to an end, there still remained the promise of a dinner date. It was possible that Jem had forgotten the agreement, or even, Kate reasoned, changed his mind. In which case she wouldn't know whether to feel relieved or slighted. Either way, she wasn't going to prompt or encourage him with any reminders.

Nevertheless, when Saturday morning came, Kate spent an inordinate amount of time selecting what to wear. She wanted to be casual and careless in her jeans, but the impending aura of Christmas suggested that she should make more of an effort. Something about the season always made Kate want to wear soft black velvet or jersey, with bright jewel-coloured accessories. It was the only time of year that she even considered wearing perfume, and would daub her wrists economically with an ancient, possibly stale, but once expensive scent. She lit spice-fragranced candles in every room. Despite Kate's agnostic point of view, and reservations about the commercialism of it all, it had to be said that on occasion, Christmastime took on the rosy glow of an old Technicolor Hollywood film. There was magic in the air.

Even in her worst years, when Christmas was an ordeal to be endured and survived, there were moments of serene calm and peace. She remembered one year in her high-rise London flat, when after a momentous struggle to provide all the fripperies required to make the season real, she had sat, hand-sewing an angel costume for Isabella. She had looked up to see her little daughter solemnly arranging and rearranging the baubles on the pitifully small Christmas tree. White Christmas was actually showing on the television, and snow was gently falling outside. The smell of warm mince pies was in the air, and the taste of sweet sherry on her tongue. A cornier scenario would have been hard to imagine, but as she listened to the soothing, undulating tones of Bing Crosby, she had momentarily felt all her troubles slide away. A genuine feeling of comfort and peace had descended, rendering even the unbendingly stark surroundings, for the time being, snug and secure. She supposed that she might have been touched by the Spirit of Christmas; *if you believed that sort of thing*.

And yet, the minute the holiday season was over, the decorations would look tired and jaded, and she would abandon her perfume once more, somehow finding the heavy, warm smell too artificial for her tastes. A spell had been lifted and the magic had gone. It perplexed Kate that such a feeling of communal goodwill could be summoned by the collective consciousness at one select moment in time, yet could not be sustained for the rest of the year. There was beauty on all the Earth and throughout the seasons. Yet most people walked around like they were bored of the world. Somehow the whole incredible fact of existence was not enough to amaze or inspire.

Snapping out of her thoughts, Kate quickly decided that she would wear a black jersey dress that was simple in style, but its skirt short and flirty. She dressed it down with black woollen tights and chunky biker-style boots; then dressed it up again with a delicate pearl choker that had belonged to Aunt Joe. Her mood had brightened considerably, and she even smiled encouragingly at the cat, which she had started to call Amelia, as it clawed defiantly at the bedclothes. She put her hair up, then feeling uncomfortable, took it down again; applied some lipstick and then washed it off. With one final inspection in the mirror, she felt she was ready. But as she reached across the bed for her handbag, the cat pounced. A swift attack, it was enough to place a fresh wound on its foe; a long itchy tear between Kate's inside elbow and wrist.

Kate and Isabella stopped off at the small delicatessen and general store in the village on the way to Jem's. The shop was run by Derry's parents, Mr and Mrs Newson. It was a charming little place, beautifully maintained, and proudly supportive of locally made produce. There were cakes, pies and pasties; salads and homemade sandwiches; quiches and a range of Cornish cheeses. The store doubled as an off-licence and Kate thought that she would bring a bottle of something, as a gesture. Although knowing Jem as much as she did, there would be plenty left to drink once the champagne was finished. As she perused the limited, but select range of wines, she heard a voice that she recognised.

'What, no Chocolate Olivers?' the voice was saying. 'Well do you know where I can get some?'

Kate peered over the top of some shelves laden with fresh bread to see Alicia Browning scowling irritably at Mrs Newson, who was shaking her head apologetically.

'Well, really!' said Alicia in barely-concealed tones of frustration, 'No Party Bites, no Brandy Snaps, no Cocktail Swizzlers, and now no Chocolate Olivers. Do you actually *have* Christmas down here?'

Mrs Newson was suggesting that she might try one of the bigger towns, such as Penzance or Truro, when Alicia spotted Kate lurking behind the bread loaves.

'Ah, Kate!' she cried with a triumphal wave of her hand. She moved away from the till towards Kate and Isabella without a moment's further consideration for Mrs Newson.

'You know, I wouldn't even bother, if I were you,' she hissed at Kate's ear. 'They've got absolutely nothing that you'd want. I've got three parties of friends all coming down for Christmas, and can I get stocked up? Can I hell! The whole thing's going to be a debacle, I just know it.'

'Perhaps your friends could bring some supplies with them?' suggested Kate, mortified that Mrs Newson could overhear Alicia's loud whisper.

'Tsk! And how would that look?' said Alicia dismissively. 'But of course I don't know why I expected anything else. I don't suppose they can even conceive of our way of entertaining around here. Between you and me, I don't know how much longer I can bear it, I really don't.'

'Really?' said Kate, feeling trapped in the conversation, and unable to find a way out. 'Why, do you think you might consider...'

'Moving back to Surrey?' interrupted Alicia. 'Yes, I must say, I am giving it some very serious thought. This is the first time we've managed to persuade friends to visit since we moved. And we *had* thought there would be hoards of them coming down every weekend—given that we are known for our hospitality!'

Kate didn't know if she should be nodding or shaking her head, so she ended up making a vague circling motion with her face, whilst trying to look earnest.

'They all promised to come down when we left,' Alicia continued in a grudging tone, 'but not a one so far. And now that they've all decided to arrive at once, can I find even a simple Chocolate Oliver? No! And of course Nigel is always too busy to notice how difficult it is for me. I'm exhausted, what with the school nativity play, the carol concert and everything else. Believe me; I don't know how much longer I can cope with these...these *primitive* conditions!'

'And you'll be next!' she barked at Kate, making her startle. 'If you get lonely, dear, don't hesitate to come over for a cup of coffee. I, of all people will understand your difficulties. And the girls can play with the ponies!' she finished, smiling benignly at Isabella and touching her cheek. Thankfully Isabella didn't flinch and pull away, but the alarm in her eyes was transparent.

Kate made polite thank-you responses, and said she'd bear it in mind. Alicia instructed Kate officiously on which wine she should buy, and then left the shop, muttering unhappily that hopefully there'd still be time to mail-order a hamper.

Replacing the bottle of red wine that Alicia had thrust into her hands, and taking a chilled white from the small fridge, Kate made her way to Mrs Newson at the counter, where she also purchased a small Christmas cake that was covered in glacé cherries and almonds instead of icing. She smiled at Mrs Newson, anxious not to be associated with Alicia's tirade.

Mrs Newson smiled back kindly, then leant forward and whispered: 'What *is* a Chocolate Oliver, dear?'

Kate laughed. 'I have no idea, Mrs Newson. I have absolutely no idea!'

CHAPTER 19

Jem's Party

Kate thought that Jem looked a little flushed as he opened the door to The Net Loft, a half-empty bottle of champagne in one hand. Greeting them, he smartly planted a kiss on her cheek, smiled broadly at Isabella, and then beckoned them both inside. Loud music and a throng of voices and laughter overwhelmed them as they entered. Kate was surprised to find what looked like a party in full swing.

'It's been a great success, I think,' boomed Jem close to her ear. Then looking quizzical added: 'Everyone *says* that they like it anyway!'

Kate wished that she could run back home. The small room was so packed with people that it was hard to perceive the full effect of the transformation. 'I thought you said it was just going to be a small gathering?' Her words were lost in the noise.

Jem took their jackets and scarves and attempted to drape them successfully on the overcrowded coatstand. Isabella squirmed ferret-like through the mass of bodies towards Finn, who stood on tip-toe waving at her from the other side of the room. The two of them joined gratefully then melted away into the nether regions of the flat. How Kate envied them. Isabella and Finn lived in another world. They were not bound by the politics and niceties of adult social behaviour; no need for them to negotiate a sea of greetings and small talk. Unable to move much further, she found herself caught in a circle of strangers just inside the doorway, who started making lots of appreciative noises about how she was "the one" responsible for the makeover. Jem plunged into the crowd with her bottle of wine and cake, calling back over his shoulder about finding her a glass.

In return for her gifts he had left Kate awkwardly clutching the half-finished bottle of champagne, which she tried hard to wield in an innocent manner. She attempted to offer her companions a top-up, but they all refused, indicating their recently refilled flutes. With some surprise, Kate noticed Jenifer Trewin smiling slyly at her from the perimeters of the group. It seemed strange that Jem should have invited her after the whole business with Lance. After all, Lance was his friend and despite his behaviour, surely deserving of some loyalty? Perhaps she had come with someone else, or even gate-crashed? She seemed bold enough.

Indeed, at that very moment, Jenifer appeared to have no qualms about so obviously listening in on a conversation of which she was no part. She made no attempt at discretion, but stood unashamedly observant, her steely eyes flitting to each speaker in turn. Yet with cool professionalism, she succeeded in having her glass of champagne raised to her mouth each time it appeared that someone might politely try to include her in the conversation. Thus she managed not to reveal anything herself at all.

'So, my dear, you must be a very clever girl,' said a rosy-cheeked woman with hamster teeth that bit down into her bottom lip. 'I don't know where you people get your ideas from. For the kitchen I mean!'

'Well, I kept it simple, really,' said Kate, abashed. 'It's based on a French bistro, or the little crêpe restaurants that you get in small towns in Brittany. My parents live there you see...'

'Ah, so you were inspired!' claimed the toothy woman.

'Well, not exactly...I wouldn't say inspired...' stammered Kate, 'I just wanted something casual. You know, informal, yet stylish.' She caught Jenifer's scornful eye and cringed at her own words.

'Well it's quite charming,' said the toothy woman's genial and similarly florid-faced companion. 'Mediterranean. Reminds me of Spain.'

'Tsk! Not Spain, Johnny, France!' said the woman, elbowing Johnny so hard that he stumbled to balance his drink. 'Don't pay any attention to him, love. He doesn't know what he's talking about. Now, I just love that little red and white checked tablecloth. Looks wipe-clean—is it? Mrs Newson sells something a bit like that in her shop. But not as fancy I dare say. Perhaps I should buy one?'

Kate forced a pleasant smile. Mrs Newson's shop was exactly where she had bought the tablecloth. She kept on grinning through gritted teeth as she noticed that the small white cotton and lace cloth that she had laid the day before at an angle on top of the plastic gingham one, had been screwed up and slung in the corner of the table. It looked as though just prior to this action, it had been used to mop up some spilt beer; no doubt emanating from one of the copious beer cans that now littered the table-top. Her strategically-placed rustic wooden candlestick had also been shoved to one side. As she listened half-heartedly, smiling and acknowledging the comments and praise being issued in her direction from the small group, Kate slowly took in the appearance of the kitchen through the crowd of bodies. What she saw filled her with dismay.

The day before she had proudly arranged the cider cups on hooks attached to the revamped kitchen shelves. Kate had completely ripped off the doors on both the wall and floor cupboards and filled in the holes where the hinges and fittings had been. She had gratefully discovered that behind the doors, the cupboards were solid wood and not veneered as she had thought, and could be sanded down and painted. She had chosen a cream colour, which she then contrasted with a warm, deep red stripe that ran across the back of each new open shelf. She had been concerned about the red; it being an unusual colour for a kitchen. In the end she convinced herself that it was quite masculine. But she stopped short of putting red and white gingham trim along the shelf edges.

Warming to her theme, she had bought some tile paints and had cheerfully smothered the old beige tiles with a high-gloss cream. She had had to dig out and replace the ones bearing the mushroom logo, but since this was a cathartic exercise in itself, it had probably been worth the sacrifice to her fingernails. The bare plaster walls were painted in a matt red, and hung with vintage posters, and a gilt mirror to add light and space. Jem's orange pine table had been replaced by a dark oak one and a pair of matching settles from Wreckers. The clothes-dryer had gone, but as a playful gesture, she had left Jem's lime-green bungee and attached corkscrew more safely hung from the side of one of the shelves.

She had discovered that Derry, when he was not surfing, was also a skilled carpenter, and the answer to her prayers considering that the omnipresent fake tweed look had also found its way onto the kitchen work surfaces. Joining her for a day—and for a ridiculously small fee—Derry had quickly and professionally replaced the hated worktop with a solid oak one, carefully cutting in a porcelain sink that had shamefully lain unused—and not even planted with pansies!—in Jem's garden, whilst all this time a hideous orange plastic one had held pride of place in the kitchen. Observing Kate struggling with the lino floor-covering, Derry had generously returned the following day to help her repair and sand the floorboards underneath. Kate had enjoyed working with him. Despite his unconventional appearance, he had an undemanding, unobtrusive character, and he worked hard and without fuss.

He was amenable in respect of Kate's half-baked dreams of self-sufficiency, and even offered, in his lovely Cornish accent, to introduce her to the local 'Freeconomy' market.

And he was not unattractive, Kate had thought as she watched him sand down a difficult floorboard with long sweeps of his hand plane. He had a strange way of dressing, seeming to prefer endless layers. On that particular occasion, he had worn a kilt over the top of army greens, and a woollen tank top over the obligatory layers of T-shirt. On his feet he wore huge industrial-style boots that had seen many years of use. *He's like some big Celtic warrior*, Kate had thought, observing the long dreadlocks and the collection of charms and amulets on a chain around his neck.

Today at the party, Derry was standing on the far side of the kitchen rolling a cigarette and chatting to Lance. He acknowledged Kate with a grin and a nod, and she returned a rueful smile. His eyes danced playfully around the kitchen and then heavenwards in silent confirmation of her unspoken address. After all their hard work, Jem's kitchen, albeit stripped of its surface grease and dust, had resumed its previous character of general disarray. The bin overflowed onto the floor; with copious empty bottles clustered at its feet. Jem's collection of gadgets and gizmos had found their way out of the shelving units to resume their occupancy of the cluttered worktop, and Kate's carefully arranged rows of glasses and crockery were already a jumble. Too late, she realised that open shelves had not been a wise move where Jem was concerned. Instead of Parisian bistro, the kitchen resembled the aftermath of a Western saloon bar fight.

She looked for Jem to rescue her. She spotted him on the other side of the throng clutching two glasses of champagne which he appeared to have picked up from a tray of pre-filled flutes. But he seemed to be trapped in conversation with a guest. Making her excuses to the group by the door, and since she had not seen Vivien, Kate wound her way through the bodies towards Derry's friendly face. She had been going to have a moan with him about Jem's wanton disregard for their efforts, but Derry took her by surprise, by slinging an arm affectionately around her shoulders.

''Ere; tell this man,' he said, indicating Lance, before pausing for a drag on his roll-up, '...tell this man that The Septix were the best band in the universe!'

Kate laughed, recalling how they had discovered a mutual interest in music—and an obscure punk band in particular— as they had worked together.

'Well, I don't know about the best...' she began, but seeing the look of distress on Derry's face, added, '...but they were certainly unique; in a league of their own. Some of their songs are classics.'

'Of course. That breakneck-speed cover of 'Winter Wonderland,' said Lance, dryly. 'I'd forgotten about that.'

'No!' cried Kate and Derry in unison. Derry released Kate from his grip to raise his arms in protest, and then covered over his face with his hands in mock shame.

'That was bad, man,' he said, shaking his head. He reappeared again from behind his fingers to reveal a broad grin. 'That was *so* bad. I guess they might have been taking irony to new levels?' It was a pitiful stab.

'Possibly,' said Lance. 'Either that or their record company were desperate to wring a commercial Christmas single out of them.'

'No, you're right, that *was* bad,' said Kate. 'But in their heyday, I mean in their first incarnation, they were inspired. Seminal, even.'

'Seminal?' Lance sputtered incredulously, and breaking into a deep chuckle. Once more Kate found herself disconcerted by the sudden drop from cool composure to animated warmth. 'I suppose they may have been responsible for the three-minute frenzied nihilistic pop song...or was that every single other punk band? I forget.'

'Very funny. But before you mock,' Kate continued, flourishing her champagne bottle at him, 'I suggest you actually listen to their early albums. They were innovative. They were experimental. They were...they were *arty*!'

'They were?' Derry said with a puzzled expression. It was a look that stayed fixed on his features as he appeared to be processing this information.

'Enjoying your drink?' asked Lance, with a flicker of his eyes to the bottle in Kate's hand. She opened her lips to protest, but instead, in a fit of pique, she nodded eagerly.

'Yep!' she said.

Then she threw back her head and took a long swig from the bottle's neck. When she could gulp no more, she lowered the bottle and tried to look defiantly into Lance's pale dissecting eyes. But the champagne bubbles were fizzing up her nose, making it twitch.

Lance appeared to scan her features, inspecting them, before lowering his gaze to fall on the fresh scratch on her arm. Kate became suddenly conscious of her bare, unpainted fingernails, still somewhat ragged from all the work on the kitchen.

'I never really thought of them as being *arty*,' said Derry, still looking confounded, and shaking his head. '...Just thought they were a good laugh, is all.'

Kate spotted Wendron Laity from Blue Wave on the other side of the crowded room, making as if to leave. Summoning up her courage, she was about to approach him, but finally Jem reappeared behind her, clutching the two flutes of champagne.

'Sorry I took so long,' he whispered huskily in her ear. He stood so close that she could smell his aftershave and feel the warmth of his body close against her back. 'Here,' he said

213

handing her one of the glasses. Kate took it, and before he could escape, inserted the half-finished bottle of champagne firmly into his empty hand. He looked at it blankly; frowned, and then shoved it onto the overcrowded worktop, where it dislodged some scrunched-up beer tins, and tottered precariously itself on the edge. Jem completely ignored the fallen tins as they clattered onto the floor.

'Where's Vivien?' he asked cheerfully.

'She'll still be at the shop,' said Derry. 'I expect she'll be along later?' he added, unable to disguise the hope in his voice.

At that moment, Jenifer Trewin brushed by, her breasts jutting from her uplift bra and tiny T-shirt. She appeared to deliberately thump into Lance's arm, causing him to spill his drink, then with a deft flick of the wrist, sent her own champagne flying all over his neck. Her cronies followed her, shooting cold-eyed, hostile looks at the group in the corner.

'Oy! Be careful!' Derry shouted above the racket at the disappearing trio of oscillating hips and raised cigarettes.

'It's like being back at a teenage party!' Kate whispered to Jem, then looking directly at him asked: 'Did you invite them?'

'Well, not exactly,' said Jem, close to her ear. 'You know what it's like in these small villages—well, maybe you don't— but word just sort of gets around.'

Kate wasn't entirely convinced.

'She's harmless,' added Jem, with a shrug. He drained his glass and then looked around. 'But I'm guessing Lance could do with a refill. Back in a bit,' he smiled before disappearing once more, and completely forgetting the half-bottle on the counter.

Kate looked at Lance, who appeared surprisingly unruffled considering Jenifer's obvious assault. She had expected him to be mortified, but his expression was as cool as ever, as he mopped the champagne from his neck with a tea towel. It was as if nothing had happened. Could he really be so callous and invulnerable? True, Jenifer's behaviour was pathetic and

214

infantile, but surely most human beings would feel some sense of humiliation? Perhaps he was the kind of man who enjoyed engaging a woman's wrath; who got some strange kind of perverse pleasure from being able to exercise such power. Kate shivered with repulsion.

When Jem came bouncing back again with a fresh bottle that he offered around, Kate felt her heart warming to him. His manner was so exuberant and uncomplicated. And maybe it was the champagne, but he was looking incredibly attractive tonight. He had lost some of the prim neatness of attire that she had come to expect. (She had thought on more than one occasion that her mother would absolutely adore Jem.) But tonight, his shirt was unbuttoned at the neck, and the fact that he wore an undone tie around his shoulders was somehow far sexier than if he had worn no tie at all. His dark curly hair had slightly outgrown its usual taming cut, and kept hanging seductively over one eye, so that he had to keep pushing it back. Tonight, Jem was looking positively ruffled; *rakish* even.

Even as she thought this, he put an arm around her waist and pulled her nearer.

Without warning, and with the effect of a multistorey concrete car park slamming down upon her head, Kate thought of Miles. Alarm bells sounded from somewhere in the shades of her subconscious: *Don't go there.* She moved stiffly away from Jem's friendly embrace, using the excuse of setting her flute down on the nearby countertop.

He didn't seem to notice, but pulled her back to him.

'Of course, the best thing about Kate finally finishing my kitchen,' he said, beaming at Derry and Lance, 'is that I finally get to go out with her!' Kate stared at him, unable to meet anyone else's gaze, as Jem continued, 'Yeah, that's right. You see, Kate wouldn't give in while she was working for me, but said that once the kitchen was finished...well, we've got a date! Isn't that right Kate?'

Kate opened her mouth to speak, but was silenced by the sudden pressure of Jem's lips on her own. The kiss was brief, but firm, and Kate was furious.

She felt compromised, and dragging Jem by the arm to the small balcony at the top of the stairs outside, she told him so.

'How could you do that?' she cried in exasperation. 'And in front of a room full of people. Not to mention my daughter could have seen!'

'It was just a little kiss!' grinned Jem. He still had a glass in his hand and now conscientiously balanced it on the narrow handrail of the wooden balustrade before stepping towards her. 'And your daughter's not here now.' He kissed her again.

'The point is,' Kate said, pushing him away, 'I haven't agreed to anything. I haven't said that I'll date you, or...or anything! And I certainly didn't say that you could kiss me!'

To her surprise, Jem, who still had his arms tightly around her, threw back his head and laughed. 'Oh Kate, you're so funny,' he said tenderly. 'So sweet and old-fashioned and adorable!' He moved to kiss her once more.

'You're drunk!' she exclaimed, emphatically. She was in danger of losing control of the situation. Despite her anger, she was instinctively tempted to respond to the warmth of his arms and the softness of his kisses. It had been so long since anyone had held her in that way, and she struggled to contain herself from an act of shameful desperation.

'You're right,' said Jem, suddenly compliant. He took a couple of steps away from her to rest against the balcony railing. 'You're right, of course. And I'm sorry. It's just that...you must know how much I like you Kate. Maybe I went about it the wrong way tonight, but I just felt that we were, you know...going somewhere.'

He paused and then said, with deep drunken solemnity, and an actorly bow: 'Madam, I beg thy forgiveness.'

216

They were both silent for a moment, suddenly feeling the chill breeze. The harbour lights glowed prettily and the crash of waves from the incoming tide upon the shore could still be heard above the noise from the party. The night sky was clear and star-filled.

'I love the smell of the night,' Kate said. Then, catching the sparkle in Jem's eye, and anticipating his joke, conceded a wry grin. 'No, I don't mean your overflowing bins, or your little rat problem. I mean that wonderful, clean, sweet night smell. It's exciting, or...dramatic. I can't quite describe it. It must be something primal. Do you know what I mean?'

'I think so,' he said, moving a cautious step closer again. 'Why doesn't it smell the same in the daytime? I think it must be something to do with the Earth being cooler at night.'

'Yes; and less busy, less...noxious.'

He tentatively put an arm around her shoulders. They stood there for a while, staring out at nothing.

Nothing except the white waves breaking on the black sea, and the vast mantle of the galaxy. Kate stood accused beneath the majestic authority of space and time, and she felt humbled. She sensed that the workings of the universe itself had contrived to arrive at this exact moment in time. What right had Kate to deny its machinations? She could try all she liked to control and make-safe her world; but at that precise moment, standing on the balcony with Jem's arm around her and breathing in the night air, she felt condemned into taking a chance.

'I will go out with you Jem, if that's what you want,' she said turning to smile shyly at him. 'But...can we take it slowly, please?'

Jem smiled and pulled her close again with both arms. He said nothing, but gently laid his head on her shoulder.

Then Kate said softly, 'It's been a long time.'

217

CHAPTER 20

Christmas Eve

Despite costing much more than she could afford on her modest salary, the silver Porsche was a source of enduring pride for Juliet. Not for her a clapped out old heap like her sister's car. There was something ultimately pretentious, Juliet thought, about obstinately driving around in an old banger. Kate, no doubt, felt that there was something noble about it, but really she was just making life difficult for herself. For Juliet, the sleek lines and polished shine of the Porsche said everything that she wanted people to know about her, and now, thanks to Aunt Joe's generosity, she had finally paid off the loan. It was all hers. Only the irksome, muddy, country lanes that they had been navigating for the last half hour spoilt her pleasure in driving. She stole a look at Parker in the passenger seat beside her. He was hunched uncomfortably in the gloaming over a hand-drawn sketch which served as their only map since leaving the A-road.

No chance of persuading him to wash the car for her; the cynical thought escaped before she could stop it. She shouldn't be so critical of him. After all, he was a model-stroke-actor, not a common labourer. So what if he couldn't unblock drains or put up shelves? The truth was, that she still felt a frisson of pleasure at the reaction that he commanded, whenever they strode hand-in-hand into a nightclub or bar. She still liked to register the salacious looks from other women. Parker really was highly desirable. He was always immaculately styled, super-cool, and knew all the right people. To cap it all, he was a genuine, bona fide, sound-of-Bow-bells East-Ender; born and bred in Bethnal—or "Befnowl"— Green; and as such, was the height of fashion. Yet Juliet was not the sort to be overwhelmed by his popularity and minor fame; but rather, she thoroughly enjoyed the prestige that came from being with him, and was confident that she was at least his match for good looks and glamour. Indeed, just as the Porsche was an extension of her persona, so Parker was the perfect accessory. He complemented her. They *went* together. And besides, she loved him, didn't she?

Parker squirmed in the seat beside her and folded his arms petulantly. Juliet rolled her eyes. He was still sulking.

'Okay, okay! I'll turn back! *If* I can find anywhere to turn around,' she said, although privately thought that it didn't look too promising, judging by the long stretch of narrow lane and high hedges that lay ahead in the gathering dusk.

'I *toldja*, it was on the left back there by the Vet's—bit of a sudden left, I give ya that,' said Parker. 'Trebarfa Lane. She's scribbled on the map that it's a bit tricky to spot.'

'Well, there you are then,' Juliet said defensively. 'Not my fault. Besides, I haven't seen anything that looks remotely like a Vet's.'

Parker sighed, emphatically. 'Like I said, it's back the other way. We passed it. Blimey, it's not like we ain't been here before. You remember nuffin' Jules, nuffin'.'

'I said okay! I'll turn around!'

They sat in silence for the an interminable few minutes, before Juliet finally found a lay-by suitable for turning in. Then they were silent all the way back again in the direction from which they had come. Juliet was tired and prayed that they didn't miss the entrance to the lane again. She had begun to have that ominous weary feeling; the premonition that, like so much else lately, this trip would not live up to her expectations. She had foolishly begun to hope that it might be wildly romantic, but so far she and Parker had bickered all the way from London.

'There it is. There!' Parker said pointing. 'That's the Vet's, and there's the lane.'

'That?' Slowing to indicate, Juliet peered at the dilapidated building. 'Well, no wonder I missed it. Looks like an old cow-shed.'

'Yeah, except it says 'Veterinary Surgeon' in a big sign on the side,' Parker said sarcastically.

Trebartha Lane was an unmade road that dipped steeply. Juliet bumped and rattled the Porsche as elegantly as possible down to the bottom. From there they took a left onto Carrick Lane, which was thankfully better-made, and passed the entrance to Kate's cottage twice before they finally beached the car in the slurry of mud that passed for the driveway. It was dark now. There were no outside lights and Kate had drawn the curtains at the cottage windows. But where the material did not quite meet, Juliet thought she could detect the flicker of firelight on Christmas tree baubles.

'What a dump,' said Parker.

'You made your feelings perfectly clear the last time we were here,' said Juliet. 'Have to admit though...it is a bit of a shack. But that's Kate for you. Anyway, we're here now. So, come on mate, put your happy face on!'

Juliet opened the car door and stoically placed her brand new and ridiculously expensive ankle boots into the mud. Kate and Isabella were at the open door now, and behind them hovered the taller, more indistinct figure of a man.

'Must be the new boyfriend,' Juliet whispered to Parker. 'He's a doctor or something.'

Isabella ran to greet them. She kissed Juliet, then threw herself on Parker, who swung her around in a bear hug. Then Isabella took Parker's hand, and led him proudly to the cottage, where he greeted Kate with a kiss on each cheek.

Juliet, still stuck in the mud, could hear him say what a fantastic place it was; so wild and abandoned. Oh, he was good.

'You alright there, Jules?' Kate cried, coming to meet her sister halfway. They embraced. And then kissed and embraced again. Juliet was surprised at how suddenly happy she was to see Kate again.

Once inside the cottage, Juliet's mood improved considerably. There was indeed a log fire lit in the living room, and a woodburner in the kitchen. And Kate had gone to town on the fairy lights and candles. The cottage seemed much smaller than she remembered, but it was gloriously cosy, and definitely romantic. Perhaps it would be alright after all. And if Parker decided to be an arsehole all week, she would just get pissed with her sister instead.

She was introduced to Jem, who politely shook her hand, and offered to open a bottle of wine. *So*...civilised, and not a pig farmer at all. Good-looking too. In fact Juliet was prepared to concede that Jem was definitely worth a shag. *Way to go, Kate.* Catching the pained expression on Kate's face, and realising that her sister was reading her mind, Juliet burst out laughing.

'Did I miss somefing?' asked Parker, returning from Isabella's tour of the cottage.

'Private joke,' said Juliet, winking at Kate, who shook her head in exasperation.

Once Isabella had been tucked up in bed with a book, a mug of cocoa and a plate of treats, the adults set about the small feast that Kate had prepared. They got through two bottles of red wine with a simple supper of quiche from Mrs Newson's shop, and a salad. Then they drank another with a board of Cornish cheeses served with fruit, nuts and fresh local bread. The slight quantity of a bottle appeared to go nowhere between the four of them, and so at Jem's insistence, they opened a fourth.

As a result of Kate's blossoming relationship with Jem, the old larders at the back of the cottage had become improvised wine cellars. Each time he visited he came laden with his favourite labels, as if he lived in fear that she might offer him something inadequate. In order to try and compensate for this largesse, Kate had stocked up on some of his favourites, and—so as not to be seen as a complete toady—a few of her own.

And so the wine flowed. Juliet and Parker were by now completely relaxed as they chatted around the kitchen table, warmed by the comforting heat from the woodburner.

Parker explained how he had always wanted to live in the country, and that he felt an affinity with the sea. He had, apparently, been born to surf. 'I jus' know it right? It's in me bones.'

Except that he had been born in Bethnal Green. 'Ain't a lotta call for surfboards in Befnowl Green, know what I mean?'

But now that he had come here, it all made sense. In fact, coming to Cornwall was a veritable *sign* as to the route his future life should take. 'Kismet, innit?'

Kate was fascinated by his accent; an estuary English that sometimes tipped over into lazy, plummy Sloane, whilst simultaneously being peppered with golden nuggets of Cockney idiom: 'Mind if I take me daisies off Kate? Warm me plates by the fire?'

Kate mused not for the first time on her suspicion that Parker Dean from Bethnal Green had in fact started life as plain old Dean Parker.

By the fifth bottle Juliet was talking intimately with Jem by the fire in the living room, and by the sixth, Kate excused herself from massaging Parker's ego to go and make up the beds. In truth, she had already done this, having relented to let Juliet and Parker have her own room. She herself would sleep on a blow-up mattress in the small third bedroom which housed the ancient computer, and which Kate had begun referring to, ironically, as "the study". But she busied herself by taking up her guest's bags, and made a pretence of saying goodnight to Isabella, who was already fast-asleep and snoring gently. Back in the study, she took a minute to herself, to sober up and collect her thoughts. She walked to the window, where a dazzling moon beamed its light into the little room. Kate felt a sense of extreme loneliness, even though she could hear the voices and laughter drifting up from downstairs. After a moment she went back down, and made some attempt to wind up the evening. She said goodbye to Jem outside in the porch in the moonlight, with a lingering, but perversely chaste French kiss.

Later, Juliet sneaked into bed with Kate in the study and demanded: 'So, you're not shagging him, then?'

Kate groaned and insisted that Juliet leave her alone until morning. But Juliet was persistent, and so being goaded, Kate confessed that her relationship with Jem was in its "early stages"—a declaration that had Juliet stuffing the duvet into her mouth to quell her laughter— and that when she felt the time was right....well, their relationship would hopefully develop into something meaningful and...and *intimate*.

Juliet was near-hysterical. 'Oh just shag him Kate! *Please*, just shag him!'

The following day was Christmas Eve, and the evening was to be the night of Kate's Christmas party. Kate had a mild panic attack over breakfast, wondering why on earth anyone would want to come to *her* party on Christmas Eve, especially since she had so recently arrived in the village. But Juliet scoffed, saying that even if it were only to be the four of them, like last night, then that would be okay. And anyway, surely this Vivien person would come? It sounded like Kate had become particularly good friends with her? Kate agreed that Vivien had indeed assured her that she would be there. And she had no valid reason to think that the others would not show up. With the panic over, the girls spent the day shopping, cleaning, and decorating the cottage, whilst Parker competed with Isabella all day on the Playstation.

Juliet was amazed at how happy she felt. She would never admit that Kate might have made a wise choice in moving to Cornwall, but something about the simplicity of life was genuinely appealing. To focus on one party so intently was a rare treat. In London, parties were only heard about at the last minute; and then you would turn up to find the same old cokeheads, and a whole bunch of other posers, all behaving like total wankoids. Yet somehow, it was still important to be there; to be seen.

And she found herself oddly buoyant at the prospect of meeting completely new and different people. Juliet was *bored*. She longed for new sights and sounds, and to shake off this...*malaise* that she could not quite pin down. She allowed herself, whilst chopping salad ingredients in Kate's kitchen, to fantasise about strong, rustic men. Swarthy, they would be, like the young Alan Bates.

Whatever was wrong, Juliet thought, as she shredded some iceberg lettuce, would be put right; would somehow make sense when she embarked upon her trip around the world. In many ways, you could say that Cornwall was the first stop on their trip. And she was sure that they would soon be gone.

Vivien was the first guest to arrive and Kate greeted her warmly. Of late her appearance had been relatively normal, but tonight, reverting to type, Vivien wore what could only have been one of her dresses from the rail at Wreckers. It was long and layered in forest green and walnut brown. The bodice was fastened with a golden lace and the sleeves tapered from the wrists. Tonight, her long hair was curled into ringlets, and on her head she wore a crown of twigs. She was the Queen of the Yule; a beautiful, ethereal woodland sprite.

When she got the chance, Juliet leaned towards Kate and whispered theatrically from behind her hand. 'Who's the nutter?'

'Now stop that Jules, Vivien looks enchanting.'

Once Kate had moved safely out of earshot, Juliet scanned Vivien's appearance once more. 'Freakoid' she muttered to herself.

Finally ready, Parker swaggered downstairs looking fashionably louche in black leather trousers and a largely unbuttoned red silk shirt that exposed an obscene amount of lower torso. As he entered the kitchen he did a little dance step and a twirl in time to the party music. But he was stopped in his tracks, his entrance apparently usurped, when he caught sight of Vivien's unorthodox appearance. Initially a little taken aback, he soon discovered that she had studied fashion, and so was in his element. He contrived, in an oh-so-casual manner, to drop the names of all the big-name designers that he had ever met, or worked for. He declared that Vivien was positively avant-garde...in a, er, *retro* kind of way... It only took Jem to arrive with another box full of alcohol, and accompanied by Angie, Don and some other stragglers from the pub, and the party was under way.

Gabe came next, with the usual entourage of Salima and Derry in tow, and just as Kate was closing the door behind them, Lance arrived with Finn. Lance was carrying a beautifully wrapped present. There was an awkward moment whereby Kate was unsure of how to greet her new guests. Back in the old days in London, it would have been with a kiss, or even a warm-hearted hug. But these people were comparative strangers. Derry and the others had blustered in, smiling cheerfully, but with no heed to ceremony.

Lance, however, stood for a moment on the doorstep, as if awaiting a formal invitation. He had one hand on Finn's shoulder, and defensively clutched his parcel in the other. 'It's for Isabella,' he said, noticing Kate's subtle, but curious, glance at the Christmas present.

'Oh,' Kate said, 'I mean, thank you very much, that's very kind of you. You didn't have to.' Oh hell, the clichés were out in full force already. 'Come in!' she added quickly, and offered to take their coats; even though she had no specific place in the small cottage for putting coats, and ended up dumping them in a pile on a chair in the living room, where the others had slung theirs.

Kate and Juliet had prepared a buffet in the kitchen, and it was here that the small party now congregated, opening bottles and idly sampling the food. Kate noticed gratefully, on entering the room, that everyone was chatting amiably, and that there were no perceivable awkward silences that might have left her the struggling hostess. Isabella, with Finn at her shoulder, insisted on opening her present right in the middle of the kitchen, no doubt so that she would be in full view of a cooing audience. Kate, keen to maintain the genial equilibrium, found herself joining in the cries of encouragement, as her daughter slowly relished stripping away the layers of Christmas wrapping paper.

'Oh,' Isabella said flatly, and clearly unimpressed, 'It's a book.'

Kate suddenly understood that particular cliché about cheerfully throttling one's offspring. She pleaded telepathically to Izzy to show some gratitude; some interest even. If Kate were to go blundering in now and force her daughter to admit that she absolutely loved the book—*say thank-you, Isabella!*—it would only serve to embarrass its giver.

'Yeah, it's a brilliant book!' said Finn, saving the day. 'I helped Dad to choose it. It's really cool. It's got pictures of the universe from like, way far out, and look,' he said turning the book's pages impatiently to a large glossy photograph of coloured clouds of light set against the darkness of space. 'This is actually a picture of stars being born! The words are all a bit boffin-y; but if you read the paragraphs in the margin, it's a bit easier.' Instinctively falling into peer-group bonding-mode, Isabella suddenly appreciated the wonderfulness of the book.

'Wow!' she uttered. 'It's fantastic! I love it!' And then more solemnly she said, 'Thank you Lance.'

'Yeah, and also,' continued Finn, ignoring the niceties, 'it gives you references so that you can look up some of the places on the computer; on Google Space. Do you want to...ah. Yeah, sorry I forgot; your computer...'

'That's right,' said Isabella, with a dark look in her eye directed at Kate, 'No disk space. No disk space, no Google Space.'

Jem was standing behind Kate. He leaned forward and whispered plaintively in her ear. 'I suppose *I* should have bought Isabella a Christmas present. I didn't think...'

'Oh no,' said Kate, turning and smiling kindly. 'I certainly didn't expect it, and neither would Izzy. Besides, if you had, she would only have been suspicious.'

'Hmm...perhaps you're right,' said Jem, 'It might have appeared a little...ingratiating.'

'Precisely!' said Kate, and they both inadvertently looked at Lance, who, luckily, was watching the children, deep in thought.

'However,' said Jem, 'I did bring *you* a present. One minute.' He dived off towards the far corner of the kitchen where he had stashed his large cardboard box full of booze. He bent, rummaging for a minute, and then apparently satisfied, pulled out a bottle of red wine. He returned with a huge smile on his face.

'There you go,' he said. 'Chateauneuf du Pape. Just for you. Save it for a special occasion. And by the way, Happy Christmas, Kate.' He bent and kissed her on the cheek.

Kate looked at the wine and tried hard not to grimace as she smiled back at Jem. Chateauneuf du Pape! Okay, it was decent enough, but in Kate's opinion, overrated. But more to the point, hadn't she told him only last week that she didn't really like French wine, with perhaps the exception of the odd Vin de Pays or a really good Côtes du Rhone Villages? Indeed, hadn't she *raved* about her favourite Australian wine, a blend of Durif and Shiraz? Hadn't he been listening? Since Kate had not thought to buy anything at all for Jem, she accepted the present as graciously as she could. All the same, she shocked herself with the errant thought that Jem looked a little too self-satisfied as he offered to refill some of her guests' glasses. She was instantly ashamed. Jem was being a wonderful host— even if that was not, strictly speaking, his place.

As soon as Jem had left Kate, Juliet sidled up to take his place at her side.

'So. Where'd you find Thor?' she whispered archly.

'Eh?' Kate asked, puzzled.

'*Him*; the gorgeous blond Nordic sex-god; don't pretend you don't know what I mean,' Juliet said, and she nudged Kate suggestively with her elbow. Kate realised that Juliet was talking about Lance.

'Juliet, please!' she said, and then sighing, continued in hushed tones. 'His name is Lance, and he's a scientist, believe it or not. Brother of Vivien and father of Finn, okay?'

It was Juliet's turn to sigh, in an exaggerated manner. 'Yeah, yeah, yeah, but is he single? He has a child so I suppose he's not gay?'

'To be perfectly honest, Jules, I don't know, and I have to say I'm not comfortable discussing him like this. And as for you,' she playfully prodded Juliet's arm with her forefinger. 'You shouldn't even be interested! You're with Parker, or had you forgotten?'

One reproachful look from Juliet later and Kate relayed, as concisely and unsensationally as possible, Lance's history as she knew it. Thankfully the music and chatter was loud enough to smother her words to all but Juliet's ears.

'Leah Greenwood? No!' Juliet gasped in a suppressed squawk. 'I've seen her, you know, in a cocktail bar in Shoreditch. And I'm sure Parker actually spoke to her. Just to say "Excuse me", or something like that, but she like, y'know, *acknowledged* him.'

'So?' Kate said, in annoyance. 'Honestly, Jules, you can be so shallow!'

'I know!' Juliet said merrily. 'Anyway, your friend Thor is certainly going to make the evening more interesting! I'm sorry, but I can't call him Lance.'

'Thank you!' Kate cried in recognition and raising her arms in equal merriment. '*Nobody* is called Lance anymore!'

Juliet grinned: 'Well, save for portly sherry-drinking company directors from the seventies. It's not even naff enough to be cool. Anyway, Parker thinks he's winding me up by being all over that Vivien, so let's see if we can't redress the balance a little, huh?'

That Vivien, Juliet had said. Kate felt a wave of disappointment at the lack of respect for her new friends. As Juliet strolled sensually away, Kate closed her eyes and prayed silently that her sister would behave.

CHAPTER 21

Love & Science

It was a fundamental law of group dynamics, thought Kate, that the atmosphere of all parties should follow a graph-like path of little upward peaks and troughs, culminating in a high-point, or summit. After that, if you were lucky, there would be a plateau of good humour and geniality before began the inevitable and sudden downslide into the muck and mire of drunkenness, high emotion, and argument. Either that or you would spend the small hours of the morning playing DJ; indulgently regaling all with your old 45-inch singles collection—which was probably worse.

By eleven o'clock, Kate reckoned that her party was already in the "plateau" stage, and as such, proceedings were likely to take a nose dive at any moment. Isabella and Finn had gone upstairs in an attempt to wring a modicum of gratification from the computer. Jem was happily holding court in the winged armchair by the fire in the front room. There was something about his manner tonight that was supremely self-assured. He sat beaming happily with a full glass in his hand, loudly entertaining Gabe and Salima with a lengthy tale about how "they" had had so many problems in getting the party ready. It was a bit soon to be playing Master of the House, thought Kate, with a bitterness that shocked her. She immediately chastised herself for once more having mean thoughts. It was *nice* that Jem felt so comfortable.

Derry, not really listening to Jem's witty anecdotes, leaned in the doorway of the living room and gazed wistfully across the hallway corridor to where Vivien was still being pinned up against the kitchen worktop by the overbearing enthusiasms of Parker. Kate, watching him, despaired that someone could hold a torch for so long. Didn't he know that he was wasting his time?

Kate was sitting at the kitchen table where, over a bottle of wine, she was attempting to police Juliet's attentions on the unsuspecting Lance. They had struck up a conversation about names, initiated by Juliet's somewhat unoriginal, indecently insincere—given her very recent comments—but very flirtatious insistence that 'Lance' must indeed be short for 'Lancelot'.

'Actually...' Lance looked at each of them in turn.

'Seriously?' said Kate, round-eyed, and trying not to laugh. 'I did wonder, but *seriously*? You're actually named Lancelot?'

He confirmed the truth of the matter with a nod and a long-suffering look.

'You read all that old stuff, don't you Kate?' Juliet said, 'about King Arthur and the Knights of the round Table. Which one was Lancelot, then?' It was clumsy by Juliet's standards. She was expert at playing dumb, and *of course* she would know who Lancelot was—who didn't? But she glared at Kate, willing her to play along.

'Lancelot du Lac was his full name, son of King Ban and Queen Elaine of Benwick; friend to Arthur, father of Galahad, and reputedly the most valiant and chivalrous of all the Knights...' Kate's voice trailed off as she registered Juliet's warning expression of impending boredom. ' ...Basically, he was the one who had an affair with Queen Guinevere.'

'Aha!' said Juliet, having received her prompt. 'There you have it! He was the sex symbol. Every good story has to have a sex symbol. I guess you must take after your namesake

231

Lance,' Juliet lowered both her voice and her eyelashes seductively.

'Er, of course Tennyson's *Idylls of the King* paints him in a more sympathetic light,' blurted Kate. 'It was Guinevere's lust for Lancelot that really caused the problem.'

'That's a very...unusual take on the story, Kate,' said Lance.

'I've never claimed to be *usual*,' said Kate with a smile, but secretly wondering if she'd got it all wrong.

'We have an early edition of Malory's *Le Morte d'Arthur* at home,' said Lance directly to Kate. 'The language is a little hard to understand, but it's very interesting as an *objet d'art*. There are some exquisite illustrations. You're welcome to borrow it some time, if you're interested.'

Kate looked at him dubiously.

The gift for Isabella had been easier to fathom, since it was no doubt meant as a polite gesture, or Christmas present from Finn, rather than his father. And she understood Lance's occasional abrupt appearances to chop wood for her, since she knew that he had been coerced by Vivien. But they had never cleared the air since their first meeting, and consequently, even small demonstrations of good manners, such as now, were tainted with an air of suspicion.

'Thank you; I would appreciate that,' she said, 'even if I *am* only capable of looking at the pictures.'

Immediately the keen, seagreen eyes were upon her. 'I'm sure your comprehension of literature is superior to my own,' he said, 'even if your understanding of the spoken word sometimes deliberately is not.'

'Of course, Kate and I were named after Shakespearean characters,' Juliet said, hastily interjecting. 'Since we're talking old literature and names, that is. Myself after, well, Romeo and Juliet, of course, and Kate after...'

'The Shrew!' Kate interrupted with a groan.

'...Katherina from The Taming of the Shrew,' continued Juliet. 'Poor Kate; of all the names our parents could have chosen from. You could have been Miranda, or Nerissa, or...well, Juliet!' And she smiled brightly, to show that she meant no offence, but was only teasing.

'I know!' Kate cried, 'But then it could have been worse...it could have been Hippolyta, or Titania! Or, I dunno, Nurse, or something!'

'Katherina is a lovely name,' said Lance.

'Bottom!' Juliet shouted, ignoring him and spilling some of her drink with a grand wave of her hand.

'Puck!' concluded Kate, and they sighed in unison, both trying to quell their giggles. Alcohol and the merry party atmosphere gave licence for them to laugh at anything.

'Well anyway, I'm pleased I got "Juliet",' said Juliet, remembering her task in hand, and turning to Lance. 'She is the most romantic of Shakespeare's heroines. And I'm always up for a bit of romance...'

Kate was frantic now, for her sister's sake. Juliet didn't know who she was dealing with. Lance would see right through her blatant attempts at seduction. Juliet was very attractive, and another man would have been flattered by her attentions, no matter how clumsy or unsubtle the approach. But Lance, Kate was sure, would despise her for it.

'Well I don't believe in romance,' Kate said, diverting the attention once more. Juliet and Lance both looked at her expectantly. 'Well, I don't,' she insisted, and frowning at Juliet's sceptical expression. 'I think that people are self-deluding when it comes to love and romance. Furthermore, I think that you can fall in love at any given time with whomever you may so choose, because that's exactly what it is—a choice. I think that if you have made a decision—conscious or otherwise—that you *want* to be in love, then inevitably, you will always be on the lookout for someone suitable to fulfil that desire. That's how you get so-called love at first sight. You already have a subconscious picture in your head of the sort

233

of person you'd like to be with, and then you meet someone who roughly fits the bill and wham! It's a thunderbolt! It's fate! And then of course once you've invested a relationship with such an auspicious beginning, you feel reluctant, as time goes on, to dismiss it for what it is.'

'Which is what?' asked Juliet.

'A delusion,' said Kate.

'So you don't think that love, or more specifically, romantic love, is an intrinsic part of the human condition?' asked Lance.

'Oh, human condition, *please!*' said Kate dismissively. 'Human insecurity, more like. It's very tribal, really. You think everyone else has it, so you want it too. Like all those really sad people who go on those tabloid talk shows. Their boyfriend has beaten them up, totally obliterated their self-esteem, killed their cat and slept with their mother, and when questioned as to why they are still with the creep, they invariably say, "Cos I love him". Romance is a luxury afforded only to those with nothing better to occupy themselves with. Do you think those people you see on the news who've endured earthquakes or volcanic eruptions are moved to dedicate the rest of their lives to searching for true love? Do you think that if you've seen your entire family butchered to death in a civil war that you give a stuff about love at first sight? It's survival that counts.'

'All the same,' Lance said, thoughtfully, 'it's something that appears to have been present throughout history. It's in the Arthurian tales that you have just been talking about. It's in every love song ever written...'

'Oh don't get me started on love songs!' cried Kate. 'All those songs about love! When a man sings "let me love you" it's usually just a euphemism for something else. Have you ever thought that it's just because when popular songs were first written, and more especially broadcast, they only said *love* because they weren't allowed to say...you know...'

'Fuck,' said Juliet helpfully, and lighting a cigarette.

'Exactly,' said Kate. 'Next time you listen to a really smoochy love song on the radio just try paraphrasing the word love for...'

'Fuck,' said Juliet again.

'Quite,' continued Kate. 'Just change the words over and you'll soon start to see what I mean.'

There was a moment's pause while the others contemplated the notion, then Lance suddenly burst out laughing. 'I can't believe you're really so cynical, Kate. If romance doesn't really exist, then why have we invented it? What need is it fulfilling?'

'Like I said, insecurity,' said Kate. 'And of course, procreation!'

It was Juliet's turn to laugh out loud, remembering to touch Lance's arm "spontaneously" as she did so. 'Bloody hell, Kate, you're priceless!'

'No, I'm serious!' said Kate, although she was laughing too. 'Don't underestimate the need to procreate. We have romantic ideas, and physical desires, that ultimately lead to...'

'Sex,' said Juliet.

'Right,' said Kate. 'And sex, whether we choose to interpret it that way or not, is purely necessary for procreation.'

'But you make it sound so clinical!' protested Juliet, who was delighted that the conversation has so easily turned to the subject of sex. 'Don't you like sex, Kate? Don't you think it's great?' She gave a knowing sideways look at Lance. Oh, it was perfectly clear that she, Juliet, definitely liked sex. She absolutely *loved* sex.

'Well, of course I do! And of course it's great,' said Kate, starting to feel the blush, 'but that's *why* it's great! To make you do it!'

'But what about gay sex?' said Juliet. 'That has little to do with procreation, I imagine?'

'Ah, but it's the same impulse,' said Kate. 'And besides, you never know. Nature finds a way and all that...' Chuckling, she raised her glass in salute and then drained it.

'I give up!' Juliet said to Lance. 'I've know her all my lifetime and I can't do anything with her. She's a phenomenon.'

'Indeed,' said Lance distractedly, and in so deadpan a tone that his meaning was unclear. Kate struggled against inebriation to construct a reply that perfectly demonstrated that she did not consider herself remotely phenomenal in any way, but suddenly Lance stood up.

'Excuse me,' he said graciously, looking at each of them in turn, and then with no further explanation, left the room.

Kate and Juliet looked at each other for a moment.

'Was it something that I said?' asked Kate, and they started giggling again.

Juliet eyed Kate suspiciously through half-closed eyes and a haze of smoke. '*You like him,*' she accused, pointing her cigarette in Kate's direction.

'What? No!' said Kate, incredulously. 'No. Believe me, you've got that one wrong Jules. Besides, haven't you been listening to anything I just said?'

'What, all that crap about not believing in love?' Juliet scorned. 'Do me a favour. You've just out-flirted me in the most outrageous manner!'

Kate was horrified. Naturally, Juliet was wrong. But it wouldn't do for Lance to think...'No,' was all she could say, again. 'Definitely not! Oh heck, you don't think he thought that do you? And anyway, you can talk. What are you playing at? I thought you were happy with Parker?'

'I am,' said Juliet nonchalantly. 'But a girl likes to keep her hand in, not to mention her options open! Anyway, I've gone off Thor. I can't see myself with anyone who uses the word "exquisite". *You*, on the other hand, I can.'

'For the last time,' Kate sighed, 'He doesn't interest me, at least not in that way.' She lowered her voice. 'There's a coldness about him. And...I don't think he treats women very well.'

'Sounds like Miles,' Juliet said. Then, seeing her sister's face added: 'Sorry, that was below the belt.'

'Oh, never mind,' Kate said, 'So long as you're clear, I am *not* interested in Lance Borlase.'

'Oh all right, have it your way,' said Juliet, 'But tell me one thing; when were you going to let Jem in on your little theories about romance? Because I should say that he might have different ideas in mind.'

Kate looked uncomfortable. 'I should go and mingle,' she said, getting up from the table. 'And check on the children...'

'Yeah, right; go mingle,' Juliet said with frank cynicism.

Jem cornered Kate in the hallway, and encircled her waist with one arm.

'There you are!' he said. 'Good party! I was just going to open some champagne. Like some?'

'No; no thanks,' Kate said quickly. 'I just have to check on Izzy and Finn—make sure they're not being neglected.' Smiling apologetically, she gently removed his arm, and then quickly ducked away up the twisting staircase.

Kate was surprised to find the study empty. The room was dark, and unlit except for the glare of the computer screensaver, a message of which huffily advised that it should be turned off. Kate obliged.

With the room now completely dark, Kate moved to the window and looked out at the splatter of stars in the cold night sky. She gave a tiny gasp as she acknowledged the spectacular intensity and clarity of this night's display. Then she saw movement in the darkness of the garden below her, and after a second's puzzlement, thought she recognised the short, shadowy figures as being those of the children. Kate sighed.

Doubtless they were not wearing coats and hats, and it was freezing outside.

She grabbed a coat from her bedroom, slunk downstairs again, and magically unnoticed by the throng, went outside. She ventured around to the side of the cottage where she had seen the children. It was very dark. She approached the bobbing silhouettes, and reassuringly, heard their voices.

'Izzy, is that you?' she called, stumbling towards them. 'What are you doing out here? I hope you've wrapped up properly, it's freezing.'

'We're just looking at the stars, Mum,' said Izzy to Kate, who had reached them now.

'Kate, it's my fault,' said another voice.

Lance moved from where he had been leaning against the woodshed and came towards the small group gathered in the cold. 'I said it was okay,' he continued. 'I should have asked you first, of course. But I have made sure that they've wrapped up warm.' Kate saw now that both Finn and Isabella were fully attired in woollen jumpers, overcoats, gloves, scarves *and* hats.

'He wouldn't let us come out until we'd put all this stuff on,' complained Finn.

'So what's so impressive about tonight?' asked Kate wryly. 'I mean, apart from being spectacularly beautiful, that is. Is there a meteor shower expected? A comet, perhaps? The Aurora Borealis?'

'No,' said Lance. 'Just, as you said, a beautiful night; very clear, although...' he paused to consider, '...it would be even better if you could have drawn your curtains.' He gestured towards the cottage, from which the only light in the immediate landscape emanated. The sound of distant throbbing bass lines intruded into the stillness of the night.

'Sorry,' Kate said. 'I should have cancelled my party. Next time you hold an impromptu Astronomical Society meeting in my garden, just let me know and I'll rearrange my social calendar.'

Lance smiled sheepishly, not entirely sure that she was joking.

'Mum *always* leaves a light on,' piped up Isabella, resentfully mindful of her own secret stargazing. 'She leaves the hall landing light on every night. She's afraid of the dark.'

'I see,' said Lance.

Kate glowered at Izzy, pointlessly, in the shadows. 'So, what's it all about then?' she continued, staring up at the stars. 'You're educated in these matters, I believe. Is there anything out there, or not?'

Lance took a step closer to her, and turning so that they were shoulder to shoulder, he too raised his face to the sky. The two children stood in front of them, their young faces similarly uplifted. They all awaited his answer.

'It depends on what you're asking,' he said. 'Can you be more specific?'

Finn, who was more accustomed to his father's ways, gave an exaggerated groan.

'Well,' said Kate slowly. She didn't want to sound trite. 'Is there life on other planets?' she heard herself asking, tritely.

Thankfully, Lance appeared to take her in earnest. 'The answer is, we don't know. It's either / or really.'

'What do you mean?' Kate said, puzzled.

'Well, consider how vast our universe is...which of course I'm sure you have done,' he added quickly, as if at pains not to insult her intelligence again. 'Naturally you will have imagined; and then consider how life exists everywhere that we look for it...'

'...from our viewpoint as human beings on Earth,' Kate interjected.

'That's right,' continued Lance in all seriousness. 'All the information that we can gather, that we can see or experience,

239

tells us that life exists everywhere. All over our planet, from the deepest parts of the ocean to the highest reaches of the atmosphere, even perhaps the rocks. And if we look through a microscope, we find more life. If we split an atom, we find yet more intricacy. Subatomic particles are like worlds within worlds.'

'Except that we have not yet observed evidence of life outside of the Earth,' Kate checked over her shoulder to ensure that Juliet had not surreptitiously crept outside and was eavesdropping. She would have a field day with this kind of talk.

'What do you mean no life outside of the Earth?' Lance looked puzzled. 'Oh, I see. You mean so-called *intelligent* life. You don't count the stars and the galaxies and the universes as life. Only humanoids or little green men count as life.'

'No,' said Kate becoming perplexed. 'Well, yes I suppose so. I mean...life as we know it.' Hell, she was pretty sure she was paraphrasing Star Trek now. 'Anyway, that was the question, when I asked it, although perhaps I wasn't *specific* enough for you. The question is, is there life—intelligent life— *as we know it?* And what do you mean, 'universes' anyway? When did it become plural? That's all science fiction isn't it?'

Lance stared at her for a moment, as if he couldn't decide whether she was inherently stupid or just taking the piss. 'Like I said,' he said after a while. 'It's either / or. Either the entire universe, as logic would decree, is teeming with life, or rather *teems intermittently* with life—it's rather possible that if any other civilisations have existed they have followed the human pattern and extinguished themselves before they ever got remotely close to any kind of contact—*or...*'

'Or what?' said Kate, Finn and Isabella in unison.

'Or, it *has* to be this big, perhaps infinite, in order to create the odds for our existence. Think about it. What are the odds of a planet evolving with just exactly the right conditions for life? *As we know it?*' Lance's last phrase was gently mocking.

240

But he had lost his audience momentarily, as they all quietly contemplated what he had said, their faces once more upturned to the starlit night sky.

'So you mean,' said Kate slowly, '...that we could be alone? In the whole universe...*alone?*" There was the smallest choke in her voice.

'Well, it *is* possible.' Lance said gently. 'In this universe, anyway. We may even be an accident; an aberration. A minor blip. A mistake.'

'There you go again,' said Kate. 'What do you mean *this* universe?' She was on the point of calling him a crank, but then remembered that he was, after all, a professor. He was in theory highly informed, and perhaps entitled to appear a little eccentric.

'It's complex,' was all that Lance said.

'He's talking about the multiverse,' said Isabella. 'Honestly, Mum, don't you know anything?'

'Right. The multiverse. Is that like, when anything that can happen, will happen, somewhere, sometime?'

'No,' said Lance. 'That's the Many-Worlds Interpretation. It's not the same thing at all.'

'Of course; Many-Worlds...thingy.' Kate cleared her throat. 'Well what about the Big Bang? You scientists can't explain what happened to make it go bang, can you? You can take it back as far as you like, but you can't actually explain why? I mean, why anything at all? Why not just nothing? Except of course, that then there would be no such thing as nothing—unless there were something for it to be the opposite *of*; if you see what I mean?'

Lance smiled. 'I see you're answering your own questions now. As a matter of fact, there may well be no such thing as nothing, but rather there are jitters...'

'Jitters?' Kate looked at him sceptically.

241

'Tiny fundamental units of time and space that fluctuate in and out of existence.'

'Like the cat?'

He smiled again. 'Yes Kate, like the cat.'

'Oka-ay...but I don't go with this whole explosion idea,' continued Kate, on a roll, and fuelled by red wine. 'I don't know why exactly, it just doesn't feel right. Do you know what I think?'

He looked askance at her. 'Is this going to be about The Reality Computer again?'

'No...' she shot him a withering look. 'What I think is...why can't the universe just have *grown*, like...like a baby grows? Or developed in a similar way at least. The way I see it is this...' she paused to allow the quietest of hiccups to be released, '...at the very first moment of existence, the universe is both the smallest and the largest thing in existence, right?'

'Er, well, not necessarily. There may be a higher dimension,' said Lance, then added hurriedly, '...but for the sake of argument, okay.'

Kate gave him a puzzled look, then continued. 'It is the smallest and the largest thing in existence. All the space and time imaginable exists within its framework. And then, it simply divides.'

'Aha, a developing foetus theory,' Lance interrupted with a chuckle.

'And then it keeps on dividing, and then *diversifying*,' continued Kate unperturbed, until all the matter in the universe is formed. Of course, I don't know what caused the diversification, but then you scientists don't know what caused the Big Bang.'

'The Singularity. We prefer to use terms like singularity and expansion. And I agree that "Big Bang" is misleading with the image it conveys of an explosion. And it may not have been one event but part of a cycle. It may, in fact, not be true at all! But to return to your theory—why do women always relate everything to childbirth, by the way?—there are, shall we say, holes. How, for example, do you explain the expansion of the universe? The fact that the galaxies are moving away from each other?'

'Simple,' said Kate, 'space isn't expanding, *we* are getting smaller.'

'What?' Lance sputtered, 'Well, relatively, yes I suppose...'

'No, no that's not what I mean,' insisted Kate

'You are *so* embarrassing, Mum,' said Isabella.

'My feet are frozen,' said Finn, 'Let's go back inside, Izzy.'

'With pleasure,' Izzy said, and the children turned and ran indoors.

'It's like those fractal images that you see,' Kate continued as she and Lance picked their way more slowly back to the cottage. 'No matter how deep you look, no matter how much you magnify, the pattern keeps repeating. I think that matter and time kind of *fold-in* on themselves. We think of time as being a straight line, but really, it's hurrying inwards. And the spaces in-between are getting bigger. Did I mention that already? As the spaces get bigger, we, as you so rightly said, become relatively smaller, but still all within the encompasses of the universe...which is still, as I said, both the largest and smallest thing in existence. It has to be—there's nothing outside of it...or something.'

'Hmm,' said Lance. He looked at her thoughtfully as they walked, and then smiled. 'Have you ever considered studying philosophy, Kate?'

His voice sounded even, but Kate looked back at him in the dark, studying his features for signs of mirth. 'You're laughing at me.'

'No I'm not,' said Lance. 'I'm serious. In many ways, philosophy is not so different from theoretical physics. It's not a popular opinion amongst some of my colleagues, but I believe it *is* a kind of philosophy, inasmuch as it requires asking some deep questions. Sometimes you have to imagine the most wild and extreme ideas, if only to prove that they are impossible. But then sometimes, the seemingly impossible cannot be disproved. That's what's so exciting. The boundaries of possibility are always being stretched. But just remember, I suggested that you study philosophy, not physics. Don't show up at any of *my* classes with your crazy ideas.'

Kate stopped to look at him, and saw that he was grinning broadly. 'Ha, ha, very funny.' She started to move on again.

But this time it was Lance who stopped suddenly, and looked at her questioningly; his expression once more serious.

'What?' Kate said, drawing alongside him again.

'Kate,' he said solemnly. 'Perhaps...I think we might have got off on the wrong foot—when we first met.'

And so; at last.

'I think I may have misjudged you,' Lance continued, 'and I'd like to apologise. It looks like we're going to see a lot of each other whether we like it or not...because of the children, I mean. I really would like to clear the air. Could we...do you think that we could try and behave as friends? Or at the least, civilised acquaintances? What do you think?'

'Friends?' Kate asked, affectedly. '*Us?*' She was hiding her instinctive nature to immediately forgive. For all her wariness and cynicism, she remained a sucker for anyone whom she perceived as having the courage to admit a mistake. 'Why, do you mean that we could help each other out, with picking the kids up from school and such?'

'Right. I get the message. I suppose it was an innocent enough suggestion.'

'Well, I may have been a little...premature,' said Kate, relenting a little.

'Overtly familiar, I thought!' Lance said, smiling cautiously.

'I had a toothache!' Kate protested. 'I wasn't myself!'

244

'Neither was I,' said Lance distantly, and then returning from other, hidden thoughts suddenly added: 'I take full responsibility. I overreacted. It's just...I had some problems with one of the other mothers down at the school, and I suppose I was on my guard.'

Kate knew that he must be referring to the affair with Jenifer Trewin, but thought better of pursuing him for details. There was a danger that she would end up disapproving, and argue with him again. She wanted to maintain this new-found truce. Life would be so much more comfortable if she no longer had to guard against every action or flippant comment that she might make in Lance's presence.

'Let's just call the whole thing a misunderstanding,' she said. 'But just for the record, and so that I can be perfectly at ease when you're around; be assured that I do not have romantic designs on you. I will try to be clear-meaning at all times; but in case I ever say or do anything in future that might be held up for misinterpretation, trust me now when I say that I'm not interested. You are perfectly safe in my company. So then; friends?'

'Friends,' said Lance, with a degree of relief that surprised Kate. Perhaps he too, had felt the burden of unresolved bad feeling? But it was a thought that she found hard to reconcile with her still-lingering impression that he was aloof. Although she might be prepared to revise her opinion that he was arrogant, or callous, even, there was something about Lance that suggested an *apartness*; a separation from all those around him.

She held out her hand ceremoniously for him to shake.

He took it firmly in his own, and then with a final, querying scan of Kate's earnest features, he nodded to seal the deal. 'And by the way...Merry Christmas Kate. It's Christmas Day.'

'So it is,' she smiled, realising the time. 'Merry Christmas...*Lancelot*,' she snickered.

245

Lance could only roll his eyes and shake his head as they strolled back to the cottage together. 'I'm going to regret this, aren't I?'

CHAPTER 22

Christmas Day

Kate rose early on Christmas morning, and managed to clear the debris from the living room, before Isabella descended from her room. In truth, it was not nearly as squalid as she had imagined it would be. The kitchen, however, was another matter. *How many bottles of wine had they drunk?* It didn't seem humanly possible. In a practised, methodical manner, she began to collect the empties into a cardboard box for recycling. Wryly, she observed that the bottle of Chateauneuf du Pape—her present—lay discarded on the floor, its contents spent.

Later, she sat cross-legged on the rug by the Christmas tree for the gift opening ritual with Isabella. Izzy was tired but benign; full of excitement. Kate had scanned the room for any dubious looking substances, but had found none. Neither were there any unconscious bodies to be stepped over. Mother and daughter enjoyed an hour of uninterrupted intimacy, before Juliet emerged, mascara-eyed, yawning, and looking for food.

The household remained peaceful as Kate and Juliet set the table for a "blow-out" breakfast for two at the kitchen table. Izzy, too full Christmas-stocking chocolates for breakfast, had run upstairs to calculate her morning's booty, and to play her brand new computer game. Parker was reputedly out for the count. The girls gorged their way through scrambled eggs, mushrooms, tinned tomatoes with brown sauce, and piles of buttery toast. They washed it down with fruit juice and—*just this once*—mugs of evil, sugary tea.

'Hmm,' Kate said, with a mouth full of toast, 'You can't beat tinned tomatoes for a hangover!'

'Yeah! But of course, this isn't a proper blow-out,' said Juliet, 'If Parker were up he would insist on sausages, bacon, and beans. Even kidneys sometimes!'

'Ooh, no. All that meat,' said Kate in disgust, 'Too dry and stodgy. Best to stick to the juicy foods: so much better for rehydration purposes. We should really have started with watermelon, or grapefruit or something.'

'Yeah, well, never mind. Still,' Juliet said with a click of her tongue and a wink. 'Tinned tomatoes, eh?'

It was a freakishly hot morning, and Kate could feel the sun's rays, magnified through the large kitchen window, burn against her cheek as she sipped her tea. A little shocked, she thought how grey Juliet's pallor was. Juliet had looked perfectly stunning the night before, but now Kate noticed that the inevitable fine lines had begun to appear around her sister's eyes. Horrified, and mindful of the fact that she was the elder of the two, Kate secretly despaired that perhaps she too, was starting to age.

The actuality of decline was the most insidious and treacherous of nature's little tricks. How to be admired was the wondrous capacity for new life, and fresh growth; but how *did* those little lines appear as if from nowhere overnight? How could it be? Was it compulsory? What invisible mitochondria altered in some silently imperceptible way so as to leave a living form forever changed? And why today and not tomorrow? As if sensing her sister's thoughts, and in typical defiance, Juliet, right on cue, lit up a cigarette.

'Christ, Jules,' Kate said in disgust, and waving away the smoke with her hand, 'How can you possibly actually want that, after a heavy night's drinking? And besides, I don't want to inhale it! Haven't you heard of the dangers of passive smoking?'

'I've heard of the dangers of passive living,' Juliet retaliated. 'Best fag of the day I say, after a blow-out breakfast.'

Kate rolled her eyes in resignation.

'So, what device did you use to avoid sleeping with Jem last night?' Juliet said, direct as ever. 'And where's he gone today anyway?'

'To his parents for Christmas dinner. And I didn't use a "device" as you put it, I don't need to! Honestly Jules, you have to realise that my position is different from your own. I have an eleven-year-old daughter. I can't just have a string of boyfriends staying overnight!'

'Oh give me a break!' Juliet drawled, 'One boyfriend! One. In ten years! Christ, even Izzy would break into the Hallelujah chorus!'

'Stop it!' Kate said, giggling; then more seriously, 'You don't understand. I have to be responsible; to myself, as well as to Izzy.'

'Well, I despair, I really do. You'll lose him, you know. He'll think you're not interested. You just need to get back on the horse, Kate, so to speak.'

They both grinned dirtily, like smutty teenagers.

'I suppose so,' said Kate, slowly toying with the teaspoon in her cup, and affecting a sulky expression. 'It's just...I'm just...I guess I'm just not the promiscuous kind.'

Juliet exploded with raucous laughter. 'No, Kate dear,' she spluttered, choking on her tea, 'you're certainly not that. I think your reputation is more than safe in that respect.'

'I'm serious, Jules,' Kate pleaded. 'I hate that women are expected to sleep with a man so early in the relationship. What's wrong with getting to know him first? That takes time, doesn't it?'

'Well, yes,' Juliet said, sobering a little, 'but what's wrong with having a little fun while you get to know him?'

'It feels wrong because it's *intimate*,' said Kate. 'I can't bear the thought of realising that someone is so totally wrong for you; that you might in fact not even like them very much, but that you've been irretrievably intimate with them. It's like losing a little bit of your soul.'

'Right. So you're frigid,' Juliet said matter-of-factly.

'No!' Kate cried indignantly, but then with a worried expression added: 'You think I'm frigid? Do you think that's what it is?'

'Look, I just think that a whole parade of mistakes; an entire cavalcade, if you will, of Mr Wrongs, can be educational. Or liberating. Yeah, liberating.' Juliet looked rather chuffed with this realisation. 'Honestly Kate, it's like female emancipation passed you by! What did they invent the pill for?'

'To liberate men, not women! The pill frees men of their responsibilities. It makes women wholly responsible for contraception and pregnancy. *And* it puts married women, in particular, in danger of catching some hideous disease.'

'How so?' Juliet looked both amused and exasperated.

'Well, you can hardly insist that your husband wear a condom if you are supposed to be in a monogamous relationship, and contraception is taken care of by the pill, can you? It would be openly accusing him of being unfaithful.'

'I suppose,' Juliet conceded. 'I never really thought of it like that before...but frankly I'd make him wear one anyway, and sod his delicate feelings.'

Kate did not mention that despite her protestations, despite even what she had said to Vivien at Captain Carter's, she had dutifully, sensibly taken herself to a doctor and obtained some contraceptive pills, just in case. She'd stared at the little innocuous-seeming drugs that had become a thing of the past for her, and tried to dismiss the notion that she was being prepared for usage. (She tried even harder to dismiss from her warped imagination the analogy of the Christmas turkey; trussed, seasoned, and ready for, well, stuffing).

The two women were suddenly distracted by the sight of Parker, who had somehow come downstairs and past the kitchen unobserved, and was now bending and stretching exuberantly on a yoga mat in the garden. Through the huge frame of the window, they watched him stiffly attempt to touch his toes, then balance on each leg in turn, grabbing the opposite ankle to stretch his quadriceps. And then standing with legs astride, he swung his arms alternately around and about his head in a whirling manner.

'Hey, there it is!' said Kate, 'It's that strange warm-up thing with the arms that men do! What *is* that meant to do exactly?'

'Shush!' said Juliet. 'Don't draw attention. I want to see what he does next!'

They sat, mesmerised with horrified fascination as Parker worked his way through a series of unlikely stretches and warm-ups. It was when he started violently into some ungainly power lunges that they once again got the giggles.

'What *is* he wearing?' said Kate more quietly, although there was little real danger of Parker overhearing.

'Don't ask,' Juliet replied wearily. 'Apparently it's the latest fashion in surfing gear. Some incredibly hip designer let him have it after a show.'

'But why? Does he think he's going surfing?'

'Probably,' Juliet said, chuckling again. 'He brought some foam thing, but it fit in the back of the Porsche so I'm not sure it qualifies as a surfboard.'

They sat back and luxuriated in the spectacle of Parker's wobbly and self-conscious movements. He wore a garish, patterned wetsuit—a thin summer short-john—topped, inexplicably, by a pair of equally multi-coloured boardshorts.

Kate was aghast. 'He can't go in the water in that!'

251

'Yeah, it's a bit Jackson Pollock, innit?' replied Juliet, dragging on her cigarette.

Kate sniggered. 'I meant he'll freeze! They all wear thick 5 millimetre wetsuits this time of year.' Kate was surprised at her own knowledge; at what she had picked up. 'But you're not wrong. Please Juliet, you can't let Gabe and Derry see him like that!'

'Oh, I think we should!' Juliet replied cruelly.

'What's he doing now?' Kate asked, as Parker's mood became more solemn, and his poses slower, and more controlled.

'Oh, Tai Chi, I think,' Juliet answered dismissively, 'or callisthenics, or whatever the latest thing is. I forget.'

'Really? I had no idea Parker was so...so *healthy!*' Kate said. 'And you're actually going to take him to the Far East? I suppose you know he'll "find" himself?'

'Well, it's inevitable I suppose,' said Juliet dryly. 'And he could do with a little more self, and a little less ego, to be honest. I don't know why I don't just take him up to the Radha-Krishna temple in Soho. Just to get it out of his system. He could do the whole spiritual thing and be finished with it by the spring.'

At that moment Parker, either sated or bored by his exercises, bounced energetically in from the garden, his yoga mat rolled up under his arm, and sat down at the table. 'Hey, Jules. You look well Brad,' he said friskily, grabbing a cold triangle of toast and stuffing it whole into his mouth.

On seeing Kate's puzzled expression, Juliet explained. 'Cockney rhyming slang. You'll figure it out...'

A little later, Kate and Juliet made the traditional festive telephone call to their parents in France. Both Isabella and Parker were summoned and put onto the phone in turn. The air of enforced jollity was infectious, and was carried on throughout (another blow-out) Christmas dinner.

Kate had sadly had to cull Parker's enthusiastic desire for a surf by revealing that it was 'flat' and had been for days.

'Flat?' Parker had queried.

'Pancakes, millpond,' said Kate, before spelling out her point: 'There are no waves.'

'No waves? In the sea? Yeah right. You're 'aving me on, aintcha? Nice one.'

After the meal the mood subsided a bit. All the feasting and requisite resumption of wine-drinking was taking effect. Juliet and Parker slumped, thoroughly defeated, on the sofa in the living room. Standing in the hallway, Kate tried to persuade Izzy to accompany her on an after-dinner constitutional.

'A what?' demanded Izzy.

'A constitutional,' said Kate. 'To get some exercise after all that food.'

'A *what*?' said Izzy again.

'She means a walk,' Juliet cried weakly from the sofa.

'A walk?' groaned Izzy, 'What for?'

'Like I said, it'll do you good,' said Kate. 'Come on, Izzy, this is our first year here. We can walk into the village and see if there's anything going on.'

'But Mum, it's Christmas Day!' said Isabella, as if this were explanation, not to mention excuse, enough. 'Besides, I want to watch Godzilla, it's on T.V.'

'Oh right, very festive,' Kate said grumpily; but then in resignation, gave it up. She stubbornly donned her coat, hat and scarf and took off down the lane and eventually along the cliff path by herself.

The unnaturally hot sunny morning had been overcome by cloud. It was colder, but there was little wind; and so it was not unpleasant to walk along the cliff tops and see the grey ocean in repose. Porthledden looked stunning, as ever, but there would be no Christmas present for the local surfers. The sea was not, this day, pounding the rocky crags of land, but was sitting quietly for once, as if it too was glutted, and taking a nap.

As she walked, Kate thought about what Juliet had said. Deep in her heart, she knew that she was stretching things out with Jem. But she couldn't understand why. She knew that she was afraid of something, but wasn't sure what.

Intimacy? It wasn't as if she didn't find Jem attractive. True, there was something off-putting about kissing someone who regularly inspected her teeth. But if he could rise above it, then so could she. Kate was pretty sure that if she were to let things go far enough with Jem, that there would be no problems in that respect. So what was stopping her? Why couldn't she just let it happen? There was some hurdle in her mind, and though she had made excuses to Juliet, she truly did not know what it was.

She looked too far around the corner; that was what Juliet said. Was always saying, in fact. Miles had hurt her badly, she acknowledged that much. But she had always maintained that her resultant attitude of mind was justified. She had learnt her lesson and was not going to get caught again. But now Kate worried that perhaps she was, even after all this time, still licking her wounds. The lesson that she had learnt was not to trust. But now she had the uneasy feeling that she had not moved on; and that in order to move on, she was going to have to let herself be vulnerable again. Perhaps that was the real lesson. It was a distinctly queasy feeling. Hastily, she dismissed the thought. It was all so much guff; so much psychobabble. The people who believed that kind of romantic nonsense were the ones who got hurt time and time again. Kate did not want the trauma in her life. She just wanted to love Isabella, and to paint. But of course...if she were genuine in this conviction then she should finish with Jem.

Yet somehow, she didn't want to let go of the clumsy, bumbling, juvenile pretence of a relationship that they had.

She liked being with him. She liked being *seen* with him. People wouldn't think that she was weird: a mad woman with a cottage and a cat, if she were with Jem. And he was easy to be with; good-natured and light-hearted. They enjoyed many of the same things. He could chat easily to her about music and films, and gossiped wickedly about anything and everyone. They enjoyed drinking wine and eating good food. No, Kate wasn't prepared to lose Jem, and decided that she would have to bite the bullet and make up her mind, before the problem became an irresolvable albatross. And there was another niggling annoyance to be dealt with, namely that Jem wasn't exactly pressuring her...

To be fair, she had asked him to take things slowly, but still...he wasn't supposed to find it *easy*. And she had picked up enough information from local gossip and her own female intuition to know that Jem was by no means considered undesirable, and could presumably take his pick. In truth, he was probably the most eligible bachelor in the village; what with Lance Borlase being not only a divorced father, but cold and weird and scientific to boot. Kate allowed herself a little chuckle at the preposterousness of the language that filled her thoughts. Eligible bachelors indeed! *Try to think differently Kate,* she scolded herself.

All the same, her thoughts now wandered, as she trod the cliff path down into the village, into reflection on her talk with Lance the previous night. She struggled to recollect exactly what had been said. It seemed like a hundred years ago. The irony of alcohol was that all of the important conversations that it fuelled were forgotten in the resultant stupor. But she did hazily remember that they had called a truce. And then, mortifyingly, she recalled that she had told Lance—a *physicist*—how the universe worked. She couldn't help but chuckle to herself.

She was still grinning like a simpleton as she made her way across Porthvean Beach and along the narrow lane into town. The village looked extraordinarily pretty. Overhead, a string of coloured lights ran the length of Fore Street to the harbour, where they continued all around the wharf. Their twinkling luminescence was all the more magical for the winter afternoon's gloaming. The shops were shut up for the day, but their seasonal window displays remained, and she passed along the cobbled street as if in a fairyland. There were, unsurprisingly, few people about. But she heard carousing from The Ship Inn; a Christmas carol.

She stopped outside for a moment. In the empty streets the smell of ale and bar-food was all the more pronounced. The archaic pub's windows were made up of many small panes separated by muntins, and the dancing amber light within flickered like the welcoming coals of a hearth fire. Beyond the singing, the sounds of chatter, of disconnected laughter and the clink of glasses made her hunger for other times. She looked out again to the harbour to where the charming fishing boats huddled, and a sea mist was beginning to form. As she gazed further out to where the sea almost indivisibly met the sky, there loomed a feeling of dark import that Kate struggled to quell. She missed her friends. She shivered, suddenly cold. Turning, without another thought or hesitation, she strode towards The Ship Inn, pushed the heavy door and went inside.

The rush of warmth and noise was immediate. Many of the inhabitants turned to observe as she entered, which she had expected, but was defiant. She would not be afraid to be alone. A sign at the bar declared they were serving hot rum punch, and she gratefully ordered a glass. Looking around, she noticed that the carousers had been the same fishermen—the wreckers of her imagination—who had cajoled her that first day outside Vivien's shop. But this time they merely nodded in acceptance and carried on with their business. They looked smarter today, their waterproofs cast aside in favour of their best fisherman's jumpers, or ganseys as they were called, and were rendered less fearful in being accompanied by wives and girlfriends. And, Kate conceded, they were not all as grizzled and wizened as she had initially thought—some were really quite young—but rather they were sea-worn, tanned and strong. She felt ashamed of her initial distrust and downright prejudice.

She made her way with her drink to the window seat where she felt she would not be disturbed, and where she could now gaze at the harbour boats from a place of comfort. As she sipped the warming punch and absorbed the fragrance of citrus and cinnamon, she began to feel at ease. It was okay. She would be left alone.

And that was how Kate O'Neill came to spend Christmas afternoon wildly singing sea shanties with a rag-tag group of fishermen and friends.

* * *

Back at Dolphin Cottage, Juliet grabbed the control and turned the sound down on the television. Then she resumed her position of near collapse on the sofa next to Parker; although this time, she resettled herself a little further away from his sleeping body. It was so quiet. True, Parker was snoring sporadically, and the occasional sound of foot on floorboard reminded her of Izzy's presence upstairs, but in all, she felt herself alone in the peacefulness of the surrounding countryside. She gazed out of the window at the stillness of the bare branches of the trees in Carrick Lane. It was perfectly possible that not one living soul would pass by along the lane all day, except of course for her crazy sister; out walking on Christmas Day.

Juliet thought about her conversation with Kate in the kitchen that morning. Kate was undoubtedly a laughable prude, but she wondered now about her own outlook on love. She knew that she presented herself as liberal-minded. What was it that she had said to Kate? That a whole parade of mistakes was liberating... That was it. A whole parade of mistakes. She looked at Parker forlornly, as he interrupted her thoughts with a sudden loud snore. And Kate had talked about intimacy. Although she thought her sister naïve in the extreme, it disturbed her now to think about those things; about affection and deep understanding. It was something that she used to feel, but which now belonged firmly in the past.

Her first real love had been a boy from school, whom she had dated since she was sixteen. Two years later when university called him away to the other end of the country, they separated, the best of friends, but more importantly, with both their egos still intact. And so it was with great self-confidence that Juliet had fallen completely in love with Steve.

Steve was a law student by day, aspiring musician by night. They had moved in together within weeks, and Juliet had taken great pride in supporting him through his—rather many—moments of discouragement. It was notoriously hard to break into the music business, everyone knew that. But Juliet had been convinced that his talent, aided by her love and support, would eventually ensure success. And so she had misspent her youth propping up the bars of smoky dingy North London pubs. And then scouring the deserted streets outside for Steve's drunken collapsed body, when—disconsolate at his performance—he would abandon her to disappear into the night. But Juliet had felt that she alone understood him. It was natural that he should torment himself with his own imagined inadequacies; because he was so sensitive, of course.

'What a wanker,' Juliet muttered to herself now, a million light years away on her sister's sofa in Cornwall. It had not taken her too long to find out about Steve's unfaithfulness, but it had taken her longer to accept that he did not love her. When they were together the feeling was so strong, so powerful, that she had believed him when he persuaded her that his affairs were just another symptom of his own deep self-loathing. Repeatedly, he begged her to forgive him and threatened to die without her. And so she had stayed another two years, until finally, emotionally battered, she could take no more, and left. He did not die, as proposed, but instead scaled the promotional heights of the law firm, and was now married with three children. No doubt he still hated himself.

Juliet's next boyfriend, admittedly a rebound, was also unfaithful to her. And the next one. And then the one after that. Juliet would not have been in the least surprised to discover that Parker was cheating on her. After all, everyone she knew was at it; friends both male and female. She had somehow found her way into a veritable society of faithless promiscuity, masquerading under the banner of equal rights and empowerment. Even she, Juliet, who had limits, and despised the degrading drunken antics of some of the younger crowd within her circle; even *she* kept her options open. Kate had denounced the existence of romance at the party; and Juliet had feigned disbelief. It had suited her interests at the time to do so, her objective being to attract the attentions of that strange man Lance. But Juliet's heart was as hard as Kate's. Oh she was still in the game, for all that she could get; but her defences were impenetrable. The silence in the small, darkening room became maddening. Drawing up her knees, Juliet curled up the sofa, and cried a little, very quietly.

CHAPTER 23

Lance

It was the day before New Year's Eve, and the mild Cornish climate had finally succumbed to the fact that it was winter. Rare frost lay on startled exotic palm trees. Ice made its presence known on the roads, and even something resembling snow clouds threatened to make an effort. As he trudged along the chill lane, shoulders hunched and hands pocketed in his large overcoat, Lance relished the memory of long-ago winter walks made magical for a child by the hot dragon's breath of exhalation. He felt that his senses were attuned to every breath, every whisper of nature. He welcomed the cold; a reminder of how exposed, how naked was the surrounding countryside. It was not for no reason, he mused, that human beings felt instinctively comforted by the welcome of a warm country pub and a huge blaze in an inglenook fireplace: it was the traveller's rest; a respite from a life lived in the elements. These instincts remained intact despite the latter-day comfort of central heating. As always, Lance felt a supreme sense of gratitude and well-being to be so ensconced in the beauty of nature. He would never have been happy in London with Leah. His sensibilities were knitted to the fabric of the land and his spirit to the seasons and the sea, to the thrill of a glassy dawn wave and the smell of the night air.

Presently, he reached Carrick Lane and turned in the direction of old Amelia's cottage. Or rather, *Kate's cottage*, as it was now, he supposed. Lance could easily have taken the car, or indeed left his son to find his way home by himself, since, in a statement of independence, Finn had taken lately to visiting his friends alone on his bicycle. However, Lance did not tell Leah this, but instead chose to walk to Dolphin Cottage in order to be out of the house for longer. He took his time.

Leah had arrived that morning, unannounced, save for a call from her mobile phone as she sped down the A303. Well, *of course* she wanted to see her only child over the holidays! What did he expect? Or so she had remonstrated at Lance's cynical allusion to the fact that perhaps she was experiencing a lull in-between Christmas and New Year's Eve parties.

Lance had not hurried Finn immediately home from Isabella's, but rather had awaited Leah's arrival. Then, somewhat vindictively, he had subjected her to his mother's interrogation, while they all sat self-consciously rattling teacups on saucers. Vivien, after a desultory greeting, had decided that she would open up the shop today after all, and had hurriedly departed. Lillian, who refused to recognise any of Leah's exploits as actual *work*, looked baffled as her erstwhile daughter-in-law attempted to explain her latest television venture.

'Well, I thought you had rather a nice little job with the Meteorological Society,' Lillian had said in puzzlement, 'I don't know why you couldn't have stuck it out with that.'

Leah had sniggered, unabashed: 'I was a weather-girl, Lillian! I read the weather, I didn't invent it!'

Lance had soon bored of this rather bitter exercise, and with the excuse of having to collect Finn, he left his ex-wife alone to fend off Lillian's remarks. He felt no guilt, but rather annoyance and frustration at Leah's seemingly undisturbed composure. The woman was hard as nails.

He reached Dolphin Cottage and thumped the dolphin-knocker sharply against the wooden door, hunching uncomfortably within the confines of the flimsily trellised porch. Then, conscious of having let Leah rattle him, he quickly checked his behaviour, and made an effort to dispel the feeling of dejection. After a minute of listening, he realised that no one was coming to answer the door. He knocked again; a little louder this time, but hopefully without an air of irritation. There was still no reply, and he could distinguish no sounds from within. Certainly, there was no sign of the rumbustiousness that he had expected to encounter, what with Kate's visitors from London and it being that time of the year. He peered through the kitchen and living room windows in turn. He saw no one, but noticed the embers of a fire dying down in the kitchen wood-burner. Had they all gone out somewhere? Kate's ramshackle old car was parked on the grass to one side; but there was no sign of the silver Porsche that her sister drove. However, he felt sure that Kate, who had proved to be diligent in these matters, would have called to inform him if they were to make off anywhere with his son. And then surely they would not have all fitted into the Porsche?

Momentarily undecided, he walked back to the gap in the hedge that marked the entrance to the cottage and stared both ways along the lane. All was quiet. Then he strolled back to the cottage and tried the knocker once more, to no avail. He felt like the lonely traveller from De La Mare's poem, with only a throng of ghostly *Listeners* in the cottage to hear him. With no clear purpose in mind, he decided to check the back of the house. Idly he recalled that on one of his wood-chopping visits, Kate had mentioned a desire to fence off the back part of the garden to ensure more privacy; but this project, like much else that she had plans for, had not yet been undertaken, and so he made his way easily unguarded, checking cautiously through windows as he went. He despaired, not unkindly, at Kate ever being able to maintain the property.

He reached the conservatory at the back, and raised a wry eyebrow at the ivy that had not only been allowed to grow high up the side wall of the cottage, but was now also invading part of the conservatory windows. No doubt Kate, with typical emotional response, thought it characterful, or even beautiful. He had noticed, in passing, her somewhat unbalanced reverence for all things natural, and only supposed that it was a direct response to the limitations of city life. In truth, these sentiments were not so very far removed from his own. However, English Ivy could be a tenacious beast, and Kate would have no light at all soon if she allowed it to continue on its unswerving path.

He stopped suddenly, as he caught sight of movement from within the conservatory. For a fraction of a second he felt like a young boy again, caught trespassing in the farmer's field, scrumping apples. Then, scorning his own ridiculousness, he moved forward to peer more closely through the ivy-covered glass. He saw Kate, standing by an easel, paintbrush in hand. Next to her was a table covered in twisted and curled tubes of oil paint, bottles of linseed and turpentine, and a collection of jam-jars containing varyingly tinted watery shades. There were also plates: piles of seemingly discarded crockery, each made blotchy with its own array of colour; where diverse acrylic hues merged and collided in layer upon layer. On the floor he could see several opened tins of emulsion, dripping lavender, cobalt, emerald and aquamarine. Each tin-lid had been sloppily tossed adrift onto the paint splashed quarry tiles. The angle of the canvas on the easel only allowed him a distorted view of the work in hand, but he could tell it was a seascape; a judgement reinforced by the similar content of the many other paintings propped up around the edges of the conservatory.

Kate's small, old-fashioned transistor radio told soothingly of current affairs, or world news, or some such. But the radio was not loud, and Lance wondered that she had not heard his persistent knocking.

He was about to tap on the window, but stopped himself short. There was something compelling about the scene before him that he was reluctant to disturb. He stared, transfixed by the slow, repetitive, yet oddly rhythmic motions of Kate's hand, and of her paintbrush, as it flowed from palette to canvas. She was wearing old jeans, faded and worn to soft comfort. She also wore, again, his own black jumper, now so irrecoverably splattered in shades of oily colour, that he concluded resignedly that it was lost to him for good. Her long hair was held up carelessly by a clip at the back of her head, and a loose straggle fell engagingly across her face. Even as he observed this, Kate suddenly blew the wild strand from her cheek with a sharp puff of breath, and then, barely distracted, returned immediately to her painting.

Lance was rooted to the ground on which he stood. He hid, guiltily, behind the ivy, grateful now for its presence. His mind raced erratically, reproving and shaming himself for the act of intrusion that he was committing, yet still drawn compulsively to the vision of Kate, painting. Perhaps it was the long graceful pose of her arm and hand, as she altered the angle of her brush to either fleck, or stroke, or sweep. Sometimes, she would come in close, gently biting her bottom lip, to complete some small and complex detail. Then she would step back again and observe in such quiet and still contemplation, that Lance feared his discovery. Any small movement now; any slight cough or rustle of leaf and the spell would be broken. But each time, Kate would return to her painting, her eyes focused, and with just the faintest of frowns on her brow. She remained locked in the deepest concentration, and it was this, above all, that kept Lance, in turn, mesmerised.

He was brought sharply back to the present by the sound of children's voices and bicycle wheels from near the entrance to the cottage. Fleetingly, he saw Finn and Isabella ride across his line of vision, and around to the other side of the house. Thankfully, they hadn't seen him. Listening, he waited until they had abandoned their cycles in the shed and returned to the front of the cottage, where they rapped loudly on the door. Darting a covert look once more between the ivy leaves, he ascertained enough movement to indicate that Kate was, this time, responding. Feeling desperately self-conscious, he waited a while, skulking between the exposing windows at the side of the house. A robin flew down to the frosty grass in front of him, but spotting the intruder, sprang back to its perch in the hedge and loudly sang the alarm.

Lance raised a finger to his lips. 'Shh,' he whispered as the robin cocked a curious head on one side. One minute went by, then another. Not being able to think up any suitable explanation for his lurking presence, should he be discovered, he decided that he could wait no longer. He strode quickly around the house and banged loudly with the poor assailed dolphin. There was no reply.

'Oh, for fuck's sake!' he muttered exasperatedly.

Suddenly the door swung open. It was Finn, with the best part of a jam sandwich stuck in his mouth. He waved hello, and beckoned Lance indoors. Lance gestured a refusal with his hands.

'We have to hurry, Finn,' he said, forgetting his earlier lack of haste, and then added gently, 'Leah's here.'

It was at Leah's insistence that she should be referred to by her Christian name, and not as "Mum" or "Mother"; not even by her son.

'Oh,' was all that Finn replied, and silently went to fetch his things. Meanwhile Kate and Isabella appeared from the recesses of the cottage.

'Lance!' said Kate pleasantly, 'I didn't hear you knock!'

'I know,' he said dryly.

Puzzled, Kate took a step or two backwards while opening the door further in a welcoming manner. 'Would you like to...?'

'No! No thank you,' Lance interrupted her. 'I'm in a hurry. Leah...*Finn's mother* is waiting to see him back at the house.'

'Oh, okay,' said Kate, and they stood looking awkwardly at each other.

So it's back to this she thought—yet another strained meeting on her doorstep.

'Good Christmas?' she ventured.

'Yes, fine,' said Lance politely. 'You?'

'Yes, fine,' agreed Kate, and they both dried up again. After long seconds, Finn finally reappeared and they said their farewells and thankyous.

'What's up?' said Finn to his father when they reached the lane.

'Nothing!' said Lance quickly. 'What do you mean?'

Finn looked at him curiously. 'I dunno. You just seem a bit odd.'

Lance was indeed feeling a bit odd. He was, for one thing, acutely ashamed. He tried to justify his actions; after all, it wasn't his fault that Kate had not heard him at the door. It was not as if he had *planned* to spy on her. But it was no use, he still felt like a creep.

* * *

Back at Dolphin Cottage, Kate had reluctantly abandoned her painting to attend to the more pressing priority of Isabella's imminent collapse from starvation. As she stood waiting for the pasta-water to boil, she pondered on Lance Borlase.

So much for our new-found friendship, she thought, and smiled sardonically. He had barely been able to utter two words to her at the door. A small, paranoid part of her worried that perhaps, once again, she had blundered? But no. Kate

266

decided that her conscience was clear: that she had greeted him most civilly, and more importantly, without innuendo. Or perhaps he regretted their pact in the dark of the garden on Christmas Day? She wondered if she had misinterpreted any part? It was after all, hazy. Or what if he had changed his mind? In the end she decided that Lance had merely been frantic to return to his darling Leah.

All the same...*typical*. And gathering the wooden spoon, she beat the frying tomatoes and garlic in the pan into a pulp.

CHAPTER 24

Leah

Lance approached his family home with a heart like a rock. Observing Finn's silence and sullen features, he searched for clues to his son's thoughts. Leah's visits were always agonising, not least of all because of her carefree manner. There were many things, Lance knew, that Finn wanted to ask his mother. Young, and not yet formed, he was unable to find the courage to confront her, or to articulate his darkest, most difficult feelings. Lance had approached Leah many times in the past, urging her to make the time and space available for Finn to talk. But Leah, no fool, was not about to walk into a situation that might undermine her equilibrium. Instead, she insisted that her son was perfectly happy, and that Lance was a just a po-faced misery. It seemed to her that Finn had more than enough attention from Lillian; and as for that witch Vivien! Well, she was practically saving that pitiable spinster from what would otherwise be a lifetime of childlessness. Leah's point of view was always that she was doing them, the Borlases, the favour.

And there she was now, waving cheerfully from one of the mullioned stone windows, from the room that they kept for her, as Lance and Finn reached the quiet crossroads in the lane where the house stood. Lance instinctively put an arm around his son, and together they entered the emotional fray.

Vivien, under protest, had been dragged back from the sanctuary of Wreckers, for dinner. Lillian had spent the best part of the afternoon intermittently hissing down the telephone at her daughter, whenever the excuse of making yet another coffee for Leah had arisen—'Lance has disappeared, and if you don't come back and do something with her, so help me, I'll put her out! I'll put her out!'—and Vivien, reluctantly, had relented.

At Finn's appearance, Lillian and both her adult children summoned all their resources to appear friendly towards Leah. And as ever, Leah felt reassured, and relaxed. It was obvious to her that they all still adored her. Lance particularly, she thought, could not hide his regret at having lost her. Oh, he tried to be cold and hard; but once dinner was under way, and under the relaxing influence of wine, his guarded reserve fell apart, and she was convinced of his deep and undiminished longing for her.

Later, in the kitchen, with the excuse of clearing away the dishes, and knowing that Leah would not volunteer to help, Vivien confronted Lance. 'How long is she staying? Please don't say she's going to be here for New Year's Eve! Does she know about the party? That we've invited our friends? It's not that they'll mind so much, and Salima will be pleased; but I can't stand what she does to you!'

'She does nothing to me,' said Lance.

'Yes she does!' cried Vivien, brandishing a saucepan in one hand and a teatowel in the other. 'She's caused nothing but unhappiness since the day you met her!'

'That's not true,' said Lance, head down, concentrating on scrubbing the roasting tray. 'There's Finn.'

'Well, of course,' said Vivien, 'but if ever a child took more after one parent and not the other...'

'You can't say that,' interrupted Lance. 'You wouldn't say that if you had...if you were a parent yourself.'

'Ouch! That's so unfair!' cried Vivien again, 'I've been more of a mother...'

269

'I know, I know,' said Lance. 'But it's not the same. You don't understand. I can't criticise her; otherwise I'm criticising Finn.'

'Huh! Finn might find something there to criticise himself!'

'Perhaps,' said Lance, thoughtfully, and drying his hands on a towel. 'But that's his right. As for me...' and at this point he smiled and put an arm around Vivien's shoulders. '...As for me, dear sister, I shall just have to welcome her. And endure her.' Then more seriously he added, 'But you don't have to. You do more than enough for me already.'

'Damn it!' Vivien suddenly vent her frustration, slamming the poor pot on the countertop. 'And will continue to do so; because I love Finn, and I love you.'

'All the same,' said Lance, moving away again, but his tone all the more earnest, 'You've got your own life to lead. I don't expect your continuing commitment, and I don't expect that you suffer Leah needlessly. I may not be able to show my true feelings, but you may.'

'No I can't,' said Vivien, after a moment's thought. 'What you said just now was right. If I care at all for Finn then I have to respect his mother.'

They both fell silent for a while. Then Vivien said, 'How's Kate?'

Kate.

Lance was thrown off guard by the unexpected sensation that the mention of Kate's name induced. He still felt supremely guilty about his earlier sneakiness. 'I didn't really get the chance to talk to her,' he mumbled, kneeling to stack the dishwasher. 'Thought I'd better get Finn home, you know?'

'But you talked to her at the party the other night?' Vivien asked curiously. 'I thought you both seemed to get on a lot better, at least.'

'Yes. Yes we did. You were right. She's really not as bad as I thought—but as for the sister!'

'Oh, she didn't like *me*!' said Vivien. 'I couldn't get away from her gaze all night. And it wasn't even my fault. Her boyfriend wouldn't leave me alone. But Kate's lovely.' She looked slyly at Lance. He said nothing but concentrated hard on obtaining the ultimate harmonious balance of dishes in the machine.

'Anyways,' continued Vivien. '...she's very attractive though, don't you think?'

There was a heartbeat's pause.

'Who, Juliet?' said Lance, 'Yes, I suppose so. But...well, don't think I'm vain, I know this sounds conceited, or in my case even paranoid, but...I think she fancied me!'

At this, brother and sister became convulsed with laughter.

'I hope you set her straight?' chuckled Vivien. 'Told her where to get off?'

'Well, of course!' said Lance, standing upright and grinning broadly. 'Bloody women, always harassing me!'

At that moment the arched oak door that led into the kitchen opened with a creak, and Leah stepped into the room. It was hard to disguise the abrupt cessation of mirth upon her appearance.

Never one to be paranoid herself, Leah simply asked, 'What are you both laughing at?'

'Oh, just something that happened at a party the other night,' said Vivien. 'You had to be there.'

'Oh? A party? Around *here*?' Leah mocked. 'Let me guess; you're all still cramming into Gabe's crumbling shack on the beach and pretending to be in California? Or at Jem's, more likely. He's never short of an excuse for a party.'

For a brief second there was a pause, as Vivien and Lance caught each other's eye, wondering which of them would proffer a reply. In the end it was Lance who spoke.

'No Leah, for once it wasn't at Jem's; it was at Dolphin Cottage, where Amelia Church used to live. The new owner Kate is a friend of...ours,' he said, smiling covertly at Vivien.

'I see,' said Leah, picking up and flicking nosily through some letters that had been left on the kitchen table. 'And is she a particular friend of yours, Lance dear? Or perhaps she's one of the women harassing you?' She smiled beautifully at him.

Vivien silently fumed at the casual and presumptuous manner in which Leah made herself at home, and the familiar way in which she talked about their friends. As if she still belonged. As if she had never caused any harm. And it appeared that she had heard them talking before she even entered the room. If so, had she been deliberately listening? Perhaps she had only overheard them accidentally, but it was typically unashamed of Leah to let them know. She always had to be seen to be in control of a situation, at any cost. Without a word, Vivien pointedly held her hand out for the letters. But rather than comply, Leah smirked and slung them wilfully back upon the table.

'Kate is Jem's girlfriend,' said Lance; but he thought his voice sounded strange saying it. 'At least...they're dating.'

'Jem?' cried Leah, clasping her hands to her cheeks in mock astonishment. 'I don't believe it! How long?' Her generous, plumped up lips twisted into a leer. 'Never mind...I doubt it will last.'

'They seem very happy together,' said Lance, ignoring Leah's scorn, but secretly concerned that he too, felt that there was something not right about Kate and Jem; Jem and Kate. No matter which way he said it, it still didn't sound quite right. It was all the more disconcerting given that his reservations were based on some knowledge of both parties concerned; whereas Leah did not know Kate, and was basing her derision on Jem's past reputation for short-lived affairs.

'I have to go,' stated Vivien, aiming a furtively apologetic look at Lance. 'I want to finish my dress for tomorrow.'

272

'Whatcha going as tomorrow, Viv?' called Leah after Vivien's disappearing back, 'Are we still doing the medieval princess thing?' Vivien ignored her and left the room.

Immediately Leah turned her full attention towards Lance. 'So...' she said, bringing herself to stand directly in front of him. '...Still no girlfriend, Lance? Or did I miss something?'

'No, Leah, you never miss a thing,' he said wearily.

She stared at him for a moment, allowing him to digest the full power of her beauty; the full lips and long, curled eyelashes; the thick sheen of her chestnut hair. Her eyes were a cool arctic-blue, like the palest of dawn light. Lance found himself thinking that Kate's eyes were also blue, but much more intense, with a ring of navy circling the iris, and a startling flash of amber around the pupil.

Leah interrupted his thoughts. 'Oh Lance, don't be cross with me. I only want what's best for you. Which is why I just feel so guilty, sometimes. I know we had our problems, but I hate to think of a man like you...well...being *alone*. And it's all my fault. If only I could have been different; could have settled down. But I'm not like that Lance. You know that's not me. There are things I want to do with my life!'

'Like Confession Box, you mean?' asked Lance.

'It's a very good job!' cried Leah. 'My profile has skyrocketed since that programme took off!'

'Congratulations,' said Lance, his expression emotionless.

'Oh Lance, why do you despise my success? After all, you have what *you* want. You have your books and your telescopes and computers. You have your crummy countryside. Why can't I be who I have to be?'

'No reason,' said Lance, so quietly and softly that even Leah, normally so insensitive, detected some deeper regret, and narrowed her eyes as she struggled to perceive his meaning.

'Look, why don't you go upstairs and see Finn?' he said, still softly, as if he were somehow grieved. 'He will be in bed now, but probably reading. I'm sure he would love a chat—just the two of you.'

'Oh. Okay. I mean of course,' said Leah. But she had been taken off guard, and sourly resented it. Nevertheless, she moved closer to Lance and kissed him gently on the cheek, before whispering in his ear: 'We'll talk again soon.'

Then turning, she strode elegantly towards the door where she stopped to shoot him her best demure look over her shoulder, before leaving him alone.

Lance felt like slumping onto a chair by the table and cradling his head in his hands. Yet, as if trapped in some emotional limbo, he remained standing, leaning against the counter, his palms tensely gripping the edges. Unwilling to focus on any one emotion, the only condition he would agree to recognise in himself was one of immense sadness. After many minutes had passed, and the rest of the house became quiet, he grabbed an open bottle of red wine and then quietly stole up to the top of the house and to his observatory, where he gratefully put his mind to some work.

Eventually, in the deepest part of the night, he succumbed to fatigue and lay himself down on the tatty red velvet chaise longue that lay haphazardly in the middle of the room. He stared up through the glass part of the ceiling to the canopy of stars, and uncharacteristically, especially for the time of night, polished off the remains of the wine. It helped, and sleep eventually came. He awoke, freezing, in the morning with a stiff shoulder and a dry mouth. He suspected that he stank. He looked at his wristwatch and grimaced when he realised that it was only 9.00 a.m. It would not have been such a bad thing if he had managed to sleep until midday. He felt sure that Leah would be thinking of leaving by then; would give herself time to get back to London for whatever New Year's Eve revelries she had planned.

Sure enough, as he staggered downstairs to the first floor of the house, he heard Leah on the telephone in the study—*his* study—barking orders, or perhaps reprimands, at her assistant Penny. Lance remembered Penny, vaguely. They had met once in London when he had had the audacity to turn up unannounced, with Finn, at Leah's agent's office in Bloomsbury. Penny was much older than Leah; a strange upper-class eighties throwback who still obstinately wore fussy collars and pearls, and Alice bands in her hair. It was as if she wished Fergie and Di had never left the palace. Lance could never understand the unlikely alliance of Leah and Penny; especially since the latter kept pushing Leah to attend the more fusty, traditional events. And thus, the game show hostess frequently found herself inappropriately and most definitely underdressed at Henley and Ascot.

On this particular occasion, he remembered, Penny had panicked and tried to usher Lance and Finn off the premises. It seemed that a well-known pop star was due to arrive at any moment, with a view to setting up a photo opportunity with Leah, so she couldn't possibly receive any visitors at that time. In the event, only the pop star's agent turned up, but not before Leah herself had emerged snarling from somewhere beyond reception and ordered them to wait for her in the café around the corner.

Lance couldn't help but pity Penny now, as he heard Leah's angry, impatient tones. The study door was ajar, and he caught a glimpse of long silk nightdress and peachy negligee as Leah paced the floor of the small room. As ever, she looked as though she had been up all night reapplying her immaculate make-up and blow-drying her hair. Lance wondered that he never saw her without a trace of make-up. Perhaps she'd had it tattooed on? The muscles in his face knotted as, tired of pacing and with a deft little jump, Leah perched herself on his desk, squashing some papers he'd been working on with her bottom. Taking a deep breath, he crept quietly past and carried on down through the house to the kitchen, where he was greeted by a sleepy-headed Finn.

'Hi Dad,' said Finn, and then unexpectedly, got up from his cornflakes and gave his father a hug.

Lance felt an uneasy mix of gratitude and concern. 'Did you have a good talk with Leah last night?' he asked casually, reaching for a pot of coffee that Vivien must have made earlier, while Finn sat down again in front of his breakfast.

'Yeah, sort of,' said Finn, idly stirring the soggy flakes with his spoon. 'She says that when I go up to London to stay with her, we'll go to Madame Tussauds, and to some kind of jungle restaurant. And she says we'll go shopping. *Shopping!*' The look of disgust on Finn's face said it all, but Lance made no comment. 'I told her I would like to see The Gherkin and The Shard. I said I wanted to climb to the very top of St. Paul's Cathedral. Apparently it takes ages, just like climbing a mountain; and when you get to the top you can see for miles; and when the wind blows, it's so strong it nearly blows you right off the top. And so, Tom says, they have to put these steel bars up, to stop everyone blowing away. But 'cos it's so windy, you still get all these faces pressed up against the bars—like this!' Sniggering, Finn made a grid with his fingers over his face, and stared obscenely at his father through one protruding eyeball.

'But *she* just wants us to go and pose for photos with a bunch of dummies,' he continued, resuming his former sulky slouch. 'How rubbish is that?'

'You'd probably enjoy the waxworks,' said Lance unconvincingly, and sitting down at the table with his coffee. 'Anyway, when's all this planned for?'

'I dunno,' said Finn, 'Sometime. Never. Who cares?'

'Finn...' began Lance, but was interrupted by Leah, still in her negligee and in an agitated state, banging open the door and stamping into the room.

276

'I can't believe that stupid bloody woman!' she shrieked, throwing herself onto an available chair at the table, where she slouched and folded her arms petulantly. 'She couldn't decide which of two parties I should go to tonight, and now I might not get into either!'

'Which one do you want to go to?' asked Lance.

'Well how the hell should I know?' shouted Leah. 'It depends on who else is going! Christ, I don't want to be seen dead at some Zed-list turnout!'

There was an uncomfortable pause, where Leah noted Lance's look of consternation.

'What?' she protested, and then understanding, turned to her son. 'Oh right. Sorry-Finn-about-the bad-language-stroke-display-of-bad-temper.'

'Oh, like you really mean that!' Finn muttered with equal sarcasm, and only half under his breath.

'Are you going to let him talk to me like that?' Leah demanded of Lance.

'No,' said Lance, who was becoming irate, but maintained his usual composure. 'Stop it, both of you. Behave yourselves.'

Leah giggled at this, but Finn glared at his father, looking injured.

'I suppose I *could* always stay here tonight,' Leah said testily. 'It would be nice to see the others again, only...it's just so frustrating! You soon get forgotten in London if you don't keep your face in the papers. Not to mention the networking opportunities I might be missing. And I had the most gorgeous dress lined up...well, piece of dress really! It'd be wasted down here.' She leered salaciously.

Finn stood up suddenly, scraping the legs of his chair loudly against the quarry tiles, and very pointedly left the room. Lance and Leah eyed each other, wondering who was going to go first.

'Can't you try to be just a little bit sensitive?' Lance asked, struggling now to keep his tone even. 'He's very hurt that you don't want to stay longer. He needs to know that you want to be with him.'

'Finn knows what my work means to me,' Leah replied flippantly. 'He's always been very understanding. Which I might add, is more than I can say for you!'

'Well, it's a shame that you can't afford the same consideration to Finn!' snapped Lance, finally losing his temper. 'Really Leah, you neglect your duties as a mother!' He regretted his comment immediately. He knew it sounded sanctimonious.

'Really? Well, perhaps I should fight for custody then!' Leah was shouting, but there was an air of triumph in her voice. There was no way that she wanted the responsibility of Finn at this stage of her career, but equally, she knew that Lance would never want to lose him. 'I could, you know,' she continued. 'But I thought this was the way *you* wanted it? You get full control; full power over my baby's upbringing.' Leah even managed a choke in her voice, revelling in her role as self-sacrificing martyr.

'I wasn't talking about who puts a roof over his head,' persisted Lance, 'I was talking about your moral obligations; about Finn's *emotional* well-being.'

'It's tough, you know; trying to build a showbiz career,' said Leah, ignoring him. 'But I have commitment!' she cried, thumping her little fist to her chest dramatically. 'I am building a future for myself that Finn can be proud of! I want to be able to give him everything, you know. The best education, the holidays...'

'Oh, *please*!' said Lance, disgustedly, 'No one even knows that Leah Greenwood *has* a child!'

They might have continued like this, except for Lillian's arrival in the kitchen, and her dignified request that they

278

refrain from shouting. 'There never used to be shouting in this house,' she said sadly before leaving the room again.

Perhaps it was due to Lance's hostility, or perhaps she had managed to make her own decision about the coming evening, but Leah was packed up and ready to leave for London within an hour. Nevertheless, as the Borlases lined up uncomfortably to say goodbye, she still harboured the notion that Lance was secretly in love with her. Oh, he was bitter, yes. But judging from the passionate responses that she always managed to incite in him, it was obvious that she still had him on the end of a very long string.

As Leah swamped Finn in a perfumed hug, Lance felt a pang of guilt that perhaps he had driven her away, and that Finn would be the one to suffer. He wished that he had held his temper. He should have been able to persuade Leah to spend more time with Finn without resorting to a slanging match. He suspected that his behaviour had been affected by his own selfishness, in wanting her visit to be short, and was annoyed at himself because of this, especially since he had preached about moral rights and wrongs.

But as the afternoon wore on, Lance's spirits lifted a little. After all, it was New Year's Eve, and all their friends were coming over to celebrate. There were times when he became tired of the same old crowd, but tonight he was looking forward to the company. He busied himself setting up the fireworks display in the garden, and was delighted to notice Finn's mood improve, as he watched and chattered to his father from an unsafe distance. Finn was looking forward to seeing Callum, Tom and Isabella who had been invited for a sleepover. There had, initially, been some dispute with the other boys over Isabella's presence, but Finn had managed to convince them that she was cool, and worth enduring if only for her vast knowledge of Playstation cheats.

Lance too, was looking forward to seeing Kate in particular, if only to try and make amends for his curt behaviour the day before. She had been so honest and friendly and funny at Christmas in her garden, a refreshing relief from his usual experience of women; and he was afraid now that she might be reconsidering whether or not he was worthy of friendship. But he would make up for everything tonight. Tonight, the dawn of a new year, would be a fresh start. Tonight he would be congeniality itself.

CHAPTER 25

New Year's Eve

It was hardly the cramped, frenzied and hellish ordeal of a London bar on New Year's Eve, but Captain Carter's was relatively crowded.

'Just a couple of drinks before the party,' Jem had said, but it didn't feel like anyone was in much of a rush to leave. They were all squashed in together on the two large settles that flanked the big table in the corner: Kate, Jem, Juliet, Salima, Derry and a couple of Kate's new fisherman friends. Gabe held court in his usual spot, a large wooden chair with carved armrests at the end of the table.

Kate felt pretty and slim in her blue cocktail dress. And there had been a look in Jem's eye when he had arrived and spotted her; a register of approval. He looked good too, she thought, in his smart trousers teamed incongruously with converse trainers, a black velvet jacket and old-fashioned, ruffled open-necked shirt. She didn't say so, but teased him: 'You forgot your medallion!'

She had initially been annoyed to see Jem accosted by Jenifer Trewin almost the second that he walked through the bar door. Jenifer had skipped over to embrace him with a hug and then planted a kiss on his lips. 'Happy New Year!' she'd trilled, although the excuse may not have accounted for the way her arms lingered around his neck. Jem had looked abashed, but not exactly annoyed. Finally setting him free, Jenifer watched him move towards the others, before settling her black-lined eyes on Kate with that predictable sneer. Kate tried not to be rankled, but it was so annoying. Jenifer must have known that she and Jem were dating. And as for Jem, it was typical for him to take it all at face value, to be flattered even, and to not see the underlying deviousness. For the first time in her relationship with Jem, Kate felt the awful demon of insecurity raise its head from its long torpor. Born out of her desertion by Miles, it had been dormant for some time now, but was always there, it's nostrils primed for the whiff of potential pain. Surely Kate was not going to let the likes of Jenifer rile her? Yet Juliet had said that she would lose Jem...that he would think she wasn't interested.

...But he had looked at Kate with a spark in his eye, and he was sitting here now with her, and not with Jenifer. She patted the demon on the head, nursing it back to sleep.

The lighting in Captain Carter's was low, but there were lit candles in old clay bottles or brass chambersticks on all the tables and window ledges. They cast a clandestine glow upon the scene, as if they were a band of smugglers, plotting in the kiddlywink. The Christmas tree by the fireplace still exuded the aroma of pine and enchanted forests. Kate sat squeezed somewhere in the middle, with Jem's arm slung— satisfyingly— around her shoulder, as he regaled the company with some tale that she was not really listening to, but rather was wondering in amazement: *What am I doing here?*

Kate had left London determined to go it alone. It wasn't easy; fonder memories of her old friends often intruded. But she had persuaded herself that friendships, work colleagues and all attachments were—sometimes painful—distractions. She did not miss all the backstabbing; the gossip and scandal; the lengthy phone calls of petty grievance and analysis. She had brooded about all the demands: social media; birthday parties and engagement celebrations; the office outings and leaving 'do's. She had always felt a sense of unease surrounding these affairs that she had put down to her penury. But more lately, with her new-found sense of freedom, she realised that they had all been aberrations that had pulled her from her course; from her true bearings.

In the private island of Dolphin cottage, happily marooned from all the impositions and intrusions, she could be herself. She had time to think, and—crucially—had started to paint again. So did she really want new entanglements? And yet there was something different about this new, Cornish gang; they were far more laid-back, more open and undemanding. And true, Captain Carter's was doing a good job of impersonating a fantastical Arcadian ale house, but surely it would be naive to suppose that she had stumbled into some joyful magical realm? The Hydra grew new heads everywhere.

Yet Juliet's words had been subsumed: she looked too far around the corner.

She observed her companions as Jem topped up her glass from one of the wine bottles on the table. Salima was rosy-cheeked and tearful from some joke. Derry, similarly convulsed, leaned against her for support, and she noticed Juliet eye him with a smile of appreciation. Parker was perched on a stool at the bar chatting with an elderly man as though he had never even heard of the catwalks of Milan.

She summoned her pain, bid it remind her of her devastation, that people were treacherous. But it didn't come. Instead, she felt a strange emotion that came curiously close to...happiness. In truth Kate was sick of herself; sick of misery and hard feelings. Sick of being a mess. She took life far too seriously, and so far it had not served her well.

Perhaps it was time she had some fun.

Derry was the first to rise, mumbling something unconvincing about not keeping their hosts waiting. Kate reached for her coat slung on the back of the settle, but Jem put his hand on hers, and insisted they had plenty of time.

'Besides, I've just ordered more wine,' he grinned.

The others appeared to be similarly happily ensconced. Derry bade them farewell, although no-one paid much attention, and then edged his way through the crowd and slipped away into the night.

Inevitably, word got around about the party. Eventually a crowd of them stumbled, en masse, from Captain Carter's into the cold, clear night and made their way along the wharf, intending to walk the path out of town towards Tremeneghy. The Ship was also full, and revellers, some in fancy dress, spilled out onto the cobbled street. Greetings and good wishes for the New Year were exchanged, and all was convivial and high-spirited.

The fresh ocean air and the wine combined to make Kate feel a little woozy. She stopped suddenly to look out at the sea water lapping against the harbour wall, and at all the pretty lights reflected in its inky depths.

A new year. It felt as though she was standing at the gateway, at the true entrance to her new life, and that all so far had only been a preliminary. But she was still behaving and reacting like the old Kate. Just who was she trying to impress? Whose approval did she seek? Was she expecting a medal for virtue; for chastity? Or did she dare to be different, to perhaps make a mistake; or even...a whole parade of mistakes?

Jem, who had strolled ahead with the rest of the crowd, noticed she had fallen behind, and turning, made his way back to her. 'Kate, is everything okay? Are you not coming to the party?'

She looked at him, as he smiled in that unsure, self-deprecating way. 'Everything is fine, just fine.' And she reached out her hand to take his, and then moving towards him, touched his face with her free hand. And then she kissed him; softly, and with more tenderness—with more of herself—than ever before. When she pulled away again, it was clear that he must have noticed the difference, for there was something new in Jem too: a questioning urgency in his moonlit eyes.

And then he pulled her close and kissed her properly.

CHAPTER 26

Fireworks

When he had finished in the garden, Lance went with Finn to help Lillian and Vivien with the food. The mood in the kitchen was cheerful bordering on joyous, such was the cloud that had lifted since Leah's departure. For a while Lance indulged in the warm affection of his family as they bantered over the preparation of crudités and freshly made dips. Lillian declared that she would not be staying up until midnight, but would go to bed with a good book, as she insisted that she did every New Year's Eve. Vivien and Lance smiled at each other, knowing full well that she would still be in circulation well past the stroke of midnight.

At seventy years old, Lillian still loved to keep up with all the gossip and find out who was doing what, and what they thought about this or that. She was brutally candid in her opinions, and therefore came as a bit of a shock to the uninitiated. There was no malice in her nature, or intention to condescend. It was more that wisdom and experience made her impervious to the trifling sensibilities of the young. They had so much yet to learn. They were as mere babies to her, and she spoke her mind freely. At least, this opinion, held by all who knew her, was far preferable to the notion of advancing senility.

Salima, therefore, and to her dismay, was openly addressed as "The one who looks like a little boy". Similarly, Derry was "The one who wears skirts", and Jem the one who didn't quite make it as a doctor, and was very handsome but "Not wed yet, you know". Gabe got off relatively lightly as "The American one", although Lillian questioned him regularly about his tattoos. Kate, if she had but known, was lucky enough to be regarded as "Quite pretty, really."

Isabella was hastily dropped off at seven-thirty by her Aunt Juliet, who had, via Kate, contrived an extended invitation to the party for herself and Parker. Juliet didn't come into the house, but instead told Izzy to offer her apologies, and explain that she had to dash back to get ready. The two boys arrived shortly afterwards, and before long, the children were all immersed in that other world that they inhabited when grown-ups became no longer necessary for either sustenance or company.

Derry was amongst the first guests to arrive later that evening, at around nine o'clock. Lillian received him at the door. Proffering a bottle of champagne, he explained that the others were still at Captain Carter's but would be along shortly. Although he did not say as much, it was clear that poor Derry was anxious to be with his beloved Vivien, but as such did little to further his cause by being so unfashionably early.

'Ah, Derry,' said Lillian, almost as if talking to herself. 'Such a sweet boy. No skirt tonight? Come in, come in. They're in the drawing room. My goodness, don't you get nits in that hair?' She took hold of one long dreadlocked strand for inspection as she spoke. 'Men always had shorter hair in my day, of course. So much smarter. But then they didn't wear skirts either. Unless it was a Scottish wedding; then they might.'

As she guided him along the corridor towards the drawing room, Derry was a little disappointed. He had actually gone to some trouble tonight, being dressed in a vintage tuxedo, finished off with a tartan bow-tie. He had felt sure that the sight of him in a suit of any description would provoke a compliment of some sort from Lillian. It was a kind of unofficial game amongst the group of friends.

A compliment from Lillian, however meagre, was worth a free night out at Captain Carter's at the expense of all the others. This was in no way a slight towards Lillian, but rather a mark of respect. She was after all a bit of a heroine, or as Derry put it, "A legend".

'There's Vivien over there,' said Lillian, pointing extravagantly to where her daughter stood chatting to a friend by the fireplace as they entered the drawing room. 'You're still in love with her, I suppose?'

The music was not nearly loud enough and several heads turned in amusement.

Even as Derry's cheeks turned a deep shade of beetroot, Lance and Vivien leapt to his rescue, offering him a drink and enquiring about the others. When her mother wasn't looking—which would only have made things worse—Vivien put a reassuring hand on Derry's arm, and with her wide blue eyes gave him an understanding *don't worry about it* look.

It was of course the wrong look. Derry did not want Vivien's pity. Not even her understanding. He wanted Vivien to return his passion, because he knew, he just knew, in his heart that they would be right together. It put him in such an awkward position, because how could he look anything but desperate? He was well aware of the danger of coming across as a sad and needy freak. Derry was not a sad and needy freak. He held his head up high in all other respects of his life. He was capable, skilled and well-liked. He could do a mean aerial off the lip of a wave. He *ripped,* for fuck's sake! Other women even paid him attention from time to time. But what could he do? He loved Vivien. He was utterly smitten. Stories, poems and songs of unrequited love, regarded as no more than tragic fables to others, were more keenly felt by Derry, being afflicted as he was by the very condition.

Under the circumstances, he withdrew a little inside himself, as Lance and Vivien chatted cheerfully away with their guests. He fought off becoming borderline morose; but all his intentions of winning Vivien over at last with his festive bonhomie and, he had hoped, handsome appearance that night, were sent witheringly back into the deepest recesses of his persona, having been once more shown up as the utter wretch that he was.

By eleven o'clock, Lance began to wonder where the others had got to. He didn't care to admit it, but it really wasn't much of a party so far, however low-key you might like to call it. Yet he remained optimistic. Captain Carter's would be open until well after midnight, and they had probably forgotten the time, not having the pressing insistence of the closing bell to drive them out.

'Who was there, by the way?' he asked Derry.

'Oh everyone,' said Derry, with just the remotest hint of his despair. The vision of the heaving throng of merriment that he had left behind in the bar did little to dissolve his self-contempt, being another reminder of his desperation to see Vivien. Pulling himself together, he attempted to describe the mood in Captain Carter's.

'Jem's surpassing himself,' Derry's rich Cornish drawl gave emphasis to the statement. 'He was even getting in a second round when I left. Must have done a couple of bottles of wine himself by then, I reckon; although Kate probably helped him out with those. Her sister's still around, and that boyfriend of hers. *He* was chatting to Old Bill Jenkins at the bar. Old Bill was spinning a yarn, pretending to be a smuggler or something. You know, regaling him with tales of the sea and all that. They looked pretty engrossed anyway. And Parker kept nodding sagely, and saying: *Oh for sure; yeah, for sure...*' Derry paused and then said 'What a tuss...' under his breath.

289

'But they are coming aren't they?' asked Lance, trying not to sound concerned.

'Hey mate, relax,' said Derry, touching a hand to Lance's shoulder in manly reassurance. 'They'll be along dreckly...'

All the same, Lance started to have the acute sensation of being at a party for very unpopular five-year-olds. Not that it was ever intended to be a full-scale jamboree, of course, more just a gathering of friends; a soirée, if you will. Yet it increasingly did not feel like the place to be on New Year's Eve. He thought of Leah at her London party, braying contemptuously at their sad little existence. But then the resounding thud of the heavy door knocker broke into his consciousness, and Lance's impending despondence immediately flew away. At least here in Cornwall they were real friends, and not the fair-weather variety. They weren't closet gay pop stars pretending to be having a relationship with you for the sake of mutual publicity. He strode purposefully towards the front door, beating Lillian to it this time, and opened it to...Angie and Don.

Angie and Don? Had they been invited? They weren't part of his close circle of friends; perhaps they'd become pally with Vivien? But swiftly Lance remembered his manners, and warmly invited them in. The newcomers drunkenly advised him that the others were on their way, before stumbling towards the drawing room and vociferously admiring the unexpectedly grand surroundings that they found themselves in. Lance suspected that Jem had assumed vicarious authority and was inviting the entire clientele of Captain Carter's.

Before long there was another knock at the door, and once more, Lance flew to answer it. Gabe, Salima, Juliet and Parker piled noisily into the house, shrieking hellos and "Happy New Year's". Sure enough, they were followed by a band of revellers from the pub. There was no alarm at the arrival of the gatecrashers, since each and every one was from the village and well-known to the Borlases. Lance was grateful, however, that Jenifer Trewin was not amongst them.

Gabe immediately turned up the music on the stereo to a level more consistent with their mood. Lance called to him over the top of the noise and the intervening bodies. 'Where's Jem?'

'What's that?' Gabe shouted back, 'Jem? On his way Bro, last I knew...'

Well at least things were a bit livelier, thought Lance as he looked at the chattering, jovial crowd gathered in the room. Parker had decided to toady up to Gabe tonight, and was attempting to bond with him via the subjects of music and surfing. Lillian appeared to be hitting it off marvellously with Don, of all people; and Juliet, it seemed, had lost interest in Lance, and was now exercising her considerable charms on Derry, as they chatted together, snug on the sofa.

'I'm not jealous you know,' said Vivien, coming up behind Lance and reading his thoughts. 'In fact, it's good to have the pressure taken off me for the night. I'm glad he seems to like her.'

Just at that moment, Derry threw back his head and laughed uninhibitedly. Juliet, who had kicked off her stilettos, sat curled up like a cat next to him, and turned slightly towards him, so that one black-nyloned leg was almost draped on top of Derry's thigh. Despite Vivien's assurances, Lance thought privately that she looked a little peeved.

It was now eleven-thirty, and still no Jem and Kate. Lance threw himself into his role as host; insuring that the drinks kept flowing, and passing around the hors d'oeuvres.

'Canapés remain old school in this house,' he joked, offering up a tray of cheap biscuits topped with cheese and pineapple, which were nonetheless greedily accepted and devoured. 'Fresh out of chocolate grasshoppers, I'm afraid; silverskin onion on a stick, anyone?'

Many commented on how high-spirited he seemed to be that night. Behind his back, some also added "Thank God," or "About time". The music was very loud by now, but Lance kept one ear strained, listening for the door knocker. And to his irritation, he repeatedly caught himself looking abstractedly out of the window into the blackness of the road outside.

The time came for the countdown to midnight, but confusion reigned in the drawing room. Someone had turned on a television, and a group who had gathered around it began to shout the receding numbers at the top of their voices, whilst others remained locked in conversation, oblivious that the whole purpose for their partying was about to pass them by unnoticed. However, at the stroke of midnight, the group surrounding the television let rip with cries of "Happy New Year!", that started to spread around the room, as they kissed everyone that they encountered. Juliet rose to the occasion by planting a smacker on Derry's lips. Parker might have been tempted to kiss Gabe, but responded instead with a languorous, laid-back high-five.

Champagne was opened, and Lance resumed his role as party host, topping up the glasses and bantering good-naturedly. After all, the party was not automatically over at the stroke of midnight, and he felt it was important to maintain the jovial atmosphere, despite the imminent threat of his own spirits plummeting.

A few minutes later, somewhat late for the occasion and without fanfare, he sneaked outdoors to light the fireworks. For some reason, he couldn't summon the energy to round everyone up to follow. He reasoned that they would hear the noise, and anyone interested enough would find their own way out. Sure enough, the children flung open an upstairs window, shouting and pointing with delight at the illuminations in the sky. One or two adults ventured out to watch some of the display, but staggered indoors again before long bemoaning the cold, or to replenish their drinks.

Lance didn't care. He crouched alone in the dark, lighting a series of fireworks in turn and then standing back to watch thoughtfully as each one exploded and disintegrated. He felt like an errant child being forced to witness the consequence of his own folly.

BANG! There went happiness. BANG! There goes hope. That strange elation that he had felt all day fizzled and died in the night sky. Yet to his credit, it was a full one hour and forty-three minutes into the brand new year before Lance conceded that Kate was not going to come.

PART TWO

The Turning Tide

"All things must change to something new, to something strange"

Henry Wadsworth Longfellow.

CHAPTER 27

New Year Woman

Kate stood by the large kitchen window where the sun's rays filtered through the dark winter branches of the ash tree, and stretched and yawned. She wore nothing but a large white bathrobe, and her hair, she knew without reference to a mirror, was definitely tousled and sexy in a most comely bed-head manner. She put the kettle on and wondered if she should light the fires now, as she absently put some mugs on a tray. She didn't want to start fussing about with her daily chores, yet it was very cold in the cottage. Kate was finding it hard to concentrate on anything much. She was distracted; and was it any wonder?

She allowed herself to squirm for a second with embarrassment and delight, before resuming an air of lofty maturity. By rights she should be wearing a cute chiffon negligee and fluffy mule slippers, but she glided around the kitchen like Doris Day nonetheless, fetching the milk and pouring some into a jug. As an afterthought, she hastily replaced the colourful mugs with two old bone-china teacups and saucers, then put some sugar into a pretty round dish and garnished it with two dainty teaspoons. She wondered whether she should serve the water in her heavy glass pitcher, but settled for pouring some directly into plain tumblers.

Kate observed the display on the tray critically. Ideally, she should put some delicate cut flowers in her small glass rosebud vase, but decided that although that sort of thing might work well in a picture shoot for a glossy magazine, in real life it was probably going too far.

In real life. Again, she took a minute to digest the fact that this was indeed real life. Kate had finally rejoined the land of the living. At last, at long last, she was a real woman again. She still wore the seductive traces of last night's perfume. Her toenails, for once, were elegantly tended and painted a spangly blue. She felt sure that she had lost weight. But more than this, she had a man in her bed. A real, delectable, attractive man was at that very moment crumpling up her white cotton sheets.

Kate's body was testament to the truth of the matter. She still tingled where Jem had kissed or caressed her, and ached where she had borne his weight. The scent of him still filled her senses. She had all but forgotten what it was like to be so *aware* of another person, almost as if you were dressed in them; dipped and coated with their flavour. And it had all happened so easily, in the end—although the vast quantities of alcohol they had both consumed had naturally helped.

Abruptly Kate sat down in terror. What happened now? What if he wanted to do it again? What if he *didn't*? In the cold light of morning, with the comforting, residual haze of intoxication fast deserting her, Kate started to panic about etiquette. Should she come over all seductive temptress, or should she sit awkwardly on the blow-up bed and chat gaily over the teacups? Having sacrificed her own charming bedroom to her house guests she was left with the undignified scenario of crawling back onto what was no more than a mattress upon the ground, surrounded by the clothes that they had hurriedly removed; her pretty party dress discarded in a sluttish, crumpled heap on the floor.

And then she remembered the brandy. Jem had insisted on a nightcap and now the bottle and their half-finished glasses sat reeking degeneracy on the rug. It would be hard to pull off "seductive temptress" in what now resembled a squalid student crash pad. Perhaps she could avoid returning to the bedroom, and the situation, at all. If, for example, she were to forsake the love-bed in the early hours of the morning to paint in her studio, might that not be seen as soulful and enigmatic?

But what was she thinking anyway? She had left her daughter all night at the Borlase household, which was fine in itself since it had been prearranged; but she herself had been expected to be there for most of the evening and she hadn't even shown up. She was painfully aware that it might appear that she had deliberately taken advantage of Isabella's absence to procure a night of passion with Jem. She would have to call Vivien or Lance at the earliest civilised time. And where the hell was Juliet?

Kate stared forlornly at the tea tray and wished that she had not risen so early. In truth, she had been too nervous to sleep. At this admission, the womanly aura that she had tried to evince a few minutes ago began to fade, and was replaced by the realisation that she was in fact exhausted and hungover. Prompted by a frighteningly loud snore from upstairs, she abandoned the china for Isabella's Spider-Man mug, and grabbing a blanket from the pile she kept in a basket, climbed out of the kitchen window to sit cross-legged on top of the garden table and drink hot restorative tea. It was cold, but the air was still, and it was tolerable. Kate tucked her bare feet under the folds of the bathrobe, pulled the blanket tighter around her, and turned her head to the beautiful morning sky. She closed her eyes briefly and took a few deep and sobering breaths of crisp air. As she sipped her tea, she slowly began to recover some kind of equanimity. She decided not to make any decisions about Jem. She would simply wait and see what happened. *Don't look too far around the corner.*

It was so quiet that Kate heard the footsteps on the lane long before their perpetrator appeared. It was a ragged, uneven step, and Kate, as still and quiet as the Ash tree, followed its progress along the other side of the hedge towards the gap that opened onto the cottage grounds. She had expected the walker to pass by, oblivious to her existence, and so was surprised to see an unkempt Parker lurch into the driveway and shamble towards her.

'Morning!' Kate called cheerfully. 'Must have been a good party! Where's Jules?' Her voice sounded strange and disconnected as it broke the morning calm.

Parker groaned something unintelligible and waved an arm at her dismissively, before disappearing into the cottage. Once inside, he did not enter the kitchen behind Kate, and neither did she hear him stomp up the wooden staircase. After many minutes of deep silence, Kate deduced that Parker had retired to the sofa, and that she now had two sleeping men in her little home. She began to worry about Juliet. Her sister must have stayed at the Borlase's all night, but why had Parker come back without her? Surely he would have waited for her to wake, and they would have returned together? She should probably send a text message, but didn't want to appear overly-concerned—at least not yet.

She twisted around to look through the window at the kitchen clock. Still only 8.15. The longer she sat on the table outside Dolphin Cottage, the more removed she felt from the events of the previous night. There was no way that she could climb back into bed now. She wanted Juliet and Izzy to return. She wanted people and activity and noise. She wanted normality, and most of all, she wanted time; time to digest and assess her situation. Compulsively, she glanced once more at the clock.

8.19.

It was going to be a long morning.

Eventually, unable to take the chill any longer, Kate climbed back into the cottage. Wandering like a lonely ghost, she discreetly threw a blanket over Parker on the sofa. She ascertained that Jem was still asleep—or perhaps unconscious, but alive—by listening quietly at the bedroom door. Quietly, she showered, and dressed in some clothes that she pilfered from the unironed mass in the bathroom airing cupboard. By 10.30, and no longer able to stand the silent monotony of the morning, Kate decided that it was a reasonable enough time to call Vivien and check on Izzy. It took a while for her to answer, and when she did, Vivien sounded tired, even a little dejected.

'No, that's fine; Izzy's fine,' she said. 'They're all still asleep, but she can stay as long as you like, there's no rush... Well, we usually go for a walk on New Year's Day, but she can join us. It's no big deal—unless of course you want her home?'

'No...I mean thank you. I'm so sorry I didn't make it last night,' said Kate hurriedly. 'Change of plans. I feel a bit guilty for not showing up.'

'Don't worry. How *is* Jem, by the way?' Vivien gave a small chuckle, but Kate could sense that the humour was forced.

Kate was concerned. 'Is everything okay Vivien?'

'Of course. Give me a call when you want Izzy home, otherwise she's welcome, as I said, to stay as long as she likes.'

There was something wrong.

'Is Jules there?' asked Kate, remembering her sister. 'Only, Parker came home earlier...'

'No, she's not.' Again the reply was taut.

'Well, do you know where she is?' Kate was really becoming worried now. She thought she heard Vivien sigh on the other end of the telephone line; a long, weary, drawn-out sigh, as though she were bracing herself for something she would rather have nothing to do with.

'She might be at Derry's,' said Vivien. 'I think she left last night with Derry.'

It was almost midday when Juliet finally arrived back at the cottage, shuffling up to the doorway on foot, much as Parker had done. Her expression was drained, but impenitent.

Kate grabbed her sister by the arm, steered her into the kitchen and closed the door. 'What are you thinking of?' she cried in a loud whisper. 'Parker's in there, on the sofa!' Kate indicated abstractedly in the general direction of Parker and the living room.

'Oh, so *what*?' said Juliet defiantly. 'It's over between us. He knows it; I know it. It's just a matter of closure!'

'Closure? Stop talking like that!' said Kate, crossly. 'It's embarrassing. You're not an American, for one thing, and it makes you sound so...so heartless. As if it's just a game, and people and feelings aren't important. I mean, there's a time and a place, Juliet. Don't you think you could have finished with Parker *first*, if that's what you really want, and only then, maybe set your sights on someone else? And not *Derry*, of all people!'

'Why not Derry?' demanded Juliet. 'Let me tell you something about Derry, Kate. He might look like a crusty, dog-on-a-string-type yokel, but he's *very* sexy in bed.'

'Stop!' cried Kate, holding up one hand stiffly, inches in front of Juliet's mouth. She wondered if her sister was still a little drunk. 'Please Juliet, Derry is my friend. *Vivien* is my friend. Okay, they're not dating as such, but there's something *there*. Don't you ever think about the other relationships involved? Why do you always have to act without thinking?'

'Who says I wasn't thinking? Maybe I knew exactly what I was doing. For your information, big sister, Derry is a top-notch, class A, total *Shag*; and that prissy Vivien is a fool to have neglected him for so long. It's her loss, and her own stupid fault!'

Kate said nothing. She wanted to cry with shame at Juliet's complete lack of remorse. Then several things happened almost all at once. Jem stumbled downstairs at last, bursting into the kitchen, semi-clad in just a pair of barely-buttoned jeans. He yawned; ruffled the curls on his head sleepily with one hand; said a good-morning to Juliet; and then grabbed Kate and kissed her passionately. Almost immediately the loud peals of the telephone in the hallway broke into this intimacy, and Kate gently urged Jem to unhand her so that she might answer it. He protested, but then good-naturedly sloped off to fill the kettle, still yawning, but generally looking very pleased with himself. Ignoring Juliet's knowing leers, Kate approached the kitchen doorway, but found her entrance was suddenly blocked by the looming and uncharacteristically forbidding presence of Parker.

For a moment all parties stood stock-still, while the telephone squealed impatiently at them. It even dawned on impervious, buoyant Jem that hostilities were abroad.

'Excuse me,' Kate said weakly, and ducking past Parker, she grabbed the telephone receiver. It was Lance.

'Happy New Year,' he said.

'Yes, Happy New Year!' Kate replied with false cheerfulness, as the baleful face of Parker glowered cynically at her from the kitchen doorway.

'I was sorry not to have seen you at the party last night,' Lance continued in his measured manner.

'Oh yes, me too. I'm so sorry we—*I*—didn't get there. Er, probably had too much to drink at the pub.' All at once Kate felt shy. Would Lance be aware that Jem had spent the night? Could he sense her coyness down the telephone line? 'How did it go, anyway—the party I mean?'

As Lance replied with the usual commonplace responses, Kate saw Jem leave the kitchen and quietly shut the door behind him, leaving Juliet alone with Parker. He shot Kate a meaningful look as he passed her, and then went to lurk discreetly in the living room. Distractedly, Kate stared at the kitchen door, but could not hear any raised voices. She remembered Parker's martial arts skills. It was possible that he had murdered Juliet silently and efficiently with one killer move. She was only half paying attention to Lance, as she strained to listen for any signs of disruption from the kitchen.

'I wanted to let you know that we're taking Isabella with us on our walk now,' Lance was saying. 'We'll just be following the coastal path along to the estuary, and then round back on ourselves through the fields and lanes. We should be back by late afternoon.'

'Thank you,' Kate said. 'Are you sure?'

'Yes, Kate, it's not a problem. The other boys from last night are coming too.' Kate could sense the pause that followed, as though Lance was silently thinking something over. Then he said, '...and you're most welcome yourself, if you'd like to join us.'

She wanted to say yes. At that precise moment she longed to escape the atmosphere in the cottage and the pressure of her own predicament. She wanted to see Izzy, and to wear off her hangover with a long walk through the beautiful countryside. She desperately wanted to speak to Vivien. She suspected that Vivien was more hurt by Juliet's actions than she let on, and wanted to console her; to reassure her that her own friendship was genuine, and to be trusted.

But what was to be done with Parker and Juliet? Perhaps she ought to leave them alone to talk. But there was the risk of Juliet escaping Parker by demanding to go on the walk with Kate, and that would be a disaster, considering Vivien. And then there was Jem. He might offer to accompany her—might insist upon it. Yet Kate didn't feel ready for this; to be so publicly together the day after the night before. She felt the familiar guilt. She should, of course, spend the day with him. Poor Jem. He had done nothing wrong, and he was, after all— she forced the thought—her *boyfriend*.

'Kate?' Lance queried.

304

Suddenly it all became clear. In all her mind's confusion there was only one, true constant in her life, and on which she could trust her instinct. Isabella. Kate became overwhelmed with the desire to see her daughter. How could she have forgotten that nothing else really mattered? Juliet and Parker were adults and should be left to sort out their own problems.

'I'd love to come, Lance,' she said.

CHAPTER 28

Strange Paths

She met them on the cliff path by the top of the railway sleeper steps that led down to Porthledden Beach. She gave them a wave as she approached, and in response, Vivien began to gather up the children who had been playing on the tiered levels of wood. Kate sauntered up to Lance and smiled amicably. He nodded in return but said nothing. She thought that, like everyone else that morning, he looked a little tired. But Kate was surprised at how pleased, almost relieved, she felt to see him. It was ironic really, after the flare-up of their first meeting that she should begin to feel anything like easy in his company now. Yet it was becoming increasingly difficult to imagine that she had ever thought him arrogant and vain, especially when held up against the likes of Parker.

But was it possible that he might yet prove to be undemanding; supportive; even an ally? There was certainly no chance of Lance pursuing her romantically. It had occurred to Kate that the whole upset of their initial misunderstanding could in fact pave the way for their relationship to be uncomplicated, and completely free of suspicion of ulterior motive. After all, they had made their positions clear at the outset. If nothing else, she was becoming less disconcerted by Lance's silences and stares, and in some small way, found them strangely reassuring. He was at least consistent.

306

And sure enough, as Vivien stepped up to join them with the children, and Kate grabbed Isabella in a tight hug, Lance was already moving off along the rugged path; his long legs setting the pace and his now familiar coat-tails flapping in the sea breeze. Kate felt oddly relaxed. So much so, in fact, that she was more ready to broach the subject of Derry with Vivien, should an opportunity arise. But first she had to catch up with Isabella. It felt as if she had been apart from Izzy for days, rather than just one night. As she watched her daughter speak excitedly about the previous evening's events, Kate only half-listened, being distracted with wonder at her own child's face. It shone with the exuberance and beauty of youth.

'The fireworks were *so* cool, Mum,' said Izzy; eyes shining, 'Better than anything on Clapham Common. I mean, they weren't as big, but they were just better. I think it was because the night was so dark, and we watched from high up in the bedroom with the lights off. Why weren't you there?'

'I'm so sorry,' said Kate guiltily. And she was sorry; she regretted missing the party. 'I got tired and went home. I called first thing this morning, so I knew you were okay. I hope you didn't feel abandoned, or anything?'

'No!' said Isabella cheerfully. 'It meant I got to stay longer at Finn's!'

Well of course, thought Kate. Life was always grand with the beautiful Borlases.

'But I'm glad you're here *now*,' her beloved added, just in time.

After a while, and as she had hoped, Kate found her personal concerns succumb to the immediacy of tramping the path. The day was still cold, but cloudless; and the sunlit sea cut a striking bright turquoise against the dark rocky landscape. The beach below, save for some dog-walkers, was near empty. The pristine sands stretched out for miles ahead, the serenity only tempered by the elemental energy of the breaking waves. Rugged, romantic, dramatic; it still made Kate gasp in wonder. It was strange to accept, in moments like this, when overwhelmed by the sheer beauty, that she was here, in this moment; that this was her home now.

'I don't know what to say,' Kate said, finally finding the appropriate moment as her stride fell in line with Vivien's. 'About Juliet, I mean. I know that your feelings for Derry are different from his, but all the same, it's still a blow when someone who... It can still feel like a betrayal.'

Vivien looked pensive as they carefully picked their way along, finding footholds in the rocky path. 'I've given it some thought, and really, I'm not angry. I have no right to be. I've taken Derry for granted. Of course he should...see whomever he wants. I can't believe he hasn't done so before now. It just feels a bit strange. You know, like your whole outlook on the world has been set permanently askew. And it'll never be the same.'

See whomever he wants. Kate had baulked at the word "see". Vivien had quite clearly meant something a lot less polite. Neither of them fooled themselves that Derry and Juliet's liaison was going to result in a permanent relationship. Suddenly, Kate felt less comfortable, and not because of any recrimination by association on Vivien's part; but rather it occurred to her that perhaps Lance, if not his sister, might judge her by Juliet's actions. Her sister had behaved shamelessly and remorselessly in a situation that she, Kate, had invited her into. And Kate herself had left her daughter all night in the Borlase's home in order to indulge in a bit of drunkenness and—as it turned out—debauchery.

Was he judging her? Suddenly his lonely striding ahead of the group was no longer a symbol of security and comfort, but rather a cause for impending paranoia. And yet he had asked her to join them, so surely she was mistaken?

'Anyway,' said Vivien with a small smile, and looking around to make sure that the children were out of earshot, 'how's Jem? You didn't answer me before.'

Kate blushed and grinned, as was appropriate; but inside felt a flicker of panic, which she quickly suppressed. 'He's fine,' she said coquettishly.

'Didn't he want to come on the walk?' asked Vivien, still smiling knowingly.

As it had turned out, Jem had initially been all for it; but after having eaten a very quick late breakfast, showered and shaved, he had had a sudden relapse.

'To tell the truth, Kate, I'm flagging a bit,' he had said. 'Would you mind very much if I went back to bed? ...Bit shaky!' And he held out one hand to show the trembles.

Kate had been part endeared and part horrified. But she assured him it didn't matter. And despite her concern over the warring couple that still occupied the kitchen, she nonetheless felt relieved that she was going to be able to escape by herself.

'I suspect he's sleeping it off,' was her elusive reply to Vivien's question, although she returned a coy smile.

The coast path eventually led down from the cliffs into sand dunes, and then turned inland by the estuary. Before long they arrived at a pub with grand sweeping views of the rivermouth and the sea beyond.

'Can we stop?' asked Finn. 'I'm starving.'

'Sure,' said Vivien. 'Could do with a sit-down myself.'

'The Ferryman? Really?' said Lance.

'It's just for a rest,' replied Vivien. 'And the children need feeding and watering...'

Once inside, Kate could understand Lance's reluctance. Despite its stunning location, The Ferryman was not as aesthetically appealing as The Old Oak or the village pubs, and as they ordered their drinks they silently communicated second-thoughts with their eyes. The pub should have been

309

warm and inviting, like some cavernous dwelling that offered a certain primal comfort from the world outside. A blazing fire would have been welcome. But instead they encountered jukebox, lino, and wilfully unaccommodating bar staff, presumably disgruntled at having to work on New Year's Day.

'I'm going outside,' said Lance, picking up his beer and promptly leaving.

Vivien looked at Kate and shrugged in resignation. 'You go too, I'll order the chips.'

Lance sat on the wooden bench by a table outside the pub and stared out to sea. His long hair drifted gently in the breeze. It was second nature for him to stare out to sea. Apart from a habitual compulsion to check the surf, the sea was an all-encompassing power that, like the stars, helped diminish all other cares. And this morning especially he was in need of that comfort and reassurance. He took a deep breath and steadied his heart to the rhythm of the small glassy waves.

Kate came outside and sat beside him, so that she too faced seawards, and caressed a glass of grapefruit and soda. She had learned her lesson about pub wines and unwieldy pints, and ruefully, was not speaking to her good friend alcohol at the moment. Lance had yet to address her directly since they had set off. The silence between them made Kate all the more acutely aware of his presence. There was something that needed to be said by one of them, but she knew neither what it was, nor which of them should speak it. Lance too, she thought, seemed at times about to comment, almost in desperation, but each time resisted and turned away, back to the sea.

And he was Jem's friend. It was a most disquieting thought. Would they talk about her? Had Lance, like Vivien, already guessed what had happened last night? Well, of course he had. *Would he judge her?* Kate's spirits suddenly and inexplicably plummeted. It was so odd to be sitting on a cold bench staring out to sea next to this brooding man, when she had so recently left the warm arms of another. She should have stayed at home with Jem, and had the courage to continue what she had allowed to begin. Instead, she had run away.

The children emerged from the pub with Vivien, each of them laden with unhealthy sustenance, and the mood changed. Kate had to squash up closer to Lance in order to fit everyone around the small wooden table. But he did not flinch or leap up—hurriedly insisting that he'd prefer to stand—as she might have imagined. Instead, he appeared to relax somewhat; so that she still could not fathom his mood.

The conversation turned once again to the previous evening's events, but tactfully, none of the adults mentioned Jem. Lance, now that he was finally speaking, was animated and friendly, and it wasn't long before Kate started to feel easy in herself again. As she looked around at the affable smiles, she realised that she was not being excluded, despite Juliet's best endeavour. And she reminded herself that Lance had, after all, and despite recent frostiness, held out the olive branch to her in the early hours of Christmas Day. As she watched him talk now, she decided that she should try hard to embrace this friendship wholeheartedly, and not forever suspect his changing moods.

Surprisingly, it was Lance who suddenly broached the subject of Jem. The children had finished demolishing their refreshments and had obligingly run off to play near the water's edge, unwittingly leaving the adults at liberty to discuss meatier topics.

'So, Kate,' he said, looking quizzically at her. 'I guess things are getting serious with Jem?' It was a brazen question; but there was, as ever, a reticence about Lance. He was trying, woefully, to sound light-heartedly playful but it was as if he were holding something back. Kate was mortified. She could not immediately find the words to answer him, and for a few seconds her eyes locked in consternation onto his. He was very close.

'Well, we have been dating for some time now...' she managed to stammer, disconcerted by the green gaze. She thought she detected a flicker of expressiveness in those eyes before the usual inscrutability returned.

'I think it's good,' he said, turning away from her and regarding his pint; although he sounded unsure, as if he was still mulling the idea over. 'Yes, I think it's good. It's about time Jem found someone...' he looked at Kate strangely once more before finishing '...someone special. I just hope...'

'What?' asked Kate, reddening.

'I hope it lasts,' Lance all but murmured to his pint again.

'Lance!' cried Vivien, reprovingly. 'What a thing to say! Can't you see you're embarrassing poor Kate?'

Kate's colour changed to ashen. Her mind raced. Why did Lance think that it would not last? Was he accusing her of a mere dalliance with his friend? Did he think that Kate, like Juliet, was prone to casual flings? Her feelings towards Lance were once more in danger of becoming hostile. It seemed that no matter how much she tried to think the best of him, he contrived a way to upset her.

'Who ever knows with these things?' she said, struggling to contain her emotions. 'All I know is that my intentions are good. I mean well. I'm not...I'm not *flighty*.' Kate was theoretically speaking to both the Borlases, but her eyes, angrily challenging, never left Lance. 'I've never been the sort of person that wanted lots of lovers. I guess some people do. They set out to have as many affairs and experiences as they can and good luck to them. But it's not for me.'

'I'm sure it's not,' said Lance softly, and turning to face her once more. 'There's no need to be so defensive.' His eyes softened again and his expression was almost sad. It was confounding.

'I only ever wanted one true love,' Kate went on, and at risk of being deemed to "protest too much". 'But it's a fantasy. It doesn't really exist. I thought I'd found it, but it disintegrated before my eyes. Consequently *one true love* never will be, for me.'

'So where does that leave you and Jem?' asked Lance.

There was a moment's pause before Kate, defeated, answered honestly. 'I don't know.'

They all fell quiet. Vivien was looking at Lance in such a way as to suggest that he should not say another word. Isabella ran over to their table and announced that she had been appointed to request further drinks all round for the children.

'No, Izzy, we're going now,' said Kate, frustrated at hearing the choke in her voice. 'It's getting cold, sitting here.' Isabella duly ran off again to deliver the verdict.

Vivien grabbed the glasses from the table and went to take them back inside the pub, calling upon the children to assemble on her way. Left alone together again, Lance turned abruptly towards Kate.

'I'm sorry Kate,' he said firmly, 'I didn't mean to upset you.'

For some reason, Kate found that she could not bring herself to look at him. He hesitated, and Kate knew that he was still looking at her intently. She kept her gaze fixed firmly ahead; her mouth set hard. She was not giving anything else away.

'You misunderstood me,' Lance said after long seconds, and then with a wry laugh, 'we're good at that, you and I. Misunderstandings, that is.'

Still Kate said nothing.

'It's not *your* intentions that I doubt, Kate,' Lance finished with a surly note, finally averting his eyes away from her and back once more to the sea.

Unable to resist any longer, Kate turned and spoke, her voice harsh. 'So it's Jem then. It's Jem that you doubt. I thought you were supposed to be his friend?'

Before he could answer her, Vivien returned, and gratefully, Kate jumped up to leave. She could feel Lance's discomfort with what she had said, but decided to let him stew.

For once Lance lagged behind as they continued on their route back home, which rendered Kate self-conscious in not allowing herself to look back, at any cost. She tried to put some distance between them, but no matter how hard she tried, it seemed as if Lance was perpetually just a few paces behind her. At one point the group muddled together at a high and slippery granite stile, along a sludgy tree-lined path. They were behind schedule, and darkness had fallen suddenly upon the lonely track. With almost ludicrous Boy Scout resourcefulness, Lance produced a small but powerful torch from one of his coat pockets, and vaulting effortlessly over the stone stile, he gallantly offered his hand to help or guide each of them over. Loitering reluctantly at the back, Kate nevertheless could not bring herself to snub him by refusing his outstretched hand. As she took it, he smiled at her in the dark, and once again threw her mind into utter confusion. As she landed beside him in the mud, Lance unexpectedly put an arm around her shoulders and gave her a little hug, before moving quickly away again, resuming his more customary position at the head of the group.

It had been a passionless, amicable embrace, and an act of some bravery for one as self-contained as Lance. It was obvious what it meant. It meant that Lance wanted forgiveness; and that he wanted their fledgling, floundering friendship to endure. And as was her way, Kate instantly forgave him. She could not help but be touched by such an act of apparently genuine sentiment. Magnanimity was her downfall and often made her a fool, but Kate was touched, all the same. As a consequence, her spirits lifted a little, and she chatted happily for the rest of the way with Vivien. Yet at the back of her mind she could not forget what Lance had said and his implied meaning. And it was exasperating how he seemed to have the power to so easily influence her mood.

Their path took them past the end of the lane that led to Dolphin Cottage, and the others said goodbye to Kate and Isabella at the corner by the Cornish hedge. Vivien gave Kate a friendly kiss on the cheek, and promised to arrange a night out together soon. Lance, following suit, took Kate by the elbow and planted a brief kiss on the side of her face. His eyes fleetingly met hers, and she sensed that he was anxious to be sure that all was well between them. But he turned away just as quickly, as if reluctant to know the answer.

As she and Isabella finally, wearily turned into the cottage entrance, Kate saw that all was in darkness, and that Juliet's car had gone.

CHAPTER 29

Derry

Kate had returned on New Year's Day to find that Juliet and Parker had packed up and returned to London. Once she had found a signal, a text message from Juliet briefly explained. Kate shuddered to think of the seething resentment that would flavour the atmosphere on that long journey. Yet Juliet's message insisted that she and Parker were "okay with each other", and even offered a begrudgingly curt "sorry about your mate" in reference to Vivien.

Kate had thought what a strange relationship theirs was. If Kate had been Parker she would not have suffered the humility of requiring a lift, but would have waited, in a hotel if necessary, until the first available train. But then a snore from the darkened living room had reminded her of her own capriciousness. It seemed that Jem had helped himself to a couple of bottles from her wine store, and so for the second time that day, Kate had spread a blanket over a sleeping man on her sofa. She had then, rather sneakily, contrived to watch a video in bed with Izzy, and they had fallen asleep together. She told herself that it was because he was drunk; and besides, Isabella was in the house.

But she couldn't avoid him forever. As the weeks went by, Kate refused to show that there was any level of commitment between the two of them in front of Isabella; after all, it was still early days. As a consequence, she was only occasionally

316

available to spend the night with Jem, usually when Izzy made arrangements to sleep over at Tremeneghy again. They still met for lunch, however, or the occasional drink. Sometimes Jem would come over and cook dinner, insisting that she "relax" while he proceeded to transform her kitchen into something resembling his own.

Jem was a spectacularly messy cook, sloshing wine with wild abandon and trampling chopped onions and garlic all over the floorboards. Small flecks of red were recklessly splattered across the grass-green walls when he boiled spaghetti sauce so fast that it gave a fair impression of active primordial soup. Great gloops of pancake batter dripped tediously in their own gloop time-speed from the ceiling, thanks to his carefree use of the liquidiser minus lid. If Kate attempted to clear up or offered to help at all, she was instantly sashayed back to her chair by the fire in the kitchen, poured another humongous glass of wine and told, once more, to "chill". And so, Kate could do little but get slowly drunk, and wince discreetly as Jem flambéed the tea towels.

Ending up in bed together was never a given; but when it did happen, it usually followed one of Jem's highly inebriated cookery evenings, and resulted in half-remembered sex, followed by passionless mornings, as Kate fought her hangover and Jem snored soundly beside her. Yet this sorry state of affairs did not seem to bother Jem in the slightest. He appeared to be more than content with his lot, and Kate found herself thinking traitorously that he enjoyed the food and drink rather more than he did her. She did not complain. After all, how do you force passion? Yet it was a disappointing denouement to the expectancy roused by months of desirous, meaningful looks.

As the colder days rolled into spring, sometimes Kate would lie awake at night next to Jem's sleeping form, wondering why on earth she allowed him to be there at all.

317

Nothing was going to plan. She had let Jem into her life inadvertently, and in spite of her best misanthropic intentions, just as she had Vivien. She had wanted to create a bubble; a safe place where only she and Isabella would live. But the world kept squashing against the edges and busting through like some great hernia.

Lance, at least, knew how to conduct a relationship at arm's length. He would no more intrude on her privacy than he would allow her to invade his own. Except, perhaps, for that conversation on New Year's Day, when he had talked about her relationship with Jem. She had barely seen him since that day except in respect of the children. It was as if she had passed some unseen barrier by becoming involved with Jem and the world had changed ever so slightly. It made her a little sad, but she repressed the feeling immediately. After all, at least they got along now.

Jem, on the other hand, was a different matter. She still harboured an unreasonable resentment at his intrusion into her life; a life that she had intended to be so well-ordered and free of the emotional trauma that she saw as inevitable in a sexual relationship. And so Kate felt guilty that she was always secretly relieved when Jem had gone home and she was left alone once more, in her own world. Yet despite herself, she always looked forward to seeing him again after a couple of days. Such was the perversity of being alone.

Not that Kate perceived that she was lonely. An early spring had brought forth all manner of previously undiscovered plants in the garden, and she spent long hours identifying the herbaceous perennials from the weeds. As the weeks passed, the garden and the winding lanes in the valley beyond became verdant, lush, and intoxicating. It was glorious. She carried on with restoring and repairing the cottage, and she continued to paint.

Derry, true to his word, picked her up one morning in the little two-seater van that he used to carry his carpentry tools, and took her to a "Freeconomy" market in a field on the other side of Pencarra.

'Hey girl, just come and take a look,' he assured her, pushing his long sandy-coloured dreadlocks back from his face. He explained on the way how it worked: that nobody exchanged money, but rather traded goods or services.

'Put it like this,' he said, 'I could mend someone's gate, for example, or hang a door maybe, and they'd do something for me in return. Like, I dunno, give me food, usually; or home-brew, or a hand-knitted jumper. I even got a tattoo once! But I usually go for the food—I like the food!—I can sometimes go weeks without paying for vegetables. Not to mention the home-baked cakes. You got to love the cakes.'

'But, how do you decide? What something's worth, I mean,' Kate asked.

Derry shrugged. 'Mutual decision. Don't think it's ever been a problem. I know some other places invent a token system, an I.O.U. type-of-thing. But that's a bit too official for me. A bit too "promise to bear the holder" if you know what I mean. The community in Pencarra is small—very close-knit—and so's we just go on agreement.'

When Kate still looked sceptical, he added: 'Look, I know it doesn't work for everything, and could soon get out of hand on a larger scale. We'd end up back where we started. You know, like Animal Farm.' he turned to grin at her, before returning his eyes to the road. 'And we still need schools and healthcare and that. Still gotta pay the rent. I got my day job and pay my taxes like a good citizen. But I'm one of the lucky ones; I get to do something I enjoy and be creative too. There's too many are working *just* to get the money, and not getting too much of it either. This offers them, I dunno... a *way*. For me, it feels good to break free of the shackles once in a while; spread a little goodwill with the neighbours, like.'

'I can't imagine what I might trade,' Kate said with humility. It was a shocking revelation to her that she did not do or produce anything worthwhile; not unless her paintings counted, and she still wasn't convinced that they did.

'You'll think of something,' said Derry.

The field was alive with the bustle of trade and the smell of hot food. Derry was accosted several times with greetings and salutations from others, impeding their progress to where he intended to set up stall. Kate stood shyly by as he was grabbed in a succession of affectionate bear hugs. Derry spoke a strange, otherworld language when questioned on surf conditions.

'Crumbly, onshore, messy,' he said with a coded waggle of his hand, and 'might get better on the push,' was met with sage nods all round. Clearly he was something of an authority.

Finally, the stall was erected and they returned to the van to collect Derry's wares.

Kate was astonished when she saw the collection of wooden pots and goblets that he had crafted on a lathe from his own designs. She picked up one large yew bowl which had an asymmetric design whereby part of the bark had been left on, yet polished smooth.

'But...these are brilliant!' said Kate, turning her attention to a giant turned candlestick, with a hand-carved ivy-leaf design twisting around its length. 'Well *I'm* having this,' she laughed. 'Not quite sure how yet, but I'm having it! Derry, you could make a fortune selling these.'

'Not quite the point,' said Derry.

'But...are you not remotely tempted? I mean; the *money* you could get!'

'Yeah, maybe. But what for?'

'What *for*?' Kate stared at him, before foolishly remembering why they were there. Foolishly remembering her own reputed intentions. Talk about being tripped up at the first temptation.

'Of course,' she said. 'You don't *need* the money. You have everything you require.'

'Now you're getting it,' said Derry.

Kate wandered around the market with mixed feelings of admiration and inadequacy as she observed the variety of goods on offer. There were plants and cuttings, second-hand or handmade clothes, tools of every description, people cutting or braiding hair, cheeses, breads, and as Derry had promised, lots of cake. Homemade beer and wine was not only being traded but freely passed around and drunk; and not in throwaway plastic cups either, but in tasteful hand blown or recycled glasses. Kate was amazed at the unconditional trust; at the cooperation.

Later, as she minded the stall, she was still feeling conspicuous at her own lack of produce to trade when Derry returned from a foray and handed her one of several bottles of wine and a round of Cornish Camembert.

'On me,' he said, beaming. 'For helping out.' Kate took them gratefully and without protest. He was accompanied by a woman whom she recognised as his mother, Mrs Newson from the village shop, but this time Derry introduced her as Kerensa.

'Kerensa's got something to ask you,' he said.

And so it was that Kate found herself guaranteed a small hamper of local groceries in return for her own promise to repaint the shop's faded, hanging sign. Kate was thrilled at the simplicity, the ease with which the transaction had been negotiated, and furthermore, she felt an unprecedented sense of belonging; of being a part of the community.

As she shook hands and said goodbye to Kerensa, Derry passed his eyes over Kate's tunic top that she wore with her jeans. It was dark red and recognisably medieval in the cut, but incongruously made up from a patchwork of recycled materials. 'One of Vivien's?' he asked.

Kate nodded, thankful that she at least looked the part today.

'She'd normally be here; runs a clothes stall...' his voice trailed off.

Kate studied him intently as he averted his gaze across the field, and her heart went out to him. It occurred to her that it was a tragedy that Vivien did not—would not—love Derry. He was thoughtful and kind and creative. He was popular and sincere. And he had not mentioned Juliet, which showed tact.

'You know, faint heart ne'er won fair maiden,' she said.

'What's that?' said Derry.

'You have to fight for what you want.'

Derry looked at her for a moment before thoughtfully rubbing his formative beard and laughing. '*Faint heart never won fair maiden*...I like that. Yeah, I like that!'

'That is of course if you're serious. And you haven't just given up?'

Derry's expression became solemn. 'I'll bear it in mind.'

'On the other hand,' said Kate hastily, '*brave* heart gets innards torn out and fed to the dogs!'

He smiled again, wryly. 'I'll bear that in mind too...'

CHAPTER 30

Hangovers

D eviously, Kate had managed to come home that day with the coveted candlestick, by way of agreeing to paint a mural of mermaids on one of the walls at Lorelei—tenuously described as the only nightclub in Pencarra, and Derry's favourite haunt—thus guaranteeing him free entrance for the rest of the year. Derry had gasped in mock horror at his protégé's crafty three-way trade.

And surprisingly, she had had another decorating request from one of the villagers, following her 'debut' at Jem's kitchen party. Rosie, the toothy red-faced woman, married to Johnny, had dragged Kate to one side in the street and confided that her bedroom needed spicing up a little. Perhaps it required more of a boudoir effect? After a day of fantasising about a career in interior design, and notwithstanding her wasted efforts at The Net Loft, she conceded that her heart was not really in it. The more she thought about it, the more ludicrous a notion it seemed to go into someone else's home and tell them what colours and furnishings to use. Kate strongly felt that surroundings ought to be personal, and should evolve from the unique and eclectic pool of individual experience. This conviction was strongly propped up by the fact that she would rather stay at home and paint.

Once again Kate experienced the nagging thought that she was shirking. "Interior design" was rather a grand term for what was essentially a bit of decorating, not to mention basic hard labour. That paid hard cash. It was of course, lovely to potter around the cottage being 'creative'; charming to be painting murals and shop signs. But she had no long-term income and would have to, sooner or later, take responsibility.

And then she sold a painting.

She *sold* a painting.

Vivien had been insistent that Kate should display a few canvasses in Wreckers, and reluctant to appear amateurish, Kate had offered a few of her finished works. As the weeks went by without a sale or even any particular signs of interest, Kate resigned herself to the fact that she had not only deluded herself as to her abilities, but was now firmly and publicly exposed as a fake.

Yet Vivien had remained unconcerned and positive. 'The tourists always buy this sort of thing,' she had said without any irony or condescension. 'You've missed the Christmas influx, but once things pick up again I'm sure all of these will go.' Kate did not feel so confident.

But then, one morning in the middle of March, she had a call from Vivien to announce that a painting had indeed been purchased, and not even by a tourist but by someone from the village itself.

'It wasn't you?' asked Kate suspiciously, and trying to contain her excitement. 'Or Jem, trying to do me a favour?' Although on reflection, she doubted that Jem would be that imaginative. But no, Vivien claimed that it had been bought by a villager, a mother of four who claimed that it was 'lovely'. It was the highest accolade as far as Kate was concerned. No passing tourist, high on the whole Cornish experience; no pretentious art critic; but an ordinary person, had bought her painting. They had actually parted with hard-earned money for her work. Kate was positively brimming with joy.

She was still dancing and skipping around the cottage when Isabella came home from school, and even Izzy's incredulity gave way to a sort of pride as she slowly accepted that perhaps her mother might be a *real* artist after all. They ordered a take-away curry that night; not only to celebrate, but also because Kate had spent the afternoon in a stupor of excitement, unable to do anything remotely useful or constructive such as provide a meal. Alarmingly, she was too nervous even to paint very well, so unbalanced was her equanimity, but this would surely pass. In her mind's eye, she was already selling bigger and better canvasses. Blue Wave would welcome her with open arms; her reputation and fame would spread; and by next year, who knew? She might even be holding exhibitions? And then the thought came. A graceful, white, ocean-liner of a thought came looming from the horizon; and yes, she dared to think it.

The Tate, St. Ives.

She would exhibit at the Tate to rapturous reviews and become universally acknowledged as the brightest new talent in the South-West. She would join the ranks of Hepworth, Nicholson, Heron and Lanyon. The Cornish tourist board would struggle to cope with the hordes that travelled to see the landscapes that she interpreted, and marvel at the inspiration that had led to such a profound talent for expression.

'So, how much did you get for it?' Isabella asked.

'Seventy-five pounds,' replied Kate, with eyes shining.

'Seventy-five pounds?' Isabella's voice was once more disbelieving. 'Is that *all*?'

Kate was unperturbed. 'Oh, you just don't understand Isabella. It's extremely hard to make a living from Fine Art. To sell anything at all is absolutely amazing. And of course it was one of my early attempts, so I can only improve. And if I sell some more, and start to make a name for myself, then, *who knows*?'

'What?' said Isabella, unconvinced, 'who knows what?'

'Well, who knows how much money I will be able to command in a few years from now?' Kate said grandly.

Jem was invited over for the Indian take-away supper; a rare treat these days since the little restaurant in the village charged prices even higher than those of London, such was its rarity; and tourists craving a curry fix ensured a constant demand. Jem was pleased to find Kate in high spirits, and offered encouragement both in words, and in large, chilled, celebratory glasses of cheap champagne. Kate felt so exhilarated that she almost allowed him to stay the night.

In the morning, Kate felt terrible. She did a quick, reflexive notch-up of how many bottles they had opened the night before and groaned. She managed to appear lucid and in control as she helped Isabella prepare for school. She was just about able to converse coherently with Angie at the school gates. But by the time she returned to the cottage, her energy rapidly dissipated. She felt distant, as though her entire being were actually in some tiny, scrunched-up faraway place, and that she was operating her body only by some integral remote backup system. She wondered if she might be dead?

Was this what it felt like? She had passed amongst people that morning like some overly-cheerful spectre; unaware of its condition and puzzled at the looks of incomprehension that it met with. Perhaps she had been babbling; or worse, slurring. The remote control system was apparently not fully operative. She sank onto one of the kitchen chairs and stared at the debris on the table. Shamefully, she found herself gorging hungrily and mindlessly with her fingers on some cold Bombay aloo.

Bombay aloo that had been left out all night and uncovered in its little aluminium carton...

Disgusted with herself, she began to gingerly clear up the mess, almost retching at the smell from an unfinished glass of wine, the contents of which she tipped hastily into the sink. Although, it was not without *some* regret that she forced herself to scrape the remains of the curry into the bin. Soon the kitchen was respectably clean again; but Kate did not feel purged, as she had hoped. What was the point of it all, she wondered? Suddenly seventy-five pounds appeared to be exactly what it was.

Very little.

They had probably spent the bulk of that amount last night just on food and wine, in the light of which her achievement did not seem so very great after all. She pondered awhile on the fact that all occasions in life nowadays were deemed worthy of instant gratification and luxurious self-indulgence. It was as if people did not know what else to do with themselves. Gluttony, excess and self-reward were the norm.

'Now, Kate,' she admonished herself out loud, 'you know you enjoyed yourself at the time, so stop being such a drip.' She could not deny that in more high-spirited mood she would embrace the joys of a heaving table of good food and wine; her attitude was distinctly "eat drink and be merry, for tomorrow we die". So she would not allow herself to feel superior; she didn't deserve to. Not having abused her liver and digestive system so wantonly the night before. Kate was still in self-imposed purgatory, and that left no place for redeeming intellectual philosophy. Instead, she resolved to feel bad about herself all day.

There was a call that night from Juliet. Kate did not mention the sold painting, but decided rather that she would casually slip it into a passing conversation at a later date, as if she did that sort of thing all the time. Not that Juliet gave her the opportunity, anyway.

'Right, well it's definitely over with Parker,' she announced flippantly. 'It turns out he fancies someone else anyway. Some tart he met on an assignment, so that's that then. Anyway I'm trying to sell my tickets for the Asia-Pacific trip...'

'It's off?' Kate interrupted. 'You won't *go* now?'

'By myself? Nah. I thought about it. You know—it might present some interesting opportunities and all that; but I'm really not into the whole soul-searching routine. I need someone to get pissed with.'

'Perhaps Parker will buy your tickets from you? He might go with his new—er, tart?' Kate ventured an attempt at laid-back cynicism.

'You're joking!' Juliet yelled down the phone. 'Who do you think paid for all of them in the first place? If he wasn't going to part with the cash then, do you think he will now? *Bastard.*'

'Oh Juliet,' said Kate gently. 'I'm so sorry, I really am. Not just about the trip, but about Parker too. It's such a shame that you've fallen out.'

'Fallen out?' Juliet asked, confused. 'Oh, we haven't fallen out, silly, we're still mates.'

Kate gave up. She did not understand modern relationships. But then, she did not understand relationships full stop.

'Anyway, since the big trip is all off now,' Juliet continued back on track, 'we thought we might come down and see you again soon. It wasn't too bad really, at Christmas, we quite enjoyed it. Well, apart from all the *stuff*. But we'll wait until the weather's better and all the gorgeous surf dudes are hanging out. What do you think Kate? Got your bikini ready?'

Kate, who was still immersed in self-chastisement, thought that she most certainly did not have her bikini ready, let alone her winter-fed, alcohol bloated body. And whom did Juliet mean by "we" anyway?

'Well, Parker, of course,' said Juliet impatiently. 'Who do you think I meant? Keep up Kate!'

And so it was decided. They would come around midsummer, before all the school holiday crowds. Kate felt utterly resigned. The world just would not go away. And neither, it seemed, would its recently rejected "bastard" boyfriends.

CHAPTER 31

Revelations

Sometimes you knew what it meant to have your bristles stand on end. Sometimes you felt, long before you acknowledged the reason to yourself, a chill in your heart, or a shadow passing over your soul. It was the truth. The truth about to be revealed, yet too soon to be universally accepted. It was the truth getting set to gnaw its way into your consciousness regardless of your own feelings and prejudices. Kate looked distinctly uncomfortable. Vivien leant a little closer.

Kate wasn't sure that she wanted to hear any more. It had been bad enough seeing Lance earlier in the evening without having her tranquillity disturbed even further. His physical guise when she had dropped Isabella off for the evening at Tremeneghy had already put her in a curious state of unease... And so it was exceptionally unnerving to have all one's preconceptions compounded and exposed in just one evening.

'Of course he didn't shag her!' Vivien hissed, 'I mean this is Lance we're talking about! And *Jenifer Trewin*, for goodness' sake. You *have* met her? Be serious Kate, Lance wouldn't go near her in a million years!'

If nothing else convinced Kate, it was the use of the term "shag"—so untypical of Vivien—that persuaded her to take the matter seriously.

It was a gloriously sunny evening, and Kate had gone with Vivien to Captain Carter's for a drink. The weather was now warm enough for tables and chairs to be placed outside on the cobbled harbour, and there was, apart from the recently departed presence of Jenifer Trewin and her friends, a warm and convivial atmosphere amongst the mixed gathering collected there. The two women drank chilled wine and nibbled from a plate of garlicky olives. Only their conversation was incongruous with the pleasant surroundings.

Vivien continued. 'Don't get involved with Jenifer Trewin; she's bad news. And she treated Lance appallingly. She lied about him in a horrible and vicious way. Lance was never very good at defending himself, and sort of let her get away with it. It makes me so mad even now just thinking about it.'

'What exactly happened?' Kate asked, trying to remember the scenario between Jenifer and Lance as described to her by Jem. She couldn't remember exactly how he had worded it. But she did remember the incident at Jem's Christmas party, when Jenifer had covertly, but deliberately thrown her drink at Lance. At the time she had thought that he deserved it.

'Lance originally took on all responsibility for Finn,' Vivien said, 'I mean when Leah left. I was far less involved at that point, and Lance did all the school runs, befriended the mothers, invited them over so that the children could play; you know the sort of thing. Anyway, Jenifer became friendlier than most, if you know what I mean?'

Kate remembered now the relationship that Jem had described. Again she felt peculiarly uncomfortable. She remembered that according to Jem, Lance had behaved despicably.

'It's not as if Finn and her boy even got on that well,' continued Vivien, 'but Jenifer was so out to get Lance that she, shall we say, *encouraged* their friendship just so that she could spend time hanging around him. But of course Lance would never be interested in someone like her. I mean, I know that Leah is shallow, but by comparison even she has redeeming qualities—and besdes, that was a one-off; special circumstances. When Jenifer realised that all her attempts to seduce Lance had failed, she told everyone that he had, you know, *used* her. I think that she had misled so many people about the nature of the relationship that she couldn't suddenly change her story. And she was so determined that no one else would get him if she couldn't, that she set about ruining his name.'

The heaviness finally set to rest upon Kate's heart. *Of course* Jenifer was not to be trusted. She had divulged rumours about Lance on their very first meeting. *Of course* the jealousy had been apparent. Only she, Kate, had been blind to the obvious intent because of her previous encounter, and argument, with Lance. But what about Jem? He was the one—she was sure she remembered—who had told her about Lance's misbehaviour. Surely Jem couldn't have got it so wrong? Even given Jenifer's spiteful nature and Lance's apparent unwillingness to defend himself, Jem was Lance's friend. Surely he knew the truth and indeed must have discussed it with Lance? It was an uneasy thought.

'Anyway,' Vivien said with a look of disgust on her face. 'She undermined Lance's reputation. Not that he loses sleep about that; but the worst thing was that it affected Finn. There was a lot of nastiness in the playground. You know the sort of thing; Finn getting picked on for his father's supposed misdemeanours. There was even a fight. Finn came home with cuts and a black eye.

Again Kate remembered Jem saying something similar and to the same effect, but there had been nothing in what he had said to suggest that Lance had not deserved the disapprobation. Her discomfort increased. If what Vivien said was true (and there was no reason to suspect otherwise, unless of course Vivien herself had been duped), then Lance had been done an injustice. Perhaps not the greatest of injustices; not one that could not be risen above or weathered; but enough of an injustice to have swayed Kate's opinion of him, and who knows how many others? She felt angry, not so much at Jenifer Trewin, but at herself, for being so easily influenced.

'Poor Lance,' she said quietly.

'Oh Lance couldn't care less,' Vivien surprised Kate. 'At least, as I said, about his own reputation. No, it was the effect on Finn that really cut him up. It was bad enough with him being the son of a so-called celebrity. Some of the other children were already half-envious and half-willing to bring him down. After Jenifer put the knife in, he became ostracised. Still is, to some extent. He's only really got the two loyal friends; well, three since your Isabella arrived in town. It just makes me so mad; how anyone can be so vindictive towards a child.'

'I don't suppose she ever meant to get at Finn,' said Kate thoughtfully. 'Lance was her target. But she's too stupid and insensitive to understand the impact on the children.'

'Yeah, well. *Bitch,*' said Vivien conclusively.

When Kate arrived home later that night, she had still not shaken off the feeling of guilt at her own collusion in maintaining Lance's tainted reputation; for at the time, she had been triumphant at Jem's revelations. And she was cross with Jem too, although she supposed that he could have acted under a misapprehension. Surely he deserved the benefit of the doubt?

That night, Kate's sleep was more fitful than ever. Even as she struggled on with *Le Morte D'Arthur*—which it turned out, *was* a difficult read, but since she had borrowed it from *Lance*, was determined to get to grips with—she found her mind returning to her apparent lack of judgement. Kate had always considered herself a fair person. *She* wasn't one to condemn or criticise. So why did she feel so terrible right now? Her conscience would not let her sleep. She felt like calling Lance right there and then to put things right. Except that she did not have the slightest clue as to how to go about it. She laid awake rehearsing conversations in her mind. She practised casual meetings and scenarios whereby she could let it be known, that *she* at least, understood his quandary. But as the night wore on, it became increasingly difficult to imagine ever converting her error. The Lance that she had known, or at least, was starting to know, had disappeared.

When she imagined her reconciliatory conversations in her mind's eye, she was ever conscious that the image of him that she pictured no longer existed—was in fact, defunct. For when she had taken Isabella earlier that evening to Tremeneghy, she had been taken aback. Lance's behaviour had been uncharacteristically amiable—he had actively encouraged that Vivien and Kate should go out; and positively insisted that he would look after the children, and not hide in his study whilst Lillian attended on duty—but it wasn't that. It was the unfamiliar face that had greeted her at the door. For a split second, she thought that it must be a cousin, or perhaps the other brother. But then she recognised the green eyes and the slightly crooked teeth and saw Lance. Only Lance as a larger version of his son.

He had had his hair cut.

Chapter 32

On the Beach

'I mean, I know it's a simple, everyday thing to do,' Kate said to Vivien as they tramped the path down to the beach. Isabella and Finn were already at the bottom and running across the sand. 'After all, he's only had his hair cut! It's just that...well, he looks so *different*.'

'I know,' said Vivien flippantly. 'It's always a shock when Lance gets a haircut. It's strange to see him looking so neat and tidy. I think he feels he owes it to the University or something; to appear professional. But it's the same thing every year. He gets his hair cut in the spring and then forgets about it for the rest of the year. It grows long and tangled and messy, but *he* thinks that he's only just had it done!'

So, thought Kate. That explained a lot. Not so much laid-back surfer-dude, but more nutty professor. It started to make sense. Yet Kate could not shake off the feeling of annoyance. True, he was still handsome in a bookish sort of way, but inexplicably, she did not like the new shorn Lance. There was no reason why she should not. She told herself that it made no difference; he was still irritating; still unfathomable. Yet she remained unreasonably bothered.

Vivien had surprised Kate by showing up carrying a large, pale blue surfboard, and surprised her even more by the deftness with which she carried the cumbersome thing. They stood aside momentarily to make way for a family of tourists who panted their way up the steep cliff path in the hot April sun. They bade cheerful, breathless salutations as they passed, expressing delight at such lucky Easter weather. Kate took a minute to survey the view of Porthledden Beach. Sunlight glittered on the azure sea and in the distance, sets of perfect waves lined up to greet the offshore breeze. Wild flowers drifted gently in the breeze amongst cliff-top grasses. A tall handsome figure in a wetsuit and carrying a surfboard turned and waved to her, before heading on towards the water. She took in the shock of brown curls and the easy grin and wondered if Jem had lied to her.

The thought was unbidden, errant; an intruder. Appalled, she quickly buried it.

Kate spent the day on the beach sketching with watercolours. It was quite an achievement since she still felt diffident about showing her work in public. And yet it seemed that each and every passer-by could not resist peering over her shoulder, and with no thought given to the interruption, feel compelled to make comment.

'Oh, you're *so* clever!'

'I wish *I* could draw like that!'

'I used to paint, but now I don't think I could create anything more wonderful than my child...'

'Oh so you're an artist are you? I *suppose* it's a diversion of sorts...'

Kate smiled and nodded appropriately, but secretly wished that she were invisible.

As the day wore on, the sea filled up with more and more familiar-faced surfers and bathers. Derry and Gabe, more usually to be found standing on the cliff top with eyes narrowed to the horizon—checking, always checking—had been *out back* for hours now, and so Kate dryly acknowledged that on this particular day, the surf was—finally—'pumping'. Jem and Finn had also long since all but disappeared into the waves, and even Vivien had forsaken her frocks for a wetsuit.

By the afternoon, Salima and Lance were also immersed in the ocean. Kate also recognised Finn's two friends from school on bodyboards. The tide was on the turn now, and the shallow, far-travelling surf spat them right up onto the beach. They screeched with insane laughter as the sand grazed their elbows and knees.

Only Isabella sulked on the land. Hidden behind sunglasses, she ostensibly read a magazine and pretended not to care. Kate felt a pang of guilt, but was resolute. It was *so* dangerous, after all. All the same, she herself couldn't help but feel like an old fuddy-duddy, as more and more faces that she recognised plunged into the waves and became barely recognisable specks of action in the far distance.

Kate had to admit to a certain surprise at Jem's capacity for the sport. There was a podginess around his belly that suggested there might be a touch of the landlubber about him. She could easily picture him driving fast cars, or playing complicated computer games; the toys of the urbanite. Never would she have imagined him to be accomplished in such a physical activity. But as she recognised Vivien casually ride a wave to its destination, she realised that this was in their blood. Surfing had been an integral part of all their lives since childhood, and as such, was commonplace. For some reason, Kate was reminded of the time when, as a schoolgirl, she had suffered the humiliation of being the only girl at the school disco in a long frilly skirt, while all her friends, normally so innocent and proper in uniform, wore micro-minis.

She became aware of sniggers behind her. Turning around Kate saw that Jenifer Trewin and the cronies had surreptitiously gathered behind to look at what she was doing, and were suppressing laughs behind cupped hands. Discovered, they sprinted off quickly towards the surf, not bothering to hide their screeching mirth any longer, and kicking sand over her work in the process. Kate watched as Jenifer—not for her a wetsuit, but an optimistically white crocheted bikini—spilled around at the water's edge, clutching her stomach in mock hysteria. Kate was mortified. Jenifer was actually rolling around the floor—well, the sand—laughing.

As Vivien had put it—*bitch*.

At that moment she noticed Lance emerge from the sea. He carefully avoided and ignored the cackling trio and made his way solemnly up the beach with his board to where he had left a towel on the wall by the surf school. As Kate watched him, she observed that he did not wear the typical, slightly gormless, but happy grin of the just-stoked surfer. There was, as ever, a touch of the melancholy about Lance; and Kate, with sudden clarity, realised that it was this quality that had led her to believe him arrogant.

She thought back to that day when they had first met, and struggled to remember the conversation. She had rashly suggested that they help each other with childcare, and Kate blushed now to recall her foolishness. And *good grief*, she had even tried to ply him with alcohol! Yet rather than politely decline, Lance had badly overreacted. He had suggested that she was making a move on him; using the excuse of the children as a means of ingratiation. She still felt a pang of anger at the injustice of his interpretation, but understood now that Lance's experience with Jenifer, and the consequent condemnation of all the other mothers in the village, would have made him suspicious and oversensitive. Angry, even. He had become a victim of his own attractiveness and whilst not actually curtailing Finn's friendships, had probably vowed never to get involved with any of the mothers at the school ever again. And then along had come Kate with her brazenly inappropriate suggestions after only mere minutes of acquaintance! There was still an element of conceit to his behaviour, but she began to understand that he had been wounded by experience.

337

Kate suddenly became aware that she had been gazing unconsciously at the subject of her contemplation, and that Lance was now fixedly returning her stare as he towelled himself dry further along the beach. His look was abstracted and unfocused, as though he might even be looking straight through her to something just beyond. She ought to look away, but instead felt curious to see what he would do.

He was still looking. He had stripped his wetsuit to the waist, and his arms and hands moved busily about his body with the towel, then up to his head to dab unconvincingly at his hair—that damned haircut! It annoyed her so! Why didn't he look away? More seconds passed, and Kate's heart beat a wild rhythm. And then suddenly, inexplicably, it was all right. It was as if they each knew they had both exceeded the acceptable respectful boundaries, and so might as well stay awhile. It was a mutual agreement for each to study the other at leisure without the underlying connotations that society decreed. She could almost believe that he had known that she was thinking about him and was responding; confirming; reassuring.

'What are you staring at?' demanded Isabella brusquely—and it was gone. In the same moment that she had averted her eyes to her daughter, Lance had turned to pick up his surfboard and walk away from the beach in the opposite direction to where Kate sat.

Later on, back at Dolphin Cottage, she wondered if she had imagined the whole thing. After all, Lance had at first appeared unfocused. Or what if he had noticed her staring at him and had merely been trying to ascertain why? And so Kate's initial instinct slowly turned to paranoia. She felt strangely anxious and her mood was snappish. It didn't help that Jem, who had returned home to the cottage with them, was in exceptionally good humour, and wittered senselessly about everything and anything.

338

There was another letter from Marsha. Kate sighed as she scanned the urgent jerky handwriting, which had certain words underlined for emphasis. And so it was that Kate learnt that she <u>must</u> contact Marsha <u>please,</u> and that she really needed to learn to <u>forgive,</u> and not be so very <u>petty.</u>

'Letter from a friend?' Jem had come up behind her and was casually reading the letter over her shoulder. 'Invite her down! You don't seem to have much contact with your friends in London, Kate. Invite them all down and we can have another party!'

'*We?*' said Kate moodily. 'What do you mean "we"?'

Jem didn't seem to notice and carried on. 'Yeah, get them all down. Your sister too, she was a good laugh. Make a change from the usual motley crew. Which reminds me, did you see The Professor get wiped out earlier? Man, it was hilarious; he really pearled it! Bet he's still coughing up sea water!'

'I thought Lance was your friend?' Kate said testily, and recalled how she had once asked the same question of Lance about Jem.

'Well, yeah, he is, but it was just so funny! You know— because he's usually so bloody perfect all the time.'

'Is he? I wouldn't have said so. What are you doing anyway?'

Jem was opening, and not shutting, cupboard doors. 'Oh, just looking for some wine. I fancy getting sloshed. Perfect end to a great day.'

'You know I keep my wine in the pantry,' said Kate.

'Yeah, I've looked,' said Jem vaguely; his back to her; his eyes scanning the contents of her shelves. 'It's all gone.'

Kate stormed from the kitchen to the little pantry rooms at the back of the cottage. Jem was right. He had indeed drunk her dry. And everywhere there were bottles; great stinking piles of bottles. A dozen or so had been washed and placed with great intention into cardboard boxes, ready for recycling;

but the vast majority were furtively stashed at the back of one of the pantry cupboards. And then, as if seeing with fresh eyes, she noticed bottles on the windowsills, and littering the sides of the little sink where she washed her brushes. Glaring into the conservatory she saw an empty vodka bottle had been casually slung on the floor and now rested on its side against one of her unfinished paintings. When had he even *been* drinking in there?

Kate was suddenly furious. She marched back into the kitchen. 'I think we need to go to the bottle bank.'

'Oh, so it's "we" again now is it?' said Jem with sarcasm. 'Ok, so it's *your* wine, but *we* have to go to the bottle bank.'

Kate's anger was given free rein. 'Why does there have to be so much drinking anyway?' she said, barely hiding the contempt in her voice. 'You think it's the answer to everything; the only thing worth doing! We never do anything without having to get drunk! We never have sex without being drunk! Have you *ever* had sex without being drunk, Jem?'

Jem's omnipresent smile finally faded. 'You've never complained,' he muttered resentfully.

'Well I'm complaining now!' Kate yelled, regardless of Izzy's presence upstairs. She couldn't quite believe the extent of her anger, and did a quick mental check to make sure that she wasn't premenstrual—no, not that. Jem looked back at her quizzically. He didn't seem to know what he had done wrong or what he should do.

He tried again. 'Look, you're quite obviously in a bad mood,' he said gently. 'I will take the bottles to the bank tomorrow, I promise. Let's forget cooking, and go out to eat. We can go to Captain Carter's...'

'No, *I* can't,' snapped Kate.

'Why not?'

'Because,' Kate paused for emphasis, 'I have an eleven-year-old daughter! You want me to drag *her* to the pub now!'

'Fuck's sake Kate, it's only Captain Carter's! You know they cater for families. Or we can sit outside with her, it's a warm enough night! You're being deliberately obstructive.'

He was right.

'Look,' she said, trying to sound calm. 'It's true; I really am in a foul mood. Perhaps we should just forget it for tonight.'

There was a pause while Jem, normally so impervious, studied her intently.

'Just tonight?' he asked in a low voice.

CHAPTER 33

Box Hill

L ove.
   1. An intense feeling of deep affection or fondness for a person or thing; great liking.
   2. Sexual passion.
   3. Sexual relations.

...The list went on. Her dictionary described the varying comprehensions and permutations of the word, but when Kate applied the fundaments to her feelings for Jem, it did not bode well. Yes, they had had sexual relations; but where was the passion? The intensity? Where, even, the deep affection?

Kate was standing at the lookout spot on top of the cliffs which was more usually reserved for Derry, Gabe, and the other hardcore surfers. It was from here that the full grandeur of Porthledden Beach could be most appreciated. The day had been sublimely hot, and now the setting sun painted the sky in beautiful coral and baby blue, with only the tiniest strokes of amethyst cloud upon the horizon. The cliffs were lined with bursts of pink sea thrift and the pungent aroma of wild thyme permeated the air. The sea was tranquil, resting. No breeze disturbed the marram grass, intensifying the exhaustive quality of the day's heat.

Kate wondered if it was time she called Izzy up from the shore, where she frolicked at the water's edge with some school friends. (Kate had been informed in no uncertain terms that *all* Cornish children Izzy's age were allowed out by

342

themselves, and that she should keep a firm distance). It was a school night, but the evening was so beautiful, that Kate decided a little longer wouldn't hurt. If only she could stop her mind from constantly replaying the events of last night. Each time she recalled her conversation with Jem, she looked for a change, a nuance that might have rendered her comment innocuous.

'*Just tonight?*' Jem had said.

It would have been so easy to say, "of course not, silly!" She could have given him a hug and said she'd call tomorrow. But instead she had opened the door to the reality of their relationship and slung the whole heavy book of doubt on it.

'I don't know,' she had said.

Jem had looked at her with a mixed expression of hurt, anger and bewilderment. Then, saying nothing more, he had left. It was an act so out of character that Kate felt equally stunned, as though her accusations and criticisms had wounded herself as much as him. She had not heard from him all day, and each time she had gone to pick up the phone to call him herself, something had stopped her.

She could have pleaded a bad mood. She could have blamed, inaccurately, hormones; a headache; any number of other worries. All she had to do was say sorry. Kate had never had a problem with apologising. If ever she misbehaved, or spoke out of turn, she liked to think that she was humble enough to admit fault. Of course she was sorry if she had hurt Jem's feelings, and apologising was naturally the thing to do in order to put things right. It was just a tiff. Jem would surely want to make up, and it would not take much effort for them to get back on track, to resume their relationship. But then again, if she apologised, they would get back on track, and resume their relationship...

343

Making up with Jem would imply that she wanted things to continue; would confirm that she cared for, wanted, and *loved* him.

As she had said, she just didn't know.

How had she got into this mess in the first place? Why had she become involved with Jem at all? She certainly hadn't fallen in love with him that was for sure, at least not in the way that she had fallen for Miles. It was odd that, despite their subsequent history, the memory of her first meeting with Miles was still a precious thing. It was as if they had, for a short period of time, been an altogether different couple; who would forever be detached from, and untouched by the calamity that was the rest of their relationship.

Kate had just started the second year of her Fine Art BA course at Wimbledon. Lauren and Marsha, old school friends, had invited her to a picnic on Box Hill. Thinking of the panoramic skies and incredible views of Dorking and the Mole Valley, Kate had immediately sensed a sketching opportunity. She invited Stevie, a theatre design student who shared accommodation with Kate and four other students in a large, rambling, and ill-converted house in Tooting.

They met Marsha and Lauren at Box Hill and Westhumble Station; not the best plan as it turned out, since it meant climbing *up* the steep incline from the valley to the top of the hill. They eventually crawled, flushed and panting, over the top of the escarpment, bemoaning the fact that they had all become *so* unfit since leaving school, and declaring the hill to be practically a bloody cliff-face. Breathing difficulties aside, some lit cigarettes as they admired the view. They walked a little and then laid down their blanket. They tore bread with their hands and shared a blunt palette knife to cut camembert and brie. Juicy ripe tomatoes were eaten whole, and strawberries washed down with two bottles of cheap sparkling wine.

344

Stevie seemed to hit it off immediately with Lauren and Marsha, and was at his rudest, campest best. Kate often wondered why Stevie had taken up with herself as his chosen buddy at the house. Without being, she hoped, a complete prig, she was however, introspective and serious. When the other housemates were about she would join in the banter and teasing with the best of them, and Stevie naturally was in his element. But when they were alone together, he seemed forced to revert to a quieter, more reflective, yet uncomfortable version of himself. He was used to loud, effusive characters in the bars and clubs that he frequented in and around Earl's Court. He was, it felt, somewhat suspicious of Kate's honesty. Often, he would assume that Kate was joking when in fact she was being perfectly serious. She would catch him looking curiously at her sometimes, as if he couldn't quite believe she was for real. And once, at college, she had overheard him remark, in that good-natured mock-bitch way, that he called her Snow White, because she was so morally perfect, and virginally innocent. Kate had been a little hurt, and had asked him later why he hung out with her at all.

'Because you're beautiful, darling,' had been his reply.

It had been a perfect day on Box Hill. Sunny and warm with a slight breeze in the air and the clouds gliding gently by in a deep blue sky. It was the sort of day that made childhood memories. Some days you knew you would always remember; almost as if you were seeing yourself now from deep in the future; revisiting as you enacted as yet unknown events. It was beyond déjà vu.

They attempted a game of scrabble, but being on an incline, the pieces kept sliding off the plane of the board. For some reason, this was deemed incredibly funny, and somehow *ironic*. Playing scrabble on Box Hill was *so* going to be the new craze. They grinned and giggled like children, although they

345

were, of course, insanely witty and profoundly intelligent. It was a wonderful feeling to be nineteen years old.

They had no comprehension of how swiftly youth, beauty and freedom would pass into history. At that time, anything was possible, and they themselves, just brimming with unlimited potential. Of course, they were idling the day away *now*—Kate had not once produced her sketchbook from her rucksack—but as Stevie reasoned, they deserved—no, were *entitled*—to their day in the sun, because they were the artists and writers and philosophers of their age. Let lesser mortals work in banks and law firms and insurance companies; in pubs and bookies and estate agents. They were to be the great people of the planet; the ones destined to forge future society and culture. It was an absolute requirement that they should endure halcyon days in order to feed their creativity and nurture their burgeoning intellects.

In time, they packed up and went for a walk. They stumbled upon a pub near a wooded car park for the more sensible visitors who drove to the top of the hill. It looked pleasant enough, and not withstanding their natural student imperative to drink at the drop of a hat, they were reluctant to end what had been a glorious day and head back to the inner city. Fatefully, they did not ingest the implication of the presence of several large motorbikes propped up in the surrounding area.

Once inside, it was too late. To have turned and walked out again would have been an act of the most mortifying, shameful cowardice. The smell hit them in the face like another climate: beer, crisps, leather and body odour. Rock music played from a jukebox, but was almost drowned out by the raucous and animated conversation of the crowd. Through thick clouds of smoke, it appeared that every other person in the poky bar was a leather-clad biker. Several of them stopped talking and turned to look at the newcomers at the door in unison. Stevie gulped; he hoped, inaudibly. The foursome stood, momentarily paralysed in the doorway, half-expecting, half-hoping, to be told in no uncertain terms, to clear off. They found themselves being unscrupulously eyed up.

Suddenly Stevie's vintage goth-chic look; the skinny black drainpipes and shirt; the lopsided haircut—black, streaked with pink—the thick kohl eyeliner; normally all gone unnoticed, now seemed to shout for attention. And then there were those red leather pixie boots that had seemed like such a good idea that morning. Even the girls, in their individual trademark clothes seemed out of place. Marsha might have been conventional enough in grey cords, tank top and shirt, but the many ornamental clips in the shape of butterflies sparkling from her afro did much to give the game away. Similarly, Lauren might have got away with it in her long droopy hippy-dress supplemented by beads and bangles, but she was carrying a couple of books for heaven's sake! Kate had not noticed her carrying any books all day! It was as if she had picked up a prop by the door. Kate herself had gone casual for the day in an electric blue fifties cocktail dress, tempered as usual with her thick black biker boots; which might have been a godsend, except that they were not real biker boots, but wholly impractical *fashion* biker boots, and as such, virtually an insult. They may as well have walked in with a banner saying: *We are students, kill us now.*

Kate's self-preservation skills kicked in. It was vital not to appear remotely intimidated. Besides, they were just men in leather jackets, after all. It was then she noticed that in fact, some of them were women, but had gone to great lengths to belie their gender. She squared her shoulders and strode with apparent confidence to the bar. Thankfully, Marsha shuffled along behind her, whilst Lauren and Stevie dived into a free table booth, which was thankfully close enough to the door should they be forced to a sudden, improvised run-for-it.

At the precise moment that Kate ordered the drinks, most of the attention that had been on them immediately dropped away, as the other occupants of the bar appeared to relax and resume conversation as before. It felt as though they had passed some sort of secret test. Gratefully, drinks in hand, Kate and Marsha joined the others at the table.

'Oh my God!' Stevie managed to screech in a whisper. 'This is *so* thrilling! This is just like a fantasy I had at fourteen!'

'Shh!' protested Kate. 'Please, just try and act natural!'

'I *am,*' replied Stevie, with a glare. 'I mean, just look at that one over there. With the dark curls and the funny necktie. Absolutely gorgeous!' Kate refused to look, but Marsha and Lauren instinctively craned their necks to see whom Stevie meant.

'Yeah, I see what you mean,' said Marsha. 'Very nice; not so tattooed or grimy as the others.'

Lauren shrugged: 'Does nothing for me,' she said sullenly. But her gaze returned, in appraisal, to the man all the same.

'I can't believe I didn't do any sketches,' said Kate, ignoring them. 'Call myself an artist? Too busy having fun, you see. I am doomed to die in poverty, my talent unfulfilled. Might as well start on the absinthe straight away!'

'They keep looking at us!' hissed Stevie. 'Oh well, at least if I die, I'll die happy...'

'Can we just go?' Lauren whispered back. She was visibly nervous. Her body language gave it away, as she sat hunched over her drink, and put her hand over her eyes as she spoke.

'Perhaps we should,' agreed Marsha with a worried expression. 'They do keep looking at us.'

'Probably because we, or rather you lot, keep looking at *them!*' said Kate, getting annoyed.

'Oh frickin' crapwiddle, one of them's coming over!' came Stevie's repressed squeal. 'What *is* it? It's like...it's like...a *monster!*' and his lips curled in genuine horror.

It occurred to Kate that the creature approaching their table with a fuck-off look in its eye had once perhaps been someone's adored baby girl. In the thirty odd years that had passed since then, any allusion to femininity had been stripped away, beefed up, and concealed by multiple piercings and patchy, inexpert tattoos. Underneath an outsized leather jacket was a sagging man's vest, which showed the woman's complete and utter denial about the existence of her large and equally sagging breasts. All this was topped off with badly dyed—and presumably self-imposed—purple cropped hair.

She hovered dangerously at their table, eyeing the four of them up through suspicious narrowed eyes, like a wild animal sniffing the air for its enemies. Then she leaned drunkenly forward and demanded in Kate's ear,"Ere, *geh-ohl!*', her south London accent refusing to articulate the word 'girl'. 'Gotta fag, *geh-ohl?*' and then she turned and looked at Stevie so menacingly that it took Kate a second or two to fully understand her meaning.

'Er, no, sorry,' stammered Kate, 'I'm afraid I don't smoke...'

'*Afraid?*' The Creature mocked, whilst trying to balance upright again, 'I bet you fucking are. Tell you what, since you ain't got no fags, you'd better buy me a drink instead. *Awright?*'

Incredibly, and to her horror, Kate found herself unable to think of anything except correcting the use of a double negative. Her mind was torn between constructing a witty riposte to this effect, and simultaneously pondering the wisdom of doing so. If she were a braver soul, she knew that she should verbally crush this monstrous person like a slug underfoot. But the very image of things being crushed stopped her in her tracks.

'Did you 'ear me?' the drunken woman shouted, 'you owe me a fucking drink!'

She looked around for approval from her companions. Some of them laughed, knowingly, but to Kate's surprise most of the bikers looked away uncomfortably, distancing themselves from the behaviour of their loudmouthed representative.

It was then that Miles had strolled, devastatingly, into Kate's life. With a lazy, laid back gait, the biker in the necktie posed his lean frame confidently next to the creature, and after a slow drag on his cigarette, presented her with his own full pint of beer.

'Here you go, Charmaine,' he said pleasantly. 'Take this.'

While Kate blinked incredulously at the likelihood that this brutish woman should have such a flowery name, Charmaine appeared to be debating whether to pursue her line of provocation, or simply grab the proffered drink while she still could. Her squinty-eyed hostility was met with a gentle smile, the bluest of eyes, and just the merest hint of amusement. In the end, the desire for a free beer won out, and she grabbed the drink ungraciously, and took off.

'Nice one Milo,' a passing biker said in a low voice, and patted Kate's saviour discreetly on the arm.

Now Miles stood casually before their table, in Charmaine's place. He appeared totally unhurried and at ease with himself. His eyes had flicked nimbly over Stevie, Marsha and Lauren before settling with conviction upon Kate. He just stood there staring at her as if contemplating. And Kate, to her great distress, found that she could not look away.

He was gorgeous. His black gypsy-curls framed a strong angular face oddly beset with a smallish, too pretty nose, and lips like a young girl's; curled, soft and generous. But it was his eyes, dark lashed, and of the deepest indigo, that rocked Kate's composure to its foundations. And those eyes were fixed on her now. What did he want, a thank-you? Kate was reluctant to admit that she had needed saving. An introduction? He said nothing.

And then he took a step forward, bent towards her, and gently taking her hand, put it to his lips and kissed it.

'Hey, Babe,' he said, with warmth; as if he had known her for *years*, 'I love your dress.' All the time, his eyes never left hers.

Kate was shocked at the power of his gaze. And in an instant, she was hooked. She knew that this man held the power to make her either delirious with happiness or disconsolate with rejection.

At last.

At last, she knew that it was all true. That you could meet someone in a crowded room and yet be aware of no one else but them. That time would slow, so that you could drink in every detail, every utterance or expression of the beloved. She knew now that there could be an aura of energy surrounding two people, so strong that Kate swore she could almost see it; touch it. That this made her want to laugh, dementedly, out loud, yet equally be rendered powerless by the strange mixed emotions of joy and fear. That finally, *finally* it had happened to her. Kate had been waiting for him all her life.

And so it didn't matter, later on, when Kate discovered that 'Milo' the dangerously sexy biker was in fact Miles Christian Bartholomew from the comfortably well-off Tobin-Baker family. And neither did it faze her that during the week he was in fact employed as a trainee stockbroker, and that he only donned his leather jacket at weekends, when he threw off the shackles of the City to let rip on his highly impressive Harley-Davidson. Neither did his revelation to Kate, that you only got mixed up with a scarier type of biker if you wore gang "colours" on your jacket—which he didn't—do much to tarnish the romantic image that she maintained of him. She merely adjusted the picture slightly to accommodate the fact that the only real danger he faced—other than being trampled to death on the stock market floor—was that he might fall off his bike.

And besides, although he might spend the evenings of his working week being rowdy in some City bar, that had to be better than being mixed up with dubious gang activity, didn't it?

None of these minor disappointments mattered because Kate knew that they were meant to be together. The magical feeling that she had experienced that day in the pub on Box Hill had been so rare, so extinct from her life until that point that she felt sure she had to trust it. It just couldn't have meant *nothing*.

And now, years later, and far away in Cornwall, his words and actions, so romantic to her at the time, were cynically remembered as corny and theatrical. And it *did* matter about the loss of the happy times, and the arrival of the bad ones. It did matter that he had once professed to love her, but that he had left her; and that he had left their child. It did matter about the pain, loneliness, and years of unhappiness.

Yet Kate could not quite abandon the memory of sheer tangible joy. If it had been love, then it should have come with a disclaimer. Instead, it had hit her like a virus, and with no guarantee of future happiness. Love was not blind, it was a fool, and it shouldn't be allowed out. Especially if it went around gratuitously making one half of the equation love and the other—well, not so much.

But it was me, Kate thought to herself sadly. I made it happen because I wanted it to.

Love was, in truth, a giant leap of the imagination. She remembered what she had said to Juliet and Lance at her Christmas party: that love was a decision. Subconscious perhaps, and guided by delusion, but a decision nonetheless. And you really didn't have to do it, not really. You could kid yourself it was magic, if you liked, but really it was your call; your choice. And it was vanity too, to think that just because you inflicted your emotions on another human being that they would, naturally, reciprocate.

It was almost dusk now on the beach and Kate shook herself awake from her thoughts. She called and signalled to Izzy that it was time to go home.

'I'm never going to fall in love again,' Kate muttered out loud to herself.

But what was she to do about Jem? Regretfully, Kate faced the truth. She had formed a relationship with Jem for all the wrong reasons. She had not been driven by love or even desire, but rather had succumbed to pressure of society. Kate had not wanted to appear weird; unnatural; a prude. The burden of her lengthy celibacy had not resulted so much in physical or even emotional desperation, but rather more shamefully, she had acted out of social embarrassment.

She had let herself down. She had slept with a man she did not love out of vanity and pride; and this, despite having resolved to exclude all unnecessary society. There too she had stumbled at the very first test by caring about what other people thought. It would be unfair to Jem to continue the lie, but she did not relish the thought of telling him. Yet, not telling him would be unfair to herself.

The small, repressed voice in the depths of her mind struggled to make itself heard: *how would she ever find real love if she were in a relationship with Jem?*

But you're not going to fall in love again, she reminded herself. *It's a decision you don't have to make.*

CHAPTER 34

Surgical Spirits

Jem was not happy. In fact, he felt decidedly edgy as he examined the nervous child's teeth. Nicky, as usual, sat on the opposing side of the patient, awaiting instructions in resentful silence. The little boy's mother protested anxiously in the background that her Kane almost never had sweets, or fizzy drinks, but had been brought up almost entirely on fresh fruit, vegetables and pure fruit juice. He drank water happily and without complaint. He had even been known to reject those awful sweets made of little else but sugar and chemicals as being 'too plasticky'. For the most part, Jem ignored her, as he despaired over how such a paragon's teeth had arrived at such an advanced set of decay in so few years. His silence, he knew, only added to her discomfort. Wickedly, he enjoyed the power. And frankly, he had heard it all before.

However, even he had to concede that in this case, it was probably all true. Kane's mother, Mary Buscombe, was indeed the type of hippy Earth-mother who knitted porridge for breakfast and grew her own fresh organic sackcloth. In all probability, the nearest the child had ever come to anything resembling refined sugar was the batch of homemade toffee apples that his mother made just once a year at Hallowe'en, "as a treat".

'There's a lot of sugar in fruit and fruit juices,' Jem said absently, still poking around in Kane's mouth, and not addressing the mother directly.

'Well yes, but you can't stop eating fruit now can you?' Mary asserted, and gearing up to broach one of her favourite subjects. 'I mean, the *junk* most kids eat these days! I'm very proud that my children eat healthily...'

'Does he brush his teeth regularly?' asked Jem bluntly, and with just the faintest note of derision.

Nicky's eyes, dull with boredom, flickered momentarily with contempt. She made a mental note to suck upon a lollipop later in reception.

'Why of course!' protested Mary. 'I bring my kids up properly, you know! Why I even...'

'What are you using?' Jem interrupted again. He really was far too busy and important for such particulars.

'Sorry?' asked Mary, puzzled.

'What are you using to clean his teeth?' Jem clarified, reluctantly. He so enjoyed these little games with his patients.

'Well...' said Mary, a little hesitant now. 'It's my own mixture. You know, I make it myself. A little rosemary, a bit of mint; mix it all together in a paste with...'

Oh yes! This was too good. Jem was no longer listening but mentally preparing his speech.

Five minutes later, Mary Buscombe left shamefaced and chastised, her darling but, so it would seem, grievously neglected little Kane in tow, and a lecture on the importance of cleaning children's teeth with a *proper* dental paste still fresh in her conscience. In her guilt, she made a considerable dent in her weekly budget buying expensive dental products from Nicky in the reception area on her way out.

Back in his surgery, Jem's brief enjoyment dissipated almost immediately, and his disquiet returned. He had been harsh with poor Mary Buscombe, because there really wasn't

355

a lot of justice in the world. He hadn't told her that his previous patient had been an incredibly smug sixteen-year-old tearaway who had been his patient for years; and who, despite an almost constant diet of cola, sweets, and highly processed sugar-laden foods, had the most pristine, strong, and gleaming white teeth that Jem had ever encountered. He had never found a single hole to be filled in the child's head. Not one. —Unless you counted the vacant space between his ears. The teenager had left the surgery with the usual self-satisfied leer on his face, happily bopping along towards his next sugar hit.

'Don't worry,' Jem had muttered evilly under his breath, 'the diabetes and heart disease will get you in the end.'

Life, Jem reflected, for the umpteenth time that morning, just wasn't fair. He was thirty-three for fuck's sake! If there was any justice at all, he should be married by now; perhaps a couple of sweet little kids. He was handsome, so he was told, and to be honest, thought it fair comment. He was well paid, in a respectable career, and he was fun, wasn't he? At least, he wasn't a *crashing* bore. He liked a party and a drink...

On that thought, Jem told Nicky to take a break while things were quiet, and once sure she had popped out to grab a sandwich, retrieved a half-empty bottle of fine malt whiskey from one of the sparkling white, state-of-the-art surgery cabinets. He would need a slug of this before meeting Kate for lunch.

He hadn't heard from Kate for three whole days, but this morning she had called and asked him to meet her at Captain Carter's. Her voice had sounded level and she hadn't given much away; given that she had, unusually, been using her mobile on the way back from dropping Izzy at school, and protesting that she couldn't hear him too well because of the wind and the noise of the waves.

But Jem had an uncomfortable feeling of dread about their meeting. It was a familiar feeling. In all honesty, it was

356

amazing really that they had lasted as long as they had. He had surprised himself in that respect. And *she* had surprised him. Kate was clever and pretty and creative. He enjoyed being seen with her, especially since she was a new face in town. There was no question of her having had a past with any of his mates. Truth told, he had been pretty nifty to get in there first, before someone else did, such as Lance.

He splashed the whiskey recklessly into a plastic beaker, and drank it down in one.

Damn it, he liked things the way they were. He liked dossing at Kate's cottage, eating good food, and drinking fine wine. She had taste, it had to be said. And the cottage was so homely; far more appealing than his miserable, grotty flat. But now it was all going to end. He could sense that he had somehow managed to mess things up with Kate. But what had he done? He was always bright and jolly. He cooked for her. And even if he said so himself, the sex was...well, *okay*, wasn't it?

A deep, bitter part of Jem suspected that perhaps there was someone else involved. Was he missing something? He had the horrible feeling of going into a situation unprepared, and the even worse sensation of perhaps having been found out, in some way. He couldn't put his finger on exactly what he might be guilty of, but felt sure there was bound to be something. Either way, it was with a great sense of impending doom and an even greater sense of injustice, that Jem left the surgery and reluctantly walked towards Captain Carter's.

CHAPTER 35

Dark Matters

K ate too, was dreading meeting with Jem. A part of her would have preferred to carry on as they were, rather than have to go through the awfulness of breaking up. Even the thought of having the conversation sent great waves of poisoned nerves shuddering through her body. Kate was no power-mad fiend. She did not relish the thought of rejecting another human being. She got no kicks from inflicting emotional pain, and was closer than she might have dared to admit to flipping a coin to escape the responsibility.

She had considered taking an appointment with Jem at his surgery. She was due a checkup, and it occurred to her that he might take the news a little better from a position of power, and whereby he might even get to inflict a little pain. She hoped to inspire in him the notion that perhaps she was not such a great loss, and absolutely nobody looked their best with their gums racked apart.

In the end vanity got the better of guilt, and she decided they should meet in the neutral territory of Captain Carter's. Even so, she wore no make-up, and had taken little trouble that morning with her clothes or hair. She had arranged to meet Jem early, before it became too busy with lunch-time diners, again hoping to avoid any unnecessary public humiliation; but she panicked a bit now as she remembered that with each passing week the town had become more and more full of tourists, and she risked chucking Jem amongst a clutter of families. Sure enough, a little girl, no more than five-years-old, at a nearby table kneeled up on her chair and twisted around to look at Kate inquisitively.

She waited uneasily, still unsure of her emotions. Finally, he arrived, and Kate could not deny a pang of regret as Jem sauntered through the bar area towards the table where she sat. She remembered how attentive he had been to her at the start; and how deliciously nervous he had made her feel. She remembered how she had almost even been jealous of Vivien, when she thought that there might be something between them. He *was* very attractive, and the fact that he had chosen her was indeed flattering.

Yet she couldn't help but wish that he looked more confident. Even now, she searched for clues that might suggest she was making a terrible mistake. But then she spied his sullen expression and general air of self-pity, as he wove his way through the tables and chairs. And thus silently and unknowingly, Jem sealed his fate.

'Hi,' said Kate softly, smiling up at him.

Jem moodily wrenched the vacant chair from under the table and slung himself down. 'Alright?' he grunted.

He was not going to make this easy. And how different this felt, thought Kate, from their early lunches together, when she had been working in his flat, and he had been a veritable bounding-Labrador of cheerfulness.

'Been busy?' Kate attempted small talk.

Jem simply stared at her, his expression a mixture of both sorrow and disdain.

'I'll have a bottle of wine please,' he smiled with mock pleasantry at the waiter who had appeared beside them. 'Anything...Merlot...no, make it Barolo; your *best*,' he snapped, as if deciding to make the most of it.

'And *two* glasses please,' added Kate, seeing as he wasn't going to.

'I'll have a whiskey and ice to start with,' said Jem.

'Yes, Sir.'

'...and make it a large one!' Jem called after the departing waiter's back.

All of Kate's prepared speeches departed like startled birds from a tree. They sat in silence for a minute. Jem feigned perusal of the menu, avoiding eye contact. The little girl on the next table, unable to sit still, climbed up and down from her chair incessantly, and once or twice wandered past Kate and Jem, smiling coyly, as if to make friends. Kate smiled back, but looked away, unwanting of the attention. Their drinks arrived and Jem greedily sank the whiskey while the increasingly flustered waiter struggled to open the bottle of wine. Jem eyed him with dark contempt.

Jake Petherick was nineteen years old and had not long been allowed to serve the wine at Captain Carter's. He was especially nervous because this was his dentist... His dentist who also happened to be his girlfriend Nicky's employer. And despite the derogatory tales that she told, he understood that it would be unwise to disrespect him, at least openly. He finally managed to extricate the damn cork from the damn bottle, and shakily poured a small drop into Jem's glass—*just enough for him to taste.*

'Are you taking the piss?' Jem snarled at the misfortunate Jake.

In truth, Jake had heard enough gossip from Nicky to know that Jem would drink the entire bottle anyway, regardless of ceremony—and that Jem knew it too.

'Thank you, it will be fine,' Kate smiled encouragingly at Jake, her eyes pleading. The young waiter dared an oh-so-slight, squinty-eyed, and thoroughly unprofessional scowl at Jem, before filling Kate's glass with an appropriate amount, and then topping up Jem's, which he overfilled. Then he slammed the bottle on the table, instantly smiling at Kate as he did so to quickly dispel any suspicion of intent.

'Are you ready to order your food?' he enquired with trained politeness.

'Not just yet, thanks,' Kate replied quickly, observing Jem's thunderous face.

'That's fine, just let me know when you're ready,' chirruped Jake, then, looking for the briefest of seconds back at Jem, 'enjoy your drinks.'

'I'll drill all his bloody teeth out next time he sets foot in my surgery,' muttered Jem at Jake's departing back.

The little girl tugged at her mother's sleeve. 'Mummy, that man's being funny!'

'Why don't you sit down and be quiet?' Jem barked at her.

Immediately the child's expression changed as her eyes filled with tears and the corners of her mouth down-turned in distress. She looked to her mother with outstretched arms, for succour, and on the verge of breaking into a wail. The mother gathered her close in a cuddle and muttered reassurances, but over her daughter's head, shot Jem a look of disgust.

'What's *wrong* with you?' hissed Kate, struggling to suppress her rising anger. 'You'll get us thrown out.'

'Nothing,' said Jem, turning his attention directly to Kate for the first time. 'Nothing is wrong with me. What's wrong with you?' He stared, challenging her.

'I think perhaps you know,' she began.

'No, I don't,' Jem insisted, and took a long draw on his wine. Then he faced her again, his eyes challenging. 'You're just going to have to tell me.'

This was not going well. Kate had imagined, or rather hoped, that he would be amicable. If this were a cosy Hollywood screenplay, he might have laughed out loud and cried: 'Guess what? I wanted to split up with you too!' They would have joked about what a right pair they were, and mutually agreed that they were only ever designed to be very good friends. If Nora Ephron could have written the script, then Jem would be muttering something about low expectations and advising her to run to the Empire State Building before it was too late. But his behaviour did not suggest an outcome nearly so optimistic. Kate struggled to think of another way of saying 'It's not you, it's me.'

'You've done nothing wrong,' she ventured.

She would not have imagined that Jem's expression could grow darker still. 'Then what's the problem?' he snarled.

Kate snapped. She had hoped to find a gentle way of explaining her feelings to him, but her innate perverseness became triggered by his growing aggression.

'I don't love you,' she said, with more coldness; more *finality*, than she had intended.

There was a moment, a hesitation in time, where he appeared not to have heard her. And then his face crumpled. For a second Kate thought that he might actually cry.

'I'm *sorry*,' she pleaded, immediately repenting the brutality of her statement. 'It's my fault; I should never have agreed to go out with you in the first place. I just wanted to be like everyone else in the world; to just be, I don't know, easy-going. *Casual*. But I'm not easy-going, Jem. I'm...I'm *difficult* and serious-minded. I can't be casual. It has to be important...'

'And I'm not important,' said Jem.

'Of course you are...' started Kate.

'...only not to you,' he interrupted again. And then before Kate could reply he added, 'It's Lance isn't it?'

'What?' said Kate in surprise, 'No, of course not!'

'Yes it is,' insisted Jem, beginning to slur. 'It always is. Lance bloody Borlase gets all the girls. Always has. *Even the ones he's not interested in,*' and he sneered maliciously, emphasising his meaning.

'I had no idea you were so jealous of him,' Kate said coldly. But she could now see it all so clearly. She could say that Jem had deliberately poisoned her mind against Lance, but Kate knew that she had willingly connived, and even enjoyed their initial idle, but pernicious chats. She had had no reason to suspect the truth of Jem's assertions, but reluctantly admitted that her readiness to accept them stemmed from her own prejudice against Lance, at the time. Kate felt a pang of regret as she realised how greatly her estimation of Lance had grown since those times. He was not the arrogant womaniser she had imagined, but rather an introvert and scholar, struggling to bring up his son, and probably still in love with his ex-wife. And yet she could not quite cast Jem as an out-and-out villain. She suspected that his jealous mind had believed what it suited him to believe; and that his real crime was to have betrayed his friend with injurious remarks.

Jem did not reject her accusation of jealousy, but merely laughed cynically, and shook his head scornfully. And then he grabbed his glass again, tipped his head back and drained every drop of the expensive red wine.

'Another bottle?' he queried, although Kate's glass was still full. His charming smile was amazingly brought back into action, as if they had not just had the previous conversation, but were on any one of their previous, ordinary dates.

Kate noted that Jake had wisely not returned to take an order for food, but busied himself with the other customers. Yet he eyed her attentively, waiting for a signal.

'No, Jem,' she said softly, 'I think I should just go...and besides don't you have to go back to work?...'

'No!' Jem cried, still smiling dazzlingly, 'Don't go! We can sort this out. I'll call Nicky and cancel my appointments. Stay. Have some food. We'll have some food, and some more wine and sort this out.' He giggled.

She stared at him; even now, unsure.

'Oh come on Kate, stop being so bloody serious! You know, that's your trouble really; you don't know how to have fun. And me, I'm a fun guy. I *like* having fun. You're just miserable and po-faced and...arty-farty...and boring! You suck all the joy

363

out of life. You need to bloody-well lighten up.' As he paused to beckon wildly at Jake for more wine, Kate placed some money on the table to cover the first bottle, slowly picked up her things and stood up to go.

'Have fun,' she said, and then left.

Her heart was beating and her legs shook all the way across the suddenly vast desert plain of Captain Carter's. For a panicked moment she thought he might run after her and grab her in anger... But then she remembered the second bottle of wine, and knew that he would not follow. And as she shut the door behind her, and took a large breath of salty sea air, Kate had to acknowledge that despite the doubt, and despite the guilt, the overwhelming sensation was one of enormous relief.

CHAPTER 36

Summer Heat

Kate's attempts to tame the wildness of her garden had not been entirely unsuccessful. She had tidied up, *a little*. And she had planted, *here and there*. She was growing courgettes, sweetcorn and peas. There were old wooden wine crates burgeoning with herbs and salad leaves. The emergence of pungent tomato plants in all sorts of odd places said little to recommend Kate's accuracy as a sower of seeds, and a lot about her innate sloppiness. But at least they were growing, she thought, as she regarded the beast before her now, rising Triffid-like from the pot of basil on the kitchen window sill. Small yellow flowers had started to form, which—she could still not quite believe—would soon become juicy ripe home-grown tomatoes. The basil didn't seem to mind either, but rather appeared to be thriving in the companionship of the intruder.

Kate had been lying low for a while, tending to her garden, and painting. She had conscientiously drawn up a timetable to accommodate these activities, which she adhered to woefully. Yet whenever she felt tempted to stroll into the village to browse around the shops, or to call up Vivien to meet for lunch at Captain Carter's, she would redirect herself to her schedule, since it served as a guide, a reminder to her purpose and her goals.

In other words, she was avoiding Jem.

Occasionally, when she became a little too stir-crazy, she would allow herself a brisk walk along the cliff tops—because exercise was important—and even to sit on a granite outcrop to stare out to sea...because it was *research* for a painting. But she always struck a path away from the village. She convinced herself that she was not hiding, but getting on with things. After all, those paintings wouldn't appear by themselves, and she had wasted enough time socialising over the previous months. She reminded herself constantly of her original plans for a misanthropic, hermitic life.

Except that Vivien was always calling over, bringing fabulous home-baked cake and tit-bits of local gossip— although perversely, no word of Jem. Lance too, seemed to be increasingly present, not to mention appear more comfortable, at her home. He would drop by with a book, or some article of interest that he had read in one of his science magazines, for Isabella. And he was always bringing cuttings for her garden from his mother. This made Kate feel guilty because she knew that she should reciprocate with a return in kind of her own, and she scrambled madly to brush up on her knowledge of plant propagation. Lillian, she imagined, thought it strange that such a cost-effective, not to mention neighbourly, pursuit was no longer undertaken as a matter of course. But equally, Kate suspected, she persisted with it as a stubborn reminder of her own generation's superior values. And so Lance delivered the cuttings, and Kate prayed that she would not murder them immediately with neglect.

She had no terrible need of firewood now that the increasingly hot summer sunshine had warmed the thick stone walls of the cottage. Most days her windows were flung wide open to the bright yellow light and hum and drone of the garden insects. But still Lance came, often bringing trunks or branches previously fallen from his own large garden, and which he would proceed, unsolicited, to chop into professionally neat, even sized logs. When Kate protested at

366

the intrusion on his time, he insisted that he enjoyed the exercise, and that she would be grateful for a good stock of seasoned dry wood once the nights started to draw in again.

On a particularly sweltering day in May, Kate sat sketching at the table outside her kitchen window. She watched Lance swing the axe and strike the thick round of tree trunk. He had used a piece of charcoal to draw a line that crossed through the centre of the block and along radiating weak points and cracks, and now set about attacking his targets with impressive accuracy. He appeared completely absorbed.

On impulse, Kate drew back the page on which she had been sketching in watercolour, and then exchanging her brush for pencil, slyly began to capture Lance's strong and graceful form as he raised the axe. They worked alongside like this for some time, in the sultry quiet of the summer afternoon. Kate observed how lean and toned his arms were. His broad shoulders and muscular chest betrayed a lifetime of paddling a surfboard through breaking waves. His legs were long-limbed and athletic, and although he wore jeans, Kate knew, from the beach, that they were not disappointingly puny under the cloth. His hair and body became wet with sweat.

Suddenly, without warning, and as if he had lost all desire for activity mid-strike, Lance threw the axe down and launched himself towards the cottage. As he approached, he tore off his damp T-shirt and shook it out.

Oh crap. Kate swore under her breath, and quickly flipped over the pages of the sketchbook. He smiled as he neared her.

'Hi. What are you drawing?' he asked. 'Can I see?'

'Oh, it's nothing,' Kate murmured, firmly shutting the book on the table, 'just sketching some ideas.'

He arranged the soggy T-shirt on the back of the wooden chair, and then sat down opposite her. Kate suddenly felt feverish... But she was also diverted. You could go around taking your shirt off in the heat if you were a lesser specimen

367

of the species, and go relatively unnoticed. But a man of Lance's obvious beauty ought to be aware of the impact of his semi-naked sexuality. She fought a sardonic smile that he should feel so comfortable in stripping off before her. She still remembered, although with less of a sting now, how he had once thought that she was making overtures towards him. It didn't matter that their relationship had improved; Kate was determined to behave with complete propriety where Lance was concerned. He was never to be allowed to forget how he had misjudged her; her pride wouldn't have it. Nonetheless, it was hard not to be discomposed by his sweating nude proximity.

She put her arm protectively across the sketchbook, which she was desperate to remove to a secret corner of the cottage. Lance's bare arm, which was also draped carelessly across the table, was so close to its spiral binding that if she moved the book even a millimetre it might scratch the inside of his forearm. His fingers were within caressing distance of the tattered bent paper edges. His eyes fell briefly, dangerously, upon the perfidious pad, but he did not pursue his request.

An anthology of William Morris's works also lay on the table and Lance gently turned the book with one finger in order to read the title.

'I'm er, trying to decide the composition for a painting. It's based on The Haystack in the Floods,' stammered Kate.

'Ah...."had she come all the way for this, to part at last without a kiss..." ' Lance quoted.

'Oh, you know it?' Kate was peculiarly pleased.

'Mr Morris's finest hour,' said Lance with another smile.

'It's my favourite poem,' said Kate shyly, 'ever since I was a schoolgirl.'

'And so you're going to make a painting...Pre-Raphaelite in style I presume?' Lance risked a little taunt.

'Actually...yes, sort of,' Kate blushed. 'Only I was going to put the characters in modern dress and environment.'

Lance's quick eyes revealed that he perceived the contradiction.

'It's kind of an experiment,' Kate gabbled. 'It will still have all the elements of romanticism; heroism, wistful looks, detailed nature and so on. I suppose I'm trying to question if these themes can only hold water in some imaginary, fantasy past.'

'Which scene will you paint?'

Trying to appear casual, Kate picked the sketchbook up from the table and enfolding it in both arms, hugged it to her chest. 'The part where Jehane is asleep on the wet haystack, I think. When she is supposed to be contemplating her decision, but is really just delaying the inevitable. She knows that she and her lover are doomed, and so just sleeps.'

'And what is it that appeals to you about that?'

Good grief, it was like being back at school! Why did he have to ask so many questions?

'The melancholy, I suppose; the sickening melancholy. The impending horror. The complete hopelessness. But ultimately, it's Jehane's refusal to...to tarnish their love with surrender or compromise. She doesn't even consider it, no matter what the consequence.'

For a second Lance's green eyes fluttered once more onto the sketchbook which Kate still held in possessive embrace. Her grip on the book tightened.

'It's...I'm still playing around with ideas,' she said. 'There's nothing of any substance yet.'

Lance looked at her curiously but respectfully, and thankfully did not continue his line of enquiry.

She got up quickly, still clutching the incriminating pad defensively close, and clambered clumsily through the open kitchen window, muttering something about a cup of tea.

'Tea would be great...' said Lance's voice from behind her, as he too manoeuvred his rangy body through the window frame, '...far too hot to sit outside for long.'

Damn it. She had to hide the sketchbook. Stuffing it under her armpit, she managed awkwardly to fill the old whistling kettle, place it on the gas hob and then strike a match to light the flame. Lance sat down at the kitchen table and watched her.

'Back in a sec!' she said brightly. He would not follow her to the loo. As she reached the bathroom door she hurled the book as hard as she could through the pantry area and into the conservatory beyond, where it skimmed across the floor and landed in undignified disarray against some paint pots.

When she emerged from the bathroom she found Lance— thankfully fully dressed again—making the tea, and was surprised to find that Vivien too had arrived, presumably via the window, and not from outer space. Kate was further amused. They certainly made themselves at home, these two.

Vivien was talking about the "Summer Ball", to be held on midsummer's day at Tremeneghy. As they sat down to drink tea, she reminded a bemused Kate that it was an annual occasion for both friends and family, and that you should wear costume.

'Think country dancing, fiddles and cider.'

'So it's kind of like a barn dance?' asked Kate.

Vivien looked thoughtful. 'More like a Georgian assembly-room ball. But usually outdoors, if the weather's okay...'

'...and in fancy dress,' Kate finished with a look of apprehension. She was already making mental excuses as to why she could not possibly go. Her major concern was Jem. Naturally he would be there, and she had no desire to cause embarrassment for either of them, particularly whilst done up in a stupid outfit.

'Costume, Kate, *costume*,' Vivien tutted. 'It's a celebration of days gone by. All the girls wear long frocks or gowns...'

'You're sorted then...' teased Kate.

'...It's largely late eighteenth century dress,' Vivien ignored Kate's mocking tone. 'Bit of a Poldark thing; that's very popular. We get a lot of serving wenches and dairymaids! The men tend to do breeches and tailcoats; but there are usually some oddities. We had a hangman one year, for some reason. And Derry once came as a scarecrow, and of course Mother berated him publicly for not bothering to dress up at all!'

There was the barest of pauses in the conversation at the mention of Derry. He had not been seen around for a while, but was rumoured to be travelling up the west coast of Ireland in search of a different, more challenging surf break. At the last report he had reached Mullaghmore Head, but that was two weeks ago, and no one had heard from him since.

'Of course, you should invite Juliet and Parker,' said Vivien, reading Kate's mind. 'If they're going to be around. You said they might be down?' There was not one hint of sarcasm in Vivien's comment. She was so kind, and Kate felt ashamed by association.

'Well, we'll see,' she said quietly. 'I'm not sure if I can make it myself.'

'Oh but you must!' cried Vivien. 'Don't worry about the costume, you know I can sort you something out. I supply lots of guests with their dresses!'

'Well...'

'Oh!' Vivien abruptly stopped pleading and instead looked unusually perplexed. 'Of course, I have forgotten, you are meant to go *with* someone to the ball. Like a partner, although you don't have to stay with them all night, you can dance with anyone who asks, but it is part of the custom to arrive with someone; so that you can be announced...'

Kate was definitely not going.

'...It's one of mother's things,' continued Vivien. She started the Summer Ball along with her sisters years ago, and

371

these traditions have stayed. Of course, I had thought you'd be going with Jem, but now...'

'...Now, I don't think I should go at all,' said Kate, getting up and starting to clear away the tea things.

Vivien became contemplative. Kate lingered warily at the sink, swilling out the teapot in a rhythmic manner. She knew that Vivien was scheming, trying to figure things out. Lance was deadly silent. Vivien's blank eyes finally honed in on her brothers green ones, and the spark returned. Lance intuitively grasped what was coming and he shifted uneasily in his chair.

'Of course!' cried Vivien, 'It's obvious. You can go with Lance! I mean, he can at least pick you up and arrive with you. Ask Kate to the ball, Lance!'

Both Kate and Lance froze in alarm. Vivien settled happily back in her chair in satisfaction.

'Well, of course,' Lance said with sudden immediacy. A second longer would have shown outright reluctance. He turned around in his chair to face Kate, who was standing by the sink paralysed with embarrassment. 'Of course I would love to go to the ball with you.'

Partly from nerves, and suddenly engulfed with mirth at the absurdity of the sentence, Kate collapsed in a fit of giggles. 'I'm so sorry,' she said. 'It's just...I feel like Cinderella! And Lance, please don't feel pressured, whatever Vivien says. As I said, I may not...I don't even know if I can make it yet.'

Vivien got up, making an exasperated noise, and left the kitchen. Kate stared after her, still amazed at the freedom with which they treated her home. Lance too stood up and drained the contents of his teacup. He moved towards the sink, and with equal familiarity, shunted Kate aside and began to wash up the cups.

'The thing is,' he said slowly, 'it hadn't occurred to me until now; I mean I haven't given it much thought; but I will need a partner for...the party.' *He was damned if he was going to call it a ball again.* 'Otherwise I'll just get tediously asked about it all night long. You would be doing me a huge favour if you would agree to come with me.' He didn't look at her, but, raising it to the light, meticulously inspected the inside of a cup for cleanliness.

Kate eyed him with grim amusement. Surely the irony was not lost on him? It was not so many months ago that he had accused her of impropriety, and now here he was, perhaps not begging, but at least pleading with her for a social favour. She sorely wanted to taunt him, but decided to be kind. She knew enough now to understand how uncomfortable Lance would be if the attentions of anyone else from the village were foisted upon him unwillingly; and equally how he would stand out if he were to attend alone. Of course the busybodies would speculate, but *they* would know that the arrangement was platonic, and unworthy of comment. She understood that this was what he wanted; what he needed; a friend, an ally, but with no complications.

'Well, okay,' she said carefully. 'If I do go—and I'm still not sure that I can—then I promise I will go with you.' She was still concerned about Jem, and wanted to keep her options open.

Lance looked sideways at her with a small, amiable smile. 'Thanks,' was all he said.

Kate suddenly wondered what had happened to Vivien, and took a scout around the cottage. She found her standing in the conservatory casually flicking through the sketchbook that Kate had sent Frisbee-like to the floor.

'I was just taking a look to see if there were any new paintings,' she offered by way of explanation. 'I've got some space in the shop if you want to hang some more? I hope you don't mind?'

These bloody people just wandering into her house! Chopping wood and climbing through windows; making tea and nosing into her sketchbooks!

373

Vivien had stopped at a certain page and was looking at it curiously, her raised brow betraying her surprise. Then shutting the pad, she looked directly at Kate and grinned archly.

CHAPTER 37

About Time

The days passed and Kate heard nothing from Jem. She felt sure that she would have heard word had he, in a fit of passionate despair, thrown himself from the cliff top, and so was secretly grateful that he had not attempted to contact her. It saved her from having to decide whether to take the call, or worse, from being drawn back in again. Nonetheless, she evaded the landline telephone in the hallway as much as possible. She took long coastal walks, only pausing to take a photograph, or to capture a colour in her sketchbook. She stopped short of turning off her already despised mobile. That would be tempting fate to bestow a calamity upon Izzy, and the school not be able to contact her. But she stuffed the phone in the bottom of her rucksack—muffled under a sweatshirt—only checking it from time to time to reassure her that no such misfortune had occurred.

She had invested in some proper walking boots and socks. The high coast path could be narrow and treacherous in parts, with loose stones ready to wrong-foot you should you take your eyes off the path to gaze out to sea. Once she had stumbled in a pair of flip-flops and nearly toppled over a sloping cliff face, whose danger was insidiously disguised by banks of wild flowers and thick gorse. She had escaped with a mildly twisted ankle and scratches, but had come out of it alarmed at her underestimation of the hazards. Now she always went prepared. She took water, a map, and the detested mobile phone, appropriately charged. Before he'd gone away, Derry—in exchange for a surf-painting he'd admired—had made her a willow walking stick, much to Isabella's derision. The stick was a thing of beauty to Kate, but her daughter missed no opportunity to crack jokes about her 'wizarding' staff.

She walked for miles each day, amazed at the sometimes subtle, often dramatic changes in the light and colour of her surroundings. Kate did not usually wear more than a touch of make-up: some eye shadow and mascara; occasionally eyeliner and lip gloss; but now she abandoned all artifice completely since the sunshine, together with the buffeting combination of wind and sea spray, always sent her home bare-faced and brown anyway. Similarly she realised the utter pointlessness of blow-drying her hair every morning, since within minutes of walking it became wild and wavy. If it rained it curled into long messy tendrils. And if the weather was hot, then Kate's sweat would see to providing the same effect as she climbed the steep cliff paths, puffing and panting and pulling herself up with the aid of her stick.

Then she would spend a day or two in the conservatory painting furiously to try to keep up with the backlog of ideas and images that had piled up in her imagination. Every now and then, she would stop, in the stillness of the afternoon, or in the gloaming of the evening, to just sit and be amazed at how lucky she was; and equally amazed that she had foolishly neglected to live here before now. It had been a terrible oversight on her part. Now that she had arrived, it all seemed so clear. It was unfair that so much beauty should be left just lying around whilst other unfortunates—the ones she had left behind—lived out their lives oblivious amongst bleak concrete walkways and forbidding high-rises. When she was not having moments of reverie, she could sometimes become so engrossed in her work that she often eschewed her habitual six o'clock glass of wine. Sometimes, for days, she even forgot to drink at all...

Izzy too, appeared to have found some new source of serenity. She had almost stopped complaining. Kate put it down to the early summer crowds, and the new, young life that they brought with them. Isabella had even run into some old school friends from London, who not only bemoaned the fact that they were only visiting for a week, but to Isabella's incredulity, expressed jealousy that she got to live here—*on a beach*—all year round!

Whatever the cause, Kate was grateful that Izzy finally appeared to have accepted her new circumstances, and was no longer mooching around in her bedroom all day. In fact, she appeared to be spending ever-increasing time at Tremeneghy with Finn, dropping in on the way home from school, and instructing Kate not to pick her up until she called her. Shockingly, Kate would get so used to these late afternoons, and so absorbed in her painting, that she would be jogged into consciousness by Izzy's phone call, only to realise that it was almost dark, and that she, horror upon horror, had almost forgotten that she had a daughter!

Isabella sometimes arrived home in a bedraggled state, which Kate dismissed as a result of running around playing football in the garden with Finn and his friends. Acknowledging her own unkempt and windblown condition of late, Kate excused her daughter's somewhat feral appearance. Yet she still pined for the imaginary Isabella with the pretty dresses and team of ducks following her around.

One day, Kate was on her way back from a long walk, this time across a public footpath that traversed fields and farmland. Today, having felt the desire to work "en plein air" for once instead of taking her ideas back to the studio, she had brought some supplies. The paints and brushes fit in her bag well enough, but she was beginning to regret her foolhardiness in carrying a folding, portable easel, and a collection of small plywood boards to paint on. She climbed awkwardly over yet another stile, and then using her stick to balance, jumped down onto a quiet country road. Unfamiliar with the route, she was scanning the hedges for a signpost to indicate where the path continued, when she heard a toot, and turned to see Lance's green Land Rover heading towards her. The car slowed down and then stopped, and Lance leant over and wound down the passenger window.

'Do you want a lift?' he enquired. 'I've got to stop over somewhere first, but I'll be heading back your way afterwards.'

Kate paused. She wasn't tired and would usually be happy to finish her walk, but looking at her cumbersome burdens, she thanked him gratefully, and he jumped out to help stow her luggage in the back of the car. Shifting the usual couple of surfboards out of the way, he looked at each painting in turn before stacking them carefully together.

'They're not finished,' said Kate apologetically. 'These are just the beginnings...I'll finish them back at the cottage.'

'I think you're very talented,' he said matter-of-factly. He was being polite of course. Kate mumbled something self-deprecating as Lance took her walking stick. He looked at it wryly, before stashing it alongside the rest of the things. Kate hurriedly climbed into the front passenger seat.

'Have you been far?' said Lance, as they drove along the sunlit lane. There was the faintest curl of his lips as he suppressed a smile. 'Merlin's cave, perhaps?'

'Oh, very funny! I take it you've been talking to Izzy. 'It's a great stick—really!'

Lance laughed aloud; in that sudden surprising way that he had, as if he had been controlling mirth and could no longer contain it.

'You wouldn't laugh if it was an expensive modern stick from some trendy outdoorsy shop!' Kate protested.

'I *would!* What's wrong with your legs?'

'I wasn't brought up with this terrain you know! And I'm not a kid anymore. My thighs are made out of...out of duvet!'

He laughed again. 'Of course; I understand. You're embracing the onset of middle age, and have taken up rambling with sticks. Very worthy of you. No point fighting it I suppose, although I think you're a bit premature. I bet you've got a compass too; and a whistle. And sing songs as you gaily march along.'

'I might!'

They were both grinning.

'I know, I must look ridiculous,' said Kate. 'And I still feel wholly pretentious wandering about sketching. I mean it's such a cliché around here. *Everyone's* an artist. You can't turn a corner without finding someone perched on a rock painting, or wistfully writing poetry in a journal. But I don't care! I'm *enjoying* myself. Although I do sometimes wonder if that's all it's about. The pleasure I mean. It's all a bit self-indulgent. How do I know that I'm not just deluding myself into having a rare old time, and that there's no actual substance?'

'Your paintings are your answer. They're good.'

Kate turned to look at him. She didn't think that he was laughing, or being polite this time.

'There's no shame in making a living out of something you enjoy,' he added.

'Well, thanks,' she said, still looking at him carefully in case he betrayed any trace of mockery, and deciding not to correct him on his assumption that she made a living. 'It can be hard to be objective about your own work. I mean, I always really love a subject when it's new; I feel really passionate, as though I never want to stop painting. But then feel equally despondent when it's finished. Not that it's *ever* finished!'

'Ah well, you've got to be tortured. After all, you're not a proper artist unless you're tortured.' He was teasing again.

'And ideally you should have had some terrible tragedy in your life, something that inspires your work.'

There was an uncomfortable pause. Kate's thoughts turned to Miles, and that crossroads in her life where it all seemed to go wrong. But even that was not completely tragic because she had Isabella.

Lance frowned. 'Oh no! You have haven't you? Kate I'm so sorry, that was thoughtless...'

'No, no,' she reassured him, 'there's been no terrible tragedy. Just ordinary heartache.' She turned away from him, and looking out across the fields to the sea, said almost to herself, '*All heartache lost in the tides...*'

'What's that?'

'Oh, it's a line from a story I once read. Can't remember the author's name—it wasn't very famous. About a flooded planet.'

'I know it.'

'You do?' Kate was pleasantly surprised. 'I used to read a lot of science fiction— when I was younger...' She added the last disclaimer as if to explain this anomaly. 'But you?'

'Hey, I'm a theoretical physicist. A cosmologist, even! Of course I read science fiction. Loads of it—even, as you say, the more obscure stories—It was Doc Verlaine, by the way. There are lots of ideas in science fiction. Ideas spring from ideas. If I recall, I think that tale—apart from the obvious environmental message—was about the ultimate futility of everything we do. But I do particularly remember that sentence: *All memory drowned forever; all heartache lost in the tides.*'

Kate stared at him in silent amazement. How odd that he should know the very line she had meant.

There was a book on the dashboard with an interesting title and cover.

'What's this about?' said Kate, picking it up and inspecting.

'Entanglement,' said Lance.

'Really? You mean like dangerous liaisons? Or just tights getting all knotted together in the washing machine?'

'Er, no, nothing like either of those scenarios at all. It's about quantum entanglement; what Einstein referred to as 'spooky action at a distance.'

'Okay... Because that sounds much more feasible.'

Lance smiled. Once more Kate revelled in the unusualness, the strange effect that the change in his composure seemingly had upon her mood—upon the world. 'It's to do with quantum particles becoming entangled—engaged. Once entangled they become forever affected by each other. They have a relationship.

'For example, a change in spin for one particle will result in a correlating spin reaction in the entangled particle, no matter what the distance. I mean, even if separated by vast areas of space—whole galaxies, or the other side of the universe.'

'How do they become entangled? And what's spin? No wait, don't answer that. It'll be something difficult and sciencey won't it?'

'It's not that difficult Kate. Stop being deliberately obtuse; it's not becoming.' He grinned.

'What's obtuse?' said Kate, with a wink.

Lance shook his head in mock despair, and continued patiently. 'The perplexity lies in the apparent immediate communication between the entangled particles. Unless the reactions are predetermined somehow—which seems unlikely—it suggests that they are relating faster than the speed of light, which is supposedly not possible.'

'Do *you* think it's possible?'

'Well...' He looked uncertain.

Unusual for him, thought Kate.

He glanced at her uneasily, as if assessing whether to continue. 'It might be possible through time travel.'

Kate raised her eyebrows and blinked exaggeratedly.

'I know, I know. I'm not referring to H. G. Wells, or London police boxes, but to retrocausality at a quantum level. Think of it like this; when you make a change to an entangled particle, it has a wave-like, ripple effect that travels back in time to when it became entangled with its partner. By communicating the change with its past incarnation, it changes the behaviour of its entangled particle and instantly alters its condition in the future, or rather the present. Do you follow? It may not make sense...'

'No, I get it,' said Kate.

She was thinking about that time, in another world now, when she had sat alone in her car in the pouring rain, insignificant in the sprawling crush of the city.

Lance stole another glance at her. She had closed her eyes and appeared to be meditating. 'What are you doing?' he asked.

'I'm sending a message to myself. To the past Kate.'

'Ha! What are you telling her?'

She opened her eyes again and turned to smile at him. 'I'm telling her everything will be okay. I'm telling her to not despair, but to leave London and her false friends and come to Cornwall. And I'm telling her that it's a beautiful day.'

Lance fell serious for a moment. 'I hadn't realised you were so unhappy in London. I'm glad you got away.' Then he smiled again and said: 'And what about future you? Those ripples go both ways you know. Any messages from an older, wiser Kate?'

'Just a minute, I'll see.' She closed her eyes again, trying not to laugh this time, but forcing her features into beatific serenity, concentrated very hard.

Lance diverted his eyes from the road again for a long second to look at her, to steal some essence while he could. He looked away again just as Kate reopened her eyes.

'She says it's all good. She's painting, and she has a fabulous studio by the sea.'

Is she with someone?, he wanted to ask. *Is she in love?*

'Glad to hear it,' he said.

'Anyway, I think I like entanglement. Forgive me, but it sounds kind of, well, magical. It's...it's *romantic*...

'Romantic?' Lance's austere look returned, although Kate thought that this time there was a hint of amusement or gentleness... 'I thought you didn't believe in romance Kate?'

'Well, I meant what passes for romance. I meant hearts and flowers; chocolates and Valentine's Day. But this...' she fell silent, thoughtful, for a moment. 'It's like...people become entangled, I think. They become involved. And once it's done, you can never undo it. Romance is dark. It's attachment against the odds, against the will. It's unrequited. It's pain and heartache. It's definitely not to be sought. Those poor entangled particles have no choice. They are doomed!'

Lance laughed aloud again.

'Romance is not the way it's sold,' continued Kate. 'Even when it's a good thing, it's not about gifts or money spent. It's not an expensive yacht, it's...it's a galleon on the high seas! It's not a designer frock but a cabin-boy disguise.'

'So... You're not romantic at all then,' smirked Lance.

She gave him an impish look. 'All I'm saying is...that your entanglement is far more interesting and exciting than a big spongy Valentine's Day card.'

They sat in comfortable silence for a while, and Kate looked absently out across the sun-filled fields surrounding them. At one point the car passed a granite farmhouse where removal men were busy packing the back of a large lorry. With sudden surprise, Kate recognised Alicia Browning's honey-coloured hair and officious manner as she gave fraught directions to the cowed workers. *So Alicia and her family were moving after all*. Isabella had insinuated as much, but

Kate had dismissed it at the time as playground gossip. For some reason now, it filled her with disquiet. Alicia and Nigel had not made it work. Would that be her in a year from now? She could not imagine ever going back.

Lost in thought, when Kate returned to the present she realised that they were by now some way from Pencarra, and heading up high into moorland. Her companion appeared unperturbed by her preoccupation, and Kate reflected on how much more relaxed Lance seemed these days; not nearly so deadly serious and brooding. Shortly, they turned off the road along a narrow country track, which slowly and gently wound up into a desolate but beautiful landscape.

'I've just got a bit of business to see to,' said Lance. 'It won't take long.'

CHAPTER 38

Chy-an-Gwidden

Kate was intrigued; what business could he possibly have in this wild and lonely place?

They came to the top of a hill, and then turned into another lane leading back down again towards the sea. Eventually, they arrived at an isolated hamlet comprising a stone church, Norman in style, flanked by a handful of ancient cottages. A granite marker by the roadside was carved with the word 'Roseglos'. Lance parked the car close to a solitary detached house and got out, and Kate, who was uninvited but curious, followed him. Lance didn't seem to mind, but rather appeared to have expected her to accompany him. With adroit familiarity, he lifted and then eased forward a tired and battered wrought iron gate.

On one of the stone pillars supporting the gate, was a slate panel engraved with the name, 'Chy-an-Gwidden'. The house was double-fronted and Georgian in style. The imposing front door, painted a chalky grey-green, was sun-bleached and peeling, and the whitewashed walls were battered by years of exposure to weather. But it withstood this faded grandeur with dignity and character. There were some dilapidated outbuildings, possibly stables or barns, and what looked like a walled section of Garden. The setting was spectacular. The hamlet was surrounded by nothing but ancient field systems, and to the west, beyond the crags and clifftops, they could see all the vastness of the Atlantic Ocean.

'Wow!' said Kate. 'What a beautiful place! And house too... Why are we here? If you don't mind me asking?'

'Yes it is beautiful, isn't it?' Lance said somewhat wistfully, and then added: 'It's mine.'

Kate looked at him in real surprise. 'Really? How come? I mean, you don't live here...'

'I bought it some years ago,' he said, standing before the house in the small patch of grass that served as a front garden. He gazed up at its facade, as if looking for answers to some long-forgotten question. 'It was when I was first married to Leah, and we were expecting Finn. I intended that we should live here, as our family home. But it didn't end up that way. In fact, we never actually lived here all together, even after Finn was born. It was a bit of wreck when I bought it, and Leah refused to move in until it was up to standard.'

Lance saw Kate's cynical expression. 'Understandably, of course, given that she had a newborn baby. She didn't want to have to struggle in a hovel. I spent most of my spare time here, in order to do the work; pretty much lived here really, while Leah stayed with Finn at my mother's house. That can't have been easy for her either I suppose. But then, things didn't work out, as you know. Leah went to London and I moved back to my mother's house with Finn, because frankly, I needed the help and support.'

'But you kept the house?'

'Yes. It seemed a shame to lose it. Leah wanted to sell, as...' his expression turned grim, '...as part of the divorce settlement. I managed to pay her off, but had to rent it out to holidaymakers to recoup the loan. It's been that way ever since.' A lost look crossed over his features. 'But I'll live here again one day...'

Kate did not know what to say. She felt compelled to touch him, to reassure. But this was Lance, and it couldn't be chanced, could it? Even now.

'However, there are problems inherent with letting property,' he said more cheerfully, and regaining his composure. 'That's why we're here. It's a changeover day, and the cleaner has lost her keys. Again. And there's a window upstairs that needs attention; won't shut or something. I thought I'd take a look at it to see the extent of the problem before calling in Derry, if we can ever find him.'

He unlocked the door, and they entered the hallway. It was sparsely decorated, with bare floorboards, and so echoed with their footsteps as if it were permanently empty, and showed no sign of being recently vacated by holidaymakers. Kate took in the grand proportions of the hall and admired the gracefully curling banister of the wide staircase.

'Gina's late,' Lance muttered in some annoyance, whilst checking that the departing family had left their set of keys on top of an old boot cupboard in the hall. 'The cleaner,' he explained. 'I'm just going to have a look at that bedroom window; hopefully we won't have to wait too long. I expect you'll want to get back soon, for Isabella. I fear I've waylaid you.'

'Don't worry, there's time yet. Do you mind if take a look around?'

'Make yourself at home. You might be lucky and find some supplies if you'd like a tea or something.'

'I'm fine; go on, see to your business.' With a wave of her hand, Kate gestured that he should carry on.

He smiled amiably and then sprang, with lissom limbs, up the stairs.

Kate moved around from room to room. Despite being only basically furnished for the purpose of letting, the furniture was tasteful and classical, and as such would withstand looking dated or tawdry. There was no overstuffed sofa in the main living room, but rather a pleasantly relaxed one, in a faded print of yellow roses. A mismatched Queen Anne chair nevertheless invited one to snuggle up with a book by the fire. Indeed the shelves on either side of the fireplace were thoughtfully stacked with books regarding local interest and history, as well as classic novels; as if to suggest that here, in this remote bolthole, you could finally catch up on a lifetime's intended reading. Kate smiled to see Moby-Dick, and The Rime of the Ancient Mariner amongst the titles.

The pictures on the whitewashed walls too, were mostly of a nautical theme; ancient prints of long-sunken ships that had met their fate on the treacherous north coast outside, or naive but charming Alfred Wallis-style scenic views of boats-in-harbour.

The kitchen was huge and startlingly unmodernised. A large black range cooker and black slate floor contrasted against the stark white tiles on the wall. This harshness was softened by a wall of open wooden shelving, containing an eclectic array of pottery, dishes, plates and cups; and a huge central wooden table and chairs. This presumably was the only work surface. Two easy chairs sat either side of the range, and the bare minimum of "white goods", a fridge, washing machine, and spare hob and oven looked incongruously dumped in a corner.

There was an adjoining walk-in pantry, twice the size of her own, which mercifully had not been converted into something depressing like a utility room, but remained, Kate thought, much as it had always been; with even more basic shelving containing clay demi-johns for wine and storage jars for preserves and pickles. Yet they were empty, forsaken. They sat waiting, unloved, for someone to fill them again. There was a door leading to the garden, with an old, outsized, decorative key in the lock. It was irresistible. She turned the key.

Outside, the immediate piece of land had been cultivated to produce a small garden to sit in, but the weathered and mismatched garden furniture sat on grass; there was no modern patio, or heaven forbid, decking, to spoil the illusion of having travelled back in time. Most of the grass, where it had not been worn by humans, had been left to its own device, and now, at the height of summer, was scattered with wild meadow flowers, and was vibrant with the hum of insects. An area had been kept mown to provide space for a badminton net. But there was no court painted on the grass; no adherence to rules, or size of space for play; but rather, just enough room to have fun.

She was surprised that Lance had not employed a gardener to maintain the grounds; presumably its wildness did not deter the holidaymakers. But then, she conceded, the eye was drawn not to the garden, but beyond it's boundaries to the deep blue ocean, and behind her, looming high above the house, to the silent, brooding moor. There was a stillness about the place that made her feel watched; as if the living moor was some giant ancient creature that she had stumbled across. The land, the rocks, the enduring sea, were all drenched in timelessness; steeped with the echo of prehistoric lives.

The two granite outbuildings were similarly neglected. One was a substantial size but appeared to be being used only for storage. *What a waste*, thought Kate. Whilst the stamp of entropy appealed to the artist in her, she had lived too long in poverty and fear of homelessness not to see the shame of it. This could be another dwelling, or at the least a workshop or a studio...

To the left of the garden was the walled part that Kate had espied from the front, and she discovered it to be an overgrown kitchen garden. Along the walls, and having nowhere else to go, leggy, straggling climbing roses supported themselves up into the sky. And following the sun to where it set, the lower branches hung their intertwined boughs across the overgrown raised beds, which had presumably once existed for vegetables, herbs, and flowers for cutting. It might have been a sorrowful sight; a tale of neglect and abandonment. But the roses were in full, profuse bloom, ranging in shade from the deepest fuchsia to the palest pinks and creams. If only temporarily, the garden had a natural, wild, summer beauty of its own.

Yet Kate was still struck by a wave of compassion for the ephemeral nature of human life. Once these beds would have been well-tended, mostly from necessity, but she hoped also with love. It might have been the source of great pride, and delight. But take away the people, the little human lives, and nature took over and ultimately, consumed. All that work, all that effort, only to eventually dissolve and disappear.

Someone ought to reclaim something of it back.

She was distracted from her melancholy by a noise from the first floor of the house, where she spied Lance still fiddling with the faulty window. She caught his eye and waved. He smiled and waved back but seemed in no immediate hurry.

Kate continued her exploration through an arch in the garden wall and saw, with some dismay, that she now stood in a small and equally overgrown apple orchard. Dismay, because Kate had always wanted an apple orchard. It was an illogical, romantic fantasy of hers. She would not acknowledge the nuisance and labour involved in collecting hundreds of rotten windfalls, but rather imagined gathering sweet pink and green apples to make pies, chutneys, and cider. And in the spring, she would lie reading a book under laden boughs of perfumed apple blossom.

Kate felt a sudden, irrational anger towards Leah Greenwood, a woman whom she did not personally know. How could she want more than this? How could fame and fortune ultimately compare when she could have lived here with Lance; could have brought up her child in this spectacular place? Even to have returned part-time; to have co-managed a career and a life in Cornwall would surely have been preferable? But to abandon all this with such little apparent regret seemed to Kate to be spoilt in the extreme. She supposed that it illustrated how people wanted very different things in life, but the less reasonable side of her still raged that Lance had fallen for, and was probably still pining for, someone so completely incompatible.

Looking up at the window again, she saw that Lance had gone, and she made her way back to the house. She found him back in the hallway, haranguing a small woman, who was puffing with some commitment on a cigarette.

'I've told you before, Gina, no smoking in the house! People don't want to rent a property that stinks of tobacco.'

'What if they smoke themselves?' Gina argued stubbornly.

'Well, they shouldn't! It's rented on the basis that there should be no smoking indoors.'

'Yeah but what if they say they aren't smokers, but they're lying? I know that's what I'd do, if it was me. How would you know?'

'I'd know, Gina, because it would stink.' The argument was exasperating, but Lance appeared to be somewhat amused.

'Yeah but, what would you do, like? You'd still take their money, right? You wouldn't kick them out or something?' Gina caught Kate's eye and gave a flicker of recognition, followed by a knowing smile.

Kate realised that Gina, inevitably, was one of the mothers she saw each morning at the school gates. *Brilliant*. There would be more rumours in the morning. Well, let them gossip. She now knew that Jenifer Trewin's original warning about Lance had been founded in malice. She was not ashamed to be associated with him...until she remembered Jem. She recalled Jem's comments in Captain Carter's. He had suggested that there might be something going on between her and Lance. But what could she do? It was a small place, and there would always be wagging tongues. It could not be contained, and her conscience, after all, was clear.

Gina looked a frail, sickly creature. Bony legs protruded from beneath her denim mini-skirt, and with her bare, skeletal arms, Kate wondered that she were capable of manhandling a vacuum cleaner up and down the stairs. The energy required to change a duvet cover might make her pass out, or indeed require a "fag" to recover.

'Anyway, here is your new set of keys,' Lance was saying. 'Please try not to lose them this time.'

'It's alright for you to say,' Gina grumbled. 'You only have to worry about this set of keys; I got twenty or more sets to worry about. I got other properties to clean you know!'

'You worry about keys? Really? Well, can't you keep them all together?' suggested Lance.

Gina frowned. 'Nah,' she admitted ruefully, as if realising a painful truth. 'Too damned heavy.'

Lance surveyed his weakling employee, and then burst out laughing. 'Okay Gina, you win,' he said, giving her an affectionate hug of the shoulders. 'But no more smoking, I insist!'

Kate shifted uncomfortably in the hallway. She still found these outbreaks of good nature strange coming from Lance, but more than that, she was irked. He'd hugged her like that once; but a long time ago now, and never since. And of course she knew it was just Gina, and only out of fondness. But all the same, and maddeningly, she still felt left out.

CHAPTER 39

Entanglement

The drive home towards Pencarra was marked by a less comfortable silence than on the way there. Kate was still brooding with an irrational rage at the fickleness of Leah Greenwood. Eventually, unable to contain herself, she spoke.

'I'm so sorry things didn't work out for you. At the house I mean. It's such a shame—such a beautiful place.' Her voice was clipped and she wondered if he suspected her meaning. But she stopped short of offering her condolences on his having married such an ungrateful harpy.

'Well, yes. Thank you,' said Lance. 'But I should have thought it through. I don't think it would ever really have worked. Leah would have been bored out of her mind. It's too remote for her. And you saw the garden; she would have found it too much. We might have employed someone I suppose, but...well, it never came to that in the end. No, it was my mistake to think that someone like Leah would ever be happy to live the simple life.'

But Kate would, thought Lance.

Kate would have loved the solitude; the coastal paths and the scenery. Kate might have struggled with the garden, but he knew that she at least would have had the desire, and the vision to try and make something of it. He stole a look at his companion.

Should he tell her? His heart thudded hard in his chest.

393

Kate said nothing. But her face was set in deep thought. (If he had but known, she was still ruminating on what a fool Leah Greenwood was).

Maybe he could just tell her, right now. But then he remembered Jem, and decided that it was too close; too soon. Lance had been very disappointed when Kate had started dating Jem. He had tried to make himself happy for them, even though they had not appeared particularly overcome with joy themselves. But he had resigned himself to the role of friend. And even though instinct told him that they, Jem and Kate, were wrong for each other, he had to admit that his own feelings must bias this instinct.

However, he allowed himself, with some trepidation, to look forward to the Summer Ball. They had not discussed it much, but rather it had been taken as resolved that Kate would be going with Lance. When it did come up in conversation she did not protest, or make further excuses about not going. He had even overheard her talking about dresses with Vivien.

So he would take it slowly. They would go to the ball, like the pair of Cinderellas that they were, and he would let their relationship grow. He did not dare think of the possibility of future, long-lasting contentment. All he knew was that right here and now, he was happy. Just being in Kate's company made him feel like a kid on Christmas morning. And it would be Christmas again tomorrow; and the day after that.

In the dark recesses of his mind there lurked the vague notion that he should tell Jem about the party arrangements. He had no desire to blindside his friend; but equally was reluctant to attach undue significance to the matter. He and Kate were going together as friends, no more than that, and it should be obvious to all. By making an issue of it he risked making it appear something more serious, and Lance desperately wanted to keep things casual: there was too much at stake. And yet...his conscience nagged at him. But he would think about it later; another time. Not now; not when he was feeling so lighthearted.

Later, back at home, Kate too, considered her mood, and decided that curiously, and unpredictably, she was happy. She sifted through some mail that she had picked up upon arrival home and dumped on the kitchen table before taking her equipment and new paintings into the conservatory studio. There was nothing much of interest, just the usual collection of bills; that stately procession of reminders of just how precarious her existence became with each passing month. She would lie awake worrying tonight, she decided, but not right now; not while she felt so light-hearted.

And there was another letter from Marsha. She recognised the distinctive pale orange recycled envelope, the florid handwriting and somewhat childish—but typically Marsha—ink stamp of a butterfly on the back. She groaned, unable to face further admonishment. Kate was determined not to have her mood destroyed. She stuffed Marsha's letter, together with the bills, on the top kitchen shelf behind an old cracked teapot, which she sentimentally could not bring herself to dispose of. She would read the letter later, when she was more prepared mentally to embrace its contents. And besides, she had the excuse of having to dash off to collect Isabella, who for once, was not stopping off at Tremeneghy after school.

Kate forgot about the letter, and the bills. As the days approached midsummer Pencarra became increasingly overrun by 'emmets', as the locals described the tourists who invaded each year like a plague of swarming insects. It was some small, subversive retaliation at having to share their beautiful county with these bringers of much needed wealth.

Everywhere was busy. No one could get a table at Captain Carter's, and Vivien was opening Wreckers until 10 o'clock every night of the week. Kate, rather rashly, had offered to help out, at least during school hours. She regretted it somewhat because she cherished her solitude. Her time alone was precious painting time. But Vivien was extremely grateful, and offered her a small wage. She also allowed Kate more space to exhibit her paintings—commission free—and it became clear that perhaps it was time to take a break from painting, and start actually trying to sell.

And so Kate reluctantly ventured back into town, and into life. In the event she was quite well hidden within the depths of Vivien's shop, with only tourists to contend with. Most of the townspeople were occupied with the business of making money whilst the opportunity presented itself. Pencarra had come alive with people selling everywhere.

The cafes, bars and restaurants were constantly full, it seemed. Shops that had lain listless for most of the year now flung their doors wide, their wares spilling into the street, each eager to grab their share of the trade. Many sold the usual seaside paraphernalia of seashells, postcards and buckets and spades. But there were also expensive, upmarket jewellery shops and surf shops that sold or rented boards and wetsuits. Anyone who didn't have a premises, it seemed, was out on the streets with a barrow selling trinkets, or offering to braid hair on the harbour front. The Pencarra fishermen had been reluctant to sell out their heritage to mammon, but one or two of them now offered group fishing trips; and the rest could hardly grumble about the demand for local line-caught mackerel at all the town's restaurants.

One day Kate surprised herself. She had been standing in the doorway of Wreckers and gazing longingly at the comings and goings at Blue Wave across the harbour way, when she saw Wendron Laity and another artist put up posters advertising a forthcoming exhibition of new works to be held in the old church crypt. The snooty woman was nowhere in sight. On sudden impulse, Kate grabbed one of her paintings from the wall of Wreckers and marched with it under her arm across the cobbled way, leaving Vivien alone and intrigued.

Twenty minutes later Kate returned, sporting a giant beam of a smile.

'I've just got myself into an exhibition!' she explained to Vivien, as if she could hardly believe it herself.

'Well, of course you have,' said Vivien. 'And not before time! I was wondering if you were ever going to do anything about it.'

Kate looked at her friend suspiciously. Had Vivien known all along that Kate was an amateur? It didn't matter anymore. Wendron Laity had even admitted to admiring Kate's paintings on a visit to Wreckers, and had said that she was most welcome to participate—provided she could supply enough paintings in time, and in accordance with the theme—and that if things worked out, they could have further discussion about her joining the co-operative. She would have to work like mad to get enough suitable work ready, but Kate was prepared to paint day and night to justify this opportunity.

'Don't worry about the shop,' continued Vivien, 'I can easily get Salima to help if I can prise her away from the beach between her waitressing shifts.'

'Oh I'll still help when I can,' said Kate, with reciprocal loyalty. 'We'll work something out.'

Whenever there was a lull in trade, Kate and Vivien would entertain themselves, like little girls, by discussing what they would wear to the forthcoming party. Kate had been through Vivien's rack of beautifully made dresses countless times, and was finding it hard to make a choice.

She liked one that was white and gold and Grecian in style; long and cool, it would be elegant on a hot summer's night. But she was also drawn to an emerald-green Georgian gown, which was made of heavier material, but had a flattering bodice and three-quarter-length sleeves trimmed with white lace. Her eyes flickered over the deep-red Princess dress that she had first discovered back in September, on her first visit to Wreckers. It was wonderful, but it was...too much; too *audacious*.

However, unlike Vivien, Kate had a limit to discussing frocks, and soon tired of trying to make a decision. The more she pondered, and despite Vivien's assurances that everyone would be similarly attired, the more she became convinced that the gowns were too fancy dress, and that she might end up looking like a pantomime dame.

But eventually, with the ball only days away, she had to decide.

'I prefer the green,' said Lance, who was there again, just hanging around. His appearance was extra laid-back today, as he slouched, arms folded, against the old table that Vivien used as a payment-desk. He wore a thin knitted sweater with faded, fraying jeans, and sported at least two days stubble on his jaw. Kate felt a ridiculous sense of satisfaction to see longer strands of blonde hair already growing scruffily out from under his beanie hat.

'Really? I'm not sure. It might be too heavy. Too sombre.'

'Try them on again,' said Vivien, with no hint of impatience. 'It's not so busy right now. Just one final try, then make a decision and stick to it.' Vivien herself was already a vision of medieval beauty, dressed in her long pale blue gown that she had worn when Kate had first met her.

Reluctantly, Kate went behind the curtain that provided a makeshift changing room with the two dresses. She had to come out again to view her appearance in the large gilt mirror propped up against a wall behind Vivien's desk. She wore the Grecian dress first, and Vivien—who naturally had a supply of hair accessories in her desk drawer—helped to pile and pin her long hair up on top of her head to complete the look. Kate did her best to look like a Goddess.

Lance mused silently, half watching the women and half-reading a brochure that he had picked up randomly from the pile of local promotions on the desk. Well, perhaps he *might* like to stay at the Sunny Vale Holiday Park one of these days.

'You look gorgeous,' said Vivien. She looked coyly at her brother. 'What do you think, Lance? Doesn't Kate look gorgeous?'

Lance glanced over Kate's appearance briefly.

'Yes,' he said.

'I think that's the one,' said Vivien. 'But try the other again, quickly, just to be sure.' Kate did as she was instructed. Although the green dress gave the illusion of being fastened and secured with stays and a stomacher, thankfully, for ease of dressing, Vivien had inserted a discreet zip, and hook and eye, at the back. And so it wasn't long before Kate re-emerged from behind the curtain.

'Okay, I think hair should be down for this one,' said Vivien, rushing to rearrange Kate's hairdo. 'Perhaps with just the front bits tied back, like this... Oh this would look lovely with a flower tiara! I'm thinking white roses with pale green accents...'

Kate gave her friend a look to suggest that she shouldn't push her luck.

'Well I don't know anymore,' Vivien pondered out loud. 'The white dress was amazing, but this is good too. You look really beautiful. Don't you think so Lance?'

'Yes.'

Kate turned and smiled blithely at Lance. At that moment the shop doorbell jingled and a fresh influx of shoppers entered. Vivien moved to the desk and gave Lance a friendly shove as a hint that he should remove himself. He clambered off, stumbling a little in the confined space, just as Kate was moving towards the changing room again. She had been stretching one arm over her shoulder to release the catch at the top of the dress, and somehow, as Lance brushed against her back, the hook managed to become ensnared in the loose knit of his sleeve.

'Hold on,' he said, 'we seem to be caught.'

Lance tried to disengage the hook, but the damn thing was ludicrously entwined. He cursed under his breath. How had it managed to become so fastidiously attached in such a short space of time and with such a brief touch? It was the same curious way that a jumble of electrical flexes or computer cables would automatically coil into a serpentine tangle; or how chains in a jewellery box would instinctively tie themselves in knots. The hook was working in a different space-time continuum and had slowly—in its own universe— weaved itself in and out of the lightweight fibres of Lance's jersey. As he tugged fruitlessly at the unfathomable attachment, even Lance began to question the laws of physics.

He held his arm awkwardly hovering above Kate's shoulder, where the low-cut neckline of the dress bared her smooth, sun-browned skin. Kate waited patiently beneath him, and usefully, she thought, moved her hair to one side to aid his view. The gesture was not at all helpful. Lance thought hard about the Sunny Vale Holiday Park.

He bent to try to see what was going on, and briefly considered removing the jumper. However, since he had nothing on underneath, he decided that the band of amused customers whose attention they had caught were probably getting enough of a side show already. Frustrated, he moved around Kate's body to face her head on, and resting his arm as lightly as he dared upon her shoulder, he reached across with the other arm and wrestled once more with the hook. Finally, in desperation, he leant forward across Kate's bared neck, his chin touching the back of her shoulder; and putting his teeth to the mangled gnarl of threads, he bit it hard, ripping at the sleeve. *The warmth from her body and the clean smell of her hair.* Sunny Vale was of no use to him now.

'Thank you,' said Kate to him, once freed. She met him with the briefest contact of her eyes, before stepping demurely to a safe distance.

Lance would have a hole in his sleeve but at least his equilibrium would be restored. 'You're welcome,' he said politely, 'and I, er, um...definitely prefer the green.'

Kate smiled and turned quickly into the dressing room. Safely behind the curtain, she tried to recover. It had disconcerted her to feel the stubble from his cheek against the nape of her neck. She had had to contain an involuntary gasp of pleasure and resist instinctively clutching at him. How embarrassasing that would have been! As if it wasn't bad enough for the poor man, being caught up in her dress; it was not as if he had a choice but to be close.

And she knew that Lance wasn't flirting, but just giving an opinion on the dress. Yet it was oddly gratifying that he should have one, and she smiled to herself again in private.

Meanwhile, a young boy of about ten stood staring scornfully at Lance, chewing gum, and Vivien was similarly considering him with hand on hip and arched brow.

'What?' Lance protested. 'I'm just saying I prefer the green one, that's all.'

'Loser!' the boy smirked before trotting off towards the beckoning yelps of his mother.

No one had noticed a figure perched on one of the harbour-side seats outside. Jem had taken a break for lunch, and sat rebelliously on the back support of the bench, his feet on the seat, eating a pasty and slugging from a bottle of beer. From his elevated height he could see right through to the back of Vivien's shop. The interior was in shadow compared to the bright sunshine outside, and customers kept getting in the way; but it made no difference. It made no difference at all.

He could see everything.

C H A P T E R   4 0

A Blossoming

It was the day of the party, and Kate was in volatile mood. True, she felt an underlying contentment, as if somehow everything in life was falling into place; and so despite her reservations, was looking forward to the evening with some anticipation. But the thought of Jem's forbidding presence caused her some disquietude. There was no way of knowing whether he would be in malevolent frame of mind, or in his more usual, jovial, element. He never could resist a party, and so she hoped for the latter condition. If this were to be the case, it would be the best environment in which to break the ice, and perhaps reinstate civilities. And she would have to face him sooner or later, she supposed.

Isabella was refusing to wear the pretty ditsy frock and broderie anglais bonnet that Vivien had suggested, and insisted on wearing a fluttery short dance skirt with black leggings and T-shirt. It was going to be either that or jeans. 'You don't understand, I'm not like *you!*' she said. 'I don't like pretty girly things like you. I'm much more, you know, *funky.*'

Kate sighed. She hadn't known that she liked "pretty girly" things, and was clearly, as a mother, not allowed to be "funky". She wondered if it was worth explaining to Isabella once more the nature of the party, but knew that she would be met again with protestations that *none of the other children* would be dressing up. And to tell the truth, Kate sympathised. Each time she passed the green dress hanging in the hallway outside the bathroom, she experienced a cold wave of doubt. In a past life she would not have hesitated, and indeed had actively dressed in an eclectic, and yes, funky manner on a daily basis. But now...now there lurked the potential danger of looking somewhat unhinged.

But there was no time to fret, or to argue with Izzy. Kate had spent a hectic morning at Wreckers covering for Vivien who was busy preparing for the party, but thankfully they had shut early for once. Juliet and Parker had arrived. It was a little awkward that their planned visit coincided with the ball, but the Borlases had been typically gracious about extending an invitation. If Vivien bore any personal misgivings about Juliet she did not voice them, but rather had reconfirmed "*of course* they're invited." They were staying this time in a bed and breakfast in the village, but stopped by at the cottage first to catch up. They had been driving since five o'clock in the morning, and looked tired.

They arrived in a colourful, shiny, and very trendy campervan, which they'd hired to accommodate Parker's spanking new surfboard. Juliet barely spoke, except to moan about missing her Porsche, but Parker was brimming with enthusiasm. It was somewhat hard to take.

He was thrilled to be back in Cornwall in the summertime. He definitely had to catch some waves while he was down. Apparently he had taken some surf lessons when recently in Hawaii, and now there was nothing on Earth that could keep him out of the water.

'It was a modelling job,' explained Juliet dryly, 'for some ultra-trendy surf clothes. And didn't you tell me that you nicked the board?' She turned her attention to Parker, with tired irritation.

'Nah, it was a freebie! Sort of. Well, no one said anyfing anyway. I got some amazing threads too. Can't wait to get to the beach!'

Juliet rolled her eyes, and Kate wondered once again at this strange relationship.

'Stoked for the party,' continued Parker effusively. 'Viv's gotta come to The Smoke. I'd show her round all the geezers in the fashion biz—not gonna lie, love her they would. Top bird. Classy.'

Juliet looked abnormally absorbed in reading the local paper and almost succeeded in suppressing a scowl.

Parker continued unabated. 'Stone me Jules, just breathe in that sea air. I'm high on it already. I'm not even joking.'

Kate could swear there was a hint of Cornish burr in Parker's already hybrid cockney accent.

'So tell me,' said Juliet, as if desperate to shut Parker up, 'who is taking Cinders to the ball? Have you made up with the dentist yet?'

Kate hid her annoyance. Juliet made Jem sound both a transitory affair by referring to him as 'the dentist', and simultaneously a foregone conclusion as her only suitor.

'Actually, I'm going with Lance,' she said, hoping to sound nonchalant.

'Oh right,' said Juliet, without a trace of excitement.

Kate had been concerned that the situation should not be misunderstood, but still found herself disappointed at Juliet's complete indifference. 'Of course it's just a convenience, since we're both single. We're just going as friends.'

'Hmm,' said Juliet, still flicking through the paper, 'I must say though, I'm surprised he hasn't got a proper date. But I don't suppose anyone round here is good enough for him.'

Eventually Juliet declared herself to be dead on her feet, and insisted that she and Parker slope off to the village for a nap before the party. No one mentioned the circumstances of their last visit, and Kate quietly hoped that Derry had been no more than a dalliance, and that Juliet might even redeem herself tonight with impeccable behaviour. Juliet, in truth, had done no real wrong; but wrong had come of it all the same.

404

Derry had, it appeared, moved on from his attachment to Vivien. No one had heard from him in weeks, and it was only presumed that he was still in Ireland. Kate suspected that it had taken this abandonment to make Vivien value, and even miss him. She may not have returned his passion, but they had shared a friendship of long-standing. It was a construct that had been built over many years of understandings and acceptances, but now was wrecked and laid bare—it had not withstood this fresh inspection.

Before they left, Juliet, who had been too tired to pay much attention on arrival, studied her sister anew. 'You look sort of different,' she said.

'I know!' beamed Kate, delighted that someone had noticed, 'I've lost so much weight! I suppose it must be all the walking...'

'No, it's not that,' said Juliet quickly. She was not about to admit that her sister's figure now rivalled her own slender frame. 'No, there's something else. You look kind of, well...' There was a difference that she could not quite place, a kind of repressed excitement. '...*natural,*' she finished, but said the word as though it were an insult. 'Your hair has got so long and...bloody hell! You're not wearing any make-up! And your skin's really brown! I suppose you've been lying on the beach for weeks?'

'Not really, I think it's more of a weatherbeaten thing...'

'It's terribly bad for you, Kate, everyone knows that these days.' Juliet's own colour came from her local spray tanning salon.

'Yeah well, it's not deliberate,' said Kate sourly, and deciding not to launch into a lecture about chemicals on the skin.

'You'll get wrinkles. I just knew this would happen. Kate, we need to get you back to civilisation for a while. Come back to London and I'll take you shopping. And you can get a decent haircut and a facial.'

'I'm fine. Really. I'm perfectly happy. And you know my opinion on facials!'

Juliet giggled. She had once booked Kate an appointment at a beauty salon as a birthday present. Once having got over her fit of giggles at being 'tickled' on the face and neck by the unimpressed therapist, Kate had left with a huge dent in her ego having had "all her blackheads" squeezed. Kate had not even known that she had any blackheads.

Eventually the visitors left, taking Isabella—in the dance skirt—with them, as they had agreed to drop her off early at Tremeneghy. Too late Kate saw how this might prove awkward, but there was a chance that Vivien would be at the shop, and that either Lance or Lillian would be there to receive Izzy. Finally, left alone in the cottage, Kate turned her mind to getting ready. No beauty salons or nail bars for her, but rather a bath, a good full body moisturise, a quick visit to an emery board and a shampoo and blow-dry. All the same...*natural.* That was the word Juliet had used. Was she letting herself go? Perhaps she should make a bit more of an effort tonight, if she could but remember how. But she allowed herself a small harrumph anyhow.

Lance was throwing hay bales around the garden when Juliet arrived with Izzy. Lillian had shown them in, and since he was in unusually good humour he greeted them heartily. He had his reservations about Juliet, but she was Kate's sister after all, and so had to be essentially okay.

'What's all this?' queried Juliet, hiding her tiredness behind dark sunglasses. She had left Parker in the car, flicking through glossy magazines.

'Bales to sit on,' he explained. 'It's just a bit of fun. There's plenty of other seating, of course.'

Isabella immediately ran off to where she had spotted Finn, Tom and Callum peering out from a house of straw made from some pilfered bales. 'Let me in, little pigs! Or I'll huff and I'll puff and I'll blow your house down!' she cried, delighted, before crawling through a small igloo-style entrance and out of sight.

'So...thanks for inviting us tonight,' Juliet offered, but without a smile. She was not going to give too much away until she was sure of her welcome.

'It's a pleasure,' said Lance as if reading her mind. It was the only reply forthcoming, but he said it cheerfully enough, and with an astonishingly dazzling smile.

'I hear you're taking my sister to the ball,' said Juliet, by way of conversation.

Lance grimaced. 'I do wish people would stop calling it that,' he said, but in good humour. 'How is Kate today? Looking forward to tonight I hope?'

'Yeah, she's good,' said Juliet, her curiosity rising. 'Very good. In fact, positively flourishing.'

Lance smiled again, only more covertly, before shyly returning his attention to the hay bales. It occurred to Juliet that he, like Kate, seemed much improved in spirit. He was somehow more ready to please, more affable. Juliet thought back to Kate's party at Christmas, when he had been reserved, guarded and unsmiling. On New Year's Eve, he had admittedly been more attentive, but in a maniacal, rabid sort of way, and had become increasingly morose as the evening had worn on. But there was nothing manic about him now. On the contrary, he seemed relaxed, happy, and yet at the same time...*excited*. And like her sister, there was an indistinguishable aura about him; a glow.

Well, well, well, thought Juliet, who was no fool. So Kate had nabbed herself the most handsome and quite possibly most eligible man in town. She wondered if her poor sister knew. And, more pertinently she wondered what Jem thought about it.

Juliet's senses, tired as they were, had secretly fired up when Kate had told her about going to the party with Lance, but rather cruelly, she had not taken the bait. It had come as a surprise to her. She had suspected in the past that Kate might subconsciously fancy Lance—after all, who wouldn't? She'd wondered why Kate was in denial about it, and had put it down to low self-esteem. Kate probably felt that he was out of her league. But it had never occurred to her before now that Lance might be interested in Kate. Juliet, despite her growing exhaustion, felt a flicker of anticipation for the night to come. It looked like this party might be more interesting than she had imagined.

She declined Lance's offer of a drink—remembering Parker stuck outside in the van like a puppy—and insisted on seeing herself out, since he was busy. In the long hallway that led to the front door, she was surprised by a tall glamorous woman who had emerged from one of the rooms on the end and who was striding towards her now, with the practiced prance of the catwalk model or most seasoned of paparazzi fodder.

Juliet, with innate if somewhat belated loyalty to her sister, wondered who this *slag* was. She casually pushed her sunglasses up onto her head in order to get a better view. The woman looked vaguely familiar, but she couldn't quite place where she had seen her before. She was sure she had not been at the other parties; and if she was here specifically for tonight's ball, then Juliet sensed that her presence did not bode well for Kate.

Leah expertly eyed Juliet up and down as they approached each other wordlessly in the corridor: *Converse, boyfriend jeans, Breton T-shirt, black leather jacket. Decent haircut. Hmm.* She was taken aback to find a strikingly attractive woman in the house, and wondered what Lance thought he was up to. However, she was not about to display her irritation in front of the woman, and so as they passed each other she

408

smiled sweetly at Juliet. But her eyes said: *I could take you, bitch.*

Just try it, Juliet's cool gaze replied with equal composure.

With no attempt to explain her presence, and in contrast to Leah's professionally leggy stride, Juliet replaced her sunglasses, and performed a rebelliously languid slouch to the door. It was only when she had sat down in the van and turned the key in the ignition that she remembered.

'Shit! Leah Greenwood!'

Instinctively Parker sat bolt upright from where he had been slumped half-asleep, and whipped off his own sunglasses.

'Where?' He cried.

'Back there, in the house,' said Juliet, more thoughtfully. 'I told you, she used to be married to Lance. She must have come for the party.'

Parker's thoughts, unlike Juliet's, were not immediately of concern for Kate, but rather he looked annoyed.

'Fuck me,' he muttered, as Juliet pulled away along the lane. 'You fink you've discovered a place, and then before you know it, Cornwall is swarming with C-listers.' He shook his head sadly. 'Lowers the tone, dunnit.'

Juliet smirked. You could never tell whether Parker was taking himself seriously or being fashionably sarcastic. 'I thought you liked Leah Greenwood?'

'Yeah, I did—but keep it to yourself. My star is on the rise and I need to be careful what manner of person I'm seen with.'

'Really?' said Juliet in mock surprise. 'I'm privileged then. What's wrong with Leah Greenwood all of a sudden?'

'She just so...'

'...So?'

'*Over,*' said Parker.

409

CHAPTER 41

Under the Pear Tree

Lance had abandoned the hay bales; it was pointless trying to lay them out in any artistic or even practical manner since the children constantly purloined and moved them around according to their own ends, and no doubt would do the same this evening. He decided his efforts would be better spent sorting out the vast tangle of outdoor lights that had been stuffed haphazardly into a large cardboard box after last year's party. Then he climbed up on a stepladder and attempted to thread a string of delicate fairy lights around the pear tree. Leah spied on him from the parlour.

She had been skulking there for some time, watching him from one of the long French windows, and trying to decide on which scheme to follow. She had not looked forward to this stupid annual embarrassment, and had only come to Cornwall for the party because of a lull in work—Confession Box had reached the end of its current run—and because of a bout of unwanted attention in the national press.

Leah usually loved pictures of herself striding from a London nightclub in the early hours of the morning, in killer heels, hemline raised to her thighs, and a corresponding lowering of lashes. It was her favourite, somewhat demure, but long-suffering look: *You don't understand the burden I have to endure*, it said. *And you never will, because you can never be me*, it said. *You are the plebs, the lucky proletariat, but it is my fate to walk amongst the elite*. She usually bore this hardship well.

But lately there had been a few pictures that she did not like so much. And there were stories being put about that, although strenuously refuted by her publicist, were beginning to chip away at her image. It wasn't her fault! Things had been going so well and she had done everything right. But fame was a fickle friend. Sometimes things changed just ever-so-slightly, almost imperceptibly, and suddenly instead of being fêted you were a figure of ridicule.

For example, Leah's hair, which she had always been so proud of, for its natural colour; its length and strength, was now being cited as somewhat outmoded. "Stale", she had been called in one particularly nasty article that led with the headline "Does this woman never visit the hairdresser?", accompanied by pictures of her taken over the last decade, exposing the crime of her unaltering hairdo. Leah had been furious. It was akin to suggesting that she had worn the same dress for ten years. Her assistant Penny had borne the brunt of her rage, despite efforts to console.

Another magazine ran an article: "Staid Maid or Modern-made—which are you?" and held Leah up as an example of the prior, whilst the latter was exemplified by one of her biggest rivals, TV presenter and "media-personality" Bette Wu. The irony being—as Leah had screamed in annoyance in poor Penny's ear—that Bette Wu also had long and natural-coloured hair; it wasn't fair! But despite her protestations, even Leah knew when she was beaten. Instead of looking groomed to perfection, Bette's hair was messy and backcombed, and would have had a struggle to look deliberate were it not set off by a perfectly straight fringe. And there was something effortlessly more up-to-date about Bette's clothes style. She managed a certain insouciance; a catch-it-before-its-gone virtual teeter on the very precipice of fashion. It

411

didn't matter how cutting-edge Leah attempted to be, she was beginning to look like a follower, and not a leader. It was the first step towards *has-been*.

At least she still had some power here. She was still the most famous person ever to have escaped from this small part of the world, and the most talked about locally. And she still had Lance, if she wanted him—and of course, Finn. Damn it, she had a *family*. And if her worst fears were realised, she could always retreat to the countryside and claim to be shunning fame and fortune in favour of the simple life. Lie low for a while. She wondered if Lance had finished refurbishing that dump of a house that he had bought in the middle of nowhere. It would be perfect for a photo shoot—people loved that sort of thing. The so-called rural idyll. And it had to be said, Finn and Lance would make beautiful accessories: the rugged yet refined husband; the adorable, somewhat semi-feral child, traipsing barefoot down the cliff path with a surfboard and his long sun-bleached hair blowing in the wind. It would, naturally, be her final recourse, but Leah felt sure she could pull it out of the bag. It would be The Secret Life of Leah Greenwood; the one no one knew about or even suspected. She would be reassessed in the public eye. She would be *fucking enigmatic!*

And there was no way she was going to let some upstart slut interfere. She went into the garden breezily. She wore a checked cowboy shirt which she had tied up at the waist to reveal her perfectly toned belly. The low-cut jeans showed off her long shapely legs, but Leah cursed herself now for not wearing those designer frayed denim hot pants with the horse motif. *Bette Wu would have worn the hot pants*. She strolled around the garden aimlessly for a bit, to ensure that Lance could check out how amazing she looked. Then she moved towards the pear tree, and with an arm up to shield her face from the sun, gazed up at him.

'Hey there,' she said, and parted her wide glossy pink lips to reveal her dainty white veneers in a radiant smile. 'What'cha doing?'

Lance sighed. 'What do you want Leah?'

'Well that's not very friendly,' Leah pouted. 'I was just saying hi. Maybe I was going to offer to help.'

Lance smiled at her fondly, as one would a child. 'Thank you, but I've got it under control here. Although I'm sure Lillian could use some help in the kitchen with the food...if you're offering?'

Leah gave him a dark look and decided to proceed anyway. 'I met your girlfriend,' she said.

For a second Lance might have looked disconcerted, but he quickly took control of himself, and leaping up into the branches of the tree, continued to drape the fairy lights around its boughs. Had she meant Kate? He wondered how they would have met. He didn't answer.

'I have to say she looked a bit rough, though,' Leah continued. 'Did you keep her up all night, Lance? And sunglasses in the house? So passé! You're letting your standards slip, my dear.' Leah was not one to publicly acknowledge any level of attraction in another woman, even when that woman, Juliet, was quite obviously pretty, despite her tiredness.

'Can't think who you mean,' said Lance, not looking down from the tree. 'Juliet was here just now, but she's a very good-looking woman—by anyone's standards.'

'Juliet?' Leah digested the information with the expression of a cat holding a tortured bird between its fangs. The name "Romeo" immediately came to her mind, but she repressed the impulse to make a crack about it. Best not to give him any ideas.

'She looks like she takes drugs.' Leah conveniently forgot her own, naturally harmless, dabbling. 'I'm not sure I'm happy about a woman like that being around Finn.' Her eyes accosted him with her most serious, concerned expression.

Lance, although by no means taken in, relented a little. He looked down at her in earnest. 'Well, there's no need for you to worry Leah, Juliet is just a friend, down from London for the party.'

'From London?' said Leah quick as a flash, and not ready to be easily appeased. 'How did you meet her?'

Lance jumped down from the tree, exasperated, and stood before her. 'Does it matter? She's Kate's sister. Kate from Amelia Church's old cottage.'

'Ah, Jem's girlfriend,' Leah nodded pensively.

The woman never missed a thing, thought Lance, in irritation.

'Actually, they split up,' he said, reluctant to divulge any further information. 'As indeed you accurately predicted,' he added, before she could get in another scathing remark.

'Of course,' said Leah but she was already bored of the subject and wanted to get back on track. 'Well, I never really thought she was your girlfriend, I was just teasing you. So, we'll be going to the party together then, you and me, as usual?'

It was true, Lance had to acknowledge, that in past years, if Leah had bothered to show up at all, that he would accompany her, for appearances only, to the party. It had suited him to sidestep the pressure and implications of having to find another partner, and had averted the awkward questions of a much younger Finn.

'Not this time, Leah,' he said firmly. 'I...have a date.'

'Oh really? Who?' snapped Leah. She was feeling foiled. he had just led her into false security, and now it seemed he had a girlfriend after all.

'It doesn't matter.' Lance turned and walked towards the house.

414

'How can you say that?' Leah followed him in angry mood. 'Don't you think I have a right to know?'

'No, Leah, I don't!' He stopped to look at her, and then spoke more gently. 'Look, we're divorced, and have been for years. Accept it. I don't want to upset you...'

'I'm not upset,' Leah said quickly, composing herself. 'Don't be ridiculous. I just want to know what kind of woman the father of my child is seeing. Is that too much to ask?'

'Yes, Leah, it is.'

'But surely I have a right?'

'Again; no, you don't.'

'Well, I'll meet her tonight anyway, so you might as well tell me.'

Lance sighed again. 'Okay. Okay, why not? It's Kate.'

'Another Kate?'

He tried not to look rattled. 'No. The same one.'

'I see. So Lance, is she a little bit slaggy? Or perhaps you're just doing her a favour? That's so typical of you. There's really no need, you know, now that I'm here.'

'I'm not just being gallant, Leah, and neither am I going to change my mind.'

'And what am I supposed to do? Am I supposed to be seen to be humiliated?'

'Don't be absurd. Besides, you're already here; just skip the grand entrance and...I don't know, stay in the background, for once, if that's possible.'

Leah looked at him as if he were mad.

He softened a little. 'I'm sure that you can find someone to accompany you if you put your mind to it. You shouldn't take me for granted just because we have Finn in common.'

Leah said nothing more. Lance was being surprisingly difficult, but even she knew when to retreat. Besides, it was obvious to her what was going on, his last statement made that clear. He felt taken for granted, and wanted to show her that he had a life. And was she, Leah, supposed to feel jealous? It was pathetic. Her natural inclination was to pretend to be wounded, but that would not do in this instance. She could do superior too. If he thought that she was going to react to his little protest then he was wrong. She could be proud; she could be cool. But still, it was annoying, and a minor defeat. She would have preferred to have had her own way.

CHAPTER 42

The Phone Call

Over in the village, Jem sat staring at his mobile phone on the coffee table in front of him. He had made a clearing in the debris in which to place it, and so it took on a more ominous, portentous meaning. Just one more drink, and then he would make the call. He slugged the wine carelessly into the glass. Jem had gone into a dark mood since breaking up with Kate, and the scene he had witnessed at Wreckers the other day had compounded his feeling of gloom. It wasn't so much that he missed her, but rather it was the overriding sense of failure that really dragged him down. He had been out on a couple of dates with girls that he had met in the pub; not local girls—God knows he had already tried most of *them*—but tourists; emmets; party girls out for a holiday shag. It only served to emphasise the pointlessness of it all. Was this all he was ever going to be wanted for? He really thought there had been a chance with Kate, but no; it seemed she didn't love him. It seemed, in fact, that he was unlovable.

And then there was Lance. Well, of course Lance would be behind it all. Oh he wouldn't have done anything untoward, of course. Lance was sickeningly honourable and Jem knew that his friend would not have made a pass at Kate behind his back. But it didn't matter. Lance just had to be there, with his tall good looks and indifferent air. Lance had a way of appearing unavailable even though he was patently single. It was as if he could not find anyone good enough, and was not going to

417

settle for anything less. And women loved him for it! That was the most galling thing. He didn't even have to try! He didn't even have to bother to go to the trouble of snapping his fingers. Lance just had to be, and the women came running; usually to be rejected. And now Kate had thrown Jem over in order to be available for Lance. It just wasn't fair. He drained the glass and poured another.

But what if this time Lance was actually interested? It had not occurred to Jem to consider this, until he had beheld the scene in Wreckers. Even he could recognise the spark of sexual tension, despite the distance, and the obstacle of the customers, which might have been fairly considered to be a reason for confusion and doubt. But there had been a moment, a second really, when Lance had looked at Kate; and Jem had seen it, and he knew. And the girls had been trying on dresses, which meant that Kate was going to the party tonight. It didn't take a great leap of imagination to realise that she could be going with Lance, even though Lance had not said anything and Jem, by avoiding contact, had heard no rumour amongst their social group. And so was he to face further humiliation? Perhaps it would be better if he did not go to the party himself. But if he didn't go it would not stop the inevitable.

In a moment of sudden panic, Jem had realised that Lance might yet tell him. The more he thought about it, the more it made sense. Lance would want to do the proper thing. He wouldn't let Jem show up in ignorance. Wildly, Jem grabbed the phone from the table and checked the time. It was 4 o'clock. It could happen any moment now; and the longer he languished in indecision, the less chance he would have of perverting the course of events. If Lance called first, it was over. He would apologise and explain, and trust that Jem was okay about it all. And so Jem, naturally would be obliged to say "No problem, mate, it's cool."

But as yet, Jem didn't know; or wasn't supposed to know. The paranoia struck deep within him. He was being taken for a fool. But he was not a fool, he was smarter than they thought. He slung the phone back on the table and raised the glass again, gnawing at its edges, seeking succour and comfort in its contents. Where was he? Yes, that was it: *smarter than them.* All he had to do was call Lance first. All he had to say was how upset he was about Kate, and that he would be heartbroken if she came to the party with another man. He would say that he hadn't known who to talk to, but Lance, one of his oldest friends, would surely understand.

He stared at the phone. He had to do it now, or Lance would surely call. And besides, he was supposed to be meeting Jenifer at five for something to eat before going to the party.

He had been surprised that Jenifer Trewin had agreed to go with him. She had shown no interest in recent years, but rather had treated him with a certain reluctance; as though she had "been there, done that". But she had shown a rekindled, highly flirtatious, interest of late—ever since he'd started dating Kate, if he was honest—and had agreed immediately to his spontaneous, somewhat drunken request in the bar a few nights ago. Jem suppressed an unwelcome thought that perhaps Jenifer was, like himself, feeling beleaguered by life. Things had not worked out for her as they might have expected when they were all teenagers together, when Jenifer had been considered the prettiest, most popular girl in class—at least amongst the boys. Now, in her early thirties and a single parent, perhaps Jenifer too was feeling jaded. They had both been cheated of life's initial promise, and were now facing increasing rejection, and ultimately, the scrapheap. So they would be two losers keeping each other company.

He stuffed the thought away and returned his diminishing powers of concentration to the matter in hand. What was it?

419

Kate...yes, that was it. *Why didn't Kate feel jaded?* It really pissed him off that she appeared so happy to be alone, to be single; to be without him... *Yeah, well maybe that was because she was sniffing around Lance*. Anyway, Kate would surely be a bit disgruntled at his appearance with Jenifer. He knew that there was a mutual dislike there. Well, he hoped she bloody well *was* disgruntled. He hoped she would be jealous. It would serve her right for thinking she could sneak around with Lance behind his back. *Oh shit and bollocks, Lance.* He had to ring him. He had to ring him right now before it was too late.

Jem finished his drink, picked up the silent, accusatory phone again, and stabbed at Lance's number.

CHAPTER 43

The Letter

Kate had, in subtle ways, adapted so well to living in the countryside that she had even left the huge kitchen windows open, wide-armed and welcoming, to any opportunistic thief whilst she had her bath. It must have been a freak gust of warm summer wind, but somehow Marsha's letter ended up on the kitchen floor, along with the disregarded and unpaid bills. Kate, tripping gaily into the kitchen in her bathrobe, scowled when she saw them in her path, where they could no longer be ignored. Picking them up, she slung the bills on the table, still destined for later digestion. But looking at Marsha's letter, she hesitated.

Later on, she would see the irony of the fact that it was her unusually optimistic mood that had prompted her to read the letter; to give Marsha a chance, for old time's sake. She wandered around the kitchen as she read, tidying up absent-mindedly as she did.

Dear Kate,

I'm very sorry that you have not seen fit to reply to my previous letters, and hope that you and Isabella are both okay? Much as I enjoy the dying art of letter-writing, you should appreciate that not everyone feels the same, and the others would happily call or e-mail if you would just send your details. Juliet says she feels guilty enough about *giving me your address, and won't tell me anything more, so I am left to appeal to your good nature to <u>please</u> urge you to reply.*

I can't believe you are punishing us all like this. Nobody ever meant to hurt you Kate. How can you throw away years of friendship over such a little thing?

Kate groaned. The letter went on like this for a further three paragraphs. Marsha was obviously not going to rest easy in her conscience until she, at least, had Kate's forgiveness. But it seemed that the only method she could devise to prompt this forgiveness was to remind Kate, at length, and with underlined emphasis, of her own failings, not only as a friend, but as a person. The conclusion arrived at was that Kate was either incredibly selfish, or must be having some kind of mental breakdown.

...Stevie is getting married in September; to Luciano (I think you met him?), if you can believe it! Well, I suppose he can, now, so he's exercising his right to. Anyway, he says he would like to invite you, but only if you really want to come (and I think you <u>should</u>). Think about it Kate, how often does Stevie get married? You ought to come. He's supposed to be your <u>friend</u>.

There's some other news that I am loathe to have to be the one to tell you, but I think someone should. Miles and Heidi are going to have a baby. It's due around Christmas, and I think that they too will be getting married, but there's no date yet. It will probably be after the baby is born. The thing is, Miles has told Angus that he really wants to see Isabella again; he feels that it's only right. After all, how can he recognise one child and not the other?

Kate sat down heavily at the kitchen table. She stared blindly at the letter in her hand for a few seconds, and then forced herself to read on.

> *...he feels really guilty, Kate, about neglecting Isabella; and you must accept that it would be wrong to keep father and child apart...*

The nerve of it! So now Miles was ready to play happy families. Now he chose to embrace fatherhood, and wanted Izzy as a ready-made sister for his new baby. She wondered, momentarily, how Heidi felt about it. Surely she wasn't going to have him give her parenting tips when he had not had any contact with Izzy for a decade? The idea was preposterous. And to suggest that it was she who was keeping them apart! No doubt this was evidence of the wilful nature that Marsha frequently berated her for. And yet...Miles *was* Izzy's father...she wondered how Izzy would feel about it.

Isabella never talked about her father. Oh, she knew about him; his name, where he came from, what he did. She had seen photographs from the brief time that her parents had been together. Kate had not attempted to hide the details of his existence or even his whereabouts. But Izzy had never asked further. Quite possibly, there was a sense of abandonment, a resentment for the man who had decided that he "just couldn't handle this". But Kate had seen no worrying signs. She had assumed that because there was no real memory of him in her life, Isabella had never missed his presence. But there had always been the possibility that she would, one day, want to know more. Kate would have preferred the request to have come from Izzy, and not her errant father; and yet that might have resulted, ultimately, in his further rejection of her. At least—or so it seemed, if Marsha

423

was right—this way it would be Miles taking the first step, and consequently he risked the rejection, which was a seriously more comfortable thought.

But what if it didn't end there? What if it should lead to access rights or even a custody battle? Kate was burning with outrage. Izzy was *her* child! She was part of her, and had been her whole world since the day she'd been born. And why now? Why, when she had finally made the effort to escape the past and start anew? She could hardly bear to finish the letter, for fear of learning what further interference in her life she would have to endure.

> *...and so, I have given Miles your address, Kate. I know you might be angry with me but I am also sure that even you, deep down, know that it is the right thing to do. In the meantime I am hoping that you will find it in yourself to _forgive_ and will pick up the phone yourself and talk to Miles. I have listed his current contact numbers at the end of this letter, in case you don't know them.*
>
> *Really, really, hoping to hear from you soon,*
> *Your friend,*
> *Marsha xxx*

Kate was stunned. She didn't know what to do, or even think. She stared at the email addresses and telephone numbers that Marsha had provided; some for work, the others private; but all of them saturated with her heartbreak and despair. It was strange how something so harmless as a string of letters and digits could haunt her, but these were cyphers that had once been her domain; would have been hers, by rights. With sudden realisation she grabbed the orange envelope and flicked it over to reveal the date on which it had been sent. Second class post; two, almost three, weeks ago. Three weeks, and she had heard nothing more. It was quite possible that Miles had not been serious, and Marsha was, after all, prone to melodramatics. It might be that he had babbled a few guilty, drunken words to Angus in the pub, and then by way of Chinese whispers they had reached Marsha as confirmation of his rehabilitation and impending sainthood.

But if he was serious...if he was serious then she had lost three weeks, and this was bound to be taken as a sign of non-cooperation. Appalled, Kate realised that she had never had to think like this before. Every decision regarding Isabella she had made by herself alone. She had had no choice, of course, but it had allowed her a certain liberty; she had never before had to deal with opposition where her daughter was concerned. It was horrific to her that Miles might now be thinking of exercising his right of influence.

She told herself not to panic. Miles had, after all, not contacted her himself; it was typically cowardly of him to approach her under the guise of Marsha's ever-willing enthusiasm to scold. But there was nothing official. It was no more, indeed, than a rumour. And she had to concede, it *was* Miles, after all. The initial news, and apparent acceptance, of the new baby may have sparked a burst of evangelical bombast on his part; but on reflection, he may have thought it better to let things lie. She told herself not to panic; at least not just yet.

The shrill bleat of the telephone in the hallway made her jump, shaking her from her thoughts and bringing her back into the present, where she still had a party to go to.

It was Lance.

'Hi!' she said, pleased to hear his voice. 'I was wondering if you would call. We hadn't decided on a time to meet tonight.'

'Actually...that's why I'm ringing, Kate.' She noticed now that he sounded odd. 'Something's come up. Or rather down, to be precise, from London.' His laugh went flat as did the attempted joke. 'It's Leah,' he said more seriously.

'Oh,' said Kate.

'I didn't realise that she was coming…I hadn't heard from her. Only now that she's here…well, it changes things.'

'It does?'

'It was expected…well *she* expected…I'm afraid that I should probably go to the party with Leah. It's easier that way. I don't want to cause any upset…'

'That's fine,' said Kate.

'Look, Kate, I'm truly sorry…'

'Don't worry about it.' She tried to sound matter-of-fact but it was hard to disguise the tension in her voice.

'We'll still see you later of course?' said Lance, equally unable to hide his anxiety. *Anxiety caused by guilt,* thought Kate. 'I know we played up the whole "must have a partner" thing, but it's really only a bit of fun. There's no reason why you shouldn't still…I'd really like to see you there, Kate.'

'Right.' She was feeling curiously emotional. *It was only a bit of fun. No need for a partner; she should still come.* Unless you were Leah Greenwood, of course, in which case you got whatever you wanted.

'Are you sure you're okay about this?'

'Of course,' she grimaced and forced herself to add, 'see you later.'

There was a short silence on the other end of the phone, before he spoke again.

'I'm sorry, Kate.'

When he had hung up, Kate stood for a while staring madly into space, transfixed by a variety of conflicting emotions. And then without warning, she burst into tears.

CHAPTER 44

Hard Feelings

Well of course, there was no way she was going now. She stared at the—now hateful— green dress hanging from the stair railings in the hallway and saw with new clarity how ridiculous she would look, and how foolish she had been. How had she ever conceived that things would go right for her? It was true that Lance had been coerced into asking her to be his partner by Vivien, and that he had agreed only out of friendship; but still, she had *valued* that friendship. She had grown to enjoy his company and had imagined that he would bring an added security tonight, especially in respect of having to face Jem. But he wasn't going to be that shoulder, it seemed. And there was something more; a disappointment...of what? Hope? She was disproportionately upset.

And underlying this distress was a churning anger that she felt rising up in her gut and which threatened to engulf her. She was possessed with rage; a wronged witch prepared to smite indiscriminately all who crossed her path.

Curse Miles and his selfishness! Damn Lance for his capriciousness! And as for Jem...he may possess the outwardly respectable persona of a dentist, but he was nothing but a lying drunken wastrel! At that moment she hated them all.

How dare Miles intrude on her life again, when she had done so much to put him in the past? The well of painful emotion that she had thought dried out had, with little effort on his part, been swiftly refilled. When Miles had deserted her she had been left with feelings of rejection that had lasted for years; feelings that had been compounded by the treachery of her so-called friends. Abandonment had changed her to the core, had moulded her differently. Her confidence and self-esteem were only superficially bolstered and patched up. When you fell, you hit the floor running where you landed. There was no choice but to carry on from the point of landing. But you never, it seemed, climbed back up to where you had started. All you could do was try not to sink to lower levels.

Like sleeping with dentists that you did not love.

She was practically a prostitute!

Kate had never felt more like a big fat failure. She had run away—all the way to Cornwall—and yet the same feelings kept threatening to overwhelm her. She had failed, not only in love, it appeared, but also in life, and in her resolve. She had thought her heart hardened, but plainly it was as susceptible as ever. Well, she would damn well harden it now.

But Vivien might call wondering where she was. Well...damn Vivien!

Kate winced; that wasn't so easy. Vivien had been a good friend and had not betrayed her. *At least not yet*. And then there was Juliet too; her presence at the party would only serve to make Kate's absence all the more conspicuous. Well, damn Juliet too.

Even harder—Juliet was her *sister*; it was practically blasphemy! Then with slow-growing realisation, Kate faced the fact of the one person whom she would not curse, and could not deny.

Isabella.

The last time the Borlases had held a party, Kate—the *prostitute*—had left her daughter there all night in order to spend the night in intemperance and debauchery. She could hardly do the same again, could she? She had an

428

overwhelming, somewhat belated, and guilty desire to see Isabella. She had of late been neglecting her daughter and her one true love, in order to indulge in vain wantonness!

But she couldn't just march in and drag Izzy out. For one thing, her darling might refuse to leave. It would cause a very negative scene, and perhaps make it appear to all the world that her heart was indeed not-quite hardened, and that she was in fact, upset. And it was inconceivable that she should go alone. She would look and feel like the biggest of losers.

She noticed that she was pacing up and down the room like some insane robot. Her heart was thudding ominously in her chest. Was she having a panic attack? She had to do something to quell this awful emotion.

It had been a while since Kate had had an alcoholic drink, but self-pity very quickly led to self-destruction. She marched to the fridge, dragged out a bottle from the back, and rebelliously poured herself a large and extremely well-chilled glass of wine. She drank almost half the glass in one go. Then she took it with her to the table and sat down with head in hands and tried to think.

By the time she had drained the glass, her intentions had been completely reversed, and now she was determined that she *should* go to the party after all, but that she would not go wounded and rejected; that wouldn't do. She must hold up her head and show all of them that she was undefeated. If only…

She needed a prop.

Kate's eyes travelled to the small business card on the kitchen shelf. It had sat there for months, seen daily but equally daily ignored. She wondered… It was worth a try. It might result in further humiliation, but if not, would be a bit of a coup. Spurred on by a restless, wild-eyed energy born of anger, she marched to the telephone in the hallway, picked up the receiver and dialled the number.

Five minutes later, she regarded the dress again and decided that that too, would no longer do. It did not suit her mood. But she still had the keys to Wreckers, and if she was quick, there was just about time...

PART THREE

Something Rich and Strange

"So comes to us at times, from the unknown
And inaccessible solitudes of being,
The rushing of the sea-tides of the soul;"

Henry Wadsworth Longfellow

PRELUDE

She walked straight in, leaving a solitary line of footprints in the sand. Unhesitating, she let the freezing water embrace first her feet, then her calves and thighs as she strove against the surf. She gave an involuntary gasp and a squeal as a rogue wave slapped against her bikini bottoms too soon, but she didn't stop. Then plunging forwards, she submerged, letting the icy sea shock her warm skin and send the message powering from nerve endings through axons, synapses and neurotransmitters until finally, numbingly, to her troubled mind.

Salt water. It was the only thing that worked; the cold, restless, implacable sea. She wasn't a strong swimmer, but each shivering stroke took her further from the affliction; from the curse. She stopped to tread the water, looking back towards the black rocks, austere in the stark morning sunlight, while she was lifted and dropped on the mighty swell. The cliffs were wounded by deep, sea-cut zawns but the boulders and crags braced themselves like warriors, ready for fresh onslaught.

Timeless, unruly, defiant nature. She was at one, but not in comfort, with it. She was insignificant; at once part of everything and nothing at all. It terrified her, but there was energy too. And so she swam; she battled against the power of the ocean until her limbs became weary and her body cried in rebellion: *no more!* And finally, just as the salt water licked and polished her skin, whitened her nails and dried her hair into mermaid's tendrils, so it also cleansed her soul. And for a while, the torment stopped.

433

CHAPTER 45

The Miner's Inn

The Miner's Inn was comfortable and welcoming, and fittingly, given its thirteenth century low-beamed ambience, claimed to have a ghost or two. But Kate had not chosen to meet him there because of the undoubted character, but rather because it was on the outskirts of the village. She reasoned that there would be less chance of encountering other pre-party revellers there, as they would more likely be meeting at The Ship or Captain Carter's. She had hired a cab to take her the short distance from the cottage rather than stride the country lanes alone in such peculiar get-up, but wished now that she had not, for after paying the driver she found herself having to then actually turn towards and enter the pub, under his mindful conscientious eye. There was no leeway to turn around and run away; no thinking space to allow her to change her mind.

Taking a deep breath, and careful not to trip on the long skirt of her dress, she lifted the latch on the old timber door and crossed the threshold into the darkness of the bar. A little blind at first after coming in from the early evening sunshine, she didn't see him straight away, but then a figure at the end of the counter moved and made a lazy gesture with his arm. Kate waved back feebly in recognition. She had half thought, half hoped that he would not show up. But there was no turning back now. Forcing a smile, she walked towards him.

Gabe had been surprised when he had received the call from Kate. He liked to think that he knew of all his potential conquests; being possessed of a certain instinct that told him within minutes whether he could pull a woman or not. He didn't exactly keep a list, but rather a mental record as to who was waiting in the wings should he inexplicably find himself bereft of female company. His judgement was exacting, but fair. He didn't delude himself, nor allow arrogance to sway his judgement; it was a refinement of years of experience and extreme honesty.

He had not considered Kate as a potential. He had known from their first meeting that she was off-limits to him. She seemed cautious of him in a way that was neither disapproving nor fearful; rather it was as if she trusted her judgement much as he did his own, perhaps based on some prior experience, and had ruled him out from the start.

And so he was curious. And curious made him interested. As she approached he looked at her with fresh eyes and wondered if there was something he had missed. She certainly looked different tonight; stunning and beautiful in a deep red silk gown, which threatened to fall off her—rather edible— shoulders and hinted that she had good and—a bonus these days—natural breasts. She wore more make-up than usual; a deep red lipstick to match her dress and some black eyeliner; but her skin was fresh and scrubbed, and not slathered in orange, foul-tasting gunk.

He looked at her approvingly. *Women*, he thought in admiration. They were amazing. They could be plain, as if at will, when they were lying low, or having a period, or generally out of sorts with the world, and not trying to grab its attention. But equally wilfully they could transform into formidable beauties. They were forces of nature. They were goddamn *witches*.

He bought her a drink quickly, and they retired to a nearby table. Dressed in their period costumes, they gave the resident ghosts a run for their money, and more than one or two other customers did a double take at the strange couple. Gabe had dressed as an eighteenth century pirate, complete with cutlass and bandana, and Kate had to admit, he looked the part. Under his shirt, his tanned chest displayed the usual array of leather thongs and pendants, and his wrists were similarly bedecked in woven and silver bracelets. They were talismans and tokens, symbols and charms. A single silver earring glinted at her from behind his long dark hair. The blood-red heart tattoo on his cheek winked at her as he smiled.

Kate promptly reminded herself of her objective, which was to arrive at the party not only with a date, but with one that might equal—or quite possibly outrank—her original. Looking at him now, she decided that he would most certainly do. Salima would be jealous of course, but she couldn't worry about that now. And Juliet would raise an eyebrow or two... But most of all, she wanted Lance to take note. How dare he take her for granted? Well, she would have her revenge, petty or not. *Gabe* was the one to be seen with. Gabe was the one who never committed; was hard to catch. And she was going to arrive at the party on his arm for all to see. She didn't care much what he did after that; by then she would have made her point.

'Well,' he said. 'This is unexpected.' His accent was an odd, transatlantic fusion of Cornish dialect and American drawl. But he was quietly spoken, and self-contained; which she imagined, in a somewhat prejudiced manner, to be quite *un*-American. He was a traveller; a world citizen, with no permanent country called home.

'Yes, I know, and I would like to thank you. You're doing me a huge favour. My daughter's already gone on, and well, my date let me down.'

'Lance?'

So he knew.

'Yes.' She couldn't bring herself to elaborate. Instead, she reached for the fresh glass of wine, and gratefully drank. It was a welcome reinforcement to her waning Dutch courage.

Mercifully Gabe simply nodded, and did not pursue the intricacies. How different from Jem he was, she thought. Jem, who relished gossip in all its gory detail. And equally, how not-so-different from Lance. Hotly, she pushed the thought of Lance away.

'And you just happened to have my number?' Gabe asked, with a faintly mocking smile.

'Well, yes. You gave it to me months ago, on your business card! You said that Izzy was interested in surf lessons, and offered to teach her.'

'Of course,' said Gabe, and nodded again in a deferential manner as if to acknowledge his own temerity.

'I'm sorry about that, by the way,' said Kate. 'It was not a reflection on your teaching, which I'm sure is excellent. It's just that I feel she's a bit young, as yet. Perhaps when she's older and a more confident swimmer...'

'Right,' said Gabe, but he looked away.

'I appreciate the offer,' Kate added, supposing him to be offended, or embarrassed.

'So why me?' he said, as if keen to return to the subject. 'How do I get to be the lucky guy? I'd kinda like to think it's not just because you stumbled upon my number?'

It was Kate's turn to be embarrassed. 'Well, sort of, actually! Let's just say that it was very lucky for me that I did.' Thankfully he looked amused. 'To be honest, it was a long shot. Frankly, I'm surprised that you were available.'

Gabe did not answer at first, but continued to smile enigmatically, whilst gazing unnervingly at her, assessing her. The truth was that he paid no heed to the silly regulations of the party; but rather preferred to keep his options open. He was not one to commit to a partner for the evening, if it could be helped, especially at an event where there might be new

438

women to be met with and seduced. But this turn of events he had not seen coming, and he was intrigued.

'I'm available by choice,' he said eventually. He was impressed by her candour and the gumption that she had shown in, essentially, asking him out. He decided such a spirit should be met with honesty. Well, at least something *approaching* honesty. 'There's no one I particularly wanted to take, and I feel no distress in entering a room by myself. Besides, I reason they would hardly turn me away.'

Kate laughed; a further much needed release of tension. 'No, you're right. I admire you for it and normally would hope to boast the same strength of character. But tonight...'

'I understand,' he said.

'It's my good fortune that you're available, and I appreciate that you've... compromised your own availability...'

So she was no simpleton. Perceptive, even. Gabe smiled again.

'...and of course I don't expect you to stay with me; feel free to pursue your own inclinations,' she paused and looked at him directly, suddenly compelled to trust him, at least for the duration. 'I just need you to get me through the door.'

'Got it,' he said. But secretly Gabe's inclinations were already being revised. Kate may insist that he was just doing her a favour, but Gabe had a mind and a determination of his own, and he liked nothing better than an unsuspecting challenge.

Chapter 46

An Eagle

'Hey, if we're gonna do this right, you're gonna have to smile,' said Gabe as he and Kate approached Tremeneghy, arm in arm.

'Really?' said Kate. 'I was thinking more of a thunderously mutinous look, myself.'

He laughed. 'Come on, girl. Illegitimis non carborundum.'

'What?' Kate shook her head in exasperation.

'Don't let the bastards grind you down.'

He stopped and eyed her critically. 'Just a minute...' He turned her bodily towards him and then, impressively, produced a clean handkerchief from his pocket. He held her chin gently in one hand and with the other used the handkerchief to dab some stray mascara from her cheek. Then equally gently, he stooped and kissed her on the lips.

'Now remember, you look beautiful,' he coached.

'Hmm,' said Kate, still reeling from the surprise of the kiss.

'Say it!' he demanded.

'I look beautiful,' she murmured.

He sighed. 'No... Damn it woman, say it with confidence!'

Kate's rebelliousness was fading fast. She needed to do something quickly to stir up the embers. She closed her eyes and imagined Miles on his hands and knees, begging her to forgive him. Somehow it wouldn't wash, being too far-stretched a fantasy. She tried again and pictured Lance, smiling condescendingly at her, putting a hand on her shoulder and apologising again for letting her down. It did the trick.

'I look beautiful!' she said again with feeling, but with a narrowing of the eyes that would strike terror into the heart of any man, and render the declaration open for debate.

'Good. Now, lipstick.' said Gabe, holding out his hand.

Kate produced the red lipstick from her small evening bag and obediently handed it over to him. He took her chin again and carefully touched up the colour on her lips. It was a very sensual thing to do, and Kate eyed him suspiciously. He regarded her again appraisingly. Satisfied, he turned and held his arm out again.

'Shall we?'

An amateurishly painted sign hung from the front door, informing them to "Party this way", followed by an arrow directing them to the side of the house. A further series of painted arrows slung along the hedgerows sent them along a narrow access track and eventually to a wrought iron gate leading directly into the garden. Lillian, an unlikely bouncer, stood at the entrance and cast her enquiring eye over each new arrival imperiously. A podium had been rigged up just inside the gate under the canopy of a rose and honeysuckle covered pergola. Lillian had actually hired a butler, clad in full eighteenth century garb and periwig to announce the names of the guests as they arrived. It was more hellish than Kate had ever imagined.

'Well, that's interesting,' said Lillian aloud, in that manner she had of appearing to be addressing her invisible sidekick friend. 'The girl who paints and the American one. I wouldn't have guessed at that. No, not at all!' And she laughed mischievously, like a young girl. The sun was lowering in the sky and the garden was cast in a smudged orange glow as Kate and Gabe stood up to the podium in the half-light. She could not spot Isabella.

'Miss Katherina O'Neill and Mr Gabriel Paco Yuma' the bewigged butler announced theatrically to the assembled guests, who turned and clapped and cheered.

'Really?' Kate whispered to Gabe in surprise. He took her hand and led her, to her great relief, down the podium steps into the garden. They were still, however, very much the subject of attention, and Kate avoided all eye contact apart from Gabe's. She especially avoided Lance's gaze, although she had been instinctively aware of his presence by the pear tree almost as soon as they had entered through the gate.

'Yes, it's native American,' said Gabe, as they strolled through the crowds gathered on the lawn. 'Paco means "Eagle" and Yuma "Son of Chief".'

Kate smirked: 'You made that up!'

'No!' he feigned hurt.

Kate was unconvinced but amused. 'So you just happened to inherit such noble and venerable names; you couldn't have been 'Snake in the Grass' for instance? Or, it's always Crazy Horse or Running Bear; never just, I dunno, 'Born with Big Nose'?

'Ah, see now that's where you're wrong; you should meet my sister Toktoomuch, or my brother Long Streakapee.'

Kate chuckled, thankful for the diversion until finally they reached the bar area, a marquee bedecked in fairy lights. More hired staff served cider from barrels and real ale in bottles from behind wooden trellis tables. The area was, needless to say, packed. Kate spied some bottles of wine in a large plastic bucket filled with icy water.

Gabe was way ahead of her. 'Two chilled Viogniers, if you have them, my man,' he requested. So: he had been paying attention in the pub. Gratefully, Kate had to admit that so far at least, Gabe was being outstanding in his role.

'Well now, what do we have here?' said Juliet, sidling alongside Kate. Irrespective of the theme of the party, Juliet knew what suited her and was wearing a satin Chinese-style dress. 'Aren't you full of surprises?' Gabe was still getting the drinks, and she nodded lasciviously in his direction. Lowering her voice, she added, in sisterly code, 'What happened to Thor?'

'He found himself a proper date. His wife, in fact; or at least ex-wife. Have you seen Isabella?'

Juliet thought again about her encounter with Leah at the house, but said nothing. There was something not quite right. Leah's presence had indeed been unpropitious; but Juliet had been almost sure that Lance had been excited at the prospect of being with Kate.

'She's around somewhere. Well, Parker will be delirious,' Juliet returned to the subject of Kate's date. 'He was right up Gabe's arse the last time we were here. Bit of a crush going on there, I think.'

Right on cue, Parker approached them and slapped Kate on the back, before grabbing her, a little too roughly, by the arm.

'You came with Gabe?' he demanded, eyes dancing with excitement. 'Blimey Kate, you sneaky monkey, you said you were coming with Lance. Such intrigue! You're the proverbial dark horse, you are.'

What he meant, Kate knew, was "How did *you* manage to pull that one off?"

'Here you go,' said Gabe, arriving with Kate's drink. As he handed it to her, he gave her a quick wink.

Parker, witnessing the exchange, stared at Kate incredulously. Then, pulling himself together, he held out his hand towards Gabe, as if to shake hands, but then appeared to think better of it and instead slapped his hand onto the other man's shoulder, in a gesture of brotherhood.

'Hey...*brah*, how's it going?' The Cornish affectation in Parker's voice was now ever so slightly tinged with an American drawl. It wasn't clear whether he was mimicking

443

Gabe, or merely getting into character, having apparently come dressed as a cowboy.

'It's going well, I think,' said Gabe, smiling as his eyes darted momentarily towards Kate's.

'Has it been going off?' continued Parker, 'I got my gun with me this time and I gotta get some stoke, man. Been stuck in the city way too long and need to actually *have* a summer; big time. Any chance we can catch some waves tomorrow?'

'Oh...my...God...' said Juliet under her breath, and shaking her head slowly at the hapless Parker.

'What does he mean, he's got a gun?' Kate whispered to her sister in alarm.

'He means his surfboard,' Juliet said dryly.

Kate watched as Gabe, with an admirable lack of condescension, explained to Parker that the surf had been blown out for days, but might improve soon if the onshore wind changed; that it was still surfable if he was desperate, but not ideal for a beginner; it could be dangerous. Yet Parker, unperturbed—and Kate thought, naively in denial about both his ability and his inevitable morning hangover—persisted in the notion that he would be up for a dawn surf. Juliet stared at the exchange in morbid fascination.

Kate took the opportunity to have a sneaky look around. The garden was already quite full, and hummed with chattering voices. Waiters, dressed similarly to the butler at the gate carried trays not of glasses of champagne, but of sherry and brandy, alluding to illegal contraband that had just been smuggled in from a hidden cove. A brace of winsome blond children implied that the Borlase family was out in force, and Kate thought she espied the older brother and sister; although Bronwen appeared taut and stressed, and lacking Vivien's easy confidence. And Tristan looked stern and critical; the very worst incarnation of his brother. The presence of so many unfamiliar faces reminded Kate of her status as newcomer, and in her present mood, she wondered

444

again if her life in Cornwall would last. Alicia Browning and her family had come and gone, unnoticed and unmissed. Was this to be Kate's fate too? Why should she suppose herself to be any less transitory in the thoughts of the people that she had met?

Many of the townsfolk, in their archaic apparel, were already doing a good impersonation of medieval peasants, drunk with bucolic revelry. Someone was singing a Cornish folk song whilst others clapped along, and a couple—Angie and Don—danced a reel long in advance of any real music getting started. Another improvised platform at one end of the garden served as a stage, where a local folk band loitered; their concentrations engaged in tuning their guitars and violins. Sudden little bursts of stringed melody accompanied by repeated twangs broke through the throng of gabbling voices. Billows of noxious smoke drifted in the warm air from the ubiquitous barbeque. However, Kate noticed that in another part of the garden there was a long trellis table beset with what looked like more traditional fare of pies and pasties, served alongside homemade pickles and chutneys; and fresh bread, cheese and preserves. She also saw that in another area, some local fisherman had set up their own alternative "barbeque"; but in this case did not use coals but wood, in what was essentially a small bonfire. Over this they had, with only the aid of a few poles of tree and some knowledge of tripod lashing, constructed a hanging pot, in which some unknown brew steamed and bubbled. A variety of cleaned and gutted fishes were being skewered onto sharpened twigs that had been stripped of their bark, ready for cooking over the fire. Kate was intrigued. Lifting the hem of her dress, she tramped across the grass to take a closer look. No sooner had she reached the small group of fishermen than Lance was by her side.

'Kate, it's good to see you,' he said, but his voice sounded tense. He wore a plain white rustic shirt with black trousers and boots; *the lord of the manor dressing down to mingle with the yokels*, thought Kate bitterly. 'I apologise again for the...change of plan. But I see that you were able to make other arrangements.'

It was there again, that note of coldness in his voice that she had almost forgotten. A sudden pang of emotion caught in her throat. Had she imagined that they had ever become friends? She collected herself, remembering her hardened heart.

'Yes,' she stated simply and then turned to one of the fishermen. 'What's in the pot? It smells great!'

'It's a vegetable broth,' the man offered amiably. 'Potatoes, carrots, onions...we'll be serving up with the fish as soon as they're done on the fire. Will you be having some Miss? Better for you than all that barbeque muck—no offence young Lance!'

'None taken; between you and me I'm inclined to agree. I always look forward to your fish stew, Tomas.' As the band finally struck up, Lance turned to Kate again, raising his voice against the noise. 'Will you be dancing tonight Kate?' He smiled nervously.

This was the part where she was supposed to be civil; to make him feel at ease at the expense of her own feelings. It was what the old Kate—pre-hardened heart—would have done; she would have hidden her own dejection in order to make him feel comfortable, and to alleviate the atmosphere. Well, she was having none of that.

'I don't feel like dancing,' she said.

'Really?' he noted her harsh expression and looked quizzically at her. 'You're not ill, I hope?'

'Oh I'm very well. At least, not suffering from anything that another couple of these won't sort,' and she raised her glass to him in mock salute before draining its contents.

He stared at her for a moment, gauging her. 'You're angry with me. I suppose I can understand that. But please don't make things more complicated. You should watch yourself, and not drink too much, especially with Gabe. He's an amazing person, but quite the libertine. You need to be cautious or he may take advantage. Trust me.'

'Trust you?' Kate's eyes were defiant, but she struggled to find the words. 'I remember you warned me off your other friend too, not so long ago. Whatever Gabe's shortcomings are; whatever Jem's are; what gives you the right to judge when your own manners leave so much to be desired?'

'My *manners?*' Lance gave a little laugh but she could tell that he was taken aback. 'Kate, despite immediate appearances, we are not living in the eighteenth century!'

He waited, hoping for the old Kate, who would have laughed back. But her expression remained stony and he spoke more seriously.

'Look, you're right; what I did was incredibly rude. But I want you to forgive me. And I don't want you to compromise yourself as a result of my actions. Things are not what they might appear. Leah...'

'Yes dear?' said Leah, suddenly slinking alongside Lance and slipping her arm through his. She ignored Kate. 'Are you missing me? I've just been catching up with some of the old friends. Hope you're not feeling neglected? You must find these things so tedious—there's nobody here of any interest.' And with barely a heartbeat she finally cast her eye on Kate.

Leah appeared statuesque in a long white dress, not unlike the Grecian one that Kate had tried on; only Leah's dress was slashed from neck to waist in a deep 'V' at both front and back, and equally deeply slashed at the sides of her legs all the way up to her bronze hips. The whole contraption was held together in the middle by a thick black gladiator-style belt.

Kate had seen Bette Wu wear something similar in the press recently.

'Kate, this is Leah; Leah, Kate,' Lance introduced the two women wearily.

'Hi,' said Kate, extending her hand awkwardly. Leah's glacial manner and body language forbade even the most shallow of superficial kissing ceremonies.

'Oh so *you're* Kate,' said Leah knowingly, and paying no heed to the proffered handshake. 'I've heard lots about *you*. You appear to be making yourself quite well-known around these parts. But then, gossip does spread so quickly in such a small town.'

Lance frowned slightly, but was otherwise inscrutable.

'I guess you would know,' said Kate, horrified by her instinct to curtsey, or flick a fan in front of her face, such was the influence of being in costume. 'But if you'll excuse me, I'd like to find my daughter,' Quickly lifting her hem again, and sensing that Lance was looking intently at her, she marched away towards the house.

Once safely hidden inside the large reception room, Kate leaned back, resting her head against the curtain that divided the long glass doors and wished that she did in fact possess a fan. She didn't know if it was the alcohol or the uneasy air of confrontation, but she was feeling distinctly flushed. The sooner she found Izzy and got out of here, the better. She had not behaved according to plan. She should have been aloof and laughed at the thought that Lance should have in any way offended her. She should not have let him *know*.

Reluctantly, she conceded that she wasn't very good at this game. In a moment of insight—a deviance from the last few hours of rage—she realised that there may have been some truth in what Lance had said. Peering from behind the curtain, she risked a look through the glass to where Gabe stood, still talking to Juliet and Parker, but scanning the garden with his

448

eyes. Was he was looking for her? He might prove quite hard to shake off...

But how dare Lance warn her against drinking! Did he not understand that it was wine's cold anaesthetic that was stemming the tide of her more powerful and damning emotions? And who did he think he was anyway? Rebellion stirring in her again, she found the nearest passing waiter and unceremoniously grabbed a glass of sherry from his tray.

CHAPTER 47

Earthly Delights

L ance had been nothing short of dismayed to receive the telephone call from Jem. And how foolish, how naive, he had been to think that it all could have been passed off as innocent. In his effort to convince Kate that he had only agreed to partner her out of friendship, he had begun to believe it himself, and as such had thought that it would correspondingly appear perfectly platonic to everyone else. He realised, too late, that he should have informed Jem immediately of the situation. He would have been upset, perhaps, but would hardly have been able to forbid. But Jem had cried, actually *cried* down the telephone to him. It was obvious that he had been drinking, but that did not render the implications any less foreboding for the party. If Jem was this upset already at the thought of Kate going with someone else, then it was inevitable that his mood would only darken and reach new depths of despair as the evening progressed.

Lance had faced a dilemma, and had had to decide on a course of action. He could have apologised to Jem there and then, and admitted that he himself was taking Kate; but something had stopped him. He could not allow himself to profess to feeling nothing more than friendship for Kate; it wasn't true. If he were to make a public proclamation of his innocent intentions, he might find himself stuck in that place forever. And Jem had said things about friendship and made garbled pronouncements about trust; he *knew* that Lance would have told him if he had heard about anything that was going on, because that's what friends were for. Lance would have been the *first* to tell him. But he hadn't heard anything had he? So maybe he was torturing himself over nothing. Maybe she would not even go?

And so Lance had decided that it would be better all round if he appeased the situation. Kate would understand. Leah would be the perfect excuse; she had been sulking ever since his earlier refusal to submit to her demands. He would not mention Jem, or the phone call, in order to save his friend unnecessary loss of face. He had been kidding himself to think that it was going to be uncomplicated—of course he had! *Of course* Jem was going to get upset, and kick up a fuss. So with a heavy heart he had made the call to Kate, reasoning that she would still come, that he would still see her that day. After all, as far as she was concerned she was doing him a favour in the first place. Yes, Kate would understand and he would still see her. He had tried to reassure himself, but was bitterly disappointed nonetheless.

And so it added considerable insult to his own personal injury to see Jem be announced to the party with Jenifer Trewin as his partner. Jem, who had been so sensible of his own delicate feelings, did not appear to be able to afford the same sensitivity to Lance's. Oh, Jenifer often showed up at the same social gatherings as Lance; it was unavoidable in such a small village. In fact he remembered now that she had been at Jem's party last year. But to actually bring her, deliberately, as his partner, when he knew of the problems that she had caused Lance, was galling to say the least.

The butler announced the names of the new arrivals, who stood arms linked, if a little unsteady, under the pergola. Jenifer looked simultaneously coquettish and smug in a revealing peasant-style dress, whilst Jem, who would have otherwise cut a dashing figure in his white cravat and long-tailed coat, was conspicuously, and no doubt inexorably, drunk. And there was no recognisable evidence of his supposed heartbreak as he lurched at Jenifer and kissed her lustily, nearly toppling them both from the podium. Instinctively, Lance looked around for Kate. What would she think of this obvious display? Would it add further to her—quite apparent—hostility? He had misread her thus far in thinking that she would not be put out by his sudden, last-minute about turn. Would it now add to her humiliation to have her recent ex-boyfriend flaunt himself with another woman so publicly? In all his concern for Jem's feelings it had not occurred to Lance that Jem, not Kate, would be the one to cause anguish.

And worse still, Kate had arrived with another man anyway, rendering his own sacrifice pointless. And for that man to be Gabe, of all people! Lance's heart had plummeted when they had arrived. The red dress had taken him by surprise. Of course, she looked incredible, but it was not *his* Kate; his Kate in the green dress that he had admired—had practically chosen. His Kate was softer, more forgiving. This one was stunning but formidable. And how had this happened again? On New Year's Eve he had lost her to Jem; a doomed relationship perhaps, but one that might never have even begun if he had not allowed himself to be so judgemental of Kate in the first place, or if he had made his consequent, dramatic change of feeling known straight away.

And now she was with Gabe. Had he risked losing her again? He cursed himself for ever hesitating or taking into consideration the sensibilities of others. Especially when that one certain other was currently not displaying a terribly fragile disposition. At that moment, Jem turned and caught his eye. For a second or two he abandoned his attentions towards Jenifer and, once more the pitiful puppy, gazed at Lance imploringly across the crowd. But Lance was no longer in the mood for Jem. Instead, he gave a brief wave and then turned and walked in another direction. He saw Vivien, sitting on a hay bale, looking quietly resplendent in her new blue gown. It occurred to him as he approached her that she had been unusually quiet of late, and that despite her insistence that he follow the tradition of attending with a partner, she herself was at the party alone. But before Lance reached her, Vivien was approached and set upon with great enthusiasm by Parker. He turned in his tracks and found himself amongst the crowd gathered by the barbeque. He became aware of eyes upon his movements; of unfriendly whispers following his back. Turning, he saw Jenifer's friends and cursed under his breath. Why the hell were they here? Immediately he knew the answer. It would be Jem; bloody Jem in the pub inviting all and sundry as usual. The two girls had not bothered to dress the part, preferring their usual uniform of high fashion and even higher heels; and were now taking great pleasure in mocking the costumes of the other, invited guests. Looking for a friendly face, Lance saw Gina and her husband Denzel eating gargantuan burgers. Or at least Denzel was eating; Gina was contemplating the size of her burger with an unusually solemn expression. The thing probably weighed more than she did, and as such was to be a serious undertaking. Seeing Lance, she brightened, shouted hello and beckoned him over. Reluctantly, but remembering his role as host, Lance smiled warmly and approached them. But it was Kate he wanted to talk to; Kate he wanted to be with. He had not seen her return to the garden. Where the hell was she?

Kate had finally found Isabella, in one of the bedrooms upstairs, together with Finn, Callum and Tom. Typically, they had found a programme on the television in Finn's room that they just had to watch, regardless of the festivities so extensively laid on downstairs. Isabella did a double take when she saw her mother.

'What *are* you wearing?' she demanded.

'It's a dress, Izzy. Yes, I am wearing a dress. For the last time, it's a costume ball. And I am a *girl* you know!'

Judiciously, Izzy decided not to draw any more attention to her crazy mother, but neither was she ready to leave. 'I don't understand. It's supposed to be a party. Why do we have to go now?'

'Another hour then,' said Kate. 'It will be late enough for you then,'

One of the boys tittered. 'Yeah Izzy, be a good girl and go to bed, it's way past your bedtime!'

'Don't forget to say your prayers and brush your teeth!'

'Leave her alone,' said Finn grudgingly. Give him his due, he was loyal; but Kate could see that his position was awkward. It was vital if you had a girl for a friend that she should cause absolutely no awkwardness whatsoever. She had to be cool at all times.

Isabella looked beseechingly at Kate.

'Oh...fine! I'll speak to you later.' Kate sighed. There was no point protesting further, it would only cause further mortification for her daughter. Instead, Kate decided she would try to grab her at a later, more inconspicuous moment. Izzy would be more reasonable without an audience. She left the room and was about to head back downstairs when she became suddenly curious. Where was this special room with the dome and all the glass windows that Lance worked in, the one with all the telescopes? She had heard Izzy rave about it for months now, but had only ever seen it from the street outside. Emboldened by drink, she managed to convince herself within about a nanosecond that it was practically de rigueur to sneak about your host's house at a party. And she could always feign looking for Izzy if she were caught. Finn's bedroom was on the first floor, but at the end of the corridor was another, narrower flight of stairs that wound upwards; confined and turret-like. Maybe it was up there? Checking

454

that there was no one about, she lifted the unfamiliar skirt once more and trotted quickly up.

The small painted wooden door at the top of the stairs looked like it had been originally designed for an attic, or servant's room. Hesitating for a second in her long princess dress, Kate almost expected to open the door to find a wicked fairy working at a spinning wheel. Certainly it was hard to envisage industrial size telescopes or cutting-edge technology being easily installed up here, and for a second she thought she must have taken a wrong turn. But the little door creaked open to reveal a vast circular open space, and the famous roof with its observatory dome. A set of French windows led out onto a roof terrace overlooking the garden. The light was fading, and the room was slightly musty with warm air, having been baked by the strong sunlight that had poured in through the glass all day.

It was not the operations centre that Kate had been expecting. She had imagined a version of "ground control" with banks of complicated machinery. Instead there was just one standard PC, the main telescope underneath the dome, and an array of smaller ones scattered about. They were professional looking, to be sure, but not the Hubble-sized giants portrayed through Isabella's mind's eye. All of the furniture, namely a cluttered desk and a chair, a floor lamp and an old chaise longue, was placed at random in the middle of the bare-wood floor space. In fact, the room was altogether archaic; dusty with papers strewn around and books stacked up in towers on the floor. Moon maps and star charts adorned the walls. Sheets of handwritten formulae—another language to Kate—littered the desk. It was the room of a Victorian explorer, not a practical modern scientist.

Approaching the chaise longue, Kate saw that there was a blanket draped half on the floor, as if it had been recently evacuated, and on its dark red velvet upholstery, a bundled up

455

jumper, which appeared to have been squashed into a makeshift pillow. The sight of the jumper made Kate suddenly ashamed, being a reminder not only of the personal space that she was invading; but also of that other jumper, lent to her months ago and still in her possession. And yet she had a perverse impulse to touch it. She stopped herself short. The jumper was a traitor; a representative and extension of its fickle owner.

She hastened instead to the French windows. From this height, the sun could still be seen setting, although for most of the guests in the garden it had already gone. The summer sky was scorched deep red on the horizon, and a planet—Mars perhaps?—blasted the reflected hot light earthwards in the remaining blue sky. Not wanting to be seen, she stood in the shadows and gazed down on the revelry in the garden below.

A scene of merriment lay before her; with fiddles and guitars, singing and laughing, dancing and drinking. It was a small crackling bonfire of human life; a glow in the dark contrasted by the darkening fields surrounding them, and the vastness of the encroaching night sky. She spotted Vivien sitting on a hay bale, being chatted up by one of the fishermen. There was no sign of Derry, and Kate supposed that he had still not returned from his travels. Nearby, Juliet and Parker stood with their heads together, engrossed in what she suspected was a swapping of gossip and innuendo. And there was Jem; not apparently heartbroken at all, but standing swaying to the music, his hands firmly planted on Jenifer Trewin's waist. Kate managed an ironic smile. She saw Leah stride regally across the grass to where Lance stood talking to Gina the cleaner, put her hand on the small of his back, and drape her body with familiar ease by his side.

They were all with the wrong people, thought Kate, as a sudden melancholy gripped her. All of them, wasting their lives away in destructive and hollow relationships. *Better to be alone*, she thought. Better to stand in a darkening room in

456

a remote part of a house by yourself than to conduct a desperate sham relationship out of fear and loneliness. She suddenly felt like Tennyson's Lady of Shallot, excommunicated from all society, and only able to watch the outside world from her mirror's refection on high, hidden in the shadows. Only Kate was not a captive, but had facilitated her own banishment.

'So, there you are!' A voice in the darkness made her jump. She had not heard him enter the room.

Gabe approached her slowly, as if not to frighten her away. Dusk now permeated the room and masked his expression. He joined her by the windows and casually leant one shoulder against the glass, arms folded and facing her. For a split second, Kate saw Miles with his easy confident manner and dangerous charisma. It was not for Gabe to lurk in the shadows like the sneak that she was, but rather he stood shamelessly in full view of anyone who happened to look or care. He glanced at her for a second, and then turned his head and peered over his shoulder at the horde below.

'The Garden of Earthly Delights,' he murmured with a slow smile.

'I wouldn't have said it was quite that much of a strange orgy,' she said, hiding her astonishment at his referencing Bosch. He certainly was full of surprises. 'Nobody's naked for a start.' She smiled wryly then added bitterly, 'well, not yet anyway.'

'Oh I dare say we'll see some debauchery yet,' he replied archly. 'It's what they all really want. To become inebriated and uninhibited; to break the mould; free themselves of constraint; to see all those polite manners drop away and...*possibilities* arise.'

'So you're saying that everyone secretly craves depravity?' said Kate, with a little false laugh. She tried to sound confident but was feeling suddenly vulnerable. The room was becoming very dark.

'I'm saying,' Gabe said, shifting from his leaning position and taking a step towards her, 'that everybody craves something. If not plain old depravity then at least freedom; at least for *something* to happen. A little action. Maybe a little romance? It's kinda dull when folk conform to manner and nothing ever happens, doncha think?'

'Well, you're talking to the wrong girl,' said Kate, turning quickly and slipping away from his gaze. Stumbling in the dark, she tripped on the skirt of her dress, recovered herself, and then promptly bashed into one of the copious piles of books on the floor, stubbing her toe.

'Nothing ever happens to me!' she said, desperately plotting an escape route amongst all the clutter. Immediately she realised it had been the wrong thing to say. She had meant to sound whimsical, but instead, alone in the dark with a highly seductive man, it had sounded like a come on, a challenge. Sure enough, Gabe changed his pace from stalking-cat to pounce, and in a few effortless long strides stood between Kate and the door.

'So, how come you're up here, all alone?' he asked casually, barring her way. 'You sure can't expect things to happen if you hide away in the dark. Or maybe you were expecting somebody? Lance perhaps? This is his personal room, is it not?'

'Actually, I was looking for my daughter,' said Kate, remembering her practiced excuse.

'Well...she's not here,' said Gabe, looking around and extending his arms in a theatrical manner and thus further blocking her path. 'And neither for that matter, is Lance.' He took a step towards her.

'Clearly. I shall have to look elsewhere for Izzy,' said Kate, sidestepping him and making a bold attempt for the exit. Surprised, and not without an element of disappointment, she made it. Hand on the latch, she turned and watched him watching her; her wary expression meeting his amused one. 'To tell the truth, I think I'd like to go home now,' she said, appealing to his candour.

'Oh come now, that's not my girl!' said Gabe. 'You can't limp away like that; you've got to show some spirit.'

He joined her at the top of the staircase and, gently shoving her out, shut the door of the observatory firmly behind him. In the poky stairwell he was suddenly too close again. Kate turned and did her best to descend, and not tumble down the steps in her dress.

'Katie, you've got to see it through; you can't just run away,' Gabe said as he followed her down the stairs and along the corridor. 'Otherwise, why the dress? Why the hair? Not to mention that you've enlisted *me*.' He stopped her in her stride by taking her firmly by the shoulders. 'I'm here to help. Use me.'

Kate looked at him with mixed emotions of gratitude and doubt. But safely removed from the confines of the observatory, Gabe no longer appeared so intimidating, but rather was gentle and reassuring.

'Come outside,' he continued, 'the night is young, and I intend to dance with you in front of everyone.'

'Oh...okay!' said Kate, an ungrateful child. She was exasperated, but resigned. Part of her knew he was right. To creep away now would undo the whole premise of her appearance in the first place. She would have to maintain the act for a bit longer. Gabe said no more, but smiled to himself as he took Kate's hand and led her down the corridor.

Passing Finn's room on the left, he gestured with his thumb and announced, 'Oh, yeah, she's in there by the way— Isabella.'

Kate glared at him peevishly. 'I *know!*' She cried, before wrenching her hand free and stomping on ahead.

CHAPTER 48

A Knight

In the press of bodies in the garden, Kate found that she was grateful for Gabe's reinstated hand, as he lead her through the crammed assembly to find a space that they could occupy. The air was still stifling despite the departed sun, and the clamour of voices, like a flock of raucous geese, almost drowned the sound of the band. Lanterns and lights adorned the trees and surrounding hedgerows. People were still dancing, which accounted for the crush on the outskirts, as room was made to accommodate leaping legs and twirling skirts. There appeared to be a gang in the know; those who knew the correct steps and movements for each new jig or reel. But most did the self-conscious side-shuffle of modern times; a half-hearted apology of a dance, largely directed by the need for self-expression via the medium of alcohol.

Gabe surveyed the situation, contemplating the options. The crowd around the drinks tent had reached festival proportions, and would have involved a tedious wait. 'This way,' he said, spotting local cider being served from a barrel in a more discreet part of the garden. He made a bee-line for it, dragging Kate after him by the hand, and forcing the crowd to part.

Kate mumbled apologies as she bumped against a succession of bodies. At the cider barrel they were given pewter tankards which were generously filled. Kate eyed Gabe suspiciously as she supped cautiously on the fusty mixture.

Despite her indignation, Lance's advice was, annoyingly, still fresh in her mind, and now she was mixing her drinks... Gabe returned her gaze, peering over the top of his tankard with a wolfish glint in his eye. She feigned another sip before casually, but firmly, planting the mug on the top of the barrel. Gabe grinned but followed suit.

'Okay, time to dance,' he commanded, taking her hand again.

'I don't know how!' said Kate in a panic, and pulling on his grasp.

'It's easy, just go with it.' And with that he led her into the throng.

They stood for a moment in the centre of things, narrowly avoiding being kicked by flailing limbs or bodily bundled to the ground, whilst Gabe stood assessing the movements of a small group beside them. There was a serious expression on his face, like a small child learning something new and complicated.

'Right. Okay, got it,' he said, 'follow me.'

And soon Kate had got it too. Despite her misgivings she found herself linking arms and reeling; skipping and clapping; laughing hysterically at her ineptitude. Despite herself she began to have fun. Gabe looked at her approvingly as he once again twirled her around by the hands. Eventually, the music finished and they stood, flushed and exhausted from the sudden burst of exercise. They raised their hands in the air and clapped towards the stage, where the band took a bow. After a bout of cheering and friendly gibes, the musicians took seats on the stage as if for a rest, except for a lone fiddler who struck up a slower, more emotional refrain on his violin. After a while, he was joined by the singer, who stood forward to begin the slow ballad. Gabe looked at Kate and moved suddenly as if to pull her into his arms.

461

'Mind if I interrupt?' said Lance stepping forward from amongst the crowd and performing a ridiculous mock bow in their direction. Then he held his hand out towards Kate, just to make it perfectly clear that there was no pressing matter of great urgency that he wished to discuss, but that he meant to dance with her. *He might well look abashed*, thought Kate; so squirm-making and unnatural were his actions. But given their attire and the general surroundings; and notwithstanding the fact that Kate had just been dancing a *reel*, of all things, she grudgingly resisted her impulse to ridicule. She had been about to reject him with a similarly ludicrous riposte—*I am sorry kind sir, but this dance is promised to another*—but saw, horrified, that Gabe was already bowing his consent with equally exaggerated histrionics. As he backed away, he winked briefly at her, conspiratorially.

Idiot! Did he think that this was in any way a good thing? Even as Lance placed one hand in hers, and put his other arm firmly around her waist, pulling her closer, Kate scowled at Gabe as best as she could over the tall shoulder that was now before her face. Gabe merely shrugged, affecting innocence, before smiling, turning and walking away.

And to think that he had purported to be on her side! Wretched, treacherous man! With ever deepening cynicism Kate wondered if they might all be in it together— some secret league of rogues.

Reluctantly, she held onto Lance with the meanest of touches. There was no grasp in her hand; though he held hers warmly enough. Her other hand necessarily had to rest upon his shoulder, but she did so with the lightest contact she could maintain—even though her arm would start to ache with the effort of keeping it stiffly there. There was little she could do where their bodies connected, except hold in her breath and suck in her stomach, as if willing every atom in her body to be distanced from him. She cursed the mutinous neckline of her dress, which had slipped provocatively from her shoulder, and which she could not reach to replace, unless he released her from his hold.

She would not speak, but stared frostily at his shoulder in sullen, tangible silence as she followed his lead and they slowly moved around the other couples. At one point she felt that Lance was about to say something, and she prepared herself to answer with cold civility. But, perhaps sensing her aloofness, he appeared to change his mind and lost the words. Or perhaps it was Jem's glowering presence as he circled the outskirts of the dancers that had stopped him. Catching his eye, Kate returned Jem's stare with an equal malevolence. If he had expected her to wave and smile, then he had picked the wrong girl on the wrong night. But it was Lance who was to feel the full force of her anger and indignation. It was Lance who had made everything wrong; Lance who had reminded her that happiness was for other people, and that she was always to be second best—an also-ran. She was the girl who was always the friend, but never the loved one. Well, she had forgiven him once before; had even convinced herself that she may have played a part in her own misconception. Such was her nature that she had given him the benefit of the doubt; had even begun to see him as tragic and misunderstood!

She had been a fool and a simpleton. It didn't matter that he smelt good tonight and that she felt a pang at the sight of his hair gently touching to his shoulder again, for he was fickle, faithless and unpredictable. It didn't matter that her hand was beginning to sweat in his, and that his closeness appeared to have sparked a bolt of electricity that spun fizzing down her backbone, and threatened to make her tremble. Only the sheer force of her concentrated fury prevented it— that and the prompt recollection that this was the man who had blithely thrown her over for a shallow, sludge-faced, surgically-enhanced media-harlot. And it didn't matter that her heart was overflowing with repressed tears at the loss of their supposed friendship; for it had been a friendship of her own foolish imagining. In her all too easy manner of being quick to forgive and to think well, she had made the fundamental mistake of supposing his feelings to be as genuine, as warm as her own, when in fact he had barely given her much thought at all. And now this dance—this dance that she was being fobbed off with—was supposed to be her consolation prize.

These were the thoughts that pervaded Kate's mind as each second of the dance dragged into interminable agony. It was these thoughts that collected and channelled her determined resentment. To the onlooker, it must have seemed the iciest, most unsmiling of dances, as if they were a warring couple worn down by long decades of married contempt. But at close quarters, the silent tension between them was anything but familiar indifference. The atmosphere was heavy with unspoken emotion, and crackling with a magnetic attraction that Kate used all her power to resist.

Finally, the song ended, the fiddler drew the last mournful notes from his instrument and the torment came to an end. Kate and Lance stood quickly back from each other and clapped politely. For the first time since the onset of the dance, Kate ventured a furtive look at Lance's face, and was shocked to see how hard it had set—whether in sorrow or anger she couldn't tell. Instinctively, she felt a stab of guilt at the possibility of causing pain; but remembering her hard heart, repressed it. Lance would merely be feeling insulted by her incivility, when he had meant, with great kindness and condescension of course, to atone for his actions by offering to dance. Well, he had done his bit now, and could swan off back to his trollop with a clear conscience.

When the clapping had finished and the band took a break, there was no choice but to look at him again, if only to nod in acknowledgement before making her getaway. She lifted her head defiantly and met his gaze full on, only to find it still cold and inscrutable. His eyes were glazed and unsmiling, and he appeared to be struggling with some inner demon; as if unable to articulate accurately exactly what he was feeling—and being Lance—would not waste words until the precise nature of his opinion could be conveyed. But more than that, it was as if he had joined her in silent, unspoken battle, and was now determined to win the war.

It was hard to decide whether the tension of the moment was broken or compounded by Jem's lurching, drunken intervention. He stumbled against Lance, and putting a hand on his shoulder to balance, leant against him in a manner that could either have been one of contrived affection, or of barely suppressed aggression.

'I knew it, mate,' he said, 'I knew there was something going on. You can't fool me, you see. I *knew* there was something going on. I *saw* you.' He swung a venomous red-eyed look at Kate before returning his attention to Lance, and all but shouting, 'I don't mind, y'know. S'none of my business. Not anymore. I don't *mind*. But how could you do this to me, mate? I'm very, very, disappointed. In *you*, mate; d'ya unnerstand? Not saying I mind, though, not saying that...'

For a second Lance looked as though he might break his icy composure and erupt with hidden rage, but when he finally spoke, he was, as usual, calm and controlled. His voice was low and soft, and betrayed just the barest quiver of annoyance. 'Take it easy, Jem. Please don't ruin the party. Think of Lillian.'

'Of course! Of course think of Lillian!' Jem was mindless, almost absent in his thoughts. 'I always think of Lillian. What do you take me for?' His tone returned swiftly to confrontation. 'It's not about Lillian, it's about you, and...and...*her!*' He pointed distractedly at Kate, as if suddenly remembering she was there, and sloshing his drink in her direction, narrowly missing.

'Well,' said Lance heavily, as if he found it hard to speak at all, 'don't worry on that score; you are mistaken.'

'Mishtaken?' Jem slurred.

'Yes,' said Lance firmly, and looking again at Kate with cold hard eyes, 'completely mistaken.'

Kate steeled herself once more, determined not to cry. After all, this was the route that she had chosen to take. She could have played the game; she could have pretended that it was nothing, and been friendly and accommodating. But she had stood up for herself and challenged him, and now Lance was fighting back and she would have to take the consequences on the chin. It felt at that moment that it was irrecoverable. Even, or perhaps especially, after their previous falling out and subsequent make-up, it now seemed inconceivable that they would ever be on friendly terms again. This would be her punishment for having been honest in her righteous indignation.

Jem might have continued his ranting, but they were all three of them suddenly disturbed by a commotion from near the entrance gate. A collective gasp of amazement and some laughter rippled through the crowd. Kate and Lance both turned to try and see what was happening.

Jem merely looked puzzled. He had had their attention, but now no one was listening to him anymore. 'Typical,' he mumbled.

Kate raised herself on tip-toe and peered above the heads. Taking her cue, Jem attempted the same and balanced uneasily on his toes, staring glassily in the appropriate direction. At first he could not comprehend what he was looking at, but since the vision did not dematerialize no matter how many times he blinked and shook his head, he began for the first time that evening to feel a real sense of concern about the amount of alcohol that he had consumed.

Standing on the platform by the gate, surrounded by roses and honeysuckle was a horse. Not just any horse, but a huge white Shire horse which was equally bedecked with flowers in its hair. It also wore a garland of green foliage and creamy white peonies around its strong neck, the colours matching the attire of its rider.

Tomas the fisherman, who stood next to Kate, nudged her gently in the ribs with his elbow. 'That be a Shire horse. Proper working animal. Not seen one of them around these parts since I were a lad—'alf-century I reckon at least. They'm all use machinery now for pulling the plough. Fine-looking beast.'

'It is,' said Kate, in amazement at recognising the rider. 'But what on earth...'

'A white one an' all,' Tomas interrupted, 'A mighty 'ansum, *'ansum* animal!'

To see the white Shire with flowers in its hair in the already surreal setting inspired reverence amongst the assembled company; they might just as well have been in the presence of a unicorn. The horse's rider was bending down to reach the ear of the startled butler, who turned to Lillian imploringly for advice. Lillian merely nodded wisely, with a small curious smile on her lips.

The butler's features struck an injured look, but with consummate professionalism, he cleared his throat and announced in a loud voice to the rapt gathering: 'Mr Derry Newson!'

The butler smiled, acknowledging the sudden burst of whoops, applause and hurrahs that emanated from the crowd. He even managed a small polite clap himself, only to notice that Derry was still looking at him patiently, waiting for him to finish the announcement and clearly in no hurry to leave the platform until he did so. Resignedly, the butler turned back towards the crowd.

'Mr Derry Newson and...er... Sir Percival!'

The crowd were even more enraptured, and let rip with more cries, whistles and catcalls. Derry appeared to hesitate, suddenly flummoxed by the steps that led down from the platform onto the grass. He hadn't planned for this. Quelling all thought of disaster, he gently stroked the horse's neck and whispered soothing words of encouragement: 'Come on Sir Percy, I know you can do this; it's only a couple of steps...'

As Derry guided the heavy horse carefully down the steps and onto the grass, the delighted horde parted to let him pass, and then followed expectantly in his wake.

'That's some clever horse all right,' mumbled Tomas, although Kate thought that even he was surprised.

Derry's costume was not that far removed from his normal attire—given that he was accustomed to dressing like a medieval peasant—but there was something unusually imposing about his appearance today. He looked almost noble in a loose cambric shirt which draped open at his chest, soft suede boots, and dark green trousers worn under the inevitable kilt-like skirt. His hair was tied back from his face by a green velvet ribbon, and hung in long sandy ropes down his back, save for the usual loose rebel strand that hung across one eye and reached down to touch his bare chest. He was suavely clean-shaven, and although there was a hint of a nervous lock to his jaw, there was also a determined challenge in his eyes. He rode bareback; a Celtic warrior home from battle— somewhat dishevelled, but dignified and bold.

He steered the great horse towards Vivien, who had jumped abruptly up from the hay bale where she had sat, uncharacteristically forlorn, for most of the evening. When he was almost close enough to speak to her, Derry dropped sleekly down from his mount. Taking the reins in one hand, he made the last few steps towards her on foot.

Kate, watching from the crowd, saw the colour rise in Vivien's cheeks as Derry produced a small posy from a pocket

468

in the breast of his shirt and held it out in offering to her. And then she watched, transfixed, as Derry went down on one knee. A quiet fell upon the garden, punctuated by some muffled gasps and equally repressed giggles. Instinctively, Kate brought her hands to her face in horror.

Oh no, Derry, no! Not like this! Her heart, hard as it was, went out to the young man before her, declaring his love in front of, well, just about everyone he had ever known. Why could he have not done this privately? Why court humiliation with such foolish, romantic and *heartbreaking* action?

'I love you Vivien. I have always loved you.' Derry spoke directly to Vivien, in a low but resolute tone. His eyes remained on her and her alone; there were no humourous asides or gestures made for the benefit of the gathered audience. This was serious. 'Please be my wife, Vivien.'

Well, at least it wasn't a long speech. The next few seconds of time were unendurable enough, but the inevitable blow that was surely to come would have been all the more painful had he rambled on at length or perhaps started reciting poetry. Kate looked at Vivien's face again, hardly daring to read the response there.

Vivien had become very still, and was looking at Derry with an expression that suggested deep shock. Kate felt her own heart beat slowly and heavily against her ribs. What must Vivien be thinking? Perhaps she was angry at the unsolicited attention, or embarrassed for Derry—embarrassed for herself? But then Kate saw that Vivien was hardly breathing; and that her eyes, although distant and thoughtful, had not left Derry. And then Kate remembered. She remembered Vivien's first love Max, and that he had asked the same question, and that the small primeval voice inside Vivien and risen up with vehemence and cried *no!* Was Vivien doing the same thing now? Was she putting this wanton, ragged theory to the test? Was she consulting the voice in her head; the deep instinctive knowledge of her soul, no less, and was she already metaphorically running away screaming in blind panic?

Poor Derry.

Derry suddenly had a sense of where he was and what he was doing. Yes, he was down on bended knee before his love with a white Shire horse breathing down his neck. He had not dared to think about what would happen next. He had the horse, of course, on which to make his escape, although it was not the sort of horse that you could dash to freedom on, leaping over hedges at a bound. No, it would be a long slow trot of shame, and he had not, in truth, envisaged leaving without Vivien; to do so might have damaged his resolve.

But her eyes had not left him, and so he pushed these thoughts aside. It was not over yet. He stood up again, and summoning his courage once more, leaned towards her and whispered some words for her alone.

'*I'll not ask you again.*'

Then he stood back and waited for his answer. He had made his move; done his worst; *plighted his troth*. And plighted it on a white horse, at that... If you couldn't win a fair maiden with a white horse anymore then there was no hope for the world and they were all going to hell in that handcart. And he had meant what he had said; he would not ask her again. And yes, it *was* both promise and threat. He saw from Vivien's eyes that she understood this. Whatever Vivien replied, it would put an end to his anguish; she would either be his wife, or he would move on. He refused to pine anymore, to languish a moment longer in a state of unrequited love. But equally, she should know that it was now or never. Derry was determined to no longer be taken frivolously. He swore to himself that if she turned him down today, right now, with all the lights twinkling in the trees, that he would turn his back on her forever.

Kate was astonished as she saw Vivien's face suddenly erupt with the widest, happiest grin.

'Yes Derry, I will marry you!'

Derry's reaction was overwhelmed by the loud cheer from the crowd. He had been initially stunned; and despite his heartfelt efforts, somewhat incredulous. But then he saw in Vivien's eyes that she meant it, and he took his girl in his arms. There was even more noise at this, and the resting band, who had been equally entranced by the scene, started up again with a newly inspired vigour.

The mood was infectious. Kate caught Juliet looking at Parker with abject disappointment, and then at Derry with an equal measure of regret. Parker, who was himself overcome with emotion, cast a wistful, teary eye in the vicinity of Gabe, who was striding across the grass to congratulate his friend; a huge smile on his face. Jem sat slumped on a hay bale consumed with self-pity and with only a bottle for company. Lillian lurked in the background, a fixed smile of contentment on her face, and for once, curbing the urge to undermine with a sharply-observed comment. Leah had grabbed onto Lance's arm again, a rictus grin failing to disguise her fury at having had the attention stolen from her. Lance had been looking at the ground, but lifted his eyelids now and briefly met Kate's gaze before quickly looking away, his features still stony.

And Vivien...most of all, Vivien looked happier than Kate had ever seen her. Initially she had been afraid that Vivien had said 'yes' to stave off Derry's humiliation, just as she had done when faced with a similar situation in front of Max's family. She had been concerned that later, in private, Vivien would let Derry down gently, leaving him to make his public excuses over time. But looking at her now, it occurred to Kate that Vivien's feelings might be genuine, for surely she would not behave so cruelly. And yet it was a shock. Kate had had no inkling that Vivien's feelings could have changed so radically. She regretted that she had not spoken to Vivien about Derry before now. Instead, she had chosen to avoid the subject because of Juliet's involvement.

She spotted Isabella, who had finally been tempted out of the house by the rumour that there was a horse called Sir Percival at the party. Jubilant to find that this was true, she stood now with Finn and his friends, admiring and petting the horse. Kate saw her chance. She had wanted to speak to Vivien, but since Derry looked to be preparing to ride off with her, that conversation would have to wait. Instead, she went to Izzy and put an affectionate arm around her shoulder. After confirming that yes, Derry had proposed to Vivien, and yes he had ridden in on the horse, Kate suggested that they might make a move to leave now. Isabella appeared to weigh up the pros and cons, which no doubt included a brief assessment of her mother's degree of inebriation. Judging that Kate might be all right for a little longer, Izzy insisted that they stay to watch the couple ride off, but conceded that after that, then yes they could go home.

The photographer hiding in the dark across the lane adjusted his long distance zoom lens and snapped merrily away. This thing with the horse and an apparent proposal was a small bonus; it would make good local news for the small weekly paper that he had slogged away on for years now. And it might add another dimension to the headline of why local girl Leah Greenwood appeared to be reunited with her ex-husband. Of course the nationals would run it as a 'mystery man', and eke the story out until finally revealing the scandal of her secret child. That reminded him, the kid had finally made an appearance—must get a good shot—they might not use it, given his age and that, but he should get the shot anyway, just in case. Yes, this was going to fetch him a tidy sum from the tabloids, and once again he congratulated himself on his great fortune on having been the one to take the call from Leah Greenwood's agency just a couple of hours ago.

Unaware of the unseen voyeur, Derry reached his arm down to help Vivien up onto the horse behind him. She held her shoes in her hand, and sat there happily astride the wide girth, her dress risen up to her thighs, and her legs dangling bare like a child's. Her arms encircled Derry's waist and she leaned against his back and appeared to whisper something in his ear. They were lost in each other, and only stopped at the gate to turn and wave to the rest of the party, before disappearing into the darkness.

Kate watched them go, and then indicated to Isabella with a reminding tap on her shoulder that it was time to go. Thankfully Isabella for once, acquiesced, only insisting that she say goodbye to Finn. Kate herself had already made up her mind that she would give her thanks to Lillian alone. Vivien was gone and she would not speak to Lance. She signalled goodbye to Juliet, who responded accordingly before returning her attention to the potential shag that she was chatting up.

It was Izzy's loud and over-enthusiastic display of goodbyes to Finn and his friends—had Kate really heard her say 'See ya brah!' as she high-fived each of them in turn?—that attracted Gabe's attention. He made his excuses to Salima, who had finally and oh-so-casually succeeded in manoeuvring herself to within his radar, only to be promptly abandoned with no more than a quick reassuring pat on the shoulder and a 'Later, gotta go.'

Salima stood, tiny in her big fluffy frock, her modern, short cropped hair and nose stud incongruous with the surroundings, and felt her ego shrivel in direct proportion to her growing sense of inadequacy. She wished with all her might that she could close her eyes and be transported back to the beach. Padding along the shore in a yellow bikini, she commanded attention. In a wetsuit, carving up the waves she was the height of cool. Here, she felt small and insignificant and ignored.

'Hey, you're not leaving without me?' Gabe said, effectively curtailing the would-be absconders at the gate. He turned briefly to Isabella.

'Hey Izzy,' he said with casual familiarity.

'Hey Gabe,' Isabella responded in the same tone. Kate shot her a puzzled look.

'I insist on escorting my date home,' continued Gabe. 'What kind of gentleman would I be if I left two lovely ladies alone, in the dark, on the road?'

'There's really no need,' said Kate testily. 'It honestly isn't the middle ages, you know, despite the illusion.'

'All the more reason for me to accompany you.'

'And besides: *some gentleman!* What use were you earlier? You left me in the lurch!'

'Ah, hiding in the shadows again. I thought you had a point to make? I left you perfectly placed to make that point.'

'Wait a minute,' interrupted Isabella. 'You came with Gabe? *Gabe* is your date?'

'Well, yes,' said Kate loftily, insulted at the incredulity in Isabella's voice.

'But he's cool! What's he doing with you?'

'Oh well, charity work, obviously!'

It wasn't that far from the truth.

From across the garden, Lance grimly observed Kate and Isabella slip through the gate and leave the party, followed by Gabe. He was staring hard at the empty spot by the gate where they had been, paralysed by conflicting emotion, when he felt a smooth warm embrace encircle his neck, and then Leah's lips pressed fully against his own. It was a sticky, chemical kiss, and the aroma of the makeup on her face filled his nostrils.

He didn't notice the flash from the hedges, discreet and silent amongst all the twinkling tree lights. And he didn't

474

notice the look of shock and confusion on his son's face as Finn watched from just a few feet away.

CHAPTER 49

Probability

Lance lay awake in the observatory as the sun rose and thought about probability. He had spent the night on the chaise longue again, an increasingly frequent symptom of a vaguely self-acknowledged custom of going into hiding. It was a trait that especially manifested itself when Leah was around.

It was with an overwhelming sense of powerlessness that he had watched Kate leave with Gabe the night before. There was an inevitability to it that was becoming part of an increasingly repetitive, unfolding pattern. He thought of all the parallel universes—if indeed they did exist—in which Kate had not left with Gabe. There might be parallel universes where she had gone to the party with Lance himself, as planned. There were those where he and Kate grew happily old together; or those where they grew indifferent and bored. Others where tragedy struck, and she died—or he did. He wondered if you ever really died, or if you simply left that world, that universe, behind, and continued your existence in another one, unawares. The loved ones that you left behind would experience your leaving, and their own loss; but you yourself would be unaware of their grieving because in your world, you had survived; and life continued. One could presumably live forever this way, skimming across parallel existences; only experiencing your loss of others, but never of your own self. Skimming...skim-boarding...surfing...there

476

would of course be those universes in which you had never existed, but you would have no awareness of them; they would not exist for you.

On the other hand, the observable world that he was living in, *thinking* in right now, was the only authentic one. Because out of all the probabilities, all those supposed other universes out there, it was the most *likely*; the highest probability. All the other universes became dreams; ghosts of what might have been, as time ploughed its way through probability, collapsing all other possibilities into one concrete, unalterable history.

Or did probability plough its way through time? Which controlled the other? Did collapsing probability create time? Was it all a diffusion of quantum entanglement? Or did time, if considered as an arrow, demand a decision from probability? Damn it, what was wrong with him? He should know this stuff!

Stiffly, he prised himself from the discomfort of his too-small makeshift bed. He couldn't think straight. His head hurt. His mind was still foggy from cider, wine and—he remembered with a groan—a nightcap of rum. He rubbed his hands over his face and combed his hair back with his fingers, then moved to the window and looked down on the remnants of the party in the garden below. That too, had passed like a dream into history, and hardly now seemed real, except for the evidence before his eyes. And was that history still developing over at Kate's house? Was every second that passed compounding the inevitability of the most probable outcome?

He had to do something.

Restlessly he grabbed his greatcoat and slung it over his peasant shirt and trousers from the night before. It was still early; dewy and cool as he marched, unseen, from the house and along the quiet lane. He stopped at the small crossroads.

477

If he took the coast path, it would give him more time. The heady air would fill his lungs and clear his head, and by the time he reached Dolphin Cottage he would have a story, an excuse to mark his presence at this early hour. But time, in this instance, was the enemy. Every passing minute might change the probable outcome unalterably. It might already be too late.

Abruptly he swung along the lane to the right, away from the coast path, cursing himself for having lingered so long. He should have pursued Kate last night, and yes, taken the consequences, however negative. Instead, Gabe had followed her. He should not have submitted to Jem and changed his own plans. He should not have involved Leah. He should not have waited, on New Year's Eve for Kate to arrive, but instead should have told her—should have *told* her!—the day that he had watched her furtively through a window. All those possibilities, gone—collapsed. These were Lance's thoughts as he hurled himself along the deserted country lane. His only companions were the small birds singing in the hedgerows, the cry of a gull circling overhead and the ever-present boom and swish of distant waves crashing against rocks. He might have been the only man alive.

The sun had barely risen, but despite the early freshness, there was the suggestion of another beautiful, golden day ahead. Before long, tourists would emerge sated from their breakfasts and take to the narrow country roads in their cars. The beaches would become full with noise and activity. In the village the cafes and coffee shops would soon be open, and any early risers might be lucky enough to find themselves in the company of returning fishermen, whose romantic tales of the sea would supply many an anecdote upon return to suburban dinner parties. The tourist shops would follow, and only the church bells would be summoning a reminder that the day was Sunday. But for now the world was asleep, and Lance a solitary, desperate knight on an ineffable quest.

Dolphin Cottage was still and quiet. The curtains were drawn and no smoke rose from the chimneys. Like the day, it had yet to stir. Only briefly, Lance hesitated; life in the mind and emotions was so different from that played out in reality. Would his words—not that he had prepared any—once uttered, appear meaningless and risible? Were his feelings real or fantasy? He had never felt so lonely. His very presence would be considered odd, and given Kate's attitude the previous evening he expected to be unwelcome, at the very least. But he had to know. He refused to think through what he would do or say to explain his presence; but instead strode purposefully to the door and knocked loudly. The sound shuddered against the wooden door, but the house, after some minutes, remained silent. With an extreme sense of déjà vu, he remembered that this was the door knocker that only resounded in another dimension. Swearing under his breath at this further test of courage, he summoned up his nerves and knocked again, with more force than before. This time he detected movement inside, and waited, with heartsick dread.

The door swung open, and Gabe stood before him, barefoot and stripped to the waist, wearing only last night's trousers which had evidently, judging from their loose state of fastening, been recently and leisurely applied to his body.

'Mornin',' Gabe smiled lazily and spoke with a sly casualness, while scratching his head. 'Come on in, you're bang on time; just made some coffee.'

Lance said nothing, but just watched as Gabe turned and sauntered towards the kitchen. Already suspecting the worst, Lance gently shut the front door behind him and followed his friend in a stupor. Gabe did not appear to be remotely fazed by his untimely appearance, and Lance was presumably expected to be equally relaxed about Gabe's highly suggestive presence.

'Take a seat,' said Gabe, as he fetched an extra coffee cup for Lance, then shuffled, with both cup and glass cafetière jug in hand, over to join him at the table. Lance felt suddenly hot in his great coat after the exertion of his brisk stride to the cottage, but he didn't remove it. It felt presumptuous, given the situation he observed with increasing dread—he might not be there very long—but more than that, he could not focus on any thought or action other than the question that was foremost in his mind. The house was still quiet, rendering every sound pronounced, each gesture conspicuous. There was no sign of Kate. Gabe sat down, putting his feet up on the table top, and idly rocking on the back legs of the kitchen chair. Lance feigned obedience and sat down, but fumed silently. How was it that in the space of mere hours Gabe was now familiarly ensconced in Kate's cottage? It was even more unbearable than Jem's rapid nesting had been.

'Great party,' Gabe was saying, 'Always is, of course, but last night was something special. I had a real good time.' His brown eyes fixed firmly and confidently on Lance's, and he smiled brightly.

Lance and Gabe had always been good friends; had hit it off from the start, despite their disparate backgrounds. Gabe's free-love philosophy regarding almost anyone except poor Salima was regarded by Lance as casual bordering on promiscuous; but it hadn't been important. It had never affected him before now, and he wondered if Gabe was deliberately tormenting him. He wanted to know how it had happened; how Gabe was suddenly with Kate and that he found himself in this situation.

'You came with Kate,' was all he could say.

'Yes I did, didn't I?' said Gabe still beaming. 'Quite a turnaround, and all to my benefit, I gotta say. Katie's great isn't she? A real firecracker! Would never have thought it myself, but hey, it's sometimes the quiet ones. But wait, I'm

480

forgetting. Weren't *you* supposed to be the lucky guy? What happened there, man?'

Lance looked away at the ground as if the answer eluded him. He didn't know any more.

'Jem happened,' he said.

'Ah,' said Gabe after a second or two, and then nodding as if with deep wisdom added, '*I see...*and Leah?'

'Leah was just there.'

Lance was still looking at the ground and did not see the thoughtful look that flickered and then vanished in Gabe's eyes. When he looked up again Gabe was draining the remnants of the coffee jug into his cup and radiating a full, satisfied grin once more.

'I take it you slept with her,' said Lance, hardly able to get the words out and hating the sound of his voice. He spoke in flat tones but it was impossible to disguise the crackle of desperation.

Gabe sipped at his coffee and resumed rocking back and forth on the back legs of the chair. *As if the answer required deep deliberation*, thought Lance. *As if there were a myriad of possible answers!* There was only one, and Gabe was deliberately prolonging his anguish. Lance fought the urge to kick the tipping chair away from under him.

'Actually...*no*,' said Gabe somewhat reluctantly, at last; the smug look disappearing momentarily. 'I crashed on the couch.' And he indicated with a jerk of his thumb the living room opposite. Turning and looking over his shoulder, Lance saw that sure enough, there was a blanket and pillow in disarray on the old sofa bed; a glass and almost finished bottle of red wine on the floor next to it. 'I walked her home; we had a glass of wine, and a chat; and then she went to bed...*alone.*'

Gabe got up from the table and moved across the kitchen to put the kettle on again. Then he grabbed the coffee jug,

481

emptied the dregs and then began rinsing it silently and elaborately at the sink.

Lance stood up and mooched restlessly around the kitchen. How to say it? The relief he felt was immense. Of course, Kate would still be angry with him, but he could explain. She was not an unreasonable person and it seemed he still had a chance to put things right—but how to convey this relief and gratitude to Gabe?

'Thanks mate,' he managed, with typical male restraint.

Gabe turned to stare at him sideways-on, a hint of caution in his eye. 'Oh don't *thank* me. Don't get me wrong, man, I did my worst; gave it my best shot. She was having none of it.'

'Oh, okay; right,' Lance was lost for words.

Gabe continued to give the coffee pot the scrub of its life. 'And don't think I'm giving up! I found myself quite taken with our Miss O'Neill last night. And I'm still here aren't I? She didn't exactly throw me out. She was being coy last night, which is fine; to be expected. I like a woman to put up a fight. But if you think I'm giving up then you, my friend, are way off-course!'

'But...I *love* her,' said Lance, mortified at how pathetic he sounded.

'Sorry dude, shoulda thought of that before. I mean, you had your chance—you blew it. As far as I'm concerned, she's fair game. And besides...' Gabe turned to look at Lance full-on and straight in the eye, '...she hates *you!*' And he raised both eyebrows, grinning cheerfully.

Lance did not later remember forming the thought in his head, but first knew that he had hit him when he felt the smacking, jarring contact with Gabe's jaw and the subsequent pain in his fist. Gabe retaliated wildly and instinctively by swinging the sparkling but doomed coffee jug into Lance's forehead. It shattered, sending tinkling fragments of glass onto the tiled floor.

They staggered apart, in some shock.

'Ouch, man!' said Gabe, with difficulty, rubbing his jaw. 'I think you dislocated it!'

'You could have blinded me!' Lance retorted indignantly, wiping the back of his hand against his forehead and then staring blankly at the unexpected blood.

In equal bewilderment, Gabe stood as if mesmerised by the remaining shards of pot attached to the handle that was still in his grip. Then both of them first of all looked up to the ceiling as they heard footsteps above, and then quietly met each other's eyes as they heard the crunch of someone hurrying downstairs, and then trotting along the corridor.

As Kate stood bleary-eyed and concerned in the doorway of the kitchen, they finally broke eye contact, and in an unspoken pact said in unison:

'We broke the coffee pot...'

CHAPTER 50

Sea-tides of the Heart

'Whoops!' said Gabe with an apologetic shrug. 'Butterfingers!' He hoped his smile was charming and boyish, and that it disguised the pain in his jaw.

Kate merely tutted absently and gingerly picked her way around the broken glass to get to the broom, eyeing Lance suspiciously as she went. 'Your forehead's bleeding,' she said, coldly, wondering why he was there at all.

'Yes, so it is,' replied Lance, touching his wound again and feigning surprise. 'Er, must have been a stray splinter of glass.'

Kate looked from one man to the other doubtfully. Something was going on. 'You'd better let me have a look at it.'

Kate shoved the broom at Gabe with a *look*, and then climbed up on the step stool in order to reach the highest shelf where she kept a small first-aid kit. She felt very aware of their eyes on her, and was glad that she had decided to pull on a pair of jeans and a T-shirt before coming downstairs. She had already managed to deflect Gabe's attentions last night, before cravenly waking and then bundling a sleepy Isabella into her own bed with her for added insurance. Neither was she going to give him any ideas by parading around in skimpy pyjamas, nor even her wholesomely fluffy white bathrobe. Even so, she hurriedly found the kit and clambered back down from the stool again.

Gabe obediently and efficiently cleared up the glass, his mind working fast. He only dared a fleeting look at Lance, for fear of giving anything away. Finished, he propped the broom up against the wall, and while Kate still rooted around the first aid kit for an appropriately sized plaster, he quickly disappeared and then reappeared fully, if somewhat shambolically dressed in his pirate costume. He moved towards Kate and kissed her on the cheek.

'I had a great time last night, Katie, but I gotta go, got an early class to teach.'

'Really?' said Kate in alarm. Surely he wasn't going to leave her alone with Lance? 'But it's Sunday!'

'Sure is, but 'tis also the season; things are hotting up. Gotta make the bucks while you can. And besides, your friend Parker is supposed to be joining me—if he remembers to get out of bed.'

'It was good of you to be so kind to him; *last night* I mean; *I'm very grateful*,' Kate looked at Gabe meaningfully.

He nodded in understanding. 'Any time, girl.'

Lance, seated once more at the table and nursing his wound, looked up at them both in turn.

'No really,' said Kate eager to disguise the true reason for her gratitude. 'You could easily have made Parker look ridiculous. You have a very generous spirit.'

'I'm not in the business of patronising; I'm in the business of teaching folks to surf. I can hardly expect everybody to be an expert now, can I? We all started out kooks.'

'All the same...' said Kate, her voice trailing off feebly. She racked her brains for a way to make him stay. All she could manage was an imploring look. Gabe smiled and moved towards her. Lance watched his every move.

'You ah...got my number?' said Gabe placing both hands on Kate's waist. 'Give me a call sometime?'

485

With the first aid box in one hand and a tube of antiseptic ointment in the other, Kate was at his mercy. But before she could reply, Gabe changed his stance and grabbed her affectionately in a hug. Eyeing Lance over Kate's shoulder, Gabe could not resist. He winked at him, eyes twinkling with merriment.

Lance glared helplessly back.

'Okay, gotta go,' said Gabe gently, and stepping away towards the door. 'It's okay, I'll see myself out. Just remember, call me; and...' he snatched a look at Lance again before turning back to Kate, '...be good!'

Outside in the fresh morning air that was just beginning to warm, Gabe rubbed and wrenched his jaw into a more comfortable position, then grinned and congratulated himself. Altruism was not a virtue that he often experienced, but he had to admit it felt good. What was it Kate had said? That he had a generous spirit? Oh yes, he liked that. And of course he didn't have an early class that morning; he had deliberately booked his first one for later in the afternoon, knowing that he would be recovering from the party. In all, it had been a very interesting weekend. He had enjoyed Kate's company and it had provided an intriguing perspective. It had been fun to be with someone who was not immediately available to him. And he liked Lance. Lance was a good friend; thoughtful, smart, and though it pained him to acknowledge it, handsome. But he was hopeless when it came to women. The guy had been alone for far too long, and he needed a shove. If a little bit of competition was required to give him that shove then Gabe was happy to provide it.

But he'd better not blow it this time; otherwise Kate, as he had said, was fair game. And with that thought, Gabe and his generous spirit struck a bold and benevolent stride towards the rest of the day.

Back in the cottage, Kate moved towards Lance, who still sat wordlessly at the kitchen table, with apprehension.

486

Standing in front of him, she could not meet his eyes, but fixedly studied the wound on his forehead in a professional manner.

'How come you're here?' she asked flatly. He started to look away but Kate grabbed his head by the jaw with one hand and firmly moved it back to face her. 'Keep still,' she instructed.

He looked up at her, and his face was very close. He moved and she felt his knee touch her leg. Kate opened the tube of antiseptic cream and squeezed a dab onto her finger.

'I came to see you,' said Lance in equally clipped tones. For a second their eyes met and Kate saw the serious intent therein. 'We need to...*ouch! That stings!*' Lance grimaced as Kate applied the ointment to the cut on his forehead. She *nearly* smiled.

'Are you sure it doesn't need stitches?' asked Lance, his thoughts turning for the first time to the extent of his wound.

'Yes. I'm sure. Don't be such a baby, it's practically only a scratch. You just need to keep it clean for a bit.' She reached for the plaster and tore at the cover.

'So I won't be scarred for life, then?' Lance, desperate to change the mood, attempted to inject some humour.

Kate placed the plaster firmly in place. 'Don't worry,' she said scathingly, 'You're still beautiful.'

And before she could stop herself, she took his forehead lightly in her hands, and stooped to kiss it. It had been an instinctive movement, a motherly impulse, as if it were Isabella sitting before her, wounded. It was a *kiss-it-better, you can run off and play now* kind of kiss. Almost as soon as her lips touched his head, she recoiled and withdrew them in horror. But it was too late; in that second of closeness, Lance encircled her waist with his arms and drew her body against his, his lips against hers, and then he kissed her.

487

In some shock, Kate responded unthinkingly, and it was some seconds before she managed to half-pull, half-push his face away from hers. But he did not release her from his arms, and it was probably still shock that left her dumbstruck and staring at him wide-eyed, so that he kissed her again. In the course of this second kiss he stood up, allowing him to increase his grasp of her, and Kate felt herself relenting to his strength and size. With a surge of willpower, she managed to prise herself apart from him and back away, staggering.

'What are you doing?' she cried. 'How can you...how can you do this?'

'Very easily, actually. In fact, amazingly easily! Can't think why I haven't done it before. Besides, you kissed me first!'

'That wasn't the same! It wasn't that sort of kiss. You...you took advantage! You can't just go around kissing people, you know.'

'Apparently, you can,' said Lance with an amazed expression. 'And I still maintain that you kissed me first. You definitely kissed me back, at least.'

Kate felt herself flush. Lance took a step towards her and she backed away again.

'Did you not see me with Gabe just then?' She pointed frantically at the spot by the door where Gabe had left, as if she might conjure him up again. 'And last night too? Does it not occur to you that I might be with Gabe now, huh? And what about Leah?'

'I don't believe that you're with Gabe,' Lance said softly. 'And Leah, other than being Finn's mother, means nothing to me. We've been divorced a long time, Kate.'

'She obviously means a lot more than I do,' said Kate bitterly. 'Do you think you can come round here and just...just *play* with me? Do you think I can be won over that easily?' She stopped. She had given away too much. She was determined not to show the depth of her upset.

'Kate, listen to me. I'm sorry I let you down, but it wasn't because of Leah; it was because of Jem. I...didn't want to cause him further distress.' Even now Lance hesitated to reveal the fact of Jem's telephone call.

'And you couldn't just have explained that to me?'

'Damn it Kate, you're making too big a deal out of this. It was just a stupid party, and it's over. Can't we move on?'

Kate paused for a moment to try and think. It was a lot to take in. She was still getting over the shock of the fact that Lance had kissed her; it was so unexpected; so out of character. But she did not get time to digest the turn of events, for within seconds she heard the thud of the door knocker, and she wondered if Gabe had returned. Throwing a last reproachful look at Lance, she turned and went with mixed feelings of trepidation and gratitude to answer the door.

'Good morning!' Juliet shrilled, with an uncharacteristically upbeat tone, and pushing her way past Kate into the hallway. Kate was amazed to see her up and so lively following a party. 'Yeah, I know it's early, but I had to come. You have just *got* to see this!'

She thrust a tabloid newspaper in front of Kate's face. It had been opened and folded on a certain page, and there, in the celebrity gossip pages, was a full-colour, completely clear picture of Lance engaged in a passionate kiss with Leah. It did not look like a discreet, ambiguous shot, which might conceivably be open to misinterpretation; but rather left little doubt as to the nature of the relationship.

Kate did not know if the feeling rising up inside her was the return of last night's fury, or a fresh well of undiluted cynicism. That old demon inside her woke with a vengeance, taunting her for her foolishness. And yet there was still shock, that Lance, of all people, should have kissed her mere hours after performing the same attentions upon Leah. Her demon laughed at her; scorned her: *Ha-ha! That's a good one, Kate!*

489

This one lasted barely minutes, before you found him out. But admit it, you wanted to believe him, didn't you? Fool!

Wordlessly and red-faced, Kate returned to the kitchen and slung the vile paper on the table and under Lance's nose. He turned it slightly to get a better view, and then stared uncomprehendingly at the picture. She waited for his eyes to lift and meet hers, then turned and left the room again. Juliet stood open-mouthed in the kitchen doorway, astonished by the realisation that Lance was there. Kate slipped on her flip-flops by the front door and muttered a few curt words to Juliet: 'Watch Izzy for me? She's still asleep.'

Then she left the cottage and fled, as fast as she could in the flimsy rubber sandals, out of the cottage grounds and down the lane. She did not know where she was going, but had to leave; compelled by nothing other than the desire to be far away from Lance. Her head was a buzz of ineloquent thoughts. Why was he doing this to her? And why Lance, of all people? Jem she might have expected this of; or Gabe, who ironically, had ultimately behaved with total respect towards her. But Lance was the last person she would have expected to play with her feelings in this manner.

She was some way down the lane when Lance caught up with her. She heard his running footsteps behind her and looked desperately for an escape route. Mindlessly, and for no other reason than it was the only one presented to her, she dived to her right along the coast path.

'Kate, wait, please,' Lance caught her arm. 'That photograph, it was nothing. I don't even know where it came from! I don't remember it being taken.'

'I suppose it wasn't you, then?' said Kate with sarcasm.

'Well, quite obviously it is; but it's not what it seems... Kate, Leah kissed *me*—'

'Right, like *I* apparently kissed you, just now. You're entirely innocent in all events.'

490

'It's not the same, Kate, you can't compare the two. I promise I only have feelings for you—'

'I don't believe you!' cried Kate with as much authority as she could muster. 'Don't you get it? I just don't believe you! Now, leave me alone!'

She wrenched her arm free and stumbled down the ladder of railway sleepers leading to Porthledden Beach. Lance still followed. Kate lurched across the sand, desperately trying to outpace his long stride, but failing dismally in her flip-flops.

'Why won't you give me a chance?' Lance was at her side again. 'I mean, what if you're wrong? What if you take everybody else away, and consider only us? I don't believe that you don't think there's something there...something...' He summoned his courage: 'Something like love, Kate.'

'You see, that's where you're wrong. I told you before, I don't believe in love, not of that kind; I don't believe in hearts and flowers and stupid romance.' Kate had raised her voice to be heard above the noise of the waves and the seagulls. Somehow it gave vent to her untapped emotions, and the venom leaked out and tainted the tone of her words with a bitter harshness. 'It's a delusion; a construct; it doesn't exist. People just imagine themselves in love because of their own insecurity. They just want attention and...and validation! Well I don't care! I don't want it and I don't need it. I wish you would just leave me alone!'

They stomped along in silence for a moment. Lance did not leave her alone, but persisted, silently fuming by her side. They were right at the water's edge now and occasionally the incoming tide hurled a random, freezing wave across their path. Kate let her feet and the ends of her jeans get wet rather than move away from the approaching waves—and closer towards Lance.

'I don't believe you,' he said eventually, mimicking her own words, but speaking in more quiet, measured tones.

'Suit yourself,' said Kate, unable to withdraw her angry tone now that the floodgates were open.

'You're the most romantic person I know,' Lance continued in a controlled manner. Kate threw him a look of incredulous disgust, but did not answer. 'You're an artist, Kate; you spend your days wandering the coast path alone, and painting pictures. You read Malory and Tennyson and Keats; you even named your daughter after a Keats' poem for God's sake! And your favourite poem is the Haystack in the Floods! How much more romantic and melancholy could you *be*?'

'But that's fantasy! It doesn't happen in real life...'

'Well, it's happened to me,' said Lance darkly. 'And what about Derry and Vivien? Do you think that's not real? And if you truly don't believe in love, then why did you finish with Jem? What are you holding out for Kate, if there's nothing better to be had?'

'Well, I'm not holding out for a man who takes me for granted, lets me down, and then comes to me fresh from another woman!'

A group of young boys playing on skimboards in the surf nearby began to leer and giggle at the couple arguing. Lance suddenly grabbed Kate by the shoulders to put a stop to her incessant marching.

'Do you know what I think?' Lance's anger now matched Kate's. 'I think you're scared. You read about love, but you haven't got the guts to embrace it in reality. You need to put the night light out, Kate, and look at some stars for a change! You need to stop being such a coward!'

Kate's eyes sparkled. 'And you need to mind your own business!'

'You need to give me a chance!'

'*You* need to get over yourself!'

'And you need to cool down!'

Without another word, Lance grabbed Kate and lifted her full off the ground, then ignoring her protests, strode

492

purposefully into the sea, carrying her over his shoulder. When the waves were hitting him waist-deep, he dropped her irreverently into the glacial sea. She gave a sound which was part gasp, part scream. Fury and indignation were compounded by the physical shock of the icy water. Then she could only watch, shivering and inarticulate with rage, as Lance turned away, and without another word or backward glance, made his way out through the white water and onwards across the beach.

Not even a backward glance! She might have been drowning for all he knew. And how dare he?! She saw one flip-flop drift off into deeper water, forever destined to be just one more piece of flotsam. Feeling her foot twist unstably under her in the current, she reached down and removed the remaining sandal into her hand. She started to haul herself out of the sea, struggling against the surf as it tried to knock her legs from under her, and untangling herself from seaweed as she went. The boys on the beach were now insensible with mirth, and they pointed and jeered and clapped as Kate, soaked and bedraggled, stumbled clumsily back to shore. She heard their rollicking laughter all the way along the beach behind her, as she slowly and shamefacedly made her way back home, clutching the pointless flip-flop to her chest, as if its salvation rendered her some small scoop of dignity.

493

CHAPTER 51

A Curse

A strange thing was happening to Kate. It had been several days since Lance had dumped her in the sea at Porthledden, during which time she had neither seen nor heard from him. She had half-expected, half-feared an apology. Given Lance's usually contained character, it had been an extreme and bizarre thing to do. Perhaps there was a wild, rebellious streak in him that she would not have predicted. She imagined that once in his senses again, Lance would be compelled to do the right thing and make amends, but she heard nothing. This sense of waiting made her deeply anxious. She could not face him yet, if indeed ever again; but not knowing if he might reappear at her door at any moment filled her with dreadful unease. She was tense and could not relax. Her mind kept going back to the events of that day: to his inexplicable early morning appearance; their argument; the shock and anger that she still felt at his sudden, impassioned behaviour on the beach.

And he had kissed her.

Sometimes she allowed her mind to wander, as one does, to speculate how she might have controlled the situation differently. She imagined clever words that she might have said to prevent his course of action, and leave her with the upper hand; or how she might have caused him equal mortification by hauling him under the water and perhaps drowning him. Her imaginings did not allow for a swift kick

494

to the groin, or other form of self-defence; the dragging influence of the sea would have rendered such a plan ineffectual. She could at least have slapped him, sharply on the cheek, like a heroine of old; but no, he had made his retreat too quickly for that. She imagined herself grabbing a chunk of slimy seaweed and throwing it at his retreating back.

Or she envisaged that he had not immediately left her, but had stayed, grinning mockingly at her. In this instance, she would have taken the stinking seaweed and casually and vengefully rubbed it slowly onto his smug head. But while she covered him in seaweed, he would take her in his arms and kiss her again. Then they would stay there for long moments, kissing, lost in their embrace and oblivious to the cold of the sea and the insistent, bludgeoning waves...

What was happening to her?!

Embarrassed by the reverie, she tried again to distract her mind by reading. But every book that she picked up seemed destined to prompt her imagination back to uncomfortable realms—everything from the poetry of Keats to tales of doomed Pre-Raphaelite sirens. Lance had been right, in his evaluation of her reading matter. Why did she surround herself with this stuff? Even Shakespeare now seemed to have forged his entire career with the sole purpose of taunting her further down the centuries with his sonnets and tales of love and tragedy. She stared, mean-eyed and challengingly at the Complete Works of Tennyson. *Give it a go.*

Flicking the book open at random, it fell upon the tale of Lancelot and Elaine from The Idylls of the King. Huh! *Lancelot*. It would be of course, Kate thought in a surge of ironic disdain. Anyway, she had already read that story hundreds of times, and so she flicked through the book again. This time she stopped at The Lady of Shallot, and paused. *Bloody Lancelot again!* But she was also reminded of her thoughts high up in the observatory the other night—she would not allow herself to call it *Lance's* observatory; every reference or thought of him would spark fresh, excruciating torment. She had imagined herself akin to this doomed woman; this "fairy, the Lady of Shallot", condemned by an unknown curse to spend her days weaving in a tower, and to only observe the outside world through a mirror.

And it had been Lancelot who had forced her finally, to look. Lancelot's unwitting beauty had sealed her fate, and lead to her lonely, resigned death. Kate had never been sure about the poem; was death itself the curse and one look at Lancelot worth the tragic outcome? And why had she compared her own life to the Lady's dismal, melancholy existence? Sighing, she slammed the book shut and shoved it across the table away from her.

She tried reading the local paper, but could not see the words. She could only stare at the picture of Derry and Vivien leaving the party on a white Shire horse, their expressions serene with mysterious contentment. She turned on the radio, only to hear the familiar chord changes of a particularly romantic love song. She quickly turned the dial to Radio 4, for once grateful to hear the passionless tones of the interviewer; a tweedy Middle-England good-sort discussing wood coppicing with a bemused young man, who had a remarkably comforting west-country accent. Kate set about tidying her kitchen to the droning intonations. But she was stopped dead in her tracks as the young man started to explain how he had taken up wood coppicing after years of drink and drug abuse, thanks to first meeting and then marrying the love of his life...

'...I've never been so happy, and would never have thought it possible. She changed my life...that and the woods...'

Kate dashed to turn the radio off. Amelia the cat, having abandoned her physical attacks of old in favour of a more subtle vendetta of contemptuous scrutiny, observed her knowingly from her laundry-basket nest.

Worst of all for Kate, was the realisation that she could not paint. This was a disaster. With the exhibition only weeks away, she had sat before her latest work, staring at it, only to find that the meditative concentration required eluded her. Her mind was stuck playing through the loop of recent events, and her thoughts overpowered by intruding romantic fantasy.

Vivien paid her a visit, finally. Kate had been busy on her hands and knees giving her wooden floors the scrubbing of a lifetime, and almost taking all the varnish off. She had discovered that ruthless housework was the only activity that her possessed mind would allow. Her heart jumped when she heard the thud of the knocker, and she peered cautiously from the living room window to identify the caller. She was grateful, if still somewhat anxious, to see that it was only Vivien, alone. Would Lance have told Vivien what had happened between them? Was she bearing some message from him? He still hadn't called.

Vivien looked younger and lovelier than Kate had ever seen her. The bright, bohemian, fairy-like creature that Kate had originally met had been replaced in recent months by a subdued, more thoughtful version of her natural self. Now, she was luminescent; overflowing with an inner happiness. It tested Kate's cynicism to its limits.

'What happened?' asked Kate once they were comfortably seated in the kitchen with mugs of tea. 'I mean, I'm glad for your happiness—if you *are* happy; you certainly seem to be. But *Derry*? You seemed so set against him, as anything other than a friend that is.'

'I know. I know! But I was a blind fool,' said Vivien, appearing in no way abashed by the hackneyed phrase. 'Thank goodness he didn't give up on me! Sometimes the mind plays tricks, Kate. I thought I knew myself, but all along I was delusional. I think Max's proposal scared the life out of me. I knew Derry had strong feelings for me and I suppose, on some

497

subliminal level, I was protecting myself from having to reject someone again. I didn't like the responsibility.'

Kate suppressed her natural scepticism. Unusually, she wanted to understand; perhaps even to believe. She said nothing, but gently sipped her tea, allowing Vivien to continue.

'Of course, when you get used to taking someone for granted, it can come as a bit of a shock to think that they might one day not be there for you anymore; that somebody else might...have them...'

A discreet reference to Juliet? Still Kate said nothing.

'...or that they might just go away forever. Suddenly, I didn't seem to see him so much. And I didn't even hear about him going to Ireland before he went. It just felt like everything was wrong! And then, when he asked me...everything was all right again. I didn't panic, Kate. I didn't want to run away screaming. There was just one thought in my mind, and that was, *I love him!*'

So, Vivien had indeed consulted her instinct, and this time her soul had not been alarmed. But Kate was still unsure.

'But, what about...I mean...it's *Derry*,' Kate broached the subject awkwardly. 'You've always said you saw him as just a friend. Do you...you know... *fancy* him?'

'Damn it yes!' said Vivien with feeling, and her hearty, dirty laugh. 'It's as if, once I started looking, I *really* started looking. I'd been avoiding the thought before, like the shutters were down or something; but *now*! Now it's like I'm under a spell; or I *was* under a spell and now it's been lifted...'

'...and you can see that the frog is really a handsome prince,' interrupted Kate with a wry smile.

'Exactly!' said Vivien with another deep laugh. 'I mean, he's gorgeous! Can't you see it?'

'Well, I've never really thought of him as a frog, you know; that was only you.'

'I know, and what an idiot I was!' Vivien stared out of the kitchen window for a few seconds, a secret smile on her lips, before turning back towards Kate with a coy expression. 'Enough of me; how about you? You came to the party with Gabe! What happened to Lance?'

Finally, Vivien had said his name.

Kate lowered her eyes to hide the emotion there. She explained that Lance had called and told her he would be going with Leah instead. '...but it might also have had something to do with Jem,' she added, upon seeing her friend's incredulous look.

'Look, Kate, I know my brother.' Vivien's tone was serious. 'Believe me, there is nothing between him and Leah, at least nothing that exists beyond Leah's imagination. She's stupid and vain, Kate. Do you really think Lance would prefer her to—'

'He married her!' cried Kate. 'And I'm sure you saw the newspapers?'

Vivien hesitated for a moment, then persisted: 'He married her because she was pregnant. He wanted to do the right thing; even at the expense of his own happiness. I think that was why he was so adamant that I should be sure of my own feelings, when Max proposed. He didn't want me to make the same sort of mistake.'

Kate flushed in indignation. 'I'm sorry but it doesn't wash. He still liked her enough to get her pregnant! If he wasn't happy with her then he should have thought of that first. How dare he play the martyr when the woman is the one who has to have the baby?'

Vivien regarded her solemnly. 'Only, in this case, it was not Leah who was left holding the baby.'

She was right. Kate's wilful opposition was drawn up short. For the first time, she clearly saw that Lance's life had taken much the same course as her own. Hapless to have become involved with the wrong person; a beloved child that nevertheless had meant long, wary, protective years spent without the love of a partner; engaging fitfully in shallow relationships only to discover an even deeper emptiness. Perhaps she had been too harsh on him. Perhaps all could be explained if she were to give him the chance. She shook away the thought. Her defences were still in place; her feelings still raw from rejection. She didn't believe him. She *couldn't* believe him. It was too risky.

When Vivien had gone, Kate tried once again to breach her creative block. She approached the work in progress surreptitiously, tidying the area around it and fastidiously arranging her brushes. The canvas didn't know it yet, but she was slyly thinking about which part she would begin to work on; which colours she would choose, secretly blending them in her mind. The painting, slumbering in innocence, might at any moment wake and discover her. She would have to move fast. Cerulean Blue; Pithalo Green; Naples Yellow mixed with Titanium White; perhaps a hint of Raw Umber.

Where was he? Where was he right now and what was he doing? Leah was still there, Vivien had said, staying in the same house. She felt a surge of emotion; a physical agony that radiated from the vicinity of her heart, but rose from somewhere much deeper.

Get to work. She began squeezing paint onto the wooden board that she used as a pallet. It no longer resembled the piece of ply that it once had been, having been covered on both sides by multitudinous coloured layers of acrylic paint; so much so that it was becoming an art form in its own right. She mixed and stirred, blended and tested. *Not quite right; try again.*

Lance had kissed her. She hadn't dreamt it, he really had kissed her. The reality was slipping away from her, and she fought to remember the way it had felt, and the exact position of his body and his hands on her. And then...*she remembered*

500

how it had felt, and how she had, through the shock and surprise, responded. What trick of her character had allowed it? Conjuring the memory, she could feel the slight growth of masculine hair on his jaw, and the insistent pressure of his mouth. If she concentrated very hard, she could invoke the warmth, the taste, the scent. She had a pang of regret that she had not touched his hair; his beautiful hair, now outgrown and untamed again.

Kate stood trancelike with her brush poised before her, her eyes unseeing, and her mind locked in torturous reminiscence and guilty fantasy. With sudden clarity she finally understood The Lady of Shallot. The curse had been to fall in love: the most wretched, painful, and destructive curse of all. No wonder the poor woman had not attempted to resist! Years of being dutiful in a tower, then wham! Try and survive *that*, if you can. No wonder she had climbed straight into the boat—forget the cloak—and let the river have its way.

Kate was consumed with desire; paralysed by secret lustful imaginings. Lance filled her every thought and action. Of course, lust was generally dismissed as a baser, lesser form of love. *It was just an infatuation*, people said, as they returned to a passionless, but safer, less painful, existence. Comfortable, familiar, enduring love was the recommended aim, the consensually valid version. There was no contest when compared with the affliction, the madness, of the other thing. The word lust indeed described a carnal desire for sexual gratification; but lust for an actual person was different. It was not just for their body but for every molecule of it; every beat of their heart and every thought in their head. Every utterance, every gesture was precious. It was called falling in love, and it was overwhelming. Kate was floored; crippled; helpless. Trying to do anything was pointless. It was as if she could not undertake one sane thought or conscious task until she had cured her sick heart and mind.

And then as she stared at the canvas before her, at the sombre black rocks and the wild waves; at the swirl of blue and green and sea-spray and storm, the remedy came to her:

The sea.

It was where she had last seen him; where the memory of their emotional conflict still lingered, a part of them both. Suddenly overcome by a compulsion to be in the salt ocean, Kate quickly changed into her swimsuit, threw a hooded sweatshirt and some leggings on top, and grabbed a towel. At the doorstep she hesitated, and then remembering a trick she had seen the surfers use, she tied her door-keys to a shoelace, which she would then be able to tie around her neck in the sea. There was no time to pause, to consider her actions, or the moment would be gone. No time to worry about what else she might need, or the sea-temperature, let alone the tides or weather conditions. It was imperative that she act now before impulse faded and reason—what little she still possessed—was restored. And so, with her head held high in determination, Kate strode defiantly towards the beach.

Chapter 52

A Wild Heart

It was incredible. How could this happen now, after all this time? This kind of love was meant to happen at first sight. It was supposed to be outside the boundaries and rules of self-determination. It was the lightning bolt; the cupid's arrow; the folly of the gods. It did not rely on rationality, familiarity, or even time—just a lazy point of the finger from an idle deity was enough. So why the long prelude? Why had she not succumbed to it months before?

Kate stared madly into the silence surrounding her. Isabella was out—again—and her life felt suddenly strange and unreal, as if she were outside of herself, observing dispassionately this deranged woman sitting alone. She had to get out, to find people and life. Even to talk to someone about mundane matters for a short time would temporarily ease her insanity. In fact the only way to ever be normal again would perhaps be to constantly distract herself with something— anything—that required interaction. She would be faking it of course, but her favourite pursuits of painting, walking and other forms of seclusion were now lethal. They said that if you smiled through depression you could make yourself happy. Perhaps if you performed your way through madness you might restore sanity.

She left the cottage and headed, bravely, in the direction of the village. She was completely terrified of running into Lance. But she was equally terrified of *not* seeing him, for nothing but his presence would ease her suffering. It was the most insatiable of itches that needed scratching.

She took the coast road, her swimsuit and towel now ever ready in her rucksack just in case the mood took her to take to the sea again. Her swims were becoming a regular feature of her routine—in some ways now her only routine. The touch of the cold salt water on her skin and having all her energy spent left her feeling purged and renewed—for the moment, at least. On this day she did not go down to the beach, but stopped at the lookout point to observe the scene below. It was late afternoon and Porthledden, although not empty, was relatively uncrowded. The next huge influx of tourists would not come until the onset of the school summer holidays and there were only some dog-walkers, couples walking arm in arm, and the usual surfers and lifeguards.

Weary with anxiety, she tried to free her mind and focus on the beauty of the scene before her. But her thoughts would not let her rest. Looking back, she realised that she might have fallen for Lance from the beginning, had she not been so suspicious and cynical to start with, and if he had not put her off with his arrogance. She had felt humiliated and unfairly judged. Once falsely accused, she had refused to let herself entertain any such desires towards him. She remembered their conversation in the garden at her Christmas party, when she had told him that he should never misconstrue her actions, because she wasn't, and would never, be interested in him. It was at this point that she had felt him relax a little, and they had started to become friends. But now she realised that she had equally been restoring her pride. She had been lying to herself when she said that she would never be interested in him; his manner upon their first meeting had brought all her defences down, and they had been so secure that she had convinced herself of the veracity of them.

Sighing, Kate tried again to clear her troubled head. She looked at the ubiquitous collection of neoprene-clad surfers littering the waves and shoreline. She recognised Gabe and realised that it was one of his classes. Gazing out to sea, she watched for a while, admiring the determination and resilience of his eager pupils. She saw one young girl hesitate, and then apparently resolute, take off and then stand up on a wave. The girl was beautiful: long-legged and lissom, strong and graceful. She rode the green wave for several seconds before tumbling into the surf, and then emerging, triumphant and grinning with joy.

Kate suddenly grasped the stone wall in front of her. It couldn't be! She peered, with fresh concentration, focussing with alarm on the subject. She ran back to the railway sleepers and then hurried down towards the shore.

Gabe saw her coming across the beach at about the same time as Isabella, and ran out of the water as fast as he could with his surfboard to meet her halfway, his spare arm raised in apologetic defence.

'I was gonna tell you,' he shouted above the sound of the waves. 'Honest I was...'

'How could you?' Kate, just metres away now, yelled back,

'She's been one hundred percent safe,' Gabe spoke more gently now that Kate had reached him. 'I'm here the whole time; I would never let her come to any harm...'

'She's ten years old!' cried Kate. 'How dare you let this happen without telling me?'

'Actually, I'm eleven,' reminded Isabella, who had caught up with Gabe and was now standing alongside them. Kate looked at her blindly for a second, wondering where she had got the wetsuit; the surfboard.

'Ten, eleven, that's not the point! I'm her mother. I should have been told!'

'You would have said no!' said Isabella, 'You always say no!'

'Hey, I'm truly sorry,' said Gabe, averting the attention from Isabella, 'but you must have seen her out there? She's great; a natural. And she truly isn't in any danger...'

'Rip currents? Jellyfish? Weever fish?!'

'Well okay, you can never account for jellies or weevers; but I would never have let her into dangerous water.'

'If you can't see how wrong this is, I seriously doubt your ability to ensure a child's safety!'

'That's not fair!' Isabella piped up again. 'He's done nothing wrong. He's helped me. This is what I want to do! Why can't you just let me?'

'Hey Whizz,' a boy shouted from further along the beach, waving to get Isabella's attention. It was Finn. 'You coming?' He stood at what was presumably considered a safe distance with some other girls and boys of about the same age. All of them wore wetsuits, and each carried a surfboard or bodyboard of some description. And they all possessed the dreamy expression of the satisfied, the exhilarated and exhausted: the *stoked*.

Isabella looked at Kate urgently. 'They've been waiting for me. They're going back to Finn's house for hot chocolate,' she said, her little chin tipped up in defiance.

Kate beheld her daughter as if for the first time. Isabella had grown tall and slender and brown, and her hair was long and untamed. Sometimes in her dark curly locks Kate would catch a glimpse of Miles; but now she saw him vividly, in Isabella's lazy, confident stance and challenging air. Suddenly Kate realised that her daughter was never going to be Isabella with the ducks following behind. She was Izzy, or Whizz, or whatever it was that they called her, and she was a surfer.

'Go,' she said simply; defeated. Isabella did not wait for Kate to change her mind, but immediately ran off towards the group of youngsters. However, she stopped halfway, and in acknowledgement, called back to assure her mother that she would not be too late home. Kate looked moodily at Gabe, who

506

stood waiting for his lecture. But she no longer had the heart. Isabella and Gabe had deceived her; but how could she justify berating them, when she herself had been shamefully negligent in checking her daughter's whereabouts and activities.

But something had changed in Kate's life, and she had not even seen it coming. Isabella had looked feral and carefree and happy. Kate could not help but feel a sense of pride. But it was a pride mixed with incredulity that this wild and free creature was her daughter. She felt something akin to bereavement. She realised more than ever that she did not own her daughter; that Isabella ultimately would take charge of her own life. Reason told her that this was natural and right, but Kate could not shake off the sense that she was losing something; that in the end, she would lose everyone. And behind all of these mixed feelings there was another of which she was deeply ashamed; was reluctant to acknowledge.

It was envy.

CHAPTER 53

A Decision

I t all came out; how Isabella had not always been playing
football or just hanging out at Finn's house, but had, for a
greater part of the time been having surfing lessons with
Gabe, who had lent her a wetsuit and surfboard. As they sat
side by side on the sand, Gabe told Kate everything; about how
he had taken pity on Isabella's forlorn figure as she had
watched the other children, helpless and mute from the shore.
He continued to apologise profusely, but in equal measure
asserted his conviction of Isabella's natural ability in the
water; that she was confident, stylish and brave.

'I suppose it's not so different from riding a Harley,' Kate
muttered, mostly to herself. 'I expect she'll want one of those,
one day, too.' When Gabe looked puzzled, she added: 'Her
father. He was a big fan of motorbikes. He never worried
about risk. I expect she gets it from him.'

Gabe said nothing but returned his attention to his
remaining pupils. They were an intermediately experienced
group, who mercifully hadn't drowned in his absence, but still
needed occasional reining in. He saw one particularly reckless
teenager drop in on someone else's wave, and swore under his
breath. The teenager was also close to the edge of the safe,
flagged area for swimmers and bodyboarders, and he could
see the beach lifeguard watching him closely.

'Hey look, I gotta go paddle out again,' he said, jumping up.
'But we'll talk about this some more, if you want? And y'know,

maybe just think about what I've said? After all, you saw her; it's a done deal, in a way...'

Kate was not forgiving enough to refrain from a reminding, thunderous look.

'And besides,' called Gabe, as he backed away from her with his surfboard once more under his arm, 'she don't necessarily get it from her dad, you know.' He turned and ran towards the sea, signalling to the miscreant surfer as he went.

Kate sat for a while longer on the beach. Rather than being a welcome distraction to her thoughts, her mind simply added this new revelation to the mix of recent events that plagued her. The affliction that she suffered from, in respect of Lance, now seemed illusive and unreal in comparison with the reality of her neglect of Isabella. Not that Isabella was complaining, but rather seemed to have flourished under self-rule.

Then there was the letter from Marsha; Kate could not help but feel bitter after her long struggle to gain autonomy in her life. Now Miles threatened to interfere, and Isabella herself appeared to be mounting her own insurrection. And thanks to Lance Borlase, she now even pined for the serenity so recently found in her painting; and in her long coastal walks. It was as if everything that she had strived for had been tossed in the air. Her thoughts were no longer clear, but a jumble of confusion; mashed and tangled; and needing unpicking from scratch. She could not even manage to harden her heart, it seemed.

She watched Gabe and the other surfers, lining up to perform their dance with the waves, and making it all seem so simple. But it wasn't simple. It couldn't be, could it? She pulled her swimsuit out of her bag, and changed discreetly under her large sweatshirt. The days were still long and sunny, but as she strode towards the shoreline in a bikini she still felt chilly, naked and exposed in the sea breeze. She had got into the habit of leaving her belongings in the lifeguard's truck so they wouldn't get washed away by the incoming tide, and she smiled at them now as they patiently, understandingly, accepted her bag. She knew that they thought her crazy, not to mention a liability, to enter the cold sea without a wetsuit; but having witnessed her survival a few times now they had grown to accept the madness. All the same, she equally knew that they shook their heads and kept one eye on her as she ran into the water.

Later, back at the cottage, Kate did not forbid Isabella to continue surfing, but made a long and protracted speech about the importance of her knowing exactly where her daughter was at all times. Suspecting that she was getting off lightly, Isabella was unusually compliant. She nodded and agreed maturely, but made a mental note that it was probably just as well, for the time being, not to inform her mother of her night-time stargazing rituals.

The following day brought Juliet and Parker's last day in Cornwall. They had been touring around the county, using Pencarra as a base, and presumably squandering some more inheritance. But now Juliet wanted to see Kate and Isabella before leaving to return to London.

'Where's Parker?' asked Kate, surprised to see Juliet arrive alone.

'Er, down at the beach, I think,' said Juliet, who seemed unusually distracted. 'I suspect he wants to see Gabe before we go. He's determined not to leave without his phone number.'

'What's up?' asked Kate.

'Nothing!' said Juliet brightly. 'But you could at least offer me a drink when I'm not going to see you again for ages.'

Kate sighed. She had all but stopped drinking until that awful day of the party, and had been sorely tempted in recent times to use alcohol's anaesthetising powers to quell the maelstrom of emotions inside her. But she had, until now, resisted, fearing there might be even more despairing depths to plunder under its influence. But given her current mental confusion, her resolve was weak and her sister's request was enough to lead her into temptation. She poured them each a large glass of wine, and then accompanied by deep self-loathing, she gratefully sipped the chill honeyed drug.

'That's better,' said Juliet, who appeared to notice no difference in her sister's demeanour, whereas Kate felt as if her torment must be obvious for all to see. It didn't just say *Mug* on her forehead; it said *Lost Forever*. How could Juliet not detect the spectacular change in her entire being?

'There's something I have to tell you,' Juliet continued. 'I've decided to go away after all; the world trip, I mean. Only I've changed my mind about Australia and Thailand and all those places. It's all a bit too predictable. Everyone does that these days. I've decided to go to South America instead. You know; the Amazon rainforest; Peru...go and see Machu Picchu, that sort of thing.'

Kate sighed inwardly this time. South America was just the new Australia and Thailand. Soon there would be no part of the world that had not been infested with tourists, and the excitement of true discovery and exploration would be a thing of the past. But she feigned an interested expression, aware that her personal state of mind was probably casting a shadow over everything.

'That's good news, Juliet,' she said. 'And I'm glad you made your mind up to finally go. Not sure I can see Parker in the Amazon though, somehow. Won't he be a little bit, well, scared?'

'I'm not going with Parker. I'm going with Jem.' Juliet casually lit a cigarette and waited for Kate's expression to change from vague interest to appalled horror.

'But...but that's...' Kate struggled for the words.

'Icky? Yes I know. But it's not what you think. We're not going as a couple, just as friends.'

Kate expression was beyond cynical.

'Honestly, Kate, it's the truth. We got talking about it at the party, after you'd gone. Admittedly he was rather drunk at the time, but I met up with him again, by complete accident, in the village last week. We had a coffee, and well, he's genuinely interested. In the travel, I mean, not in me. It will do him good, Kate. He needs to get out in the world a bit. He's in danger of— no offence— becoming stuck in a small town rut; in danger of becoming, well, *desperate.*'

'But...even if there's nothing in it now, you'll be travelling together, practically living together. There's always going to be the chance that something might happen. Are you sure he's not just doing this to spite me?'

'Don't care if he is,' said Juliet. 'It's not happening. I might even enjoy winding him up a bit. Seriously though, I've decided to take a leaf out of your book, sister.'

'What do you mean?'

'Celibacy,' said Juliet. 'I'm going to give it a go, try and get back to just being by myself; see what I really want out of life without having to consider someone else. Jem can tag along if he likes, I'll be grateful I'm sure at times for the company, but I'm not interested in anything else. I just want to kind of...get back to the beginning.'

'Beginning of what?'

'Beginning of me. I want to get back to the point where I lost my way, and start again. And I think that that requires a period of abstinence. There's a saying, you know: "if you don't like what you're getting, change what you're doing."'

Kate was momentarily reminded of her own theories of having gone down the wrong path. She was still highly sceptical of Juliet's intentions being carried out in practice, but she didn't say so. She understood, at least, the premise. 'Don't let Parker hear you talking about losing your way,' she said. 'He'll help you find yourself.'

Juliet laughed. 'So are you okay with this? If you're really uncomfortable about it, then I'll change the plan. But like I said, I think it would do Jem good. He needs to...start to feel a bit better about himself.'

'You're probably right,' said Kate absently, although she secretly wondered if Jem would actually go.

'Besides,' said Juliet, reverting to character, 'it wouldn't be the end of the world if I *did* shag Jem, would it? I mean, these things do happen. And after all...' she looked Kate square in the eye, a delicious curl of smoke adding movie star drama to her sultry expression, '...it's not as if you ever really loved him.'

CHAPTER 54

Raining in the Heart

It rained for days on end. The promise of a long hot summer had literally evaporated into hot steaming piles of cumulonimbus clouds, sending torrents of heavy water to lash down upon the land. Kate nearly wept with despair to see her vegetable plot become sodden and waterlogged, and her tomato plants bend and droop under the relentless battering. More than that, the constant downpour acted like a curtain, a wall between Kate and the outside world. She had never felt more isolated and alone. Nobody called, nobody visited. She was an imaginary person, who had dreamed all her life until now, and did not truly exist.

Finally, in defeat, she cursed herself for letting everyone know that she eschewed mobile phones. Every time her phone signalled a new text she would grab at it only to find that it was yet another message from Izzy, whose parting gift from Juliet had—much to Kate's disapproval—been her old mobile. She even found herself checking for e-mail messages, despite her knowledge that no one would insult her by sending an electronic communication. Kate performed the practicalities of her life in this same dazed manner, only finding solace in the occasional evening chat with Isabella, when she deigned to be around. But the long hours when Izzy was at school were filled with continued frustration and impending madness. More than ever, she wore *his* jumper; slept in it. It provided as much torture as comfort, but she wore it nonetheless.

514

Then finally one day, the clouds lifted, and the sunshine returned in glory. Her tomato plants simultaneously and cautiously raised their heads again, as if to wonder what had happened, and Kate could smell their strong loamy fragrance on the air as she thankfully escaped the confines of the cottage and entered her garden again. She breathed in the warm, damp air and begged life to take pity on her, to give her another chance. She had been doing so well, and was sure that she could start over again, if only she could be freed from this chronic, disabling sickness.

To think that she had practically ignored Lance at the party, when she longed for one precious moment of his company now. She recalled now almost every moment they had spent together; every incident, every chance meeting, and wondered how she had not *known*; had not savoured every delicious second. No wonder she had been so upset when he had apparently discarded her for Leah. Her defences were indeed strong to have fooled her own powers of perception, to the point that even after he had kissed her, she had rejected him. It broke her heart now to think that she might have caused him any pain.

But now it was too late. She still had not heard from him, so convincing must her protestations and denials have been. It occurred to her that perhaps she should contact him, but her nerves failed her. What if he had moved on, angry since that day on the beach? What if he had fled into the arms of Leah? Kate was still not convinced of the truth of the matter; her love for him was not in any way based on either rationality or blind trust. She was in love despite his inconstancy, and despite her own doubts.

But she managed a smile imagining the way that conversation might go, if she *were* to tell him. How pathetic she would seem, to have to retract all her assurances that she wasn't interested and wanted to be left alone. Well he had certainly complied. And how desperate too, to go chasing after a man who on their last meeting had so literally dumped her; had humiliated and left her alone to fend for herself. All things considered, it was actually rather typical of her to lose a man mere minutes after finding him. She had of course messed up her life many times in the past, but this had to be something of a record. Spectacular, abject, professional stupidity!

She made herself busy tidying and restoring the tattered garden, finding some release in the hard work. But before long, she heard the telephone ringing and practically hurdled her way over the vegetables back into the house. Her heart thumped all the way and a surge of cold white adrenalin raced through her body.

It was Vivien. Would Kate and Isabella mind joining her and Derry on a walk tomorrow onto the moors, to a place where they were thinking of performing their marriage ceremony by some ancient standing stones? Kate, chewing mindlessly on the cuff of Lance's jumper, struggled to keep up with the details: Derry was really into ancient monuments and considered himself something of a pagan; there would be an official ceremony on the day of course—something about 'handfasting', whatever that meant— but tomorrow they just wanted to check out the venue; ensure the 'vibe' was right. Vivien continued to talk about the arrangements, but Kate could hardly take them in. *Who else would be there?* That was all that she needed to be told.

By the time Kate hung up the phone, she had her answer. It would be a small party; they would drive part of the way, to save time, Vivien had said, and someone would pick up Kate and Isabella in the late morning—Lance, probably—since there was no point in all of them driving and wickedly squandering the planet's resources. Her heart pounded and she felt sick; Kate was almost deranged with nervous excitement. She would see him again! But "probably", Vivien had said. That meant it might not be him. He might even decline to come. His attendance might even have been subject to her own, and of course, once Vivien confirmed Kate and Isabella's attendance, he would naturally make polite excuses: feign urgent business or mortal illness. Yet the thought of a trudge on the moor without the promise of seeing him made her equally senseless, only this time with misery. And so, she fretted and worried madly.

The irony, not remotely lost on Kate, was that the nature of the affliction meant that she was behaving in no way like her usual character; and that if she did not get a grip, then any potential admirers within a given radius would pack up and run, thanking their lucky stars to have seen her true, dribbling neurotic self. Again, she thought of all the previous months when, basking in denial, she had behaved naturally and casually in Lance's company, and how she had taken such self-composure for granted. Now she might never feel so comfortable again, but have all their future meetings marred by self-conscious lunacy.

They rose early the next morning; Kate because she was too overwrought for sleep, and Isabella because she was restless and bursting with new-found energy. They breakfasted at leisure, with Kate trying her best to remain jovial and light-hearted, and to keep her latent hysteria hidden from her daughter's sharp watchful eye. Afterwards, she attempted to show a disinterested Isabella their destination for the day on an Ordnance Survey map.

'See here, it's called Bos...kew...Boskewjek. No idea if that's how to pronounce it, but it's megalithic. Don't worry, we're not walking from here, I think the plan is to drive part of the way.'

Isabella sat at the kitchen table idly toying with the dial on the old transistor radio. She appeared to be enjoying the rapid change in musical varieties, and fascinated by the intermittent buzz of static. 'Do you know, you can hear the sound of

517

radiation from the Big Bang in all that noise, if you listen hard enough,' she said, putting her ear closer to the aggravating hiss emanating from the radio.

'Well, it may well be there, but I doubt you'd hear it through the radio, you'd need far more sophisticated equipment...'

'No, it's true! It's the Cosmic Microwave Background.'

'...anyway, I was talking about Boskewjek. It should be an interesting walk. I've been meaning to visit.'

Isabella looked at Kate blankly, as if she had just started speaking an alien language.

'It's the stone circle. Don't you realise Cornwall has some of the oldest remaining Neolithic monuments in the world? Apart from megaliths and menhirs there's quoits, longbarrows...'

Isabella's dark head dropped onto her shoulder as if she had been suddenly hypnotised, and she emitted a loud exaggerated snore.

'Oh, very funny,' said Kate, pretending to clout Izzy on the back of the head, but secretly relieved that she had been stopped in her tracks from delivering a lecture. It was alarming how quickly and quietly her life had evolved from girl to mother, and as she turned back to the map, for a split second she had a deep awareness of herself in that moment in time. Here was Kate as a thirty-one year old mother, and here was her daughter Isabella, eleven. Isabella: a whole human being who had not even existed twelve years ago, when Kate had experienced a similar feeling on top of Box Hill. It was a brief respite, but the moment passed, and Kate felt all her anxieties come rushing back.

They packed two small rucksacks with waterproof jackets, warm hats and gloves, and bottles of water. Kate, after a further study of the proposed route, shoved the map in a side pocket. In the hallway she went to reach for her willow walking stick, but just as she did, a text message pinged on her phone. Thinking it might be from Vivien, or even perhaps Lance, she hurriedly went to open it. But no, it was from Izzy, who was only next door in the kitchen.

The message contained the single damning word: *Merlin.*

She turned to see Izzy grinning at her from the kitchen doorway. She sighed, but all the same, thought better of the stick.

By the time Lance's car swung into the muddy yard, they were beyond ready, and Kate had been on the verge of cancelling everything, forever. But he was here; and it was him. She felt the by now familiar rise of panic at the thought of their finally meeting again, but Kate's feelings were strangely ambivalent as she also experienced a sense of relief that the torture of separation, whatever the outcome, was soon to be over. Nobody left the car, but Lance sounded his horn abruptly, to summon them out. It was not a good sign. Kate locked up the cottage, and then trudged with heavy legs towards the Land Rover. Isabella, who had run ahead, had already joined Finn in one of the two large seats accessed by the door at the back of the car. Kate climbed in to one of the other passenger seats, grateful to find herself seated next to Gabe, who had shifted over to let her in. In doing so, he moved closer to Salima, who should have been delighted, but appeared wary as she smiled and waved hello at Kate. In dismay, Kate realised that the final occupant of the car was Leah, who sat with an air of appropriation in the front passenger seat next to Lance. Leah did not turn around to acknowledge Kate in any way but continued to talk and giggle in a mannered fashion to Lance. All too late, Kate saw that this was a terrible mistake. She felt like an intruder and wanted to run away.

'Everybody in?' said Lance, as Isabella finished securing her seatbelt, and Kate caught a brief glimpse of his eyes in the rear-view mirror, before he diverted them back towards the track, and carefully drove away from the cottage, and her last chance of escape.

'Where's Vivien and Derry?' Kate asked Gabe discreetly, under the noise of the children's chatter.

'They've gone on,' he said. 'Only room for two up front in the Derry love-mobile.'

'No horse today then?' Kate attempted some levity.

'Ha! No; no horse, but I fully expect a congregation of pixies and giants. A dragon at the very least.'

Kate laughed nervously, and Gabe poked her gently in the ribs with his elbow. She felt a sudden wave of affection for him; he was an unlikely, but reassuring ally.

'What was that?' asked Leah, turning around to face Kate for the first time. She did not smile, but appeared to take the opportunity to assess Kate's appearance unashamedly. 'Surely you're not mocking the happy couple?'

'Nothing they wouldn't expect,' said Gabe, saving Kate from the answer. 'And nothing I wouldn't say to their faces.'

'I wonder what Vivien will wear on her wedding day,' said Leah, turning right around in her seat and addressing Salima. '—I mean the get-up she usually goes about in—seems to me she pretty much wears bridesmaid dresses all the time. I can't see how she's going to make herself look special on the big day.'

'Hmm...' Salima smiled hesitantly. She was eager to please Leah, but equally concerned about not repelling Gabe. The result was that she was hardly able to speak at all.

'Perhaps she'll dress down for a change,' said Leah brightly, but with a curl of her lip, '...like Derry.'

'Hmph!' managed poor Salima, still gurning unconvincingly and shaking her head in a wry manner.

'Well, it makes it difficult to know what to wear to the wedding,' continued Leah, pouting now as if posed with a genuine problem. 'I mean, you're not supposed to upstage the bride, and well, that's going to be hard enough as it is, but if

Vivien is determined to wear sackcloth...well... I think you know what I mean!'

From her seat behind him, Kate sensed that Lance had been about to say something, but checked himself. Instead, he continued to silently concentrate on the road ahead. Neither did the others respond, but Kate wondered that Leah had been invited to the wedding. She was sure that Vivien was not fond of her. But then, she was Finn's mother, and—for all Kate knew—had been passionately reunited with Lance in the weeks since the ball.

'It's a shame Jem couldn't come today,' said Leah, changing course at random. But her pale blue eyes had reverted back to Kate. 'Then it would be all the old gang back together again.' She sighed dramatically and then turned back around in her seat.

'No sweat, we'll be seeing him next week for a send-off before he hits the road,' said Gabe. 'Have you forgotten?'

No one replied and again Kate sensed an undercurrent, an unspoken script. She stared bleakly out of the window at the passing countryside. She longed to be free of the repressive confines of the car, and the uneasy atmosphere. The early promise of sunshine had once more given way to grey skies, subduing the lustre of green fields, yellow gorse and summer hedgerow flowers. It was probably going to rain again.

'It's cool you decided to let Izzy continue surfing,' Gabe spoke again, this time directly to Kate, disturbing her back into the world. He quickly glanced at the two children in the back and lowered his tone. 'I know I did wrong, and this is me sticking my neck out again, but you gotta admit; she's stoked on it! Look how happy she is.'

'Your daughter's quite pretty,' said Leah, turning around again and apparently unable to not hijack every conversation. 'But a bit wild-looking. I could give her some tips if you like. I don't mind, I've little else to do while I'm here. She looks like she's never even seen hair straighteners. Oh, if I'd had a daughter it would have been so much fun...'

Kate thought she sensed Lance tense again in the driving seat. She saw his eyes dart to the rear-view mirror again, only this time, they did not fix on her, but anxiously on the face of his son seated in the back of the car.

'Mind you,' continued Leah, and still looking directly at Kate, 'it must be a nightmare to see your daughter grow up and get more beautiful, while your own looks go to seed. I think it's important not to let yourself go after having a kid. I think it's really crucial to be your own person, and to have a career. And anyway, I could never stay at home and do *nothing;* I'd just be bored.'

'Really?' said Kate. 'That's odd. I'm never bored. In fact, there don't seem to be enough hours in the day to do all the things that I want to do.'

'What? Like watch daytime TV?' scoffed Leah, seemingly blind to the reality of her own part in the most distasteful of television programmes.

Kate was reluctant to protest; why should she humour this rude, insensitive woman? She didn't have to justify herself.

'Actually, my mum is an artist,' said Isabella without warning, and to Kate's surprise.

Leah laughed dismissively. 'Isn't everyone?'

'And she grows all her own vegetables.'

'Oh sweetie, that's so cute of you. But you can *buy* vegetables you know. From a *shop*.'

Isabella glared at Finn's mother, but perhaps with her loyalties divided, appeared to decide not to pursue her line of defence. Kate shot her an affectionate, appreciative look, before turning back to gaze longingly at the back of Lance's head and neck, and then more lustfully at his broad shoulders. He was so close, and yet so silently, unapproachably distant. The unpalatable truth could no longer be stemmed: she had blown it. She had blown it, and this was going to be awful.

CHAPTER 55

Malcontents

The clouds were beginning to spit rain by the time they arrived at a small car parking space on the outskirts of the moor. They met there with Vivien and Derry who were waiting, and now jumped out of Derry's small van to greet their friends. Vivien looked somewhat disappointed, presumably because of the impending bad weather. But perhaps because she noted the equally subdued expression on Kate's face, made a beeline for her and gave her a friendly hug.

'Thanks for coming, I realise it was short notice,' she said. 'It's not too far from here, and hopefully the weather will hold.' She looked askance at Leah, who was standing nearby zipping herself into a figure-hugging jacket, and exaggeratedly flicking her long hair free from its collar. She wore matching close-fitting leggings and top-of-the-range extra-light hiking boots. Kate had imagined that she would wear something impractical and pink. But annoyingly, Leah was a picture of effortlessly glamorous hiking chic. Despite what the French manicure and pumped-up lips suggested, she was, Kate conceded, still a Cornish girl, familiar with the demands of the landscape and the vagaries of the weather.

'Don't read too much into it,' Vivien said under her breath to Kate. 'It's not easy to give her the slip.'

Kate looked at Lance, who admittedly did not appear to be paying any particular attention to Leah; but then was equally withdrawn from each of his companions, as he leant against

523

the bonnet of his car and silently studied a map. The plan was to follow a waymarked public pathway across the fields and along the lanes until they reached a small farm, from where a further footpath gave access onto the higher ground.

'So what will your marriage ceremony entail?' Kate asked Vivien once they were under way.

'Don't worry,' said Vivien. 'There will be no sacrificial rites involved, human or otherwise! Handfasting just means the binding of our hands together. I believe the original idea was to stay bound together for a year and a day, to see if you could actually last the distance together, but nowadays it's really just symbolic. Shame really; I think it would be kind of sexy to be tied to Derry for a year and a day!'

Kate looked at her in amazement, still regularly surprised at the turnaround in Vivien's feelings. And then she remembered her own sorry plight, and admitted to herself that all things were possible.

'We just want to be sure that the stones will be the right place to make the commitment,' Vivien continued. 'We're both agreed it should be outdoors. You know, to connect with nature.' She smiled mischievously at Kate, anticipating her derision. 'I expect we'll get around to the boring legal bit too, a registry office or something. But this will be our spiritual bonding; our joining.'

Vivien managed to be simultaneously dressed for both hiking and pagan ceremony. She wore black skinny jeans topped with a simple hand-knitted jumper; but over the top of these, a black hooded mantle, lined with dark green velvet. Her hair was tied back with gold braid into a long plait and she wore a plain thin gold band on her head like a crown. Today she was a fairy princess on some mission for good: an undercover emissary, masking her splendour in practical disguise.

Lance typically led the way, and Kate gazed with love at the familiar, swinging tails of his army greatcoat. Like his sister, he had not succumbed to the temptations of the latest technological stay-dry fabrics, base clothing and other nouveau accoutrements. A good pair of walking boots, a map, and a knowledge of one's own limitations were the only requirements. Kate felt amateurish and fretful in her sensible layers and cagoule; but at least they were old and known to be of good use. She might not be dressed at her most characterful, but at least, she consoled herself, she did not have to be a walking clash of designer brand names in order to venture onto a hill.

The rain became heavier, and Kate hoped for Vivien's sake that it would have passed by the time they reached their destination. The route was not at this stage hard going, but Leah lagged behind with Salima, with no apparent sense of immediacy or concern. Occasionally a giggle arose from the two women and drifted on the wind to the rest of the party further along the lane. Several times they all stopped to wait where there was a fork in the road or an indistinct signpost across a field, in order to signal the appropriate direction to the stragglers. Presently they arrived at the farm and waited again for Salima and Leah to catch up. Kate noticed Vivien talk quietly but anxiously with Derry, as the rain began to fall with more deliberation.

The atmosphere was becoming increasingly discordant. With a silent diplomacy that belied his frustration, Gabe leant against what shelter was provided by an old barn; hands in pockets and collar turned up against the breeze. Lance wandered off by himself a short distance, as if to survey the way ahead. It was impossible for Kate not to feel hurt by such sustained disregard, especially considering the way he had behaved when they had last met. But Lance said nothing; acknowledged nothing. She made herself appear occupied and unconcerned by chatting to the children, who were in danger of losing interest in the whole idea because of the change in weather.

As the two women eventually strolled towards them, Kate sensed from Salima's grieved expression and forcibly restricted gait, that she did not share Leah's leisurely attitude, but would far rather have been upfront with the others, and in particular, Kate suspected, with Gabe.

Leah took a small plastic groundsheet out of her rucksack and, having scouted around for the perfect location, placed it delicately on the ground of a sloping grass verge, before positioning her perfect little bottom on it. Then, the height of geniality and self-sacrifice, she motioned for Salima to join her by beckoning and patting the spare space alongside. Salima dutifully obeyed, but sat down with a face of perfect abject misery.

Leah proceeded to make a great job of tying her hair back in a tidy bun. She then pulled a neatly folded wide-brimmed rain hat from her bag, and carefully placed it on her head, ensuring that each and every beautiful hair was protected. When this operation was complete she made a protracted performance of untying and retying her boots, feeling her feet carefully for any pressure points or potential rubbing. It was only when she ferreted a hand mirror from the bag that Lance finally intervened, and insisted that they press on.

'Oh you never change do you?' Leah responded. 'It always has to be an enforced march. It's not a competition, you know. I don't see why you can't wait until everyone is ready, and rested. I mean, *you've* all been here for ages; Salima and I have only just got here.'

'I'm concerned about the weather,' said Lance, eyeing the approaching darkening clouds. 'According to radio reports earlier this morning, it's supposed to worsen later on. I suspect we might be in for another deluge. We need to make more progress.'

'Perhaps we should abandon for today,' said Vivien, unable to hide her disappointment. 'We should turn back and try again another time when the weather's better.'

Derry smiled reassuringly at her and put a sturdy arm around her shoulder.

'Well, of course that's up to you,' said Lance. 'If it doesn't feel right then we can come again another time. I understand that you want the atmosphere to be right in advance of the ceremony.' He spoke, Kate noted, without the slightest hint of ridicule when discussing the proposed "ceremony". 'But I don't see why we shouldn't continue the walk, even if it's just as a walk for its own sake. If we get a move on we should miss the worst of the rain. Otherwise...well, we'll get wet.'

Kate thought there was the flicker of an instinctive smile; the nearest to one she had seen from Lance that day. But once more, he appeared to inhibit any expression, as if determined to feel slighted.

'Yeah, c'mon guys, let's get going,' agreed Gabe, stirring himself to action. 'The day is what you make it.'

Clearly peeved, Leah got to her feet and carefully refolded the groundsheet into her rucksack. 'I suppose we had better go now, or we'll be knee-deep in mud,' she acknowledged grumpily.

They left the farmyard behind them and started to slowly wind their way uphill. The remaining journey was not a great distance, but it was here that the land began to steeply incline. The ground felt soft and boggy underfoot after the days of continuous rainfall. Kate, who had at the last moment left her walking stick behind thanks to Izzy's scorn, now regretted it as she picked her way through the rough uneven grass and contemplated the rising moor ahead. Occasionally they came across running water; not established brooks or streams, but excess runoff from the deluge which the moors had not been able to absorb, nor its rivers accommodate. It made the stones and exposed granite rock slippery underfoot. And it continued to spit rain; not heavy yet, but steady and persistent.

They were suddenly startled by a scream from the back of their ranks. Leah sat awkwardly in the mud, gripping her ankle and moaning. Salima agonised unhelpfully beside her.

'Help!' Leah cried. 'My ankle! I think it's broken! Lance!'

Oh for God's sake, thought Kate, ungraciously. *Not that old stunt.*

Lance turned, and with an air of practiced stoicism, made his way back down the hill towards Leah. The others looked at each other in turn, then with equal resignation, turned and followed. Only the children expressed their annoyance.

'Oh I can't believe we're going *down* again!' said Isabella. 'We'll never get to the top at this rate.'

'This walk sucks,' said Finn.

They all gathered around as Lance inspected the ankle. Leah grimaced as he held it in his hands and gently turned it this way and that.

'I knew I shouldn't have come on this stupid, fucking walk!' shouted Leah. 'I'm supposed to be doing a photo shoot next week. What the hell am I going to look like with a stupid fat busted ankle? Stupid, bloody, fucking countryside!'

'Leah!' pleaded Lance, dismayed at the look of chagrin on Finn's face. 'There are children...'

'You try being in this much pain! Can we just think about me for once? Just this fucking once...'

'...I don't think it's broken,' said Lance, 'but it might be a sprain. See if you can put some weight on it. Try standing up.'

Leah stopped raving to give him a wounded, insulted look.

'I'll help you,' he said.

Deftly, he bent and hauled Leah's slender frame up from the ground, then supporting her under one shoulder, let her lean on him while she gingerly tested the impaired ankle.

'Owww!' Leah cried, 'It won't work! It's broken, I tell you!'

'I'm sure it's not. Try again,' said Lance patiently.

Leah tried again, but this time did not cry out. Instead her blue eyes became watery, and she sobbed piteously. 'It's no good, I can't do it! I can't walk. It's not my fault! What shall I do?' She blinked, teary-eyed, at Lance.

Tell me he's not going to fall for this, thought Kate. But she knew it was an errant, jealous thought. She had experienced an ankle sprain herself in the past, and reluctantly conceded how potentially painful and disabling it could be. And Leah certainly appeared distressed enough. *Be kind, Kate.*

'Well, I suppose…' said Lance, casting an apologetic look to Vivien and Derry's sad faces. 'I suppose I'll have to take you back to the car. Do you think you can walk with my support?'

'I told you, I *can't* walk!' screeched Leah.

For a second, a shadow passed over Lance's face. 'Then I'll have to carry you. Do you think you can get up on my back, piggyback-style?'

Leah pondered this proposition. Perhaps, Kate imagined, she was musing that she would far rather be carried in his arms. Or maybe have him sling her over his shoulder in a manfully assertive way, as he had done with Kate.

'Okay then,' Leah conceded moodily.

Lance bent down and Leah climbed up on his back, encircling his neck with her arms. As she did so, she looked at Kate once more with those blue eyes. And then, just for a fragment of a moment, she smirked…

Kate could only stare, foolishly agape, at the audacity.

'Oh Salima!' Leah called from her mount; '…carry my bag for me?'

Salima was devastated. She didn't care about the rain and the mud. She didn't care about the standing stones. Truth be told, she didn't much care about Leah and her twisted ankle. She just wanted to be with Gabe, and was prepared to walk miles in slippery treacherous mudslides, wounded and bedraggled, just to stay by his side.

529

'Can I come with you, Dad?' asked Finn, 'This walk just isn't happening, is it?'

'I want to go with Finn!' said Isabella, in an instant.

'Right,' said Lance, with a note of defeat. 'I'll take Leah and the children back to the car, drop them off at our house, then come back and wait for the rest of you.'

'Actually,' said Derry, looking at Vivien, who nodded her consent. 'I think we may as well all go now. Finn's right, this just isn't working. Sorry everyone; and thanks for the support, we both appreciate it.'

Gabe shrugged in resigned agreement, and as he joined their deflated procession back down the hill, Salima's heart was restored from her mouth back to its usual anxious position in her chest. Only Kate remained unmoved. She touched Vivien's arm as she was turning to go to get her attention.

'I'm going on,' she said flatly. Vivien was about to speak her concern, but Kate interrupted her. 'I'll be fine. I just need to be alone. I'll find my own way back; it's not that far from civilisation. And so long as you don't mind looking after Izzy for a while?'

Vivien nodded frantically, but remained worried-looking. 'I don't think you should go alone, Kate, what if something happened to you?' She turned to look to the others for support, but they were already too far off and concentrating on their downhill footholds to notice what was going on.

Looking back again, she opened her mouth to continue her protestations, but Kate had already turned and was making her way determinedly up the hill again.

'I'll be okay,' she called back over her shoulder. 'And tell Izzy not to worry. I'll call someone if there's a problem.' And so she made the breakaway before anyone could persuade her otherwise.

CHAPTER 56

Illumination

Kate would not feel guilty, as she bolted up the hill. She knew that she was being irresponsible, but something in her had come apart. She was filled with restless energy and fuelled by angry adrenalin, which she felt she could only purge by punishing, physical action. Besides, it wasn't that far, and why should she not be selfish for once? Kate was convinced now that she had just witnessed a masterly display of extreme selfishness, and was no longer remotely persuaded that Leah's injury was serious. But she expected that the recovery would be protracted nonetheless, and could not bear another moment of seeing Leah skilfully steal the attention from Vivien and Derry. It was the sort of behaviour that Kate despised. Leah didn't care if her actions were annoying or even blatantly obvious. They obtained the required result, depending as they did on nobody else being assertive enough, or rude enough, to question them. And moreover, Kate was jealous. Damn it, of *course* she was jealous! Leah was now receiving Lance's full attention—hanging off his back no less—while she, Kate, had foolishly stood by.

The rain began to fall with more authority as Kate began the steepest part of the ascent. Again she thought with regret of her lovely willow walking stick, sitting forsaken in Dolphin Cottage, and which she had eschewed in vanity. Part of the path became little more than a rocky stream which flushed and gurgled around her as she began to climb almost on all fours, and using the perilously wet rocks as a handhold where possible. As her anger started to subside and self-preservation took over, she began to accept that perhaps this was not the best idea that she had ever had.

She paused, momentarily doubtful, if not quite panicked. Was this the right path? It would be ill-judged to consult her map now, in this precarious position. Better to continue upwards, and trust her previous observations. She had, after all, checked the route several times before setting off. And despite the rain, the weather was still mild, with only a little wind. Suddenly realising she might lose the signal, she searched her mobile out from the bottom of her rucksack and sent a reassuring text message to Izzy, who immediately replied: *No worries, I'm fiiiiine!!! Lol!*, in her usual manner. Then, anticipating more concern from Vivien, she switched the phone off.

Adrenalin alone gave strength to her weary muscles, still not fully adapted from years of sedate city living. It was only when the path suddenly eased into a more comfortable, grassy stretch, that she noticed her heart thumping fast against her chest and the heavy exhaustion in her limbs. But then as her pulse rapidly subsided she felt a warm calm descend and her breathing became deep and energising. Oxygen raced to every part of her body, to every molecule of her skin. It felt like she was breathing for the first time. More relaxed now, Kate took in her surroundings. A single, strange-looking tree looked lost against the darkening sky. She was surprised and a little disturbed to see some peculiar type of cattle grazing.

Kate had recently been alarmed to hear a radio programme discussing the danger of walkers being attacked by cows-in-field. Previous to this information, Kate had wandered across many a field of cows with carefree abandon, but was now not sure that she could ever do so again without being more than a little wary. And this particular breed had very long, sharp-looking horns. But the cattle ignored her, and Kate continued bravely on until the moor levelled into a vast plateau, high above the now distant valley below. From here, she could make out the coastline, and the steely expanse of the sea. Finally, in the distance, Kate saw the Stones of Boskewjek, standing somewhat dilapidated, but still stately in their small circle. Exhilarated, she pressed on easily now, across the broad expanse of the moor.

It was quiet, but for the continued, quickening pelt of the rain, the occasional low moan of the wind, and Kate's own footsteps. The wind was much stronger up here, having few obstacles to impede its rush, and it played freely with the direction of the rain, creating a new percussion to accompany its own singing notes. She became very conscious of her own breathing. But even as her anger and frustration abated, she was still acutely aware of the continuing grievous presence of her affliction. She had been holding herself together throughout the afternoon. She had tolerated the fact of Leah's continued presence, and close appropriation of Lance. She had even tolerated the coldness in Lance's bearing, given that she had recently behaved in much the same way towards him. She had told herself that there would be a moment during the course of the day, an opportunity, to talk alone with him; or to give him some signal, some slight intonation of meaning that might let him know...

But now that he had gone, his attention having been effortlessly commandeered by Leah, she regretted everything. It had been a mistake to come. Or having come, she should have spoken to him immediately. But foolishly, she had waited, instead of acting. While she had bided her time, Leah had coolly and professionally played the situation to her advantage. That was why women like Leah always, always won; regardless of what was fair, what was deserved. Never had she felt more unsophisticated, more lacking in wit or

533

charm. With sudden lucidity Kate understood what Juliet had been trying to tell her all her life: that she was hopeless at this sort of thing.

Kate could not flirt, could not manipulate; could not in fact use any of the supposed womanly wiles. When Kate cried, it was not because she wanted to contrive to appear vulnerable, or to get her own way, but simply because she was sad. When she liked a man she could not use guile to slyly influence or encourage his affection. Instead, she was more likely to either blurt out a declaration of her passion, sending said man running for the hills; or to do the exact opposite and shyly hide her feelings so successfully that he would not think her remotely interested. She had in her lifetime, been thought of as both desperate, and an ice queen. She had never managed to secure things her way.

Miles had been the only exception, or so she had thought before his act of desertion. With Miles she had been completely true to herself; heart on her sleeve and honest words on her lips. But now she wondered if her value had diminished in direct proportion to her sincerity. Had there been an underlying suspicion on his part of her worthiness? Had he been initially flattered, but then bored, by her ready surrender to him? And had she been more accomplished at game-playing, might he have found her more exciting, and stayed?

It was ironic, Kate thought, that she should appear needy and desperate when in reality she hardly ever fell for anyone, and only ever let her feelings be known—for better or worse— once she was absolutely sure of them. And it was her same compulsion for honesty that had made it so hard to employ any subtlety when it had come to finishing with Jem. Instead of letting him down gently, as was traditional, she had cruelly, if truthfully, declared that she did not love him. Even now, she did not have the slightest clue as to how to extract Lance from Leah's far more competent clutches. She did not possess the

534

requisite skills for the battle, nor even knew if her prize wished to be rescued.

Finally, deep in thought, Kate reached the circle of stones. She walked slowly around the perimeter, touching each one as she passed. Most of them, including the centre stone, were surrounded by pools of water, where presumably the ground had been worn away by animals using them as scratching posts. But she found one that was reasonably dry, and taking off her jacket, used it to sit down upon, cross-legged with her back against the cool rock.

Incredibly, for the moment, no rain fell on that part of the moor, but Kate could see it coming down in grey sheets all around her and in the distance. Dark clouds rolled overhead, but thankfully, at least for the time being, passed her by. It felt surreal, to be sitting in the dry at last, as if there were a virtual roof over her head, while the rain battered and pounded the rest of the moor.

The wind gently lifted her hair and began to dry it. Many of the stones were leaning; whether by design or interference, Kate could not tell. She had read that it was common for ancient standing stones to have to survive the 'helpful' restoration schemes of many a well-meaning Victorian archaeologist. Not to mention generations of farmer's failed attempts to remove them for more 'practical' use. But they were still here. Kate had no idea how old they were, but felt humbled by the longevity, and by the intention; the meaning of which had long since been lost in time. They knew how to make something last, these people, whoever they were. She thought about the pyramids of ancient Egypt and Mexico. Those structures and these stones would probably long outlast the buildings of Kate's own era in time. And more than that, they spoke volumes. They said: we know who we are, where we are, and how to do this; we know about science, astronomy and mathematics. Long after everything that was familiar to

535

her was lost; after even the vast cities of the world had collapsed and decayed back into the Earth; even after the last remnant of human existence had rotted away in its landfill site, these stones might well still be standing here. They were a sign: not a sad and sorry reminder of the past, but a defiant claim to existence.

We all have our little stones, after all, thought Kate, *at the end of our lives.* She thought about the sombre declarations on gravestones. At the end of it all they were a desperate, last-minute melancholy statement that this one human soul had existed. I was born on this day; I died on this one. This was my name, and I was here.

Suddenly, in the sky to the west, the sun broke through the dark cloud, and scattered its light across the wide expanse of the moor. Kate stood up, and shielding her eyes against the blinding rays, contemplated the enormity of the Earth and her own insignificance. The sombre rainclouds still promenaded overhead, but the land in all directions was revealed in reassuring pools of brightness. A path of fractured radiance forged its way across the grey sea to the horizon. And Kate herself, in her miraculously rain-free stone circle, was caught in the beam, as if she were being offered a private gift of light. Beyond the sun, the universe stretched out in all directions with unknown import, and the wheels of her own little space in time and relativity were revealed to be so small, so intricate, that they appeared to stop.

None of her worries or torments meant a thing. Not one single anguished thought was of any consequence. There was no past, no future. The people who made this circle of stones may all be long gone, but in some way, so was she. They were all of them already dead, in mankind's small sliver of existence. There was nothing other than this moment right now. She had had just a glimpse of this feeling earlier on in the kitchen with Izzy; the sense of being fully aware of *being* in that moment in time. She had felt it all those years ago on Box Hill.

And yet...there was something else, something she had been missing. She had been looking at things all wrong. She had tormented herself with the past, with the mistakes that she had made and with the heartache and betrayal; had allowed these things to influence the *now*. And so they never really went away. She was hauling all her regret and hard times with her into the present like an ever-increasing burden. But now she saw with great clarity that it was the other way round. The past was gone, did not exist. But the future...

She thought of future Kate painting in her studio by the sea, fulfilled and content, but vaporous and unresolved; her very existence dependent on her, on *this* Kate, and on what she did right now. It wasn't the past that influenced the present, but the present that influenced the future. *She had been looking the wrong way.* She owed it to future Kate to bring her into being. She liked her. Now Kate was amused that she could see it so clearly. She stayed for a while, for time no longer seemed to matter, and watched the universe turn above her as her planet hurtled through space. She listened to the wind and the encircling rain.

The sun, the moon, the wind and the rain.

And then she was back. The sun's rays were subdued once more behind a gauze of black cloud. She felt the wind pick up and the rain at last threaten to intrude on her roofless shelter. The excess rainwater continued to run off the moor to the sea. The wheels of time ground into motion again and the Stones of Boskewjek became lonely relics of the long since dead.

Yet Kate felt in some way altered. Just as on that day when she had wept alone in her car, she experienced a renewed energy and sense of purpose, and her thoughts were clear. She would have to take Lance on board, that much was obvious. She wanted her life back. She wanted to paint again and to wander carefree once more. She did not want to be the lovelorn martyr; the Lady of Shalott. If she wanted to be able to carry on as she had been, she would somehow have to incorporate Lance into her world. She would have to pick him up as necessary baggage, essential for her journey, and carry him with her. Everything else she would leave behind. It was all so simple.

And she was wasting time. Now that the space-time continuum had restored itself in this minuscule fragment of the universe, every moment was precious, and to be lived intently. Kate was filled with an overwhelming urge to get off the moor as quickly as possible; to get down that hill and back into the wonderful adventure of her life. Not without a little self-consciousness, she silently said goodbye to the stones, and then all but fled from the scene.

She tore through the buffeting wind and rain, praying but yet somehow trusting that she remembered the direction. The light was failing, and although not quite alarmed, Kate realised the potential for disaster. She found the stream-path and half-scrambled, half-slid down its rocky terrain. Her mind worked fast, with instincts primed and alert to danger. As she neared the end of the stream and the incline became less steep she found herself picking up speed again, estimating danger spots and secure footholds with a sharp, fast, accuracy. By the time she reached the lower lush ground above the farm she was practically running downhill, confident with some intuitive awareness.

She only paused to observe when she saw a lonely figure slowly picking his way up the path on the lower slopes of the valley below. She focussed on the tall meandering shape. His tread was steady but his bearing somewhat disconsolate. His long blond hair was wet and bedraggled, but flew, dancing in the wind, like his coat-tails. He was the most beautiful man that she had ever seen.

538

Something like love... Those were the words he had used that day on the beach, she was sure of it. The past was fading, dissolving; but the memory of that encounter was vividly engraved on her heart. Something like love. It was her only reason to believe. It was hope.

Kate moved on again but at a quick pace rather than a run. She became aware of her breathing once more; and now, only now, felt her legs wobble and ache, threatening to give way underneath her. It was as if the sense of urgency had just dropped away, and the adrenalin that had spurred her on had been withdrawn instantaneously the second that she had seen him. Instead, with rescue in sight, her body began to fail, and her nerves returned. Her heart began to beat with something other than exertion. She felt that every heavy step down the hill towards civilisation was a step away from the awareness experienced on the moor, and back into the thick maelstrom of real life, with all its complications and difficulties.

It was only when she reached the path, and was just paces away from Lance that she saw from his expression that he was very, very angry.

CHAPTER 57

After the Deluge

'What the hell were you thinking?' Lance yelled at Kate. 'Have you any idea how irresponsible that was? I didn't realise what you'd done until we'd reached the car. If I'd known sooner I would have turned around and dragged you off the moor myself!'

Several guilty thoughts passed through Kate's mind, not least of which was the idea of being dragged anywhere by Lance. She thought to say that he might have noticed sooner had he not been so studiously avoiding her, or been so preoccupied with Leah. She thought to say that she was after all, an adult, and had only gone for a walk. She could have done the entire "I'm a big girl now" speech. But she didn't want to argue with Lance. She struggled to think of something non-confrontational to say.

'I'm sorry,' she said.

'I've been texting you. I don't suppose you had a signal—something else you don't appear to have considered.'

'I...turned off my phone,' she admitted. 'I'm sorry,' she said again.

Lance looked surprised. Kate supposed he had been expecting a fight. He stared at her for a moment as though waiting for *the rest of it*; for Kate to protest her reasons and justifications. When she stayed silent, he frowned and then turned to head back down the hill.

'So...you came back to look for me?' she enquired hopefully to his departing back. He ignored her. She followed behind, trotting to keep up and forcing her legs to action again.

'You're absolutely soaked,' he muttered curtly as Kate caught up alongside him.

Kate stared at him in disbelief for a second or two, and then shaking her head, let out a deep ironic laugh. 'Yes. Again! Becoming a bit of a theme, for me.'

Lance did not stop his marching stride but looked at her suspiciously, as she stumbled along beside him still grinning in amusement. His puzzled, slightly worried expression suggested that he thought she might have finally gone completely mad. But his incomprehension was short-lived, and suddenly, it clicked.

'Ah, right,' he said, 'I see what you mean. I...don't know what came over me.'

Kate waited a few seconds, thinking he might expand, but Lance returned his gaze determinedly ahead and continued his brisk pace.

'Well, never mind; I was all right,' said Kate. 'Lost a flip-flop, but otherwise...I survived!'

'Of course you survived!' Lance said with a hint of disdain, but refusing to look at her again. 'There was barely a wave. And you weren't in that deep. You were in far more danger just now on the moors in this weather. Don't you realise you could have got hopelessly lost? Or...or fallen down an old mine shaft or something?'

Again, Kate held her tongue, despite wanting to protest that she was not a complete idiot.

'So, no apology then,' she said eventually, almost to herself. She wasn't angry, just curious. 'You're not sorry?'

Lance still wouldn't look at her. Still he gazed fixedly ahead and kept on walking. Then, just as it looked like he might not answer her at all, he spoke. 'No. I'm not.'

They carried on in awkward silence until they reached the car, which Lance had this time left in the farmyard.

'Do you want to put something down on the car seat?' asked Kate, hesitating at the open door. 'Like you said, I'm saturated.'

'Just get in,' Lance barked.

He was clearly still mad at her. The idea that she perhaps had more right to be mad at him did not seem to occur, and once again, Kate found herself holding back her emotions. Obediently, she got in. Then like an admonished child dutifully buckled her seat belt and sat timidly beside him as Lance negotiated the car out of the muddy yard.

In the silence between them, and despite the residues of his anger, Kate found herself deeply aware of his close presence. At this moment in time, they had not actually argued. He was here, and she was with him, finally alone. Before the seconds and minutes and hours stole him away from her again, he was here beside her, with his legs and his arms, and his long fingers, and his adored hair and his green eyes. She chanced a look at him and drank in the sight of the familiar crease-lines around those eyes. She gazed, endeared by the way his mouth curled over uneven teeth. He appeared to notice nothing, but she was guiltily absorbing him, recording the essence of him to her memory.

This was probably an appropriate time to attempt to flirt.

Kate racked her brains. What was she supposed to do? She ran a few lines by in her head.

'Thank you for coming to save me, I'm very grateful...' Except that Lance would undoubtedly assert that he hadn't technically saved her and that he had only returned out of duty.

'I think I may have hypothermia. We should ideally pull over, strip off and share our bodily warmth...' No! Pathetic!

'I'll have to get out of these wet clothes soon...'

'I think my T-shirt's shrunk—look!'

542

'*I'm very, very, wet...*'

Urgh! Kate cringed. It was no good. There was no way on Earth she could deliver those kinds of lines, even tongue in cheek. She just could not carry it off. She thought again about how he had come to kiss her. And suddenly she wished that she was one of those efficient mothers who perpetually carried a first-aid kit, or more precisely, a box of plasters. Perhaps if she were to casually slap a plaster on his forehead and then sit back and eye him seductively he might just get the message. Kate raised an appreciative speculative eyebrow; it was the best idea she had had yet.

'What is it?' snapped Lance, noticing her strange expression.

But she didn't have a box of plasters. Perhaps she should just try emanating general sultriness.

'It's nothing,' she said, dropping her voice an octave and attempting an air of mystery. Then she simply smiled at him.

Lance necessarily averted his eyes back onto the road, but when it was safe to look at her again, he did so not with inflamed passion but rather, once again, as though he suspected derangement. Realising the folly in attempting to be something that she was not, it occurred to Kate that she might just be honest. The memory of the perception that she had experienced on the moor was still with her, and she reminded herself to live in the moment. Perhaps she should just say it.

'*I love you Lance. I'm desperately, obsessively, hopelessly in love with you. What's that? Yes, that's right, just because you kissed me once. So, what do you think? Could you like, you know, help me out? Please?*'

Oh yes, that would work.

'*Lance, we need to talk. I know I said that I didn't believe in it, but it seems that after all I do, because in fact, I love you...'* Wait a minute. Kate interrupted her own rambling thoughts.

'Where are we going?' she asked. 'This isn't the way to Pencarra.'

'Chy-an-Gwidden,' said Lance. His voice was still terse but she thought a little softer than before. 'My house at Roseglos, you remember? While you've been yomping around the moor, the rivers have been in spate and the roads are flooded. I've taken the others there for the time being. Thankfully it wasn't let out this week. And yes, Izzy's fine, before you ask.'

'Oh...' was all Kate could say, digesting this information. Then, having been reminded of the others, she couldn't resist... 'How *is* the ankle?'

'*Don't,*' said Lance, menacingly. 'You're not allowed. *You're* still in trouble.' And he eyed her sideways with a warning glint in his eye and, she was sure, the slightest of smiles tempting the corners of his lips.

Kate put her head down in mock shame, but grinned openly. It was going to be all right. It had to be all right. She might have to be brave; she might have to take a chance and cast herself open to ridicule and rejection. She might have to be a little brazen. Turn the night light off and look at the stars. Kate was utterly terrified, but she told herself that she was ready. There really was no other way, since the alternative would be to suffer her ailment alone.

Chy-an-Gwidden lost none of its presence in the rain. The pale house stood plain, dignified and ghostly against the dark amethyst sky, as they pulled up outside. The stark natural beauty of the landscape in this silent, timeless hamlet was haunting. They sat for a minute, wordlessly, in the car as the rain beat down overhead, as if both needing some quiet private reflection before entering the thick soup of noise and demands that lay within the house. Once again, Kate was reminded of the day that she had sat madly in her own car, sealed and cosseted from the grim reality of the inner city housing estate. The day that she had decided, with no way at the time of seeing a means, to leave London.

'I'm glad I came here,' she said to Lance, and smiled.

He looked at her searchingly. Kate thought that he looked tired and she wanted to pull him close and let him rest against her. Lance turned away from her again, but still made no move to leave the car. Instead, he sat slumped, surveying the sea and the land and the weather. He looked careworn and defeated, and Kate's heart longed to reassure and comfort him. But there was still a doubt; a scared, mean and hapless voice from deep within her that threatened to undermine with its criticism that he still wanted Leah.

Then someone at the window waved. The front door swung open and Isabella stood there. She called, and beckoned her mother in, all breathless and excited at the discovery of this new setting. But Kate wasn't really listening. She saw that the moment was being lost. Lance reached to remove the keys from the ignition.

'Oh well,' said Kate, looking at him intently, and frantically willing him to meet her eyes. 'Into the fray...'

And then she moved to touch him gently on the arm. But just as she did so, Lance opened the car door and was already moving away, so that only the tips of her fingers reached him. He got out of the car and then, for a brief, elusive moment, she thought he hesitated. But he slammed the door shut and turned towards the house.

CHAPTER 58

Shelter

They took their wet coats off and hung them from the pegs in the hallway, Kate dumping her rucksack alongside the pile left by the others. Far from finding an atmosphere of weary gloom and damp disappointment, they were surprised by a scene of some revelry taking place in one of the living rooms. Despite the summer, it was apparently cold enough to have justified turning the heating on, and someone had managed to start a fire in the old cast-iron grate. Kate's return was barely remarked upon, let alone her dishevelled appearance. A boisterous conversation was taking place which, judging by the accumulation of small brown empty bottles, was being fuelled by a crate of ale which Derry had just happened to have in the back of his van. Gabe, even more fortuitously, appeared to have conjured up a guitar, and sat on the floor by the fire with his back against the old winged armchair, gently strumming melodious chords. The others sat or lay sprawled on the floor around him, comfortable in the welcome glow and lick of the flames. Only Leah reclined on the sofa, regal in her suffering. Her one good leg trailed on the floor as if to emphasise the tragic uselessness of the other, which was stretched out upon the sofa and propped up on a cushion.

Isabella, clearly unimpressed, announced she was going back upstairs, where Finn remained, but not before she had cautioned her errant mother for her disgraceful behaviour. Kate could only apologise.

'Hey Lance,' Derry called above the noise, 'Grab a beer.' And he threw a bottle towards the newcomers which luckily Lance managed to catch. 'Want one Kate?'

'No thanks,' said Kate, 'I think I'll get dry first.'

'Actually, it comes to my notice that we're running a bit low,' said Derry perusing the fast-emptying crate and rubbing his chin with grave concern. He turned to address Lance again, with a look of innocence. 'Don't you er, keep wine, or some such hereabouts...somewhere?'

Lance sighed. 'Yes, you know very well I do, securely locked up in the cellar.' Lance grinned with evil power. He knew damn well that Derry had already been rattling at the door of the cellar in manic frustration. But the discouraged look on his friend's face was piteous. Obviously the party was not ready to be over. 'But luckily, I happen to have the key on me,' he said in mock relief.

'Nice one!' Derry's smile instantaneously returned, as Lance handed him the precious trinket. He jumped up eagerly and ventured off in merry search of hidden treasure.

'You'd probably like a shower,' said Lance turning to Kate, who felt herself balk at the sudden change in the tone and expression of his voice when he spoke to her. 'I'll go and find you some towels. Holidaymakers usually bring their own, but I generally keep some here for when I stay myself. Hopefully Gina is up-to-date with the laundering.'

Kate nodded in grateful agreement. A shower would indeed be heaven. And she refused to be downhearted by his demeanour; she must not panic, must not give up. 'Shall I come with you?' she asked.

'No it's fine. Get warmed up. I'll be back in a minute and then I'll direct you the bathroom.' Lance set the bottle of beer carefully on a bookshelf, and then left the room. Kate was

547

aware of Leah's suspicious stare as she went to sit cross-legged by the fire, where Vivien had shuffled over to make a space.

'You managed to get found, then,' Leah spouted at Kate with unashamed bitterness from her perch.

'I was never lost,' said Kate, but understanding that Leah assumed her independent flight to be no more than a ruse, akin to one of her own fiendish machinations.

'All the same, we were worried,' said Vivien with genuine affection. 'Especially Lance,' she added slyly, 'Lance was most distraught.'

'Oh that's just pooh!' said Leah, her face a picture of disdainful authority. 'He was furious, that's all. Silly little emmet, taking herself off on the moor without any proper equipment and probably not even a map...'

'He didn't say that,' interjected Vivien.

Leah ignored her. '...totally, *so-not-what-you-do* in the countryside. He had a mind to leave you there, to find your own way back. Don't you think he was worried enough about my ankle, without having to abandon me to go and search for a silly little fool?'

'Oh come off it Leah!' cried Vivien.

'Ladies, ladies, please!' said Derry who had returned with a couple of bottles of wine and a stack of small glass tumblers. 'No harsh words! Life is too short, man. Make merry, for tomorrow we die. Be stoked, dudettes! Get the aloha vibe!'

Gabe, who had been watching Derry intently, waited for him to run out of corny platitudes, then sat up straight and with great seriousness, strummed the first chords of a familiar tune, and began to sing. Everybody groaned.

'No! Not *Trelawney*!' Derry said whilst handing round the glasses. It didn't stop him joining in raucously with the chorus of the Cornish folk song and national anthem. Soon they were all singing or clapping along.

'I was just messing with you!' said Gabe, when they'd finished, laughing and laying back to strum idly again. But the

548

situation had been diffused and even Leah managed to look cheerful.

Salima giggled with delight. Then, as she looked at Gabe, with her face lit up in sheer happiness, he smiled back.

In the darkened upstairs corridor Lance had easily found some fresh towels. He grabbed a bundle from the linen cupboard and carried them to the bathroom. There were signs of it having been recently used; some of the others must have already had showers. He placed the load of soft white towels on a chair, and then stooped to pick up a couple of discarded ones from the floor. He opened a window a touch to release the condensation. He saw a make-up bag left spilling open on the shelf and some greasy cotton wool balls that had been discarded into the washbasin. Leah's travel-hair-straighteners, complete with adapter, balanced precariously on the sink edge, still wastefully emanating heat where she had plugged them into the electric razor socket. Cursing, he reached to unplug them, marvelling that the fuse hadn't blown or the house burnt down, even.

He had a quick tidy up, and felt to check that the radiator was hot enough. Then he carefully arranged one large bath towel across it to warm. And then struggling to think of a way to create more time, he sat down on the edge of the bath and did nothing. He could faintly hear the noise from the gathering downstairs, but it was relatively quiet up here. And Lance needed some quiet; he needed to think.

He had done a lot of thinking since that day, when in frustration, he had ridiculously and shamefully carried Kate into the sea. But very few of his thoughts had been constructive or clear-headed. They were mostly defeatist, and why not? Lance was sick of being noble. He was sick of always doing the right—the honourable—thing. And he was a man for God's sake. He had waited long enough to meet someone important, only to be rejected. Why should he not give up on

549

the whole sorry idea and, well...*get some*? His previous experience with Jenifer Trewin had scared him to death; but damn it, dating was not his only option. Other men paid for it, didn't they? Other men exerted a right to have sex above and beyond all other problems and limitations in life, so why shouldn't he?

Except that he would be concerned that the girl might be too young. Or exploited, or trafficked, or fed with moral-warping drugs; or someone's sister, someone's child. She would be a *person*. It might be the oldest profession, but that did not make it the most desirable, or least lamentable. So he had tried dating, of late—random women that he had met by chance. Instead of his usual caution, he had gone against instinct and taken chances; had played the field, as they said. He needed to stop being such a wuss, and behave in a more predatory manner.

Except that he didn't approve of being predatory. That was how Leah had ensnared him and altered his life irrevocably. Jenifer Trewin had failed to do the same, but her humiliation at his rejection of her had still resulted in trauma, only this time for Finn. How could he begin to treat another human being in the same way? Lance had been a little shocked at the eager readiness of the women that he had dated. He had hoped for a battle; a succumbing of the demure to the overpowering attraction of his maleness. Even a little pretence at selectiveness might have been alluring, but these women behaved as though sex was a foregone conclusion, and expected of them.

Or maybe it was him.

Maybe somewhere along the line, Lance had forgotten how things were; had spent too long dreaming of what they might be.

Maybe Kate was right, and it was a foolish fantasy to believe in love.

Maybe it would be better to go back to Leah.

Leah had not left Tremeneghy since arriving for the Summer Ball—with the inarguable excuse of spending time with Finn—and was doing her unsubtle best, for some unknown reason, to tempt him. He could not understand why she had, so obviously, set up the photograph of them kissing. It was clearly a publicity stunt, but why him? And after all this time? Perhaps she was trying in the only way that she knew how.

And she was Finn's mother. It would be so easy to slide back into a familiar, if fractious relationship. He would get laid, and Finn would have his mother back. But for how long? Lance was still troubled by Finn's frantic questioning of him following that kiss, and the subsequent picture in the tabloid newspaper. Could he risk confusing him all the more?

And then there was Kate. She had made her feelings absolute. It hurt him even now to think about it, and so he refused to. He had been wrong, that was all—get over it. And yet she had behaved differently, strangely, today. He had expected her to be offhand and indignant, and was surprised that she had even agreed to come. Instead she had been oddly non-confrontational; uncharacteristically docile. *Was this a new trick?* She had been pleasant, almost, under the circumstances of their meeting again. He remembered her smiling, laughing, even saying sorry. *And had she reached out to touch him in the car? Had he imagined it?*

But then, he was not impressed by her walking off on the moors alone. It smacked too much of attention-seeking, and the sort of behaviour that he was accustomed to enduring from Leah. Maybe they were all the same. Maybe there was no difference between Leah and Kate, except...

Except that one of them was the mother of his son.

CHAPTER 59

A Happy Gathering

'Oh, I think I'm getting a headache,' moaned Leah from the sofa.

She naturally had to maintain her status as heroic invalid, but Kate suspected that Leah now regretted being removed from the close intimacy of the party gathered by the fire.

'Salima? Salima? Can you bring me my bag please, and a glass of water. I think I have some painkillers in there. It's in the hallway, I think.'

'That's a stroke of luck,' said Kate, as Salima sorrowfully gave up her position next to Gabe and went in search of the bag. 'It's unfortunate you didn't remember them earlier, when you hurt your ankle.'

Leah shot Kate a poisonous look. But any retort was forgotten when, upon Lance's return into the room, her attention snapped with laser-like precision back onto his every move. He beckoned to Kate, who stood and walked towards him. He spoke discreetly in her ear and then she left the room. *Probably nothing*, thought Leah, just directions to the bathroom and towels. But you could never be sure. As she gazed wanly at Lance, she gave him her best smile of endurance. Then she slunk a little lower in the sofa to give a more wanton look to her already languid pose. She relaxed her legs apart just a fraction, and turned ever-so-slightly in order that she might expose the best view of her protruding breast

552

where the top buttons of her shirt were undone. And then she considered her options. She might just have to take action with Lance, which was a shame really; she had enjoyed toying with him.

Lance slouched into an armchair on the opposite side of the room and sipped at the glass of wine that Derry had handed him. On the surface of things he appeared to be enjoying the conversation, smiling and nodding in places at a comment or observation, but his mind was still deeply distracted. He was thinking that he was almost sure that Kate had touched his arm in the car. It didn't necessarily follow that it meant anything. Worse than that, it might have been pity. That, of all things, he could not bear. Rejection was one thing, but he could not have Kate feel sorry for him. But she had smiled too, and been friendly. *Of course, she had been friendly, idiot! She just wants to be friends!* No matter how much he was tempted, Lance could not allow himself to be persuaded that Kate's feelings might have changed. But then...

She had reached out to touch him in the car...

'Lance!' called Vivien for the second time. 'Food! The kitchen? We're thinking of raiding it. Do you mind?'

'No, no, of course not,' Lance answered quickly, 'but I doubt you'll find much.'

'Are you okay?' asked Vivien. 'You seem out of sorts.'

Leah's radar picked up a notch. She quickly propped herself up on one elbow, and regarded Lance intently for any giveaway clues.

'I'm fine,' said Lance. He swiftly jumped up from the chair. 'Hungry though! Come on, let's see what we can find.'

They all got up, possessively clutching hold of their glasses of wine, and made to move to the kitchen. At the same time Salima returned the other way with a tumbler of water for Leah, which she dutifully held out with the found rucksack.

But Leah dismissed her with a wave of her hand. 'Excuse me!' she called from the sofa.

They all looked at each other in turn, before it fell, once again, to Lance to offer his support to the plucky patient. As he grasped her arm and helped pull her up to stand, Leah made a tactical wobble. Then as he grabbed her to stop her falling, she manoeuvred one soft and manicured hand onto his chest, where it lingered, before she gently moved it away, stroking the length of his body. Lance regarded her dryly. He was getting used to this sort of thing happening lately. Leah met his eyes full-on, making a promise that would be hard to back out of.

Upstairs, in one of the sparsely furnished bedrooms, Kate found an old hairdryer sitting alone in a drawer, and attempted to set about drying her hair. She had had a speedy but refreshing shower, and her clothes had dried quickly on the radiator. Now all she had to do was persuade this ancient device to get on with the purpose for which it was intended. It whirred and screeched submissively enough; it complied as best as it could with the demand that it should pass air through its apparatus, and it made a damn good effort to make that air warm.

Kate longed to get downstairs again; it was imperative to make her feelings known to Lance. Finally, deciding that the pretend hairdryer had done its heroic best, she quickly cleared it back to its drawer, and then hurried from the room to the stairs. She paused, however, at the tall hallway landing window that framed the garden and the fields and then the sea beyond. The driving rainclouds still threatened ominously overhead, but what light there was created a surreal and magical scene. *Such a beautiful place*, Kate thought to herself once again. Everything she wanted in the world was so close, almost there for the taking, and yet maddeningly elusive. Then, hearing children's laughter from upstairs on the second floor, and despite her urgency, she turned around and followed the staircase to the top.

She found Isabella and Finn in one of the two attic rooms at the very top of the house. Finn was at the window looking through the inevitable telescope. Isabella was lying on a single bed atop of a multi-coloured crocheted blanket, and with her legs posed idly up against the wall, but jumped up when she saw Kate.

'Mum! Mum!' said Isabella excitedly, 'Finn says it's too late to go home now and that his dad's probably drunk anyway, so we can stay here tonight! I'm having this room, and Finn's having the other one. I love this room, Mum, can I make my room at home like this?'

Kate looked about the room in puzzlement. It was as barely furnished as the one that she had just left; more so when you considered that there had been two single beds in the one downstairs. Here, apart from the one bed, there was just a small dressing table in one corner, and a bedside table and an armchair. A massive wooden trunk—looking temptingly like pirate treasure or a dressing-up box—stood in another corner. But the walls of the room were boarded with wood and painted white, and it had a simple, characterful charm.

'I think that you could easily make your room look like this if you threw out all the truckloads of landfill that you feel obliged to collect,' said Kate. 'And I don't think Lance is drunk! I'm sure he's only had a beer. He should still be able to drive.'

Isabella ignored Kate's words, but tugging on her mother's arm, dragged her to a part of the wooden boarding that turned out to be a hidden door. 'Look,' she said, pulling at a small hole in the wood, 'It's a door, see? It's like a secret tunnel that goes into Finn's room! We've *got* to stay here, I'm telling you! In fact, can we move here? We could live here instead of Dolphin Cottage...'

'Whoa!' cried Kate, 'Slow down. Don't get so carried away! What's wrong with Dolphin Cottage anyway?'

'Nothing,' said Isabella, matter-of-fact. 'Although...this house is much warmer!'

Finn fiddled with the focus on the telescope, seemingly unconcerned. He was a strange boy, thought Kate; taciturn like his father. What must he make of this discussion about moving into their house? Nonsensical to Kate, it had the potential to be related through a child's eyes and vocabulary as a plan of action; a plot, even. And did he harbour hopes of his parents' reunion? It would be perfectly natural to do so, and she, evil woman, was hoping to snatch his father from right under the feline jaws of his mother. With sudden realisation that Finn's good opinion of her was paramount, she tried to catch his eye with a guilty smile. To her surprise, after a second's curious hesitation, he suddenly and disarmingly smiled back.

'What are you looking at?' she asked.

'Oh some boats out at sea, just practicing,' said Finn. 'There's gonna be a big full moon later tonight and Whizz—Izzy—wants to look at it. If the clouds go away that is. And if we can stay...'

'I see,' Kate eyed Isabella suspiciously but added, 'sounds like a good plan.'

Then taking her daughter by the hand, she led her back to the bed and sat down next to her. 'Seriously,' she said. 'Are you okay? Are you happy?'

Isabella looked at Kate with a familiar, dubious expression: where was this going?

'Did I do the right thing in bringing us to Cornwall?'

'Well, duh!' said Isabella. 'I mean, yeah! Course you did. No-brainer.'

Kate kissed her daughter on the forehead. Then she got up and went to leave the room.

'By the way,' Izzy called after her, 'is there anything to eat?'

'Yeah,' said Finn. 'We're starving!'

Kate grinned. 'Let's go and see, shall we? We might have to forage for nuts and berries!'

As they all thumped their way hungrily down the stairs, Izzy turned to Kate and said, 'So we're staying here tonight, okay? That's *settled*, right?'

Back downstairs again, Kate found that the others had moved camp to the large airy kitchen, where Derry and Vivien had formed a production line for the making of jam sandwiches. Thick slabs of processed white bread were in turn daubed with too-hard butter, and then slathered with the sticky, sweet glob. They had also found some dried pasta, a tin of pulped tomatoes and some oregano, and Gabe stood at the cooker concocting something hot.

Tasting a teaspoonful of his efforts, he winced. 'Needs garlic and chilli man, but hey, I'll do my best.'

Other bounty filched from the kitchen cupboards included a packet of chocolate and marshmallow teacakes—only slightly out of date—a bag of crisps, a tin of pilchards, some rapidly hardening cheese, and two apples. It was a sad collection of holidaymakers' rejects and leftovers, yet there was a certain childish charm to the makeshift picnic—a conviction abetted by ravenous stomachs. Isabella and Finn eagerly piled their plates high with sandwiches and teacakes.

Derry had already made another raid on Lance's private cellar and the generous, quaffable glasses of wine that he continually poured helped to appease otherwise fussy appetites. Lance was busy feeding pre-cut wooden logs into the range, but the drafty kitchen was still chilly, and upon seeing Kate, he moved to offer her a blanket from a pile on a chair. Most of the others seated at the table were already cosily wrapped in the heavy woollen mantles; except Leah, who was not sufficiently frozen enough to compromise her sexuality, nor to be blind to the advantage of the sharp air on her suddenly perky nipples.

'You ought to know,' said Kate to Lance in a low voice as she gratefully accepted the blanket, 'that the children are plotting to stay the night. They've already decided you're drunk, for *my* information, and I expect they will come up with a different ruse for your hearing—insist it's all my idea, or something.'

'Right, thanks for the warning,' said Lance.

'Hey, what's that?' Gabe said, unexpectedly, as he stirred his sauce. He was not usually the unsubtle eavesdropper. 'Plans to stay the night? Well, why not? Might be fun. Besides, the roads are still gonna be flooded, and I reckon judging by those clouds the weather ain't done yet.'

'I don't think so!' Leah said hurriedly, and in disgust. 'I can't stay the night, I've got nothing *here*.' There was a moment's collective stunned incredulity as they all secretly contemplated the ingeniously packed rucksack that had so far managed to produce hat, groundsheet, hair products and straightening irons, of all things.

'Yeah, I agree,' said Derry, addressing Gabe and ignoring Leah. 'After all, we missed out on the walk today; let's stay here and party.'

'I'm up for it,' said Vivien.

'Me too!' said Salima, although she was careful not to catch Leah's disapproving eye.

They all looked at Kate, who merely shrugged. 'Happy to go with the flow,' she said.

Lance left the range to join the others at the kitchen table, but said nothing.

'Of course, it's down to you, brah,' said Gabe, taking charge, and blinking at Lance with coy righteousness. Then he took another wine glass from the shelf and strolled across the room to join them. 'After all, it *is* your place, and you are the man with the wheels. If you want us all to leave, then that's cool.' And then, the embodiment of compliance, he not-so-subtly placed the empty wine glass on the table in front of Lance.

'Well, *I* certainly can't drive,' said Derry, draining the dregs of another bottle into his glass. He turned to Vivien. 'If we don't stay here, then you may have to. Otherwise it's the back of the van for you and me, my luvver.' Vivien embraced his arm and smiled wordlessly at him.

'There is no *way*,' protested Leah. 'For God's sake, we are not teenagers anymore, crashing out on the floor! I mean, if I had known, I would have brought an overnight bag. Or even a clean pair of knickers! It's disgusting. *Salima!*'

But Salima was too delirious with the idea of an extension of Gabe's company to contemplate supporting her friend, and—deciding it best to not actually speak—merely smiled apologetically.

'Well, as I said,' repeated Gabe, demonstrating a chivalry that cleverly belied his role in starting the whole thing, 'it's up to Lance. Only...you better decide now, man, before you have another drink.'

Right on cue, the silence of their attentive focus on Lance was broken by a loud pop as Derry uncorked yet another long-held and possibly treasured, fine red wine. He held the bottle aloft tentatively, while Lance's long fingers gently toyed with the empty glass in front of him. His gaze never left it, nor did it alight on any of their expectant expressions as he appeared to silently turn the matter over in his mind. They all halted mid-feast; their poses frozen as they awaited his decision. Leah attempted to bore her way into Lance's mind with a furious, put-out stare. Suddenly Lance stopped playing with the tempting goblet and looked up at Derry.

'What the hell...' he said holding the glass up to Derry's delighted administrations.

There were cries of 'Hurrah!' and 'Yay!' from the children, and an—almost—collective sigh of relief from the others. It seemed they were going to be allowed to continue to play.

CHAPTER 60

Ghosts

As the kitchen warmed and the darkness gathered in, the small company in an isolated kitchen on a wilderness edge of the Cornish coast huddled together and told stories. Empty wine bottles were put to use supporting dribbling candles, which flickered softly, casting an ethereal light over the contours of their faces. The candles had been suggested as an ecological alternative to burning away power through a light bulb, but neither did anyone object to the comfort and romance shed by the golden light, adding to the mood of late-night companionship. The children had, ostensibly at least, been 'put to bed'.

'Don't worry,' Finn had whispered to Izzy on their way upstairs, 'I think Gabe is wrong about the rain. I think we'll see your moon.'

The remnants of food had been cleared away, but they all continued, if in a less frenzied manner, to imbibe reckless quantities of wine. Kate listened fascinated to tales from their youth; anecdotes of previous misadventures, and complicated yarns which bore new fruit in the telling to a newcomer, who had not heard them a thousand times before. Inevitably, as the black shadows gathered behind their backs, the stories turned to ghosts and the supernatural. Derry told a tale about how, as a teenager, he had taken his dog for a walk in the churchyard on the hill behind Pencarra.

'This dog was no highly strung pedigree mind,' he said. 'She was an ordinary, down-to-earth, old mongrel bitch. She'd had three litters of pups, and even looked at me and my brothers with a tolerant, world-weary eye. She weren't prone to excitability. Well, we were walking through the churchyard one summer's evening, and there was no one else there, but it weren't, y'know, odd in any way that I'd noticed. But then we came to an old grave; you know one of those that are like a sort of stone sarcophagus, surrounded by old rusty railings. Like a...like a tomb, I suppose, only above the ground. Do you follow me?'

They all nodded encouragingly.

'Well anyway,' continued Derry, 'As I said, I was passing by with Wilmot—that was my dog,' he added for Kate's benefit, '—when I noticed that the stone lid of this tomb structure had been broken in two, and that one part had fallen off and was wedged between the grave and the railings. I still didn't think anything of it. Just vandals, I supposed. But then Wilmot starts growling and pulling on the lead in the exact direction of this grave, and all her hackles are up; and then she starts just barking and barking at the site. And no matter how I pulled her away, she kept on making a racket in that direction. And even though it was a warm summer's evening, I started to feel really, y'know...shivery.'

'You were probably coming down with something,' said Leah with a tut. 'Or more likely, still on something.'

'No, I wasn't,' said Derry firmly. 'But I can tell you it gave me the creeps. Took all my strength to pull her away, and even then she was still growling and upset, like.'

'Mighta been a rat,' suggested Gabe.

'Well, maybe, but I dunno,' Derry scratched his stubbled chin thoughtfully. 'True, she could have got all excited over a rat, but would have been a little bit more joyful-like, about it! It would've been a different kind of bark. But no, there was something warning, something aggressive in her manner that I never seen before, nor after.'

'And then there was the smashed tomb lid!' Kate joined in, enjoying the spooky atmosphere. 'It would have taken quite an effort to do that—even for vandals.'

'So what exactly do you think it was?' asked Leah sarcastically.

'Don't know,' said Derry. 'Don't wanna know.'

'Didn't you look?' giggled Salima. 'Didn't you go and look inside the broken grave?'

'No chance!' said Derry. 'I got out of there as fast as I could drag the dog away!'

'I'm still getting my head around the fact you named your dog Wilmot!' Kate laughed.

'I had an experience once,' said Gabe, slowly rolling himself a cigarette. 'I was camping in the Mojave Desert...'

There were serial groans all round, and Derry threw a box of matches at him.

'Of course you were,' said Lance.

'It was somewhere off the old Route 66,' continued Gabe, ignoring them. 'I was on my way down from Vegas to Joshua Tree—going to meet a girl as it happens—before heading on through to La Jolla for a surf...'

'I swear you make this up!' cried Derry, 'You just made at least three popular American cultural references in one sentence!'

'Well, that's the way it happened, man. I can't account for your sheltered lives.'

'So, you were camping in the middle of the desert,' said Kate, eager to hear the story. 'Go on...'

'Well, can't say for sure, that place is extreme; plays tricks on the mind. It might have been a dream; but I don't reckon so. I was just lying there in the dark, looking up at the stars, having a smoke and thinking the big stuff; you know: how awesome it all is—how fuckin' big! And then, I don't know if I nodded off, or just went into some kinda meditative state, but suddenly, the stars seemed to all come together and collect into a...it was like a glittering ball...and then my eyes refocused, so that I could see that the stars were still in the sky, but yet above me was this thing, this...*amazing* globe of lights that just shimmered above me, I mean right above my head. And I felt no fear; in fact the opposite. I was filled with a sorta peace, and everything seemed really, y'know, *obvious.*'

'You were *definitely* on something,' said Leah.

'What happened next?' asked Kate.

'I raised my arm out to touch it, like this,' said Gabe; and he stretched his arm out overhead towards some imaginary image in his mind's eye. 'But as soon as my fingertips met it, it disappeared...kinda dissolved.' He withdrew his hand reluctantly, as if with some remembered sense of disappointment.

'Plainly a dream,' said Leah.

'No, obviously an alien encounter,' corrected Derry, 'UFOs! They're all over the place in those desert areas.'

'Or the spirit of your Indian ancestors,' said Kate slyly.

'Is it just me,' Salima sniggered, 'or didn't all that happen in The Lion King?'

'Okay, okay, mock away,' said Gabe. 'Bunch of heathens. But I reckon you're closest to it, Katie. I sensed it was some kind of spirit.'

'Or a dream,' repeated Leah.

'Well, it if was a dream, then it's one that I've never forgotten. I mean outta all the dreams of all the nights of my life—and I dream a lot!—it's been the most vivid. It stays with me. Why would that be?'

'How about you Vivien?' said Leah, diverting the attention, 'I can't believe you don't see spirits all the time?'

'Oh I do,' said Vivien in a heartbeat. 'They're all around us right now.'

'Seriously?' said Salima in hushed tones, her eyes bright and wide.

'Of course,' said Vivien, quickly hiding a smile as she observed one or two of them glance uneasily at the dark shadows behind them. 'But they're not really spirits, in that they're not exactly dead. They're just occupying this space in their own time.'

'What?' said Leah, her face twisting as she attempted to inject as much scorn as she could summon into one word.

'She may be right,' said Lance. 'Time—or at least the measurement of time— is an abstract concept. There may be no past, no future; just the *moment*. On the other hand, there is a physicality to space-time—gravitational waves cause ripples—that goes beyond the superficiality of clocks. And I believe there is some connection in the present with past and future embodiments, if only on a quantum level with entangled particles.'

There was laughter all round.

'He says practically nothing all night and then comes out with that!' chuckled Derry, shaking his head. Only Kate stopped laughing and found herself suddenly struck by what Lance had said. It exactly described what she had felt up on the moor; what she had felt less powerfully sitting alone in her car in London and at countless other fugitive moments in her life.

'Bollocks!' said Leah, with startling aggression. 'Utter tripe and bollocks. Of course there is a past, because you remember it. And why do you not know the future? Because it hasn't happened yet! It's so simple, I can't understand why you bloody scientists and boffins have to make it sound like it's something complicated.'

'Well yes, it's hard to ignore the very conspicuous trail of information left by increasing entropy; by time's arrow...' began Lance thoughtfully, '...although technically the laws of physics don't rule out its reversal. But there can be no evidence of a state of low entropy because it leaves no trace; we would have no memory of it...' Lance looked around at the blank faces and reconsidered. 'Okay, perhaps that's a little abstruse. How about this: for argument's sake, consider that memories are just experiences that are filed away in your brain, and as such the past only exists in your mind...'

'What about all the evidence?' said Leah. 'Dinosaur bones? Photographs? Just about everything? I think it's pretty obvious there's been a past!'

Lance finally relaxed into a smile. 'Of course, you're right Leah. There are indeed huge steaming mountains of evidence. But I might contend that this evidence exists in the here and now; in the present, not the past.'

'Oh shut up!' cried Leah.

'No, I think I understand what Lance means,' said Kate slowly, trying to formulate her thoughts. Immediately the ghost of Juliet was at her side, triggering alarm bells. *Careful*, said Juliet's spirit in Kate's mind. *Say something girly. Say something fun. For once in your life Kate, say something fucking dumb.*

'Time, as we experience it, is just the...the pocket that we play our lives out in. It's not relevant on the grander scale. Or there may be larger, or smaller pockets that we are unaware of, that we can't conceive. It's...relative.'

'As indeed Dr. Einstein informed us,' said Gabe.

'...And if entropy is progressing to both high and low states simultaneously, it kind of...meets in the middle. In the present.'

The imaginary Juliet slapped her hands to her head in despair.

'Nope,' said Derry with a grin. 'I'm out. My mind was boggled way back at "physicality of space-time".'

'*Pocket?*' said Leah, once again gasping and squirming as though the word pained her to express it. '*Pocket?*' But Kate noticed a flicker of interest from Lance; one that she suspected, or perhaps hoped, he had been trying to suppress all night.

'Er, did I say pocket? How can I explain?'

'You think the universe has pockets?' continued Leah. 'You're crazy. The universe is just stars and stuff. And that's all. Just what it says on the tin. What's the big mystery?'

'Of course,' said Lance. 'You're right. Don't know why I've been wasting my time all these years.'

'Do you not think it is a wonderful mystery? The very fact of existence?' Kate rallied against Leah's criminal lack of imagination.

Uh-oh. Juliet, supposing that Kate had done her worst, had metaphysically sat back in her chair to inspect her nails, but was now back at her shoulder, willing her to stop.

'Seriously? You're not even the slightest bit awed?' Kate, it seemed, was unstoppable. 'You think that everything just happens for no particular reason other than to allow you to, I don't know, shop for overpriced handbags?'

'Sure, why not?' grinned Leah. 'It's just there, that's all. Why not? I suppose *you* believe it was all made by a higher being?'

'No, not as such, I believe the universe itself *is* a, erm, higher being—for want of a better term.'

That's it! You're on your own now; Juliet's spirit turned her back on Kate and sulked.

There was a silent, loaded pause, before Kate battled on. 'Think of it as Gaia theory, only on a massive, well, cosmological scale. Just as the Earth can be considered a living entity, so can the Universe.'

'So...if the universe is alive, as I think you are saying,' said Leah, 'then what are *we*? Little invisible bugs, crawling around on its skin?'

Kate paused for a second, and then staring at her empty wine glass, for the first time pondered the wisdom of so explicitly exposing her thoughts. *Oh, what the hell.*

If she wasn't true to herself, then what else mattered? Anything achieved through falsehood or pretension would never satisfy. Admiration, or by equal turn, ridicule and loathing, should at least be inspired by her actual character, and not some insipid, cowardly version.

'I think that everything is connected, and that we, and everything else, are different ways of the universe experiencing itself. And as it experiences itself, it creates and expresses itself.'

'Excuse me?' said Leah, leaning forward aggressively and turning one dainty ear towards Kate, as if to imply that of course she must have misheard her.

'The universe gains knowledge of itself, of what it is, through our individual experience, but also through that of everything else, whether it be a tree or a rock, or a galaxy. We are all just manifestations, or expressions, of one thing. It's...kind of why I paint. To...manifest.' Her voice trailed off weakly.

Leah slunk back in her chair, a Cheshire-cat grin on her face. She did not need to say any more, her prey being firmly entrapped in her paws. The others shifted uncomfortably.

'I think what Kate's trying to describe, in her own particularly idiosyncratic manner, is a form of philosophical Panpsychism,' said Lance, and everyone groaned again.

Kate looked at him uncertainly. 'Well, I'm sure I haven't explained it very well; in fact I know I haven't.'

'Oh, you didn't do too badly,' said Lance. 'You might be formidable if you actually studied your subject.' Was that a flicker of a smile? Was he supporting Kate or mocking her?

'Well, *I* think it's a sign that we've all drunk too much and should go to bed!' said Leah, with sudden good humour, and everyone wryly agreed. One by one, they got up and began to clear away the mess on the table in an awkward silence. Kate wondered if this sudden, mutually agreed halt in the evening's proceedings was to save her from further making a fool of herself. With creeping mortification, she slowly collected up some bottles and added them to the stash of empties in the pantry.

'I suppose we'd better sort out the sleeping arrangements,' Lance said, but sounded as though he were thinking aloud. 'The children are on the top floor and there are three bedrooms left, sleeping six in all...one is a twin room. The other two are doubles.'

'Well, we're having one of those!' said Vivien, grabbing Derry lasciviously.

'Hey, Sal,' said Gabe, who had already done the maths and was way ahead of them all, as usual. 'What do you say you and I camp down here by the fire in the living room? I'm not ready for bed just yet, not while there's still good wine to be had.' He grabbed a bottle still half-full by the neck, and swung it gently between his fingers.

Utterly startled, Salima could barely speak for anticipation. The wine bottle dangled like a toy before a kitten. 'Yeah, sure,' she managed, with a nervous laugh.

As Gabe turned to leave the kitchen, Kate was sure that, for the briefest of seconds, he looked at her with a wicked flick of his eyebrow.

Salima did not wait to be asked again. Looking tiny wrapped up in her blanket, she scurried after Gabe, and before the dream evaporated, carefully shut the door of the front room behind them.

CHAPTER 61

Leap of Faith

So, it looked as though Salima was finally going to get lucky with Gabe, observed Kate, as she passed the firmly closed door, and followed the others upstairs to the first floor, noticing wryly that Leah had momentarily forgotten her limp. With the benefit of some prior knowledge, Vivien and Derry called a quick goodnight and then dived into one of the bedrooms. Lance guided the two other women to the bedroom where Kate had attempted to dry her hair, and led them in. Kate followed, but Leah lurked by the door.

'Here you are girls,' said Lance. 'The beds are small but quite comfortable, although you might need your blankets if it gets too cold. No en suite facilities I'm afraid, just a small sink in the corner. But you both know where the bathroom is.' He moved to leave. 'Try not to quarrel. The pair of you,' he said, but to Leah's face, as he reached the door.

She stood defiantly in his way. 'Er, is this a joke?' she said, smiling sweetly up at Lance. 'I mean, you've got to be kidding me?'

'What's up Leah?' Lance asked pleasantly.

'You don't really think I'm going to share, do you?—not with her anyway!'

Lance looked at Kate apologetically. Leah's tactlessness could be a shock to the uninitiated.

'I mean, this was once my house too you know,' continued Leah, 'We were going to live here. You don't think I'm going to settle for this crummy room when I know perfectly well there is a master bedroom down the corridor!'

'That's my room Leah,' said Lance.

Leah smiled once more, and then, mobility miraculously restored, took a step closer, touching his chest again with one hand as she did. 'I know,' she said, with a leer.

Kate might as well have been invisible, so extraneous was she to the conversation. She forced herself to look away as Leah began to run both hands up and down the length of Lance's arms. She moved to the window and, drawing back the curtain, peered out uselessly at the night, trying not to hear.

'I want to sleep in your bedroom,' said Leah. 'I won't take no for an answer.'

There were intolerable seconds where Kate fought the urge to shove them both from the room and slam, bolt and barricade the door shut.

'Right,' said Lance softly.

Kate sensed their movement, and turned slightly to be sure. Lance took a final look back at her, and then followed Leah from the room, shutting the door behind him.

So that was it. For long seconds Kate could not move, could hardly breathe. The well of emotion inside her was too great to know of a way of sufficiently expressing itself. And then slowly, noiselessly, she began to cry. She would not howl, desperate to hold on to a crumb of pride, or at least the semblance of pride after having so readily exposed herself to ridicule earlier. She had tried her best, or at least, the best she knew how; which was to be herself, and to be honest. It was really quite pathetic. It was time to admit that there had been a moment of madness on Lance's part where he had shown an interest in her, and that she had foolishly dismissed it. Now it seemed that he had no regrets, and perhaps even considered he'd had a lucky escape. And Kate would have to summon all her courage to tolerate the knowledge of his being with Leah in a nearby room. He had started something in her, stirred up her emotions, and reminded her of how it was supposed to be. But now it seemed she would have to endure those feelings alone.

She would just have to find a way. She had to find a way to be able to function, to get her life back, but without him. She made herself go upstairs to check on Izzy, her limbs heavy with disappointment and hopelessness.

'I saw the moonrise mum, Finn was right!' Kate could sense Isabella smile happily in the dark.

She kissed her daughter's forehead and tucked her in, barely hearing her chatter through the fog of her depression, before stumbling downstairs again to the lonely room. Exhausted with grief, Kate stripped to her underwear and poured herself a glass of water from the small sink. She rinsed her mouth, expunging the remnants of the red wine that had made her so bold and so artless. And then in an act of self-loathing, went against habit and turned out the bedside light. Feeling a little nauseated and needing to breathe, she opened the window slightly and then crawled into one of the small single beds. She curled up on her side and cried silently, internally, for a while, before turning restlessly onto her back and staring into the dim nothingness. The house was mostly silent, but creaked with distant unfamiliar noises; and beyond that, ever present, was the continual, insistent surge and drag of the sea.

Maybe she really didn't have a clue. Perhaps if she had been foolish enough in revealing her most absurd, ridiculous meditations on life, then she was equally foolish, mistaken even, in her emotions. After all, she had always thought that there was an element of decision in falling in love. And if so, then there would be a way out. She would get better; she would find her way out of this awful illness and make a full recovery. She had to, or it might cripple her forever.

But it was Lance. Her heart was not yet ready to imagine her life without him. It was going to take years to climb out of this one.

Long minutes passed in sleepless, troubled mind; so that at first she thought that she had imagined the handle turn uneasily, and then the door slowly open. His large figure crept in silently in the dusky light and then carefully shut the door again behind him. Kate's heart beat an unsteady rhythm. He said nothing. Perhaps in the darkness he could not tell that she was still awake. She watched transfixed as his shaded form quickly undressed and then climbed into the remaining bed.

Lance too, lay on his back, crossing his arms above his head and supporting his head in his hands. He too stared blindly at the nothingness. They lay there together in silence for measureless moments, during which time Kate thought it must be impossible for him not to realise that she was still awake. If it wasn't for her movements, however small, and her breathing, which was far from deep and relaxed, then it seemed certain that he should be able to read her very thoughts in the intimacy of the small darkened room. She could bear it no longer. She propped herself up on one elbow and looked at him as best as she could.

When Kate had drawn back the curtain earlier on, it had been a pointless action because the artificial light had rendered the outside night a black screen. Now, with the lamp off, Finn's promised full moon permeated the room with eerie light to create a diffused, silvery glow. A gentle breeze from the open window carried the scent of the sea. He was only yards away from her.

'I don't understand,' said Kate, her voice still choked with emotion. 'What about Leah?' For a while he didn't speak, and she wondered if Lance was being his usual reticent self, or if perhaps he was after all, asleep. She almost giggled, for it would be entirely in accordance with the way things had gone so far.

'Don't know,' he said at last. His voice sounded bizarre; unreal; as if his speaking finally confirmed the reality of his presence. 'I presume from the absence of hysterical histrionics that she has gone to sleep.'

'But...I thought...she said...'

He turned slightly in the half-light and looked towards her for the first time since entering the room. 'She said she wanted to sleep in my bed. I didn't agree to be in it.'

It took Kate a while to absorb this. 'So, you didn't...'

'No,' said Lance firmly.

The initial joy that flowed through Kate's heart was tempered by a fleeting indignant sense of sorority. The thought of Leah raging silently in Lance's bedroom was one that gave her a certain amount of unworthy pleasure, but even so, she could empathise with the dreadful humiliation that her adversary must be feeling. And yet, ultimately, and with selfish abandon, she could not help but feel the rapidly spreading warmth of relief.

'So, since you left you've been...'

'Locking up. Checking on the children. I did spend a while in the garden looking out to sea.'

She could have hugged him.

And so she did. In one swift movement, Kate left her bed, strode the short space between them, pulled back the covers of Lance's bed, and climbing in, lay down and held him close in a warm embrace. During the course of this action, she resisted all attempts by her saner, more cautious self to consider the consequences. Having so recently been convinced of the alternative, she would not allow anything to affect her impulse. Now was the time; this was the moment. She breached the barrier.

Initially, Lance did not return the embrace, but neither did he withdraw in abject horror or disgust, even though there was no choice but to be close in the tiny bed. Then slowly, he brought one of his arms down to enclose her, and began to gently and absently stoke the side of her hip.

'Hussy,' he whispered in her ear.

'Yes, I know,' said Kate, in resignation. 'I've thrown myself at you after only, what, ten months of knowing you? A complete slapper. Well, you told me when we met that you weren't looking for a good woman to look after you, so perhaps you'll accept an old slut?'

Lance laughed, and in doing so, appeared to finally relax. In an act of sudden acceptance, he turned awkwardly in the limited space, and grasped Kate with more assurance, enfolding her in his strong arms. A shiver, in equal parts fear, anticipation and pleasure shuddered through Kate's body.

'You're trembling,' said Lance.

'Yes. I'm absolutely terrified.'

He kissed her then, for a long time. When he finally broke free to look at her with an urgent, inflamed look in his starlit eyes, she couldn't help herself. She was still, after all, Kate.

'I thought I'd scared you off forever with my performance downstairs,' she said. 'I suppose, as a scientist, you must find my ramblings about the universe incredibly naïve; I know I don't really know what I'm talking about, I just have my own ideas...'

'Your ideas are charming,' said Lance kissing her again.

'That sounds patronising...' said Kate, breaking free and immediately forgetting that she was in a passionate embrace with the man she loved.

'Kate,' said Lance impatiently, and to her dismay moving slightly away from her. 'I think your ideas are at best uninformed, and at worst, crazy. But at least they are ideas. I like ideas. If you must know, when you were desperately struggling to illustrate the meaning of everything...'

575

Kate clasped her hands to her face and groaned 'Oh no, I really did, didn't I?'

Lance beamed; that exceptional, spectacular grin. 'I can't wait for the TED talk... The slideshow; the diagrams...'

They both collapsed in fits of suppressed giggles, anxious not to be heard; longing to maintain this delicious intimacy.

'Anyway,' Lance continued, 'I think it was then that I knew absolutely, if I didn't already, that you were the woman for me. I don't know about "higher beings", but I would never censor or ridicule a discussion about the possibility. If science ever does the same; stops asking questions, then we're in trouble. There isn't a word for what I believe.'

'I'm with you...' said Kate, nodding in agreement. 'But to be fair, it wasn't me who brought up "higher beings"; I mean that sounds like something from Star Trek. I never actually said...'

'Kate, may I ask you something?' said Lance, with great seriousness.

'Yes,' said Kate, whilst longing for him to move closer to her, to kiss her again.

'Can we talk about this in the morning?'

Kate smiled, and finally shut up. After all, there were closer, more pressing, matters to attend to.

Epilogue

The swell suddenly dropped and there was the sense of a lull; a breathing space in time between the sets, while the waves took a rest from their relentless attack on the shore. Kate sat up on her board and, having reassured herself that the flattening did not signal a rip, took a moment to absorb her surroundings. She wore a shorty, and the cut off wetsuit revealed a satisfying flex to her thigh muscles as her bare suntanned legs dangled lazily in the sea. Her skin felt alive, beaten smooth by a summer of sea salt and sand; her naked face adorned by nothing but a smattering of freckles. She tilted her head, eyes closed, towards the late afternoon sun, basking in the welcome warmth of the rays that had kissed her brown hair golden.

She turned and looked back towards the land. She waved to Isabella, who was larking about on a wooden bellyboard further inshore, where there was still a little white water from the last set. Isabella waved back, before hurling herself onto her board flat on her stomach, and riding an idle wave to the shore. Kate watched as her daughter exploded with giggles at the silliness of being cast up upon the shore, only to be left marooned there in the sand by the receding foam.

Kate's board was a long one—a log—which Gabe had advised would help her catch more waves, and therefore speed the learning process. They had become good friends, she and this board, over the endlessly long and blissful summer days. And now it was September, and a full year since Kate had moved to Cornwall. It felt like a lifetime, so much had changed. The exhibition had been a success, and she practiced her art with more confidence as a result. But it was not just her environment and lifestyle that had become altered beyond recognition; she herself was somehow intrinsically transformed. She barely knew herself, but feeling renewed, took great joy in the experience of each new day.

She had had another e-mail from Juliet that morning. Kate had reluctantly succumbed to the advantages of technological communication, since it kept her in touch with her only sister. But she still refused to answer all but the most important missives, and Juliet's, of course was one of those. An attachment of photographs showed Jem and Juliet at Machu Picchu, weather-beaten and smiling, with the awesome landscape of the Peruvian mountains in the background. Jem looked tanned and thin, but more than that, there was a radically stress-free and relaxed appearance about him.

He looked happy.

Unexpectedly, there was a footnote added to the message written by Jem himself. He hoped that both Kate and Isabella were well, and announced his intention, upon return, to volunteer for charity work in Africa: *'It'll be tough—worst kind of dentistry—heard tales of machete attacks and horrible diseases—but someone's got to do it, might as well be me.'* Despite the limitations of e-mail, Kate could detect in the hurried prose his sense of excitement; of *renewal*; there was potential there for fulfilment. The message was also an unspoken forgiveness, and she was grateful.

In the spirit of embracing communication, but this time returning to her preferred method of a handwritten letter, Kate had finally replied to Marsha, promising to make an appearance at Stevie's wedding, for old times' sake. Privately she knew that she would be making an early exit. It wasn't her intention to rekindle the old relationships, rather she hoped to mend any remaining hard feelings, in order that they might let her gently slip away from them, and unnoticed, get on with her life. And she had decided, internally at least, that she would not object if Miles pursued his purported intentions towards Isabella. There would always be the risk of Isabella getting hurt; *but*, Kate thought, *she would handle it*. Her daughter was made of stronger stuff than the likes of Miles Tobin-Baker could destroy. She watched as Isabella strode splashing with her board out to sea again; happy and brave and free.

On the beach, near deserted now after the departure of summer holidaymakers, Finn was scrambling barefoot up the black rocks as his father tended to a small fire. She could not see Lance's features clearly at this distance, but knew that he would be engrossed in maintaining the exact proportions of kindling required for long-term sustenance of heat, and the resultant perfectly cooked mackerel. It made her smile, but then most things made her smile these days.

They had talked about moving to Chy-an-Gwidden so they could all live together, but nothing had been decided. In the meantime, Kate was perfectly happy at Dolphin Cottage. Marriage had been discussed, but more in the way—and much to the relief of both—to confirm that it wasn't important. To carry on as they were, taking each day, each moment, as it arrived was reward enough. It might even be that in time, their love would fade, and they would each move on to another era; but they would always be changed forever in character for having known each other. Right here and now, all that mattered was the moment; here and now all was complete, and right.

The swell picked up again, and as if from nowhere, the ocean began to throw up some waves, moderate and dissipating to start with, but in the distance, Kate saw, becoming seductive, clean, glassy lines. She let the first ones go. Then a wave caught her eye, and she turned and waited, looking for the moment, the exact instance which would make all the difference to a successful launch.

And then she changed her mind. Not this one. Some imperceptible alteration to the size and course of the wave caused her split-second decision. It was impossible to say why, for her thoughts were working on some different, intuitive level. She let it roll under her, and watched as the next surfer in the line-up caught the breaking wave at precisely the right moment. The next one was similarly disappointing, but then she saw it, and this time she knew.

This one; this was her wave.

With her heart thumping and her mind calculating wildly, she manoeuvred into position. She felt the familiar rise and swell of the ocean, and almost sick with adrenalin, her heart lurched in fear and excitement at the scale of its power. And then leaning forward on her board, and summoning all her strength, she began to paddle like mad.

There is a pleasure in the pathless woods,
There is a rapture on the lonely shore,
There is society where none intrudes,
By the deep sea, and music in its roar:
I love not man the less, but nature more,
From these our interviews, in which I steal
From all I may be, or have been before,
To mingle with the universe, and feel
What I can ne'er express, yet cannot all conceal.-

George Gordon Byron

20043354R00350

Printed in Great Britain
by Amazon